Praise for *The Nowhere Man*

'It's great that this lost gem has been rediscovered, and at a time when Markandaya's acute delineation of displacement, alienation, and the scapegoating of immigrants is so pertinent once again. Perhaps for a decade or two, the novel might have seemed 'dated' to many, falsely believing that we inhabit a 'post-racial' world. It is, in fact, a novel that will endure not only because of the depth of understanding it brings about the immigrant experience, but also because Markandaya has, in Srinivanas, created a remarkable, indelible character.' **Monica Ali**

'This is a remarkable story that resonates in our Brexit times. Race, immigration and a British society seeking a return to a lost, glorious, world it cannot define are all sensitively portrayed.' **Mihir Bose**

'It's a travesty that this novel has been erased from British and international literary history. It is just as relevant today as when it was published - perhaps even more so. It has absolutely vital things to say about England and Englishness, race and racism, identity, belonging and prejudice. It struck many chords as I read it. Anyone who loves literature and cares about diversity in our cultural life . . . bite re he by what is happening in our cou . . . immediately.' **Bidisha**

'A British . . . depth of u . . . . . . view

'A book for our times written half a century ago is a fair definition of a classic. This brilliant if unjustly forgotten London novel combines the moral clarity of *To Kill A Mockingbird* with Markandaya's own understanding that words are all it takes to set a society ablaze.' **Maya Jaggi**

'*The Nowhere Man* was Kamala Markandaya's favourite of all her works - no doubt because the story featured something she observed frequently in England, her adopted country: racism. By addressing that issue frontally, she paved the way for novelists like Salman Rushdie and Nadeem Aslam. The novel is a richly rewarding and compelling narrative - I will leave you to discover for yourself its hellish ending.' **Charles R. Larson**

'This is a compelling, delicate portrayal of a brutalising time. A love story between a couple who defy caricature confronted by hatred rooted in stereotype. Powerful, human engaging and appalling.' **Gary Younge**

Kamala Markandaya (1924–2004) was born in Mysore, India. She studied history at Madras University and later worked for a small progressive magazine before moving to London in 1948 in pursuit of a career in journalism. There she began writing her novels; *Nectar in a Sieve*, her first novel, published in 1954, was in international bestseller. A contemporary of Ruth Prawer Jhabvala and R.K. Narayan, Kamala Markandaya is now being rediscovered as an essential figure in the post-colonial canon.

THE NOWHERE MAN

KAMALA MARKANDAYA

With an introduction by
Emma Garman

SMALL ✕ AXES

HopeRoad Publishing
PO Box 55544
Exhibition Road
London SW7 2DB
www.hoperoadpublishing.com

This edition first published in 2019 by Small Axes, an imprint of HopeRoad

ISBN 978-1-908446-99-2
eISBN 978-1-9164671-4-9

Printed and bound by Clays Ltd, Bungay, Suffolk, UK

10 9 8 7 6 5 4 3 2 1

Introduction

When Kamala Markandaya wrote *The Nowhere Man* in the early 1970s, she may well have imagined that the fault lines of British society she portrayed would, half a century on, be a bygone aspect of less enlightened times. Set in 1968, the year of Enoch Powell's 'Rivers of Blood' speech, this intricate, perceptive tragedy of alienation centres around the violent racism sparked by post-war immigration to Britain. A vivid reminder that progress is not a straight line, the novel is full of conspicuous parallels to our messy present, not least the Trump/Brexit attribution of economic woes to the presence of a maligned outgroup. Writing ahead of one's time risks cultural neglect, and *The Nowhere Man* was all but ignored on its publication. Nevertheless, it was Markandaya's favourite of her own works. She knew, with the defiance of the true artist, that she had created a subtle masterpiece. With this new edition, it finally takes its place as a classic of diaspora fiction and will find appreciation with a new generation of readers.

Arthur Miller wrote that 'the tragic feeling is evoked in us when we are in the presence of a character who is ready to lay down his life, if need be, to secure one thing – his sense of personal dignity.' In *The Nowhere Man* this character is Srinivas, an elderly spice importer, native of India, and decades-long resident of a leafy South London suburb. Along with many newer arrivals from South Asia and the

Caribbean, Srinivas realizes with horror that, at nearly seventy years old, he has been marked as a pariah, 'a convict on parole'. At first, the danger signs don't quite penetrate his consciousness. He is by nature dreamy and peaceable, not given to assuming the worst of people. And he has always regarded England as a haven of tolerance and sanity. 'My country,' he calls it. 'I feel at home in it, more so than I would in my own.' But eventually, the ambient threat turns palpable, and he begins to hear of 'a new gospel,'

> a gospel he had not heard since those echoes from Germany before the war. He recalled them now, almost phrase by phrase, presenting hate as a permissible emotion for decent German people. Not only permissible but laudable, and more than that, an obligatory emotion, which they summoned up subtly and starkly from a reading of a checklist, or charge sheet, of the differences between men, their customs and observances, their sexual, religious and pecuniary habits, sparing nothing as they peeped and probed, neither bed nor bathroom nor tabernacle, citing in the end, without shame, the shape and size of their noses, lips, balls, skulls, and the pigment of their skin.

The novel opens with Srinivas's pariah status manifesting on his body: he has developed the 'medieval' illness of leprosy. Already unwanted in his newly hostile neighbourhood, which is daubed with 'hang the blacks' and 'blacks go home', Srinivas must now participate in his own ostracization. His GP, Dr Radcliffe, advises that 'it would be as well if you did not visit any public places'. It's all a far cry from the calm and companionable existence Srinivas had once envisioned unfolding with his wife, Vasantha, and their sons, Laxman and Seshu. As we learn via extended flashbacks, the young Srinivases left India for England in 1919 and rented 'a succession of rooms and flats', before deciding to buy 'a gaunt old building' large enough to welcome their sons' future wives. But Srinivas's name, which means 'abode of good fortune', turns out to be ironic. Seshu, at age nineteen, is killed by a German bomb while driving an ambulance during the Blitz. Soon after, Vasantha dies of tuberculosis. Laxman, who has settled in Plymouth and absorbed himself in his own family and career, barely keeps in touch.

Isolated and bereft, Srinivas is afflicted with a depression bordering on catatonia. In the kind of perfectly turned metaphor that induces a shiver of recognition, his life is described as 'a dust bowl of being. Empty. Without meaning. Scooped out, picked clean, no climbing up the slippery sides.' He neglects his business, his appearance, and his house, which sinks into squalor:

Bluebottles buzzed around the dustbins, and litter from the unswept yard swirled over other people's tidy properties, severely trying the patience of housewives. A few – those most affected, like Nos. 3 and 7 – made sharp wounding comments, but generally people were charitable, knowing the history of the widower at No. 5.

Those earlier post-war days, remarks the omniscient narrator, were 'decent' and kindness was still the norm. Laxman, however, is less than kind. A fully 'English' young man who measures human worth according to financial success and 'potential,' he cannot comprehend his father's melancholic passivity. He tells Srinivas to pull himself together, 'and felt indeed that this aptly described what had to be done, as if his father were some slack old bag whose strings must be pulled tight before the entire contents fell out.' Srinivas is painfully aware of the unbridgeable gulf between himself and his son, compounded by both generational and cultural differences. He 'saw himself as his son did and as his son's children would ... an ill-dressed ancient Indian, deficient in good living and small talk, with whom they would have nothing in common.'

Previously, when the newly-wed Laxman brings his wife, Pat, to stay at No. 5 for a week, he is indeed embarrassed by his parents' lack of sophistication, by the way they dress and speak, by his father's valiant attempts to fill the awkward silences with talk about business. 'Drooling on', thinks Laxman, 'about his rancid spices'. Pretty blonde Pat, meanwhile, tries her self-congratulatory best to manage the social strain of the visit. She tells Laxman how 'nice' and 'sweet' she considers the Srinivases, 'believing she was being the kind of wife any man would want, the sort that would never come between him and his parents'. Laxman, irritated, says he finds them impossible to talk to. The conflict and sense of separation that can arise between first and second immigrant generations would, thirty years later, be explored to great effect in Zadie Smith's *White Teeth* and Jhumpa Lahiri's *The Namesake*. But at the time Markandaya was writing, it was a subject few novelists had confronted.

Salvation comes to the widowed Srinivas in the unexpected form of Mrs Pickering, an impoverished divorcée, older than him and almost as down-at-heel. Chance encounters in the street lead to walks in the park and conversations that are tentative, yet freighted with significance. Their gentle rapport relies on a mutual, delicately observed tact. 'I hate people who pry,' says Mrs Pickering, 'and force themselves upon you for their benefit and pretend it's for yours.' A partnership is forged, at first platonic, yet no less committed and affectionate for that. Mrs Pickering – we never discover her given name – moves into No. 5, and soon the house is as clean and tidy as when Vasantha was alive. The neighbours, reassured to see the 'shine on the doorstep', confer respectability on the odd couple by referring, fastidiously, to 'Mr Srinivas, the landlord, and Mrs Pickering, his tenant.' To Srinivas, resurrected from his emotionally comatose state, their easy togetherness feels both miraculous and like the most natural thing in the world. This moving and credible portrayal of a romance between two aging, unglamorous outcasts, whose love lacks passion and excitement yet utterly compels the reader, is an exceptional writerly feat.

When racist hatred shatters their hard-won tranquillity, Srinivas and Mrs Pickering's divergent reactions dramatize a common theme in Markandaya's fiction: the clash of Eastern and Western sensibilities, and the persistence of cultural values despite deracination. Though he is 'cut off from his roots' of Indian Hinduism, Srinivas's *ahimsa* – his honouring of all living beings – endures. A stamped-on mouse dropped on his doorstep by Fred, the local racist lout, causes deep distress: Srinivas feels responsible for the creature's needless death. That tiny grey mouse, he thinks, 'has entitlements no less than a man'. The same attitude was held by Markandaya. A lifelong defender of animal rights and vegetarian, she detested cruelty to animals and treated it, in her writing, as an auspice of general brutality. But to Mrs Pickering, Srinivas's anguish is ridiculous. 'Really, some people,' she thinks, 'the way they tore themselves to pieces over nothing.' Her priority is to resist and fight back against the mindless prejudice, which she does doggedly. Srinivas simply says: 'People will believe what they want to.' It is a measure of Markandaya's mastery of character and voice that neither approach to life seems less noble. And the hostility's shocking culmination, foreshadowed as though by gathering storm clouds, is in any case unstoppable.

Nor are the story's antagonists cardboard villains. Whilst we're not asked to pity down-on-his-luck racist Fred, Markandaya takes us into his mind and depicts, with convincing psychological realism and a hint of compassion, the underpinnings of his siege mentality. Emasculated by unemployment, resentful of having 'lost his place in the housing queue' after an abortive move to Australia, and desperate to maintain his 'reputation as a proper bloke', Fred casts around for someone to blame for his circumstances. To his immense relief, he realises that everything is 'the blacks'' fault. 'They came in hordes', is the spiel he seizes upon, 'occupied all the houses, filled the hospital beds and their offspring took all the places in the schools.'

This rhetoric of politically expedient nationalism has scarcely altered over the decades, although in 2015 migrants were described as 'swarms' rather than 'hordes' by both David Cameron and Nigel Farage. (Donald Trump prefers 'invasion'.) The other beacons of xenophobia flaring in Srinivas's world are no less familiar in our current social landscape. Mrs Pickering, intercepting the post to shield him from abusive missives (though they receive equal amounts), finds that the neater the writing, 'the worse the contents: the more innocent the envelope, the more vicious the enclosure'. Now it would be emails/Direct Messages, and in place of neat writing and plain envelopes the curious phenomenon, experienced particularly by women in public life, of the politest and most grammatical introductions presaging the vilest attacks. And when Dr Radcliffe reads a published letter about immigrant staff in the NHS, the sentiments precisely echo those often aired in English newspapers today:

> It concerned itself with the welfare of the sick, who might fall into foreign hands. On their behalf it inquired into the qualifications of those who tended them, their medical skills, their command of English. It hazarded – for facts were facts, and must be faced – that these might not, perhaps, come quite up to the standards of Britain which the world envied.

Perhaps this unerring diagnosis of British society's fault lines from a perceived outsider – a woman and a foreigner – felt disconcerting or even impertinent to 1970s readers. Could that help explain *The Nowhere Man*'s commercial and critical neglect? Markandaya, a rarity in the mid-twentieth century as an internationally read Indian novelist, was previously known for finely-drawn portraits of her homeland. Her debut, *Nectar in a Sieve*, published in 1954 when she was thirty, is a *cri de coeur* on behalf of South Indian tenant farmers whose fates, in Hardyesque fashion, are buffeted by forces outside their control: industrialism, colonialism, heartless landlords, droughts and floods. The title is taken from a Coleridge sonnet: 'Work without hope draws nectar in a sieve,/And hope without an object cannot live.' An international bestseller, an American Library Association Notable Book, and a Book of the Month Club main selection (worth at the time $100,000), *Nectar in a Sieve* also appeared on the curriculum at many schools and colleges. 'Most Americans' perception of India,' maintained the literature scholar Charles Larson, 'came through Kamala Markandaya.'

In the United Kingdom, her adopted country, Markandaya made no such splash. She always regarded it as her toughest market, and blamed the inevitable snobbishness towards an author from a former, and very recent, British colony. It was soon after Independence, in 1948 when she was twenty-four, that Markandaya moved from South India to England with the ambition of becoming a novelist. Like many writers, she could contemplate her homeland with greater clarity and perspective from a distance. Her daughter, Kim Oliver, remembers that at their home in Forest Hill, South London, Markandaya wrote longhand drafts in exercise books, then typed them up on a manual typewriter. She was, says Oliver, highly disciplined, a firm adherent of the philosophy that books get finished through a daily routine of hard work. She didn't romanticise her calling as a fragile, sacrosanct activity, and never objected to her small daughter's regular interruptions.

After the 1956 publication of Markandaya's second novel, *Some Inner Fury*, set amid India's turbulent campaign for self-rule in the 1940s, a journalist asked if she might write a book about England. 'No,' she responded, 'I don't know England well enough, and don't think a static society – that is to say a society which has solved its problems in a mild and satisfactory way – can prod me into writing about it. I regret to say I have to be infuriated about something before I write.' A decade and a half would pass before her greater familiarity with English society, and its increasing volatility, inspired *The Nowhere Man*. It was her seventh book. Presumably discouraged by the reaction – or rather the lack of reaction – to her harrowing portrait of modern Britain, Markandaya returned to India for the setting of her subsequent four novels (including *Bombay Tiger*, published posthumously in 2008).

But Markandaya was never to match the sensational success of *Nectar in a Sieve*, and her name gradually faded from literary prominence. Not that she ever sought the limelight, even in her heyday. A deeply private person, 'she rarely talked about herself, or her background, or her writing', says Oliver. Markandaya wrote under a pseudonym: she was born Kamala Purnaiya and became Kamala Taylor when she married her English husband, Bernard Taylor, in 1948. She rarely granted interviews, and brushed aside suggestions that her novels contained autobiographical details. For example, she claimed that unlike Srinivas, she had not personally experienced any racism in Britain, although the subject preoccupied her. A particular irritation was the Western coding of Christian as virtuous. 'Britons condemn bad behaviour as un-Christian,' she said, 'and it is unconsciously offensive. Barbarity strikes as barbarous to anyone, not just to Christians.'

Her most autobiographical novel is *Some Inner Fury*. Like its heroine, Mira, Markandaya came from a prosperous high-caste family, worked as a journalist, and fell in love with an Englishman. But whereas Markandaya's cross-cultural relationship led to marriage and a child, *Some Inner Fury* has no similar happy ending. Mira's romance with Richard, an Oxford-educated civil servant, cannot in her opinion withstand his being 'of the ruling nation' and her own passionate nationalism. 'There is no in between', she thinks ruefully. 'You have shown your badge, you have taken your stance, you on the left, you on the right, there is no middle standing. You hadn't a badge? – but it was there in your face, the colour of your skin, in the clothes on your back.' *Some Inner Fury* drew comparisons to E.M. Forster's *A Passage to India*, and one US critic called it 'actually a more valuable study of Indian upper-class life and problems than Forster's great novel.' Another review characterised the story as 'essentially a woman's viewpoint, and the expression of that viewpoint in very moving terms is Miss Markandaya's forte.'

Markandaya, understandably, had no wish to be patronised as a female author, and the 'Indian novelist' label felt similarly restrictive. 'I would prefer,' she said, 'to be called just a writer, not a nationality. No critic has ever actually said "she writes surprisingly good English for an Indian" – but the subliminal message was there, and duly received.' How galling, then, to be in effect forced into retirement for being the wrong kind of Indian novelist. In the 1980s, the magical realist innovations of writers like Salman Rushdie and Amitav Ghosh gave Indian literature an exciting and lucrative new image, and Markandaya was deemed passé. Publishers, seeking the next *Midnight's Children*, offered her no more book deals.

Markandaya continued to write regardless, and she also served as an Arts Council adjudicator. But for the twenty years before her death in 2004 at age seventy-nine, she disappeared from public view. She is still remembered by some as the pioneer who, the author Manu S. Pillai wrote, 'told India's tales to the world beyond, and brought a young, new nation into the global literary conversation.' And with *The Nowhere Man*, Markandaya wrote a British state-of-the-nation novel whose acuteness and depth of understanding resounds eerily today.

Emma Garman

(A version of this essay first appeared in *The Paris Review Daily*.)

1

THERE WAS A SCREEN BEHIND WHICH PATIENTS dressed and undressed. Usually they did not take long: but his Indian patient would, Dr Radcliffe surmised, from the layers of clothes he would now be resuming against the chill English evening. There had been, he thought, no need in fact for the stripping ritual, because while a whole spectrum of illness could present bewilderingly similar signs and symptoms, there were some whose pointers were as coldly and precisely aligned as those of the Pole Star. The two stars, (α) and (β), of the Ursa Major constellation, for which navigators looked. Which pointed unmistakably. Uncompromisingly, as in this case.

Dr Radcliffe tapped his pencil softly against the leathercloth of the surgery table, studying the medical history sheet the nurse had set before him, on which, presently, the medieval name would be written in the appropriate column. A long column this, making provision for the many ills to which flesh is heir; but the entries in it were few. His patient, then, had been a fortunate man: nearing seventy, and hardly any illnesses to his name. Either that, or one whose disciplines would not allow more than a cursory attention to the body. In all, three entries spanning the twenty years he had been registered as a patient: all three in his handwriting, the first going back to 1952, the last one dated 1965, three years ago.

Nineteen sixty-eight, the year almost done, was blank. The blankness lay waiting under his hand, though he would not, for the moment, sully the innocence of the paper. Because of the darting perceptions of his patient, which were scored on his mind and against which, already, he was arming himself. Because of the knell that sounded, even in his own trained breast, so how could he harp convincingly on about the advances in modern medicine to this stricken layman? Lame man, helping a lame dog over a stile, with the distinct possibility of stile turning into Spanish mule, slicing his man astride in half as the Inquisitors had done with heretic and infidel. Only in their case it had been intentional. In his case, as he recognized with some pale sproutings of gratitude, no ineluctable fiat compelled him to take risks. There were other courses open, carefully charted to help the patient, along which he could be conducted to the truth, accepting it as one accepted the fact of death over the long slow processes of living, the grains drawn out like spun sugar and the shining heap dwindling.

Or was it to help the doctor?

Dr Radcliffe tapped his pencil again, which was useless, since the form demanded completion in ink, which would not wash out. The tapping kept time, he gradually became aware and stilled the pencil: kept time with the artery that beat at his left temple, of whose ceaseless pulsing he was never conscious except – sometimes, not too frequently – when he cared. As happened in spite of the callousing that, examining himself dispassionately, he knew had taken place. A professional requirement that covered, or protected, extensive areas of himself. Those areas that objected to creating pain, yet stood by while the trembling guinea pig was taken from its cage, its shaven skin which the fur no longer concealed rubbed up like raw meat with induced ulcers, screaming at sight of white coat and needle: while the still-living frog was crucified, the frail webbed anguished feet clutching and curling around the holding pin. All done in the name of healing. It could only be done in that name. Only sometimes the line was crossed, the callouses underwent degenerative changes. Under the same hallowed name, then, with the blessings still falling as thick as hail, curiosity edged in. Cold and calculated, and scientific, that powerful modern absolution for atrocity.

Watch it, said Dr Radcliffe, watch it. Not the hardening that laid traps for other men, but the softening that never quite ceased to become his particular cross. Which Marjorie his wife had stumbled upon and lashed herself to, to provide explanations for the maladies of their marriage.

'You have to be different.' Her voice, like her attitudes, which marriage had altered. Her plain speech voice. 'For God's sake, why? Why can't you be like other men?'

'I believe I am. As much as one man can be like another. Though each pattern does happen to be unique.'

'Unique. Yes. That is your trouble. Our trouble is, we both have to live with it.'

A little of what was slung always stuck.

Now, abruptly, Dr Radcliffe turned his attention to his patient. He had not emerged yet, but would not be long. The outlined figure, blurred behind the screen, was bowed, engaged in a last business of tying its shoelaces. In a few seconds the figure would come out, becoming an old man who was here to consult him. The brown, contained face, which he could not read, would confront him across the table, searching his own for the truth. Dr Radcliffe lowered his gaze to his papers and shuffled them, to prepare himself.

There were certain attitudes one fell into, which were designed to help. This was one of them. He adopted another as his patient came in, leaning well back in his chair, placing the tips of his fingers together to form a little steeple.

'Ah, Mr Srinivas. Sit down, won't you?' He hoped he was not being unctuous, but failed to convince himself. That, too, was an attitude: a result compounded of medical-school training and the gibbering fears and inanities of the people who came here, men and women divested of clothes and dignity and reduced to – to beings lesser than oneself. Even if one tried to have it otherwise, which was difficult to do, because it was that much easier to be superior, an aloof and superior being to whom virtues, but no flaws, were to be ascribed.

'Thank you.' Srinivas took the chair that was offered, which being intended to save space by stacking was constructed of bent steel tubes and plastic slats, which did not suit the framework of the man. A spare figure, with hints of some dovetails of structure that could have lain within the cranium, or in the velvet functioning of well-turned ball and socket. A thin body, wearing tight white trousers and a black coat – the tunic-and-tights uniform, copied by young women in brilliant fabrics, that one saw flash past by the thousand in the streets of London. To which this old man, with his serene eyes and composed bones, clearly did not belong. Repudiated, in fact, with his quiet airs, at ease in a situation which could demoralize, as Dr Radcliffe knew. And was disconcerted, both by his patient's poise and the seeds of his own knowledge, the two conspiring to rob him of those prevarications which his professional training informed him were words that were suitable. So that Srinivas, having waited, had perforce to make the first move.

'I hope, doctor,' he said, in the thin voice of his age or race, and with the precise enunciation of a man who has learned a language later in life, 'that in coming here I have not been guilty of wasting your time.'

'Not at all.' Dr Radcliffe smiled faintly. The conventionality of the words restored him; a good many of his patients made this identical little speech, even those who turned out to be mortally ill, so frequently did injunctions not to waste the overworked doctors' valuable time assail their ears. 'Not at all. That is what doctors are for. I mean, of course, for consulting.'

'I took that meaning.' The old man returned his smile. 'Time being valuable to all men, it is, of course, too precious to squander.'

Once more Dr Radcliffe, who had believed himself restored, felt curiously dispossessed, as if the man who had come here for help had in some strange way usurped the dominant role of his helper.

'This being so,' pursued Srinivas, propelling them out of the doldrums into which this clashing of spheres had cast them, 'you will doubtless have no objection to informing me the nature of my illness.'

Dr Radcliffe looked up. There were ways of looking, through glass that one manufactured, to preserve one's insulation, and he set the process in motion.

'At this stage,' he said formally, but retaining those plums in his cheeks that rendered his voice both fruity and kindly, 'it is difficult to make a precise diagnosis.'

Then he perceived that the glass was holed: some defect of construction, like impurity in the silica content, had left gritty perforations like Judas windows through which his patient could, and was, scrutinizing him. Dr Radcliffe lowered his eyes and, drawing his pad towards him, began writing rapidly. When he had finished he signed the form, blotted it carefully, folded it according to the printed instructions, and sealed it. Then having no other recourse, he looked up.

'I am arranging for you to see a specialist,' he said carefully, through the glass that refused to mend. 'The hospital will notify you the date and time when you should attend. In the meantime it would be as well if you did not visit any public places.'

He paused. What public places could this old man visit, where he might conceivably be considered a danger?

'Such as public houses,' he said, and stopped short, stunned by the baroque quality of the statement and aware that he had similarly clobbered his patient. Both men were speechless then, struggling to resume communication but hampered by glass, which finally succumbing to the double assault fell pulverized, soundlessly, in a soft cone like volcanic ash. The silence, now, assumed a different nature, assumed in fact its inherent balance, placing both men on one level so that they could connect. Then Srinivas held out a hand, whose palm was dry and powdery with the sallow pollen of age, and Dr Radcliffe placed in it the envelope with the printed address uppermost, glad to be done with palaver, or as freed from it as one like himself could be.

'You will see,' he said, 'I am referring you to the Hospital for Tropical Diseases. Because, you understand, one rarely comes across the condition in this country. Those few cases I have encountered have been in India, where I served for a brief period.' He paused. 'It was many years ago,' he said, 'I am not entirely familiar with the clinical features. I am afraid, however, the possibility remains that my suspicions may be confirmed.'

'You need not be afraid, doctor,' replied the old man gently. 'I do not believe, either, that the symptoms admit much error. I am, you see, entirely familiar with the disease, having spent a fair part of my life in India, that is to say the first twenty impressionable years.'

'But there have been some fifty since,' said Dr Radcliffe dryly, 'which add up to almost a lifetime.'

'Nevertheless it is the early years which are most deeply etched,' said Srinivas, 'and the memories persist and are not subject to fluctuation.'

Then he rose and held out a hand, on whose back the leathery nodules had traced their first faint irregular outlines that would later on be filled, which Dr Radcliffe, subduing an unruly revolt of his flesh, after a few seconds took.

'There are a number of cures,' he said, and felt that the words reduced him, or perhaps it was the integrity of the man who stood opposite, opposing his felicities it seemed, as if flesh might prefer rubbing up by an honest grater to the application of these suave emollients.

'It is not incurable,' he said, to make it better, but dismally conscious of serving up an even worse hash.

'No,' Srinivas agreed with him. 'But it is rather late, doctor, do you not think, for a man of my age?'

'Nevertheless, if I were you, I would not abandon hope,' said Dr Radcliffe, and cleared his throat, and stood up to see his patient out; a thing he could not remember doing before in the many years he had practised in this surgery.

'Even without that,' said Srinivas, who saw that the leathercloth sweated where the doctor's fist had rested. 'Even without hope, one would not feel abandoned,' he said gently, and went out.

2

'YOU'RE LATE,' MARJORIE RADCLIFFE TOLD HER husband. 'Again.'

'Am I?' Dr Radcliffe looked at his wristwatch, which he wore but seldom consulted, finding it pleasanter to use time than to section it, allowing the arbitrary wedges power to impinge upon living.

'You know you are,' said Marjorie, and suppressed her emotions, which had once been light, a froth of annoyance over the amiable waves of new marriage, so that it was possible for her to pout and say, 'Darling, you're late, you're horrible, you've deflated my lovely soufflé.' But now they were heavy from the years' accretions, layer upon layer, the laminations reaching, she felt, into her soul.

'Yes, I suppose I am,' said Radcliffe. And he, too, suppressed the natural flow which, in fact, had dried up over the years to this, which was next to nothing. Then, lucid springs that bubbled and ran free. Telling her of this case and that, the dilemmas and perplexities of his calling, while she listened, in sympathy, he presumed. Until suddenly one day he knew she had ceased to listen. If she had ever done so. If it had not all been pretence. He could not be sure, because he had not been watchful, but he became. He saw when the thick solid gaze clarified, grew transparent as she thankfully wriggled her mind free of him while her eyes still engaged his; and watched and waited for her fingers to begin, which would straighten a hem, or the fringes of antimacassars laid upon chair backs, fretting and teasing, and at length grow still so that he could tell when she had finally succeeded in submerging his concerns, allowing her own to surface. These were to do with matters he could not find compelling, although he was prepared to acquiesce. Matters like houses, for instance, into which they moved in fairly rapid succession, and the bigger and better gardens that went with them; and better neighbourhoods, with more expansive and salubrious views and airs; and cars that expanded to match, though not their physical selves, which remained, in fact, the same size. Or so he put it, contentiously, to his wife.

'It is to do with status,' she answered him. Distantly, since it went against the grain. Having to spell out in words what everyone knew in their hearts, because of this wilfully blind man who queried so shamelessly.

'One's standing in the community,' she elaborated. With distaste, because a principle was being violated, which decreed that certain things ought not to be said. Only what option have I? I have been forced, you bear witness, she complained to that other half of herself with whom she communed at length and, on the whole, satisfactorily.

So he knew, having been bluntly told, and put up with, not having been endowed with that cast of mind. Sometimes, after they had loved, and were tender, he could even persuade himself that he understood her excessive needs, although this understanding sprang more promptly, not to say strongly, for the washing machine and TV wants that eased the drab lives of his patients. Primed by knowledge, he learned to listen, not without some quirky satisfactions of his own, for herald phrases: pronouncements – varying

little over the years save in what followed the preamble –
that preceded each move, accumulation, or aggrandizement.

'With what John is earning now we could easily afford,'
she would tell the company. A home-help or a home
extension, another car or carpet – whatever. Implying it
was virtue, or good housewifery which ran a close second,
that obstructed them, whereas in fact they could not at that
particular time have afforded what, apparently, they lacked.
But shortly would, as both knew, from the diligent efforts of
the powerful union that looked after his pay. Each desire of
hers one step ahead, as if to ensure, he sometimes thought,
that it could not be encompassed: reach exceeding grasp in a
public demonstration of poverty, although it could also have
been deficiency, though of what he preferred not to define.

So now there was the house, in its landscaped setting,
and the rose garden, and the sunroom which vacillated
between icebox and the solarium it was intended to be, and
the double garage, while Marjorie went around wanting.
Roamed the streets of the tidy suburb in her marigold mini,
in an activity she called visiting, vigilant for the additions
and acquisitions of her friends. Restless behind the gloved
wheel of her car, the fever masked by vivacity in the homes
they went to, her bright eyes darting. Cataloguing, he came
to realize, in accordance with current custom: making lists
from which items could be detached and dangled before
him like desirables or, it could be, indictments.

'The Maitlands – are you listening, John?' Because, it is
true, sometimes he didn't. 'The Maitlands have just bought
a nice little villa in Spain. With its own little beach. And a
maid.'

'Have they?'

'Yes. Didn't you see?'

'The maid?'

'Is it likely? The *photographs*.' She sniffed. 'There were enough of them around. I must say, they don't mind parading.'

'I'm afraid,' he confessed, 'I didn't notice.'

'You wouldn't,' she said, with the stiffness that presaged, while he waited for the storm, or the leaden silence, which was worse, to descend upon his head. Or that painstaking dissection that shredded the fibres of which he was made, which was worst of all. 'You wouldn't, being you. Most people would. But then, you're not like other people, are you?'

'I suppose not,' he said, and waited. Thinking about the member of royalty he had read about once, who had had a go at shearing a sheep. Sporty like, a Royal having a go. And the sheep had emerged as shredded sheep, the Royal was reported as saying, which was funny, coming from a Royal. He had not thought it funny. It had made him wince, and finger the blue tingling planes of his shaved jaw, though his hands did not tremble when he lanced a boil or dressed the weeping tissues of a burned child.

'I'm telling you,' she said, 'for your own good.' Pushing back the hair from her brow, which was pure. Not to move him, though, since that was past; it was one of her leftover gestures. 'You're odd. Odd man out. Nobody goes around like you, not interested in anything.'

'There are a good many things,' he managed to protest, though even this human exchange between them was receding, 'that interest me.'

'Things,' she said. 'Everybody's interested in things. They go to making life gracious. But not you. It's wrong. Something's wrong with you. There must be, for you to

be the way you are. You look around,' said the exponent of
gracious living, 'that's what you need to do, then you'll see.'

Then he saw. Taking her advice, since he was genuinely
concerned to preserve even those few tatters of fabric which
was what remained. Saw that cataloguing and collecting were,
indeed, rife, and that he was indeed the odd one out. Pondered
on his plight, and even gave himself a painful push or two
in the direction of the tribe from which he was isolate, but
concluded he had no driving desire to rejoin it. Nevertheless he
twisted his inclinations into some sort of conformity, creating,
in effect, a roadworthy if ramshackle vehicle on which both
could ride. But he was aware, now and then, of being rattled
to pieces, and turned to the woman who bumped along beside
him, but found she had no time for him what with having to
hang on, and lumbered with two since she could see she was
fated for life to carry his weight as well as her own.

Sometimes, when she dwelt on her lot, Marjorie had to
complain. Plaintively, to her well-heeled friends, who went
to the hairdresser twice a week and put plastic trees in their
shoes, knowing these top-and-toe points were crucial to the
immaculate woman. Women who, through their female
insight, could understand better than any man what it could
be like.

'Darling, I can't think how you cope.'

'Well, someone has to.' At times the words rang familiar,
but Marjorie could rely on the accommodating memories of
her friends. 'I run the house, I answer the telephone, I make
the decisions.' Here she paused, to make sure there were no
stirrings of envy, such as had dislocated the discourse on
one or two previous occasions, but found it was in order
to proceed. 'If I didn't, who would? John? You don't know
him! Why, he simply has no mind of his own.'

'It must be wearing.'

'It is. My dear, I can't tell you.'

There were other things Marjorie could hardly tell about but did, creating impressions and auras that were necessary to her, which involved taking her friends aside one at a time, such was the intimate nature of the communication.

'There's no peace. Those dreadful patients. The telephone never stops. At night too. Sometimes when he's in my bed ...' And her lips and linings would swell, rounded out by the passionate fantasy, the thin pink lips and flowery inner membranes which in the early days had received and accepted, at first pretending, then stoically enduring, and finally reverting to original puritan positions which rejected all his advances.

'Whatever does he do?'

'He dresses and goes,' said Marjorie, flatly, aware of anticlimax, but unable to improve the story.

But this at least was true. When a summons came he went. It was one of those points she chalked up against her husband, not that it affected her health, which it could scarcely do, considering the infrequency of the happening, but because she felt that these priorities of his somehow worked against her, her interests.

'Do you have to go?'

Thumping the pillow resentfully, the dislodged currents scraping against the Japanese paper shade with wafery sounds, like wind through pampas grass.

'I'm afraid so, yes.'

She hated it when he said I'm afraid. It meant nothing. He was not afraid of her. Whatever she said he would go on his way regardless, leaving her to get along on her own as best she could. She turned her back on him, on the sour knowledge, but could not resist turning again to have another go.

'I suppose,' she said huffily, and plumped up a pillow for support, 'I suppose someone's dying.'

'Someone's very ill.' He buttoned his fly, and amused himself by watching her avert her gaze. Virginal modesties, which at one time he had found beguiling, time had reduced to meaningless, middle-aged grotesquerie. Its core, which had damaged him, remained an impenetrable frigidity: prim stony wastes, well disguised, such was the pressing need to be led to the altar, in which little could grow.

'I must say,' she said, eyes distant, fixed upon the picture rail from which festoons of valance descended upon the heads of their two beds, giving a semblance of oneness, 'I must say, they do pick their times.'

'I hardly think,' he rejoined, 'one has much choice in the matter.'

'You always stick up for them.' Her voice had begun to rasp, rubbed up by a sense of injury which was to do with the past as well as the present. 'What about me? Do you ever stop to think about me? I'm still your wife, aren't I?'

He did not answer, because these were precisely the areas about which he was in some doubt.

'What about me?' he heard her say, steaming in the hall, his hair moulded by damp into drakes' tails, moisture dripping off the proofed herringbone and spotting the polished parquet while he struggled to comprehend, his mind filled by the creased lineaments of the old man upon whom he had that evening pronounced sentence.

'Alone in the house all day,' she complained. 'It's past eight, do you realize? You might at least have telephoned. It would have saved me.'

'From what?' he dared to ask.

'From waiting,' she said. 'I've been waiting to tell you.'

'What?'

'Oh, nothing,' she said, offhand, 'nothing that won't keep.' So that he understood it was one of her concerns, which she suspected might not engross him, and so would wait for a more hopeful moment in which to reveal and embroil.

'I'm sorry,' he said, following her into what she called the breakfast room, a large and glassy offshoot of the kitchen. 'I was detained. By a patient,' he said, making his apologies to the old man, thoughts of whom, and not the man himself, were what had kept him rooted to the surgery chair.

'I might have known.' She was busy with things, the bar which had to be pivoted from under the counter, and wiped down, and mats laid upon it, and nothing made easier by his planting himself there, plumb in the middle of paths she must take.

'It was an unusual case,' he said, not without difficulty, so many obstacles blocked their lines of communication.

'Oh,' she said, and brought out the meat pie, whose crusts had frizzled from warming too long in the oven. Though what else can you expect, coming in at all hours, she wanted to say to him, but shut herself up in the interests of what she was nursing.

'An old man. An old patient of mine,' he pursued, impelled by some need, whose thrust he could neither resist nor explain, and saw that her face had grown blank. Smoothed free of his oppression, with an opaque quality to skin like cheese crusts beneath which lay a curdling and maturing, and her gaze grown vitreous under his eyes, or perhaps it was the fizzy clarity of light that streamed from fluorescent tubes.

'I found it a little disturbing,' he finished, consuming what words were left.

'Patients.' She took him up, and was reanimated. 'Patients these days are so demanding.'

'This man,' he said, 'made no demands on me.'

'Tiresome,' she continued, 'as I said to Julia only today. When she called. Julia called today,' said Marjorie, and waited. But he merely continued to eat, sawing at crust on which bursts of gravy were annealed, so that she had to go on, she could see, or go without.

'Do you know what?' she asked.

'No,' he answered.

'Julia,' she said, rounding out lips and syllables for the grave words to fall, grapeshot from a round tower. 'Julia is going to tea with the Queen. On the occasion of the opening of the new maternity wing.'

'Oh,' he said, which was all, tussling with pie and amazement, he could find at the time to say. Afterwards he understood that this was the point at which he recognized he and his wife were living in sinful marriage; but for the moment the search for appropriate murmurs pressed more urgently.

'Is that all you can say?' she asked him.

'It is an honour,' he managed.

Then she seemed to uncoil and spring at him, although actually she continued to sit at the bar, opposite him on a foam-padded stool.

'An honour,' she said, or even half shouted, the shrill notes edging in under middle-class clamps which shut out the common virago. 'You're right. It's an honour all right. For Julia and Ken. What is it for you and me? A slap in the eye.' And here, indeed, he saw that her eyes had begun to water, and would have proffered, but felt she would have no use for small services, and returned the handkerchief to his pocket. 'That's what it is,' said Marjorie, dabbing with her own small square of lawn, 'only you don't seem to realize. You're the senior partner, aren't you? Not that anyone would know. The way you carry on. The way you let them treat you. Why do you? And me. I'm the one that has to bear it. Now Ken's invited, and Julia's invited, she brought the invitation specially for me to see. She carries it,' said Marjorie, twisting the soaked ball of handkerchief, 'around with her, in her handbag, in a see-through wallet.'

'If you wish,' Radcliffe began, and changed it to avoid injury which, he saw, lay so easily within his power. 'Since you wish, I will arrange with the Management Committee. There was, I am sure, no slight intended. It is just that Ken has been rather more involved in this particular project.'

As you should have been, but you prefer your broken old men, ran Marjorie's indictment, though her words were different.

'Sitting on committees,' she gulped. 'Leaving the dirty work to you.'

'I preferred that he should.'

'Hogging all the attention, collecting the honours and invitations.'

'If I had thought,' said Radcliffe, desperation dulling his faculties.

'But you never do,' said Marjorie. 'If you did, you'd know what it's like. Julia sitting there, queening it over me. The Maitlands. One thing after another. Now this.' She mopped and blew. Most of the powder was gone, and the pinky-beige foundations were slipping. In this light, designed to illuminate the well-finished article, the damage was plain. He would have liked to restore what had been scored into, and even eaten away, but understood it was not only a question of light, but also of what went on: the scrambling for and the scratching around, surrounded by plenty; lariats being cast, closing on nothing and returning empty to empty, trembling hands. Creating dust bowls of soul, while the visible plains were crammed.

'I expect you think I'm silly,' she said, also becoming conscious of ravages, but ascribing it elsewhere, and fetching out her compact to pat and repair.

'I just didn't think,' he replied, and was gentle, with that detached and professional gentleness which he brought to patients he knew to be sick and beyond his skill to cure.

3

BECAUSE THERE WERE A GOOD MANY THINGS TO
consider, Srinivas made straight for his room in the attic
instead of pausing as he usually did to look into the room on
the ground floor reserved for communal friendliness. Gaining
the second landing, he bent down to remove his shoes and
socks, then carrying the cast-offs resumed his ascent of the
last uncarpeted flight, the planed timber under his bare soles
giving him a pleasure that seldom failed to surface, pleasure
which he had once been at pains to subdue, though with the
passing of years his efforts had relaxed. For it was a pleasure
which went back to an old wooden dwelling, in a country
left behind, whose recrudescence now he greeted with relief,
as a sign that normalities were to prevail, despite some blows
which might be dealt by weightier matters.

Once in his room he drew the curtains on the murk
outside and sat on his bed, which consisted of a wooden
base with a bald biscuit on top and was also a link with
the past, to think. There was, indeed, a good deal to think
about, as with some regret he now acknowledged, because
of the clutter. Not so much the hardware which was, and
had been kept, at a minimum, and would have disgraced
the most modest removal van, but the human clutter. Souls
with bodies attached whom he had accumulated, rashly it
seemed to him now, one or more to each floor of the tall
gloomy house. Though at the time it had appeared to both

of them to be the sensible solution, for what else were they
to do, since so much had turned out differently, except fill
the space that they had?

His wife had been the moving spirit behind the
acquisition. Left to himself he would simply have continued
living in successive rooms and flats as he had done since
landing in England: even in those early days the inclination
towards simplicity was pronounced. When his wife joined
him, and even later, after the children were born, he assumed
his family would fall in with this way of life, and so they did.
Until suddenly one day there was his wife, the composed
Vasantha, planted pillar-fashion in front of him. Not to be got
around or overthrown. Confronting him and demanding,
the form he had thought of as pliable concealing, as he knew
but of late had mercifully forgotten, a framework with steel
in its structure.

'I am tired,' she told him, plaiting together fingers which
showed, he observed, no sign of failure or exhaustion. 'Tired,'
she said, and was picturesque, as she could sometimes be, 'of
moving from pillar to post. As if we were gypsies. It is time we
bought a house and settled down. There is no nomadic strain
in us, that forces us to wander. Although it may well manifest
in our children if we continue this vagabond existence.'

'What is vagabond,' he inquired, 'about moving now and
then, when the need arises?'

'There is no need,' she replied. 'We will buy a house. We,'
she said, 'my family, have for generations been accustomed
to living in a house.'

'So have mine,' he was driven into claiming – fatuously,
since, as he knew, none was better aware of this than she.
Theirs had been, after all, an alliance between families with
long-established links.

'All the more reason,' she said, unashamedly fastening upon this imprudence, 'why we should do the same. It is unsettling for a family to live in a flat.'

'Hundreds of families live in flats,' he informed her. 'In Bombay and Madras, not to say London.'

She fixed him with brown eyes in which there were flecks, metallic, it appeared to him.

'What Bombayites and Madrasis do is their concern,' she said. 'As for the other, can you really imagine I am a Londoner?'

It seemed, indeed, unsound for him to do so. She did not look the part. She wore her hair scraped back in a bun, through changing styles of bob and beehive and pageboy and waist-length tresses: long hair, that took six hours to wash and dry in the winter; and sandals on her smooth-skinned feet, with thongs and a toe-loop, except when snow covered the pavements; and silks whose static raised the hairy nap of tweeds and wools the sensible islanders wore.

These, which were after all only the outward trappings, might have been overcome, but the thinking was different. Vasantha was a Hindu, born and bred in a subtle religion whose concepts, being on the cosmic scale, made no concessions to puny mankind: a religion that postulated one God, infinite, resplendent, with a thousand different aspects but One: God the creator, preserver, destroyer, union with whom was the supreme purpose and bliss. She found herself accosted by practitioners of a religion that appeared, by contrast, to be positively parochial, riddled with good deeds and childish miracles. Or so it seemed to her, listening to theses advanced by flushed, not to say flustered, expounders of enlightenment who felt they had been unfairly caught on the hop. Although, of course, it could also have been the language that obtruded, mysteries having to be reduced beyond their irreducible element for her benefit, as well as in consideration of her elementary English.

She would not have been moved to comment, however, but for the continuation by those friends who, having found themselves ill equipped to elucidate their own faith, now began voicing opinions of hers which they based upon missionary handbooks borrowed from nonconformist premises. So that Vasantha was provoked to a pronouncement.

'Their religion,' she said, within her family circle for the sake of harmony and out of consideration for her host countrymen, 'is excellent for ten-year-olds.'

'There is somewhat more to it than that,' said her husband, having met some who were lucid, and even a few who had advanced beyond handbooks. 'It is, in its way, one of the great religions.'

This did not prevent Vasantha from persisting in her opinion, particularly in view of her sons' example.

These two boys, born in a Christian country, attending Christian schools, remained ardent professing Christians until the age of ten even to the extent of never lifting a finger on the Sabbath. After that age, in common with a great many of the children in their class, they became happy pagans, not returning to the austere planes of their parents' thinking until many years later, when they were grown men, and involved in the war, which caused them to re-examine, such were the convulsions.

So they bought the house, a gaunt old building in South London, which was not difficult to do in that nervous year before the Second World War, when there were more sellers than buyers. Vasantha selected it, basing her requirements with an eye to the future when her sons, at this point aged thirteen and fourteen, would be grown up and married. Then the loving mother-in-law would allocate one upper floor to each son and wife, and the ground floor reserved for themselves, ageing parents who would be past climbing the stairs. All this despite certain distinct possibilities, which she accepted, and having done so sailed serenely past the rubble. What had to be, would be: meanwhile one had to plan.

Srinivas was astonished. Was this the girl he had married, who in her early London days would have trembled to make a dentist's appointment a week ahead, for fear of tempting fate? He gazed, marvelling, at her face, beneath whose supple ovoid such changes had been wrought, under the skin which people called olive, although he could discern no absinthe tints, except (later) when bile had entered the system. And saw, of course, that she was no longer the girl she had been at their wedding, but a woman of thirty-one. A practical woman, who acquired and discarded with some finesse, who perceiving the advantages of British method over messy Indian ways had no hesitation in adopting the foreign and forsaking her own. Not wholesale, however, nor without propitiation, and some hauling in of God's name. As now, as she outlined her intentions for the gloomy old house done up in brown paint and stringy ecru lace.

'Laxman,' she said, a mist or bloom, which to Srinivas resembled rather an obscuring fog, fallen over her sharp brown eyes. 'Laxman being the eldest shall, God willing, have the whole first floor for him and his.'

'His what?' demanded Laxman, who had no patience with what he suspected was his parents' inability to come to grips. With facts, for instance, of life. And clear admissions.

'While Seshu,' continued his mother, who had this capacity for sailing on, felt Laxman, regardless. 'God willing, he and his shall have the second floor. Then the three families,' she said, and spread the pleats of her sari, over the clutch of what she was hatching, or perhaps to gather in and secure the future, 'can live harmoniously under one roof. Without problems of young and old, such as are rampant in this country.'

So the house was acquired, under whose rafters Srinivas now sat. A house with basement and attic which they had not wanted, which were immutably linked with two-storey structures. Or so it seemed to them as they hunted, with Vasantha clamped to her vision, and Srinivas who followed her cavilling and impeding, though he would not actively thwart his wife. When the deed was done, and No. 5 Ashcroft Avenue was theirs and the building society's, and they sat among their cases in the front reception whose bay was hung with soot-heavy trusses of tattered ecru, Vasantha said with pride: 'At last we have achieved something. A place of our own, where we can live according to our lights although in alien surroundings: and our children after us, and after them theirs.'

Srinivas experienced no such emotions. He did not feel like a founding father. It seemed to him that what they had done was to shackle themselves to bricks and mortar, and it filled him with misgiving. So long as they were mobile, he liked to believe the way back to India, from which events and people had driven them, lay open. In his innermost recesses he accepted that this might not be so: each year that went by laid its mark, ineffaceable rings upon the bark of his children, making it increasingly difficult for them to thrive in another climate; and the passing years, too, inexorably decimated, leaving fewer and fewer members of families upon whom the tendrils of new life could be twined. But open acknowledgement of truth was another matter. Every man, he told himself in these secret discourses, was permitted, if not entitled to, one or two delusions. These the house was now in the course of shattering, although the true extent and nature of the catastrophe it housed was not then apparent to him.

Chains, said Srinivas, glum amid the tea chests and buckled fibre suitcases. We have chained ourselves to four walls and a roof.

But these restraints were as nothing, compared to those twisted if invisible shackles that were later to be forged.

They called their semi-detached *Chandraprasad*, after the house in India which Srinivas's grandfather had built and in which they had all lived, whose beams and doorposts were made of teakwood cut from the forest he owned. The timbers of the new house were oak, to which Srinivas could not become easily accustomed after all those years of teak. But, teak or oak, the solid weathered woods continued to support the structures long after events and inmates had risen and subsided, the Indian one surviving the clearing of the forest and the reorienting of lives, and the English triumphantly withstanding the destruction that, night after night, poured down upon its hideous gables.

But it never took to its name, or its name never took on. To the postman and the neighbourhood it remained No. 5, and the family in it remained 'the people at No. 5', although towards the end of the war a few brave souls did venture to say 'the Srinivases'. By then, of course, they were becoming accepted, perhaps because of the bombing which ripped away veils, not to say whole walls, revealing weeping surfaces and intimate interiors, and making it difficult for conventions to rule with their previous inflexible rod.

There was also the matter of the basement, whose gloomy emptiness they had wondered what to do with and were now answered as the bombs began to fall. Into this cobwebbed womb or tomb, as some wag later called it, with a heap of rotting deckchairs in one corner, and an old boiler festooned with rusty pipes twisting up to the ceiling in another, the Srinivases retreated when the sirens sounded, together with an assortment of friends and acquaintances, asked and unasked, whose numbers suddenly multiplied. Vasantha did not mind, being used to large gatherings and human congress. In fact she enjoyed it, welcoming strangers in and dispensing tea she made on top of a primus to the acclaim of the assembly. It warmed the place too, which had no gas or electricity, although later they did discover some coils of rotted electric wire, and later still, as an act of fellowship, the son of a neighbour who had shared their shelter wired the basement for them free of cost and with purloined material, and was reduced to incoherence when they acknowledged his kindness.

By then, however, they had all grown a little blasé, a little tired of turning out of their beds at night. If it's got your name written on it, they said in common with the neighbours; and they took to sleeping downstairs, all four of them in the front bay, and pulled the pillows over their ears to shut out the sinister fracas, and seldom went down to the basement except on the very worst nights.

Then, suddenly, there were only the two of them. The boys, who had been schoolboys, suddenly one day, or so it seemed, were grown men who intended to go to war.

'Who would have thought?' said Vasantha, and Srinivas saw the yellow tones in her skin, under the purplish tints the cold weather brought. 'It has turned out differently,' she said.

Many things, in fact, turned out different. They slipped out like shapeless blancmanges, for all that some care had gone into preparation, reinforcing old views that it was presumptuous to plan. Only, they had taken to the ways of the West, and the habit had become too strong to succumb entirely now.

'When the war is over and the boys are back,' said Vasantha, and forgot to finish, though plans filled her mind as she packed, or perhaps she crammed them in for fear. 'There is so much to do,' she complained, and continued her struggle with the zip, whose stubby silver teeth refused to lock, trim but obstinate under fingers grown incompetent. Or possibly the fault was the bag's, whose canvas hung in folds from being half empty, like a pauper's skin about his rattling bones. Not that there was much to rattle, since Seshu took out most of what she put in.

'Pyjamas and a toothbrush,' he said firmly, removing the jars she had packed, the home-made Indian pickles, and the cake guaranteed to travel, and a pot of jam from a neighbour. There were a few other things too, which were not wanted, the training depot being well stocked, or so Seshu said.

'They look after you,' he said, 'like farmers look after their animals. Otherwise they wouldn't be fit for consumption. Remember how Jesus fretted over one lost lamb.'

He had this gristly kind of humour. It distressed his mother, who should have been used to it but sometimes felt she would never be, attributing her loss, with sound instinct but some uncertainty, to the effects of a different climate.

So Seshu was gone, at eighteen like his elder brother before him. By 1942 both were on their way to war, Laxman an engineer with the army, Seshu training as a navigator with the Royal Air Force, leaving the older pair to soldier on in their semi. Which they were not incapable of doing, having ridden out similar battles of will and strength, but possibly felt it more now, being older, and the previous struggle having taken its toll.

'As before, one is thrown back upon oneself,' said Vasantha, stroking the planes of her face, which had begun to cave in.

Srinivas was surprised. Oddly, because he knew quite well she had gone through what he had, which was the basis for such discoveries. Only, it was all so long ago, while she was still a child in years, that he had imagined she might have forgotten.

'You were so young,' he said, 'I would not have thought,' and was silent, for he saw that that was the crux of the matter, he had not thought. The two of them, then, acknowledged Srinivas, had gone through one struggle, and now were involved in another.

Towards the end of 1943 Laxman, the elder, came home on leave from his R.E.M.E. posting somewhere near Plymouth. He had grown up, filled out, the shadows of a stranger were encroaching, so that his parents felt they hardly knew this thickset booming man in khaki, to whom the army aura so palpably appealed. He spent five days with them and then went back to Plymouth where, he told them, he had friends, and an interest in an engineering firm, though he did not specify. Nor did they ask him to, since they saw that he, like many other things, had been taken out of their hands.

Seshu came home that Christmas, cycling up from the airbase at Kent. He was quieter than he had ever been, thinner too, but handsome in his uniform of air-force blue, and with a real war under his belt. By then he was a fully fledged navigator, flying in Lancasters that went out over enemy territory. They had bombed Hamburg and Berlin. He told them about it, in the laconic way they had grown used to in their anglicized children; but his thinking was independent, indifferent to English run-of-the-mill which could be shaped, by emotion, or sometimes even by propaganda. 'A thousand tons a night over the city,' he told them. 'We must be killing as many civilians as they did.'

'It does not seem right,' said Srinivas, 'whether done by their side, or ours – ' Here he faltered, embroiled in a matter of possessive pronouns which he had not yet satisfactorily untangled, and might never, he sometimes suspected, from an exchange of role and country. 'Or anyone's,' he finished.

Vasantha, convinced only that all killing was wrong in whatever circumstances, pursed her lips but kept silent, knowing what fiery coals could be heaped upon dissenting heads. 'What would you do if a German soldier raped your daughter?' they would ask. Dealing in extremes in which alone, apparently, one could function, minds narrowed in suspicion, eyes glinting dangerously. Just as they had said, in another continent, but equally appalled, 'What will you do if your daughter marries an Englishman?' in those dire days before she had come to join her husband in England. It was unanswerable. Except that in the one case, which was not quite the same, their resurrected spirit had woven a glittering defence as potent as chain mail to save them. And in the second, there had been no daughter. Only two sons, and this second one the apple of her eye, and he now involved in murder.

'The thing is, one does not connect what one does with people,' said Seshu, and stared at his mother, who said not a word. Did not wish to say, believing such matters were for each man alone. So she began instead to prepare their supper, bringing out butter and eggs, and bread, which was brownish these days, distressed about quality and quantity and such smaller woes, which might serve to keep the larger at bay.

'Such coarse bread,' she complained, 'like the kind the missions fed to the poor. The missionaries ate the white bread,' she told them, 'and gave these brindled loaves to their servants, telling them it was healthier. As if, if it had been. But it is not human nature.'

'The missionaries were not human,' said Srinivas. 'In some ways they were superior. In certain others they were somewhat inferior.'

'Do-gooders,' said Vasantha, surprisingly, but inaccurately, since she intended it as a compliment to redress some previous asperities.

'I have never met a missionary,' said Seshu, and considered the two who were his parents, who had crossed oceans and exchanged countries, if not identity, between whom lay vast areas of experience he would never more than touch, and then with a sense of unreality. 'The nearest to a missionary,' he said, 'is the chaplain we have. Attached to the air station. A decent sort,' he said, and fell silent because of the ways of this man of God, who left his bed in the raw dawn to welcome their return, and turned out again in the chill blackout before take-off to bless the bombers, and the men who flew them, and the men who bombed, and those who plotted to bring them to the target, which was not always military. 'A decent sort,' he repeated, 'who flies with us sometimes, on bombing missions, to go through what we do, you understand,' he said, and raised his face which they saw had been drained or bled, a death mask with holes in it for eyes, whose jellied slub was beyond the power of wax to mould. Then Vasantha at least knew, but continued to spread the meagre butter on muddy slices of bread, such being the way of life.

4

A FEW MONTHS LATER LAXMAN BECAME ENGAGED TO a girl called Pat, who worked in a munitions factory in Plymouth. The letter came in the cold depressing month of February, further depressing Vasantha, who would have liked to have a prior say in the matter, and whose choice in any case would not have fallen upon a girl called Pat. Not that she could possibly object to this girl without knowing, which she did not, since Laxman had supplied only these two items of information. But still. Vasantha twisted her hands, upon whose backs the veins had begun to bulge, and reread the letter until the blue-black characters swam, and went away at last to work at it, being face to face now with what to do, now that her son was marrying an Englishwoman.

'He may not marry,' said worldly-wise Srinivas. 'In wartime young people form liaisons. It may come to nothing.'

'Yes,' said Vasantha, and looked through him, and tried to visualize this city called Plymouth, and this girl who was sprung from it, its pallid teeming soil. I must go there and meet her, she determined. But Laxman. Foreign in khaki, and eyeing her. His sustained speechless stare, towering over her, while she in her sari and bun. Listening to him while he tried to be kind, and hearing the impatience sawing away under the banter.

'I do not know what to do,' she confessed at last, and smoothed her lap, on which she had cradled her infant sons, and it had all been that much easier.

'What is there to do?' said Srinivas, and arranged a few cushions behind the back that was bowed, there being little other comfort he could offer. 'What would you wish?' he asked her.

'Only to have been able to select,' replied Vasantha, and leaned against the bolster he had provided, 'since I would have selected the best.'

'As this girl may be,' Srinivas ventured to say. But he knew that it would not do, since what was upset was not concerned with Pat, but with certain maternal rights which Vasantha had believed were hers.

That was February. In March, Seshu wrote to say that he was done with war. Outdoing his brother, who had given them two facts to go on, as against this one line of writing. Vasantha was pleased, seeing it as an end to her son's complicity in murder, although she fully expected him to be imprisoned for his act of peace. Prison, however, held no terror. She had touched its bars, and had discovered that they were nothing. I will visit him, she resolved, and her mind moved over old memories of what had been received with most pleasure, and leapt forward to similar parcels she would take her son, passing them under the grille which no doubt would separate them.

Srinivas, less sanguine, in his worst moments visualized firing squads, and sent a long and anxious missive to Seshu's Wing Commander. A reply came at once, a lengthy letter acknowledging Seshu's service to his country, as well as the common right, on grounds of conscience, to curtail or modify it. Srinivas was astonished, he could scarcely dare to hope. He threw himself into his work to restrain any premature upsurges.

Insofar as he could, that is to say, for actually there was not much to do these days in his import–export business.

People, it seemed, lost their taste for spices in wartime and anyhow he had not much to offer them from the meagre supplies that now trickled in. As for exporting, this had shrunk to almost nothing, from the strictly limited allocation of shipping space. Nevertheless it was a discipline, not to say soothing, to walk into his office at eight every morning, and sniff the air to which scents clung, an essence of spices exuding from the drums and packets in which they were stored, despite linen and brown paper wrappings, and wax and resin seals. Or talk with friends, like Uijtterlinde the Dutchman, or the Zanzibari Abdul bin Ahmedi, whom war had marooned in England. Business friends, Srinivas liked to call them, although it was the friendship that thrived, while business was perceivably anaemic.

'No matter, it will recover, the war will not last forever,' said Abdul, and rocked in confident rhythm, and the silky tassel swung from his scarlet tarbush to confirm his faith.

'True,' said Srinivas, and brought coffee, in which he discerned flavours – though it could have been his imagination – of the cloves that Abdul had once consigned, the ball-and-claw Zanzibari cloves whose pungent aromas and oils no other could match.

'When the war is over,' said Abdul.

Then both looked forward, the Zanzibari, under whose thin black skin lay jam-packed memories of flags that had followed the spice trade and the crimes committed in their name, who wanted and would work for an end; and the Indian, whose sprigs being involved was not overmuch concerned with the trade, although he too had seen the links between the fat profits that were made and the poor man's rattling bones.

'If only they would come home safe and sound there is little I would not give up,' said Vasantha. As others were saying, though possibly with added truth since there was little she coveted, that was easy to come by, in this booted and suited English-speaking country-at-war.

'It will not be long now,' assured Srinivas, who had no great confidence, but felt it was incumbent upon him. Though neither could believe.

Two months later, to confound them, Seshu came home. In civvies, and carrying the same old navy canvas bag that his mother had packed and zipped up for him. Older, the two of them, bag and its owner, and both showing grave signs of wear, although Seshu was not even twenty-one.

'They've chucked me out,' he said, 'classified L.M.F., which is a euphemism for cowardice. I am now, or shall soon be,' he told them precisely, 'a registered conchie.'

They could not quite understand it. They never could understand all that their grown-up sons said. But the main fact was clear, that whether from lack of moral fibre or whatever other reason Seshu's flying and fighting days were over. Vasantha was delighted. She ran about, unpacking and making up beds, and carrying in titbits on a tray for her thin and washed-out-looking son. Srinivas was delighted too, for complex rather than simple reasons. He pondered on it, and felt his guts twist, or perhaps it was that old strangulations were at last working free, to think there could be this kind of sanity. In this country, from which one did not expect, being more used to the somewhat different quality of its Indian dealings. One sees they have changed, he said to himself, and it renewed his faith in redemption, whether of individuals or nations.

From this time on Srinivas brought a new zeal to his role
as fire watcher. Each evening, now, he strode home with
purpose, put on boiler suit and tin helmet, and ascended the
creaky ladder in the attic which gave access to the roof. Here
he stayed, buffeted by wind and rain, vigilant under the stars
and diffused grime in the sky, until the last second of his stint
was up. He had always, of course, performed these duties
conscientiously; but now personal interest added keenness
to his eye. England was becoming his country.

The registered conchie meanwhile was driving an
ambulance. A come-down, people said, from being in
bombers. But they said so soberly, knowing his history,
besides which the fashion for presenting white feathers was
past, buried with the dead of a previous war. What he had
gone through, they said. They could not know, however,
since Seshu would not reveal. He locked it away, in his heart,
in the cab of the screaming white vehicle he drove, whose
seat grew hot from the blasts that fanned out of the burning
citadels of London. Sometimes his throat grew constricted.
With acrid smoke from the blazing buildings, and thoughts
of the Wing Commander who had upheld his rights. The
right to call a halt, the right to say no, though he could not see
the sense of either himself. A man of luxuriant moustaches
and dazzling teeth, who had gripped like a bulldog and held
on, soup strainers bristling as he shook them all into silence,
if not agreement. So in the end the dissenter could go his
lone way, released with honour into the ranks of civilians.
Honour. Seshu had not thought it could matter, not after
one had pinpointed the town and seen the bombs go, stick
after stick, night after night, saturation bombing they called
it. But it did, as the Wing Commander had known, and so
had done battle for him. Not one battle, a series, against

those who wished to persecute, which Seshu's father knew nothing about – how could he? His son did not tell him – and so preserved his picture of England sweet and sane.

Until, of course, much later, when events discoloured the edges.

Some time before it happened, people guessed. Garnering secrets from the air, it appeared, since there was the strictest security, not to mention feints and alarms to, it was earnestly hoped, mislead the enemy. Certainly Laxman got wind and acted, an early indication of decisive gifts that lubricated his later progress. A good three weeks before his unit struggled ashore in France, and a full prudent fortnight before D-day urgencies suspended all leave, he married his girl in Plymouth.

Vasantha got the telegram. She held the envelope that chattered in her hands, and shivered in the May sunshine, and lowered her lids to avoid the messenger's eye which he had already averted, being in a similar sweat of embarrassment. But he stood his ground and delivered, mumbling that the reply was prepaid. Laxman, apparently, expected instant congratulations.

'There is no reply,' Vasantha managed. And continued standing until a passing neighbour saw her cemented to her own doorstep and paused irresolutely, inhibited by rules of minding one's business, but took pity and shepherded the frail figure in.

'Bit chilly to be standing about in,' she stated, to explain her audacity. 'Not bad news I hope, dear.' Eyeing the envelope, and not without sympathy. But still. The way these Indians went to pieces. Different from one's own kind, who would close the door and pull down the blind decently, not stand about letting the whole world see.

'I don't know,' said Vasantha, and turned her stark gaze upon her neighbour whom, in her misery, she did not recognize. 'I haven't opened it.'

'Best to,' said the practical woman. Because, really. 'What I say is,' she said, 'nothing gets better by keeping.' And scuttled before the deed, just in case, and feeling herself unequal to dealing if, as anticipated, this vacant-eyed Indian did fall to pieces. At least – she had seen to it – it would not happen in the public view.

Vasantha, however, had elements in her that would keep her upright, not only now but later, when the blows were not imaginary, and crowded them, or so it seemed. It was just that it took some time, and some calling upon inner resources, for unlike her alien-bred sons, she had no instantly available disguises to clap over her nakedness.

A week after D-day they had a guarded communication from Laxman. He was somewhere in France, he told them; in fact the battalion was within a few kilometres of Caen, as Seshu rightly surmised. He had, he said, been lucky enough to get a few days' leave for his honeymoon, but not so lucky since, having been slightly wounded, though his mother was not to worry. as he was well on the way to recovery. Vasantha, of course, worried. A slight non-healing wound, rendering her son *hors de combat*, would have been more conducive to her peace of mind than this quick recovery and return to the field of battle.

On the same day – it was a thirteenth, she was to remember, having glued this English superstition onto a Hindu stem that bore accretions enough of its own – the first flying bomb fell on London. So that the war, which since the landings in Normandy everyone had assumed was as good as over, was after all, it seemed, to continue.

Of all the trials they had been through, these impersonal machines of destruction that droned over the city, and cut their motors, and allowed fear to build before they fell, these Vasantha and Srinivas, in common with the inhabitants, found the most exhausting.

'Since not even God,' said Vasantha, 'warns you that you are about to die.'

'A matter of split seconds,' said Srinivas.

'There is no earthly way of measuring them,' she rejoined, with which he could not argue.

If Vasantha had had her way she would have marshalled them all in one room, preferably the ground floor bay, where they could be together while they waited in the uncanny silence for the bomb to fall. It was a tactical grouping of strength her mother had learned to employ, rousing the relatives, assembling the family so that waiting did not scour away reserves and it was the police who came who crumbled, confronted by this upright circle of stony monoliths it had been intended, at some inconceivable season, their uniformed presence should intimidate and destroy. But that was long ago, in India, when she was a child, and one roof had spread to cover root and branch of families, and foregathering was easy. Here – Vasantha sighed, and glanced through the window for signs of her husband returning – there were problems to assembling, in the shape of two ambulant sons.

By nightfall, there was only one. Seshu, speeding to hospital with the human wreckage from one explosion cramming the ambulance bays, was blown to smithereens by another together with his vehicle and half a terrace of shabby back-to-back houses on which a flying bomb had impersonally and wastefully landed.

5

THEY ENDED THE WAR WITHOUT FURTHER CASUALTY.
It could have been worse, people said, seeing they still
had a roof over their heads, and only one boy gone. People
who had lost more than one, as well as four walls behind
which to be decently bereaved, but who spoke without
envy, only stating sober facts in sober voices which had
suppressed anguish, and could not be mouthpiece to any
meanness. But they could not know, as the people of No.
5 did, what it meant, the extent of its ramifications. For
this loss encompassed the break-up of a unit, tough enough
and tightly knit, but lacking the intricate marquetry of
relationships that established and supported the natives.

Four of them, and now three. But the third was settled
firmly in Plymouth, a pale brown Englishman with a pale
pink wife. A fair-haired, pretty girl this, anxious to please,
and be friendly, who tried, but could hardly be expected,
any more than her mother-in-law, to vault over hurdles
this high. Sometimes in the unyielding silence they
wondered who had built them – both participants, the
mother and the daughter-in-law, their desperate glances
colliding over the thickly thatched head of their loved
one. But neither, after some searching, could feel guilty.
It was not of their doing, and neither, for that matter,
belonged to the category that would have looked about
for scapegoats.

Only, there was the awkward business of getting, somehow, through this visit which, in a false moment of immoderate emotion, had been scheduled to last a week.

Laxman, newly released from the acceptable bonhomie of his army days, accustomed to the flip repartee of his father-in-law's factory, at which he was adept, could not help looking askance at his prim, not to say provincial parents. Sitting side by side on the divan with the ridiculous roly-poly bolsters, and his mother with her bun. And her clothes, like the robes Jesus Christ wore, only worse with the cardigan. Her face, scrubbed clean and yellow like a plain deal table, and her English, which was not the country's or his own. As if, complained Laxman silently, after all these years she could not; although when his wife asked he could not say exactly what he wanted of his mother. But something: anything that she could do that would sink her indistinguishably into England, instead of sticking out like a sore thumb.

Vasantha, however, with no intention of sticking out nevertheless clung to her identity. What else could she do? She would, she felt, merely look ridiculous if she painted her face and put on a skirt and stockings, and only a widow, which thankfully she wasn't, would lop off her hair. So she smoothed her lap, and poked a protruding hairpin back into place under the tetchy eye of her son, and thought of Seshu, whose sensibilities were for things of a different nature, while Srinivas pushed the conversation along. Sometimes, goaded by circumstances into unfair thinking, he felt he was the only one who tried, as he searched for sentences, and scoured his mind, which seemed to have been picked clean, and stared at the blue jowls of his son which in the right company could shake like the dewlaps on a flighty cow, but now were set firm and offered no assistance. And this girl Pat, with her nervous hands and flat single syllables, her pink dry mouth which she had to lick before she could utter. And Vasantha, who apparently had been stricken dumb.

But when he looked at Vasantha something in him dissolved and he could not bear to continue, seeing the marching lilac shadows, and the falling planes of her face, which the evocation of her loss could make manifest. Then he spurred himself to rout the ruinous silence, selecting topics on which he was informed and could hold forth. Drooling on, Laxman described it to himself, about his rancid spices.

Afterwards, in their bedroom, on the first floor which had been turned over to them in its echoing entirety according to Vasantha's original plan, though she hadn't visualized it working out exactly like this, in the intimacy of bed Pat said to Laxman, 'I do think your parents are sweet.' Feeling it was expected of her, and with some sweetness in her own nature which made it ready to oblige, dealing out appropriate sentiments without undue awareness of departures from veracity.

'I find them impossible,' said Laxman. 'To talk to,' he qualified, and wondered about his wife, whom on the whole he would not, before this night, have considered moronic.

Pat cogitated. She had little mind of her own, and would have preferred to devote that little to deferring to her husband's opinion. But there were other considerations.

'I think they're nice,' she said, and glowed, believing she was being the kind of wife any man would want, the sort that would never come between him and his parents.

'I'm glad you think so,' said Laxman, and was ungracious to her with his body, which usually he deployed with skill, making her wonder what she had done wrong as she bumped up and down in no kind of rhythm with him.

Though no one planned it that way, there were no further visits. For by the following year the couple had acquired a house in Plymouth and were too busy settling in to trek down to London. The year after, there was the baby. Laxman wrote specifically to say they were not to come up yet as Pat's parents were staying to tide Pat over – there had been complications after the birth – and there was only the one spare bedroom.

'What does that matter?' asked Vasantha, bewildered. 'Is a room essential? I would have slept anywhere. In a corridor, or the kitchen. Just to see the baby.'

'They don't do things like that in this country,' said Srinivas.

'A dozen people, sleeping in one basement, during the war,' she reminded him.

'The war is over,' he said.

Largely owing to her pleas an invitation to visit was eventually issued, and accepted, for the summer, six months ahead. By then Vasantha had developed tuberculosis and, clearly, could not go anywhere near a vulnerable infant.

Although they were both registered as National Health patients, Srinivas insisted on calling in a doctor privately.

'What for?' demanded Laxman, who had come down on a flying visit to do his duty.

'Well,' said Srinivas, and stopped. He had a feeling, but it was as yet too amorphous to explain. Later – long afterwards – it crystallized; when it did the crystals had sharp, cutting edges.

'You get first-class treatment on the National Health,' said Laxman, looming tall in the sitting room above the low divans. 'All you get by paying is a few fancy frills. These one can do without,' he suggested, meaning his mother could, and citing his wife, who had done very well without them, although keeping these sentiments to himself since he found there were brakes on what he could say to this parent.

'Frills did not enter my mind when making my decision,' said Srinivas.

Then Laxman was more than usual at sea, until he remembered certain outspoken homilies, with which his unembarrassed parents had blighted his childhood.

'You think it's something for nothing,' he said. 'That's it, isn't it. Well, it isn't,' he said shortly, one concerned inner eye focused on his dwindling patrimony. 'You pay your taxes like everyone else. You're as entitled to it as the next man.'

Srinivas did not argue with his son. He has moved too far away from us, he told himself. And Laxman, in a fleeting moment of illumination, perhaps brought about by some sadness in the occasion, saw his father as a man of sound but monumentally useless principles. They parted. Laxman returned with relief to his congenial Plymouth factory. Srinivas engaged, privately, a doctor whose fees he paid in advance as firmly requested. Vasantha was deluded, briefly, into believing in her recovery.

'When I am better,' she said to her husband, 'we must return to our country. There is no reason, now that India is free, why we should not. Nor,' she said painfully, 'is there anything, really, to keep us here any more.'

Srinivas agreed, almost wordlessly. He was amazed that his wife, a perspicacious woman, should be so gravely in error about her condition. In his anger he turned upon the doctor, a kindly man who was only doing his duty, as he saw it and of course in the patient's interest, of concealing and deceiving so that the patient could die happy.

'But don't you see, one has to make one's peace,' said Srinivas, but realized as he spoke that these words would have little impact and altered his thrust. 'One has to make one's dispositions,' he amended.

'I understand,' said the doctor, and continued delicately. 'I had, of course, no reason to suspect that your wife is a wealthy woman.'

'She is not,' said Srinivas.

'Then there seems little point,' the doctor began, but was cut short, in his opinion quite unjustifiably.

'You have no right,' said Srinivas, and trembled from the strength of his feeling. 'You, a human being, have no right to keep the truth from her, or anyone.'

The doctor drew a long breath. This man, he could see, was a difficult customer. A bolshie. Disputing rights which everyone knew belonged to the doctor.

'Very well,' he said. 'You tell her.'

In fact there was no need. Vasantha's doctor-induced euphoria did not persist. She was, basically, too honest a person to resist when the truth began, however feebly, to bulge through the tissues of concealment. Srinivas, watching her sink, wondered whether, when his time came, he would be able to match the serenity with which she bore the ebbing of her life. It seemed to him intolerable. He was then in middle life: forty-nine, and Vasantha was just past forty.

Sometimes he asked himself which of the two, the body or the woman herself, had given up, and at these times he attempted to rally her, to rouse that will which had upheld them during all those years of misery and stress in India. But in his heart he knew that the mortal blow had been dealt much earlier, in the year in which Seshu had been killed. Seshu, with his tormented conscience and fine-ground sensibility, and the surprising strength lodged in his thin body, Seshu the younger son, who had been the apple of his mother's eye.

In her last weeks it was his name she called most frequently, her eyes very bright and clear, high spots of colour purplish under her yellowed skin. Srinivas heard her cries, night after night, lying on the narrow camp cot rigged up next to the double bed, and was wracked. For there were no ready-made comforts to hand. Their faith offered no anodynes, no cheery resurrections and ascensions and meetings-up with cherished ones in heaven: only a formidable purification through rebirth, and the final ineffable bliss of divine union.

Towards the end, however, peace returned to Vasantha. She was very calm, very lucid, putting her affairs in order insofar as she could, though with a certain detachment, as if the concerns and liaisons of the world had fallen into place, if not insignificance. Yet they were close: closer perhaps than many couples, since there had been no alternative vines and supports to which each might have attached.

'It has been,' said Vasantha, hoarsely, the breath from her ruined lungs coming up rough, 'a happy marriage.'

Srinivas could not speak. He clutched at her hand, whitening her bones with the strength of his grip, and rebelled at her going.

Outside the crematorium chapel a green-coated attendant handed Srinivas the casket. It was very light. Five pounds, or so, of ash. The finest human ash, for they had raked through the embers and taken out unsightly gobbets and unconsumed bits of bone and sieved out the rest.

'It's all done up, guv,' he said. 'Sealed, so you won't have no trouble with spillage.' He paused, considering, then came out with it. 'Now don't you fret yourself,' he said kindly. 'I mean it comes to us all in the end. If you take my advice you'll scatter the ashes. It don't do any good brooding over them like.'

'I shall take your advice,' promised Srinivas, and got on a bus with the casket. It was a difficult thing to do, for besides the casket he was carrying Vasantha's sandalwood box which she had filled with earth from India and brought with her, and her hair-oil bottle half full of Ganges water. Laxman should have carried these but Laxman was in bed with influenza. So he managed, somehow, on his own.

At London Bridge he alighted. There was a catwalk, and steps leading down to the river. The tide was in, there was not far to go: five or six steps, and the sluggish Thames was slopping over his toecaps. Srinivas put down the box and bottle while he broke the seals on the casket. Then he opened it gently, and leaning out as far as he could so that they should not be washed back, he tipped the ashes into the river. Afterwards there remained only the small service she had asked of him and this he performed, sprinkling earth and Ganges water onto the ashes being borne away on the Thames.

He was, at that period of his life, beginning to lose the fetters which tied him to any one country. He was a human being, and as such felt he belonged to a wider citizenship. Yet, in this moment, he could not help feeling with Vasantha, who in her breath and bones had remained wholly Indian. She would have liked her remains committed to the currents of an Indian river, though she had scrupulously refrained from such onerous impositions; and now, watching her ashes drift away downstream, he wished he could have found some way to avoid consigning them to these alien waters.

A sauntering policeman, pausing to lean over the parapet, observed the proceedings. He waited for Srinivas to come up and said reprovingly, 'You are not allowed to tip your household rubbish into the river.'

'I would not dream of doing so,' said Srinivas.

'I'm sorry, sir, but you did,' accused the policeman. 'I saw you. If everyone carried on the same the river would soon be polluted.' Here it occurred to him that it already was: a very fine array of floating debris was being shunted gently along by the tide. The constable averted his eyes. 'Well, just see you don't do it again,' he said, and prepared to move on. 'The river's not the place for rubbish.'

'It was not rubbish,' said Srinivas, and found to his dismay that his throat was working painfully. 'It was my wife.'

Joker, eh, thought the policeman tersely; but the sharp words died on his lips as he whipped around smartly, because he could see that the middle-aged Indian before him was weeping. Or was as close to it as any man could be, in the presence of another. The constable reddened, being young, and decent as the young often are; then he touched his helmet, awkwardly, to the stricken man, and walked on.

6

THAT PERIOD, FOR SRINIVAS, WAS A DUST BOWL OF being. Empty. Without meaning. Scooped out, picked clean, no climbing up the slippery sides. A skull, from which all matter had gone. Sea urchin shell, from which the living lights had been brutally plucked, leaving the pearly skeleton to serve as an ornament for the mindless, the surf-riders of life.

Sometimes the skeleton rattled off down to the spice shop to see how things were doing. Not, indeed, from any overpowering interest in keeping body and soul together, but reminded of human connections. By Laxman for instance, whose blood pressure rose when he thought of these things. 'I hear,' he wrote sternly, mentioning no names, 'that the whole place is going to pot. It seems a pity that a thriving business, built up over a decade or more, should be allowed to die for want of a little attention.'

Srinivas stared at the letter, sitting at his desk in the empty office, and waiting for the words to start prancing on the page as he knew they would. As, being meaningless, they soon did, for the truth of the matter was that it was a dying trade. The war had dealt some hefty blows, and the restrictions of the austere, immediate post-war years had almost completed the killing. Laxman had been wrong in saying it needed a little attention. It needed a great deal, of the kind and quantity a young man with his faculties and energies intact might have provided. Srinivas was neither. He was nearly fifty, and the cumulative losses of his life – even more than he knew – had denuded him.

Abdul the Zanzibari, sniffing around in England for signs of rejuvenation in the spice run, diagnosed more accurately.

'Hold on, man, trade will come up again like sunrise, you see if I'm lying,' he said, and gazed at this friend of long standing to assess him, and pursed his lips over what he saw. 'But if your heart is not in it,' he said, and left it open-ended for the other to finish in any way he chose, and Srinivas chose silence. Then Abdul rose, and went to the small room next to the office and brewed coffee on the stove that languished there, and carried the cups in, brimming, with a head of frothy bubbles on them as Srinivas himself would have done it. And Abdul sipped, and smiled, and pondered, and his black monochrome face began to grow mottled, reflecting certain emotions, until at length he felt he must declare possibilities, which excited him, and would, he hoped, spark this inert Indian.

'The trend,' he said, 'is turning. Full turnabout, because folks are fed up with basics. What they want – they don't realize yet, but they will – is comforts and luxuries. Silks and limousines and such, and rich food, rich sauces and spices ... Any time now, they'll start yelling. And our folks,' he said to the silent Indian, 'yours and mine, they'll be coming here – right here to England – to take up their share in the prosperity which was built on their backs. Only the islanders won't see it that way. The little English, they won't hear what the whole world's saying. Stone deaf is what they become when you talk about what they owe. As to what they believe – that's sure good for a belly laugh.'

Abdul smiled, at the naive laughable beliefs of his English acquaintances, who told him that the object of having colonies – indeed the whole business of empire – had been purely for the benefit of the natives, a holy business. Then Srinivas was caught up too, and taken out of himself despite his debilitating misery, and smiled back at the polished ebony features of the African, and as the infectious merriment soared Abdul began to chuckle loudly, firstly because of the joke they shared, and soon from certain thoughts which he outlined.

'Our people,' he said, 'yours and mine, when they come here they will not be able to endure the British diet. Which is insipid, even the natives admit. No. They'll have cravings pretty bad, like a pregnant woman. For red-hot curries and oily fries. For coconuts, chillies, spices, breadfruit, okra, and akki rice. Those who can give them what they want' – Abdul prodded Srinivas to share his relish, his trader's ambition – 'will grow rich, and buy big houses, and be reviled.'

'Who wants to be?' asked Srinivas.

'It is quite pleasant,' Abdul assured him. 'To be poor and reviled, that is one thing, but rich and reviled, entirely another. One can easily put up with the one for the sake of the other. Take the British: did they not find their empire so sweet one had to have crowbars to prise up their fingers?'

'They gave it up with some grace,' said Srinivas.

'How do you know, you were sitting here in England,' said Abdul contemptuously, 'listening to their delusions, and swallowing the pious talk they specialize in.'

After this there was silence, both men conscious of some heat, but soon Abdul returned to the prospects of trade, which after all was nearest to his heart. Srinivas listened dutifully, feeling it was in his interest to do so, but somehow echoes of the past kept intruding. Voiced hopes, strong and bold in the beginning. Declaring the bent towards scholarship, the intention to follow in his father's footsteps. The ambition, sown in ancient nurseries: I am a Brahmin, a scholar, I intend to take my rightful place in the ranks of the learned. Nurtured by prizes, certificates, the bright gold medal. Kept intact through all the confusion and corrosion of the nation's struggle, and on the long sea flight from the convulsed continent. And then the English voice at the interview.

'Failed BA, eh? Ha-ha.'

Failed BA, that old, old joke, so deliciously comical there was hardly a novel or tale retold in which it did not figure. How it hurt. Years afterwards that pain, unlike others, was not gone beyond total recall.

'I did not,' the young flayed man who had been himself had said, 'have the opportunity of taking my finals.'

Afterwards he knew it would have made no difference if he had sat for his finals, and passed, and acquired an Indian college degree. The joke would still have been there, it would merely have altered ground slightly to make the university its butt. Then, he did not know. He continued to offer his learning. There were more interviews. More – similar – voices and verdicts. One day he knew. Quite suddenly. One moment he was preparing for yet another interview, arranging dogeared and much-thumbed certificates neatly in a folder; the next, he knew that he would not go. Not now, not ever. Methodically, and fairly calmly, and without delay, he began dismantling the screens with which he had shielded himself.

Shortly afterwards he became a trader, taking over the foundering import–export agency of a friend who was returning to India. It was a superimposition, this business of trading: a graft upon a natural bent for meticulous intellectual organization. But it flourished. Necessity, it seemed, could work wonders.

Had Vasantha been of a different cast of mind Srinivas would have expanded the business: not to prove anything to himself, or because curiosity in his powers had been piqued, but simply as a consequence of momentum generated by opportunity and good management. Vasantha, however, deliberately kept their standards modest, in keeping with the beliefs of her countrymen, who learned to connect the pomp and circumstance of the few with the misery of the many.

'Buying cheap and selling dear is the foundation of our prosperity,' she told her husband, 'and human beings – their colour is quite immaterial – are involved in both transactions. If we live rich, like it or not, it is at someone else's expense.'

She was good at nailing connections: not merely spotting them and then keeping mum, but feeling the need to identify and declaim against them if necessary – a curse which did not descend upon Srinivas until later. Their marriage, a happy one, might conceivably have been even happier had he become the scholar he had wanted to be, rather than a merchant. Though he had never entered the category which apparently, he heard himself being assured, now lay open to him.

'Princes, rolling in riches, that is what we shall be,' Abdul was saying, carried away by a double infusion of enthusiasm, one for himself and the other to tempt this moony companion. 'Trade will soon be on the upturn, there will be opportunities galore, opportunities for us on the grand scale, such as there have never been. All we shall need is the ability to grasp them. A *leetle* expertise,' he wheedled, 'a *leetle* energy ...' And gradually fell silent, aware from sundry twinges that awkward truths were nibbling to get out, and dropped his hands, on whose dusky fingers the rings had flashed in emphatic gesticulation. 'It will not be easy,' he said at last, simply. 'Sometimes, when I think of it, I am afraid. If one is not strong, there is no place here for him. Better to leave the country.'

Srinivas stirred. 'Yes, why not?' he said. 'That is what my wife said we ought to do. Just before she died, you know. Yes, perhaps that is what I should do.'

But the thought of the process of leaving – the form-filling, the packing, the selling-up and going – made him flinch. When I have the energy, he promised himself. When, however, some of his energies did dribble back, he found he had no notion of where to go to in India, or what to do when he got there, since so much had been destroyed or given up – self-respect, livelihood, family cohesions – during the struggle for independence. In the absence of these robust lifelines the decision to leave did not survive.

Srinivas himself survived, after a fashion. That is to say, he continued to exist, in a state of some squalor. A neighbour or two sometimes rang the bell, and asked if they could help, and shuffled awkwardly on the doorstep while Srinivas stared at them blankly, and finally brought out that no, he did not think they could. Then they went away, rather relievedly if the truth be told, although if called upon they would have been happy to oblige, in those days which were decent. Meanwhile the squalor grew. Bluebottles buzzed around the dustbins, and litter from the unswept yard swirled over other people's tidy properties, severely trying the patience of housewives. A few – those most affected, like Nos. 3 and 7 – made sharp wounded comments, but generally people were charitable, knowing the history of the widower at No. 5.

Nobody, except Laxman, called the house a pigsty.

Laxman, concerned like Abdul in the revival of trade, had squeezed a few days from his own busy schedule to travel down and see for himself, and was revolted by what he saw. He had never approved of his mother or her ways, but she had kept the house spotless, rambling and gaunt though it was. His wife, in the brand-new house they had bought, on an easier wicket, was equally competent. Now, poking about in the kitchen (he was hungry: Srinivas, having forgotten he was coming, had made no preparations) he saw the signs of neglect, the stained oilcloth cover on the table, the greasy sink, dust and dead flies on the windowsill. Worse still, the only food he could find was stale bread in a bin, a few blackened bananas, a half-bottle of milk. Carrying this, and much put out, Laxman emerged, his mouth wry with disgust.

'The place,' he announced, 'is a pigsty.'

'It is not,' acknowledged Srinivas, 'as your mother used to keep it.'

That is putting it mildly, said Laxman to himself. 'You must get help,' he said aloud, and walked about pointedly, like a housewife with cobwebs on her mind. 'A charwoman, for a few hours a day. You cannot carry on like this.'

'I doubt if I could afford one,' said Srinivas, and hesitated, knowing what he had to say would pain his son. 'The business is failing,' he confessed.

'Are you surprised?' asked Laxman, and stopped perambulating, seeing that things were worse than he had feared.

'No. Not really,' said Srinivas, and looked down at his hands, those incompetent things, which at one time had been capable. 'It demands more than I am able to give it,' he said.

'So what are you going to do?'

'I don't know what to do,' said Srinivas. 'I feel empty,' he said, and stared at the back of his son's neck, where a roll of fat had begun to flow over the collar. 'Completely empty, that is the trouble.'

Laxman stifled his impatience. 'You must pull yourself together,' he said, and felt indeed that this aptly described what had to be done, as if his father were some slack old bag whose strings must be pulled tight before the entire contents fell out.

'Yes. I can see that that is what I shall have to try and do,' said Srinivas.

Laxman could see that it would not be done. He was getting more and more skilled at weighing men up, he could gauge their potential almost to the last ounce. So presently, six months later, sighing at the prospect, he took time off from his own concerns to travel to London to close down his father's business, and to prop the old man up in whatever niche could be found.

By then, however, Srinivas was standing up on his own. The shackles that the loss of his wife had laid upon his mind and energies were dissolving, melted in the warmth of human commitment.

7

IT HAPPENED IMPERCEPTIBLY: A CASUAL MEETING growing and branching into an established state that, when it was done, Srinivas had no intention of disturbing.

He was walking, as he often did, to get away from the house, or perhaps from himself, when he became aware of being impeded. Annoying though it was, he kept going, tripping and stumbling now and then but, in the suspended state these walks induced, unwilling to investigate causes. Then he heard a voice, which seemed to him familiar, no doubt from the fact that it had addressed him several times.

'Excuse me,' it said, sounding exasperated. 'Excuse me, but your shoelaces are undone.'

Srinivas looked down at the trailing laces: not merely undone, but threaded only through the last two holes.

'How careless of me,' he said. He felt ashamed: forcing good citizens to haul him up like this. 'I'm afraid I didn't notice,' he confessed, sitting on the curb and tying tight knots.

'I know. One gets like that,' said the voice. A woman's voice. A middle-aged woman's face, broad, putty-coloured, looming over him in the gloomy light.

'You know?' he asked, surprised.

'Yes. Why not? It's not unique to have problems.'

'No,' said Srinivas, and felt crushed, for here was this woman with her brisk voice, who had problems and knew what it was like but could cope, while he drifted, tripped up by simple things like shoelaces. He hunched himself still lower in shame, staring at the shins which were level with his eyes and, he saw, rather thin and encased in thick stockings which were holed, the holes exposing small hideous protuberances of puckered flesh.

'Come on,' said the woman, and nudged him – with her knee, he imagined, feeling the jar of bone on bone, kneecap against shoulder blade. 'You can't sit here all night. They don't like it, you know.'

'They,' he said, and continued to sit. 'Whom do you mean? I don't think there is anyone who cares what I do.'

'The police,' she answered.

Then he cowered, retracted his head into his shoulders, and crossed his arms above to take the baton blows, and so, cringing before dangers that did not threaten, was converted from a figure of loneliness into a madman. As almost instantly he realized, and got to his feet, still shaking and sweating, so heavily had memories marched, but returned to the manners of sanity, which demanded apologies.

'I am sorry,' he offered. 'I don't know what came over me. I have been a little run-down lately.'

She eyed him; making up her mind, he surmised, whether bouts of lucidity and madness alternated, if a change of cycle was now due.

'I do not often behave like that,' he ventured, to put the matter straight.

'Past nightmares,' she said.

'What did you say?' he asked, and grew a little agitated. 'What did you say?'

'The past has a way of catching up,' she obliged, 'sometimes at the most inconvenient moments.'

He looked at her more closely, this ordinary woman who could say such arresting things, but whatever there was was safely put away, behind a plain face which did its best to escape notice. If I saw her again I wouldn't know her, he thought a little sadly, and tried to stamp her image into his memory; but as if to thwart the intention she averted her face, presenting only a blurred profile freakishly lit by the blue mercury street lamps which had begun to flicker on.

'I must go,' she said, and he thought, I have transgressed, the English do not like their reserve invaded; but her next words, though conventional enough, cleared his dejection. Very small things, then, could tilt his balance.

'Look after yourself,' she said, and nodded to him and was gone, leaving an impression of holed stockings and a shapeless hat, and some unusual cadences of nature.

Contrary to his expectations he did in fact recognize her when he saw her again. He was walking, rather less aimlessly than heretofore, and indeed in the hope of a meeting, when he saw the shapeless hat, and, his eyes travelling rapidly downward, the somewhat scraggy shins clad in familiar stockings. Basing himself upon the holes, for which he could have vouched, though less sure about form and features, he would have launched himself upon her with glad cries, this being the first reaction of his blood, but England intervened. England, with its unvoiced interdictions, which had laid halter and curb on him, cooling the riper manifestations of emotions. Instead of falling on her, therefore, he advanced diffidently, ready with a bold remark about the weather, to which no one, not even the English, could take exception.

Perhaps it was as well. Afterwards, when he knew her better, and each had sized the other up to some extent, he realized she would have fled a more spirited approach. She almost said as much. 'I hate people who pry,' she told him, 'and force themselves upon you for their benefit and pretend it's for yours.'

Srinivas did not wish to pry. He did not know what he wished or wanted, unless perhaps it was human company of the unquestioning, unforceful kind she described. Like her, he had no desire to ask or answer questions. His wife, his sons, the past that had brought him here – he thought about these things often enough, but he did not want to talk about them. One day, perhaps; perhaps not. He could not foretell. She, likewise, seemed far from yearning to learn anything, or to tell all.

On this male, uncommitted basis they were content to jog along together. Without planning anything, they nevertheless contrived to meet, and went for walks in the local park, and sat side by side on benches, the middle-aged man and the still older woman, at whom one or two looked askance but most passed by, both being of an age in which few took interest, and fewer still, in that era before racial evil was unleashed in England, to compare with hostility variations in the colours and textures of hair and skin.

One day, lapped in the warm silence which sometimes welled between them, he was moved to confide in her. Impelled, rather, as if it was now necessary for his own recovery to yield a part of himself to another.

'I am a widower,' he informed her. 'Come Sunday, my wife will have been dead four months.'

'I guessed you might be,' she rejoined. 'The blow seemed recent.'

He waited, but she said no more, and he felt an illogical chagrin that she should offer nothing in exchange. Then he remembered the time he had allowed himself in which to reveal, or preserve intact, and wordlessly returned to her these freedoms, restoring to airs which had become congested between them their old, sweet quality. Soon after this she told him she was divorced.

'I am sorry,' he said, distressed. His marriage had made him naive, unable to think of bitter partnerships.

'I am glad,' she said. 'It was a miserable marriage. I was never so happy as the day my husband left me.'

He was wordless. He left her to continue, hardly able to imagine so barren a living.

'It was a relief,' she went on, and turned her eyes on him, pale ellipses from which most of the colour appeared to have seeped away, merging iris into eyeball. 'Such a relief, when it was over. Like a lot of knots being undone,' and she stretched out her limbs in re-enactment of the memory, raising her arms and shooting out both legs heedless of passers-by, and exclaiming at the damage now plainly on display, whose rims she traced with a finger.

'It's no good sewing them up,' she explained, 'it only increases the tension elsewhere and you have a lot of little holes, instead of a few big ones.' Though in truth, as Srinivas could see, there were several big ones, but he pretended with her out of consideration.

So he was initiated into the ways of stockings, which Vasantha had never worn, and possibly also into certain aspects of his friend's living, for it occurred to him that their tattered condition might reflect her financial state. He did not, however, investigate the matter. After a while, in the true spirit of their unspoken pact, it even passed from his mind.

Winter retreated, spring came muted and uncertain between snowdrop and daffodil. One day, instead of the old felt hat topping the familiar figure, he saw a nodding straw. It was lemon yellow, with a droopy brim and a lacy edge which, on closer inspection, he saw were stalks of straw which had become unravelled from the main weave.

'Do you like my hat?' she asked him gaily.

'It is very charming, if rather fragile,' he said sincerely, thinking it was next door to disintegration, but reassuring himself (since Vasantha had never worn hats) that he was not equipped to form valid judgements in these matters.

'I hope it will last,' she said, as if he had plainly voiced his doubts. 'I paid rather more than I liked for it.'

'Is it new?' he asked, aghast.

'I bought it in a sale last week,' she said, and fixed him with an eye. 'In a church jumble sale.'

The atmosphere, which the eye had created, told him that this was an admission of some kind, but of what he could not tell. They – he and Vasantha – had never gone to church, nor, consequently, to sales that shored up tottering spires, or paid for the removal of deathwatch beetles from the beams, or other worthy causes. He therefore did not know that these sales were a godsend to the poor, who could kit themselves out completely from jumble; and she did not choose to enlighten him. They rested. Soon the air which had been charged returned to normal. Whatever he might have gleaned, or she confided, was left.

Confidence, indeed, hardly entered their scheme of exchange. Each knew the other had lost a spouse, and suffered blows whose details were not revealed. Each knew the other's name, and concluded from the number of times they ran into each other that both must live in the same neighbourhood. Neither found further revelations essential, although, such was the bond between them, each understood disclosures would not be difficult, or a violation, if and when the time came to make them.

Returning from his office one day, to which he paid some cursory attention in deference to his son's wishes, Srinivas caught sight of the lemon straw bobbing past the railings of his house. He was delighted. It meant he could rid himself of the dreadful weight of responsibility these office visits roused without feeling unduly guilty. Pocketing the key he had ready, he ran down the steps, the clouds that menaced his heart magically dispersed.

'Mrs Pickering,' he sang, 'Mrs Pickering!' And he bounded after her, for she was a brisk walker, in all weathers.

Mrs Pickering stopped and looked around. Her broad face, battered by the seasons, beamed upon him.

'Why, it's you, Mr Srinivas,' she said – her tongue twisted quite easily around the name, he had noticed.

'Another minute and I would have missed you altogether,' he told her.

'There would have been another time,' she said practically.

'But today is important,' he said, 'since one lives in the present. I needed something' – he paused and searched his mind, which was full of feelings which would not be chivvied into words, until a neighbour's phrase came to the rescue – 'to take me out of myself.'

'A necessary proceeding, sometimes.' She nodded. 'I gather you have had a difficult day,'

'I have been to my office,' he confessed. 'It depresses me. It's worse when I get back. Sometimes I can hardly bring myself to go in.'

'Then why do you?'

'Where else should one go?' he asked. 'It is my house. I live in it.'

'Yours?' They were outside his neighbour's.

'That one.' He pointed, seeing it on the instant through Laxman's eyes. The state it was in. A house fated, it appeared, to grimy curtains and peeling paint. 'The crumbling one with the blistered paint,' he said masochistically.

'Things need looking after. But it's not so bad.'

She was being kind, he thought. She was a kind woman. He wished he could invite her in, both of them standing as they were virtually on his doorstep. His hospitable instincts urged him to but he felt he knew better. A pigsty of a place. That was what Laxman had said, and Srinivas heartily agreed. One could not invite one's friends to enter a sty. His determination grew, while the silence lengthened, and they continued to stand. All his small talk – such as he had – was gone.

'It's a lovely day,' she said at last, throwing him a lifeline. 'I thought I'd go for a walk in the park, it's so nice.'

'It is,' he said gratefully. 'May I accompany you?'

The park was about half a mile away. They walked side by side, but independently, she considerately reducing her speed, he accelerating so that they could be in step, as well as in the rhythm of their similar natures. In this harmony, which was more than the total of its parts, they walked down the road, past the brick-built houses and scarlet pillar boxes, past small corner shops and a freshly painted turkey-red kiosk and a bomb site of close on a third of an acre bright with meadow flowers and weeds sprung up above the rubble.

'How quickly the land returns,' she said, pausing to admire the rosebay, 'to its natural state, once it is left alone.'

'One soon reverts to the jungle,' he agreed. 'It needs very little.'

'Do you mean we do?' she asked, and clapped a palm to the crown of her hat, which was threatening to take off in the rising wind.

'Perhaps we too; I wasn't really thinking,' he replied, and looked at the sky which, as forecast, had become afflicted by variable cloud. 'Perhaps we ought to turn back,' he suggested.

'It will soon clear; it is a capricious climate,' she said, and almost at once the sun came out. 'You see,' she said with pleasure, lulled into removing her hold on her hat, which immediately lifted and spun away leaving a few remnants of straw skewered by a hatpin.

On to the bomb site it sailed, the lemon straw with its holed crown; over the rubble and the rosebay and goldenrod, tangling here and there with the taller weeds but freed by the wind and whirling on. Mrs Pickering, only momentarily hesitant, darted after it. Srinivas followed. Before either could reach it four youths appeared, ruffled from lying about, and perhaps by this disturbance of whatever they had been engaged in doing. Youths with the sullenness of their adolescence and idleness upon their faces, who stood uncertainly, whose urges might have been bent one way or another. Then circumstance directed, bringing the hat to rest at the feet of one of them. He eyed it, this lad in the brown leather jacket and winkle-picker shoes, then tentatively inserted a pointed toe and flicked up the straw. Clowning, thought Srinivas, and intending to dive under and receive it on his head. But the hat soared away: a ball, a woman, a fleeing animal; and winkle-picker's face lit up at the thought of a little sport livening his petrified day.

'Lady's lost her hat. Come on, mate,' he called, and winked, and plunged after the straw.

Even then they did not understand, the two of them. They stood in their innocence, waiting for the hat to be restored, which to one of them at least was important. But now it became apparent that the figures that leapt and hounded in pursuit were not as they had imagined but participants in some sport of whose nature, or consequences, they were unaware or indifferent. Skilfully deployed, passing skilfully on the run, they bandied the hat about between them, playing it as their betters might have played a hare or a bull. It bobbed and dipped, this quavery straw, shedding its trimmings as they kicked it from one to the other, and flopped down among the weeds and in grimy puddles but rose again to air currents and the thrust of determined toecaps, though with diminishing buoyancy.

It had happened quickly, so quickly that neither Srinivas nor his companion could realize and intervene in time; but now Mrs Pickering rushed forward to retrieve her hat, or perhaps the situation which had ballooned so monstrously.

'Stop!' she cried, 'Stop!' Taking hold of lapels and whirling fastenings to jackets, her thin shoes clattering over stones and fallen masonry. And her face. As if she was being beaten, Srinivas saw, and the hat were more than woven straw which had been shaped to a skull, with a brim. So he followed her, queasy in the stomach, but raging, a rather short, mild-looking man of whom no one should have been afraid, but were. Breathing fire. They felt it, the four flushed youths who had ridden high, and expressed what they felt in words familiar from their pulp magazine reading, and aimed a few last nerveless kicks before departing, telling themselves that anyhow the game was over.

As it was. No more fun to be had from the hat, which lay on the ground with its crown crushed to a pulp, and would clearly never rise and float freely again, even on the stub of a boot. Nevertheless, Srinivas bent to pick it up, though his fingers flinched from touching the bedraggled object; but Mrs Pickering stopped him.

'Leave it,' she said in her matter-of-fact way. 'It's of no further use.'

'Those louts,' he said, and trembled in anger.

'I do not suppose they had any idea,' she said, 'what it meant.'

Then, suddenly, she seemed to crumple, and sat down abruptly on the rubble beside the ruined straw.

'It's just that it was an expensive hat,' she said, and her voice was so thin and strained that Srinivas was afraid to speak in case it broke, the high-pitched voice and on its rack this woman who had become brittle, like glass, spun glass with a flaw in the blowing which would shatter it at the slightest exposure. So Srinivas was concerned not to expose, and even tried to screen her from her own disclosures by interrupting with news of the weather.

'It has turned out fine after all,' he said, and studied the sky.

But now Mrs Pickering was too far gone, or possibly recognized that the moment had come, since she had always acknowledged she would not hold back her confidences when the time was ripe, when further hoarding and withholding could impair a relationship.

'Expensive hats and gloves and shoes,' she said. 'One always had them ... when we were girls, my sister and I. It seems silly, doesn't it, but I think I missed them almost more than anything else ... I mean after my husband had gone, and most of the money too. Of course one gets used to things. Most things,' she qualified. 'I would have said all things, until now. But one does not know oneself, not after all the years of probing, does one?'

'No,' he agreed. 'It takes more than a lifetime,'

'I could tell it came from a good milliner,' she continued. 'I didn't think that could mean anything, but you know, it did. After all these years having a good hat meant something to me.'

'It is human,' he managed.

'Despite its state,' she said. 'But, then, what can you expect in a jumble sale? All those hands, rummaging. Searching for cheap things. It was a cheap hat,' she said, and nudged the fallen straw, 'if you judge by what I paid. But the quality was there.'

Srinivas had nothing to say. He simply sat beside her on the waste ground, mutely offering the comfort of his company while the shadows of rosebay willow which shielded them from the public gaze lengthened and became tinged with lilac from the darkening sky.

'It is time we went home,' he said at last.

'I have no particular home to go to,' she told him.

8

SO MRS PICKERING ENTERED HIS HOME AND BECAME part of his life. She still was. He could not imagine the house without her in it, nor his life without her presence to consolidate those intimations of grace and ultimate meaning which were vouchsafed him as he grew older. Yet he accepted that this too, like so many, could be an illusion: for had he not encountered a similar unimaginable desert of existence after the death of his wife and survived and come through to the other side? Only, he had been younger then; and there had been Mrs Pickering to rehabilitate the scorched and dusty creature that emerged.

A need, and a fulfilment, it turned out to be. On both sides. Simply achieved.

'If you have nowhere of course you must come and stay with me,' he had said, issuing the invitation, to his pigsty, the very thought of which had earlier given him palpitations. He remembered quite exactly his words, and the angle irons of someone's bombed-out fireplace upon which he sat denting his buttocks.

'With you? In your house?' she asked.

'Yes. Why not? I have no one either,' he replied.

'Your son,' she reminded him.

'Yes,' he said, and paused to shape an answer not too flagrantly a truth or a lie, for loyalties still held, although the bonds of blood had withered to next to nothing, worked on by an alien culture. 'There is my son. But, you see, we have grown apart. He has his concerns and I, of course, have mine.'

Even then Mrs Pickering – in the stress of her hat and her naked admission – did not probe. She rose from the pile of crumbling mortar onto which she had subsided, brushing off dust and grains that clung.

'If you are sure,' she said.

Srinivas was sure, with that absolute weight of certainty that occasionally invests a decision.

Very soon the pigsty was transformed: cleaned, washed, polished, shabby but shining – despite his shamefaced protests that it was his responsibility.

'I hope you don't think,' he said painfully, watching her one day, seeing the dust and fluff and shrivelled-up spiders she had poked from corners and assembled in the middle of the room ready for sweeping up, 'despite the evidence, that I am a dirty person.'

'I didn't think you were,' she replied, and continued sturdily to work.

'It is just,' he said, and stared at her, wondering if that capable frame would know, perhaps from experience. 'It is just that one cannot make the effort. One slides down. Into some kind of bog, from which it is almost impossible to heave oneself out.'

She put down pan and brush and rested. 'It seems so at the time,' she said, and her bleached eyes darkened, but, curiously, they also revealed, depth after depth like waters parting. 'It is a dreadful time, and an endless one.'

Then Srinivas began to ache as he had ached when he had seen those violet shades, destruction seeded under his wife's brown skin; and as before felt pinioned, believing there was nothing he could do. Although, in fact, he did provide some sustenance, of which he grew aware as the days went by, from a rounding-out he detected in Mrs Pickering, a softening of her brisk ways which, he began to see, had been a brittle crust to guard her vulnerability.

This did not mean, however, that she relaxed in any way her efforts to make the house as spick and span as the neighbours'. She swept and cleaned and mended and weeded and repaired, sometimes, to his amazement, to the point of exhaustion.

'I don't want them passing remarks,' she said.

'Who?' he asked, surprised.

'The neighbours,' she enlightened him.

'They're very nice people, I'm sure they wouldn't,' he said.

Mrs Pickering considered this. She began to say something, but changed her mind and stopped and began again.

'If one lives in a foreign country,' she said carefully, 'it is best to fall in with the ways of the natives, as far as possible.'

'This is my country now,' he said with some pride, and felt as he had felt when they championed the cause of his conchie son, warmed by the experience of tolerance and sanity. 'My country,' he repeated. 'I feel at home in it, more so than I would in my own.'

'All the more reason not to offend,' she said bluntly. 'Squalor is offensive to the English.'

Srinivas felt ashamed. It had not occurred to him that the results of these months of neglect, which his son had made clear revolted him, might also have been a sore trial to his neighbours. English neighbours, who had helped and put up with and never complained, at least in his hearing. The

English, who had made him free of their country; and in return he had trampled on their feelings.

'It was not intentional,' he said humbly. 'I would not willingly offend anyone.'

Although in fact he did, quite deliberately: but this was later on.

Whatever his shortcomings as a householder, no one faulted (although they would later on, after tuition) his fastidious personal cleanliness, those finicky habits he had carried with him from India and clung to despite the difference of equipment in England. He gargled and washed and spat, for hours on end, it sometimes seemed to Mrs Pickering as she waited to use the bathroom; and performed delicate balancing feats on the lavatory pan as he cleansed himself with water; and bathed under a shower he installed himself, an inept affair with a zany spray, so that when he had finished the walls dripped water and there were pools on the floor and damp patches on the ceiling of the kitchen, which was directly below. If Mrs Pickering noticed – she could hardly fail to – she did not comment. She restrained herself, though Srinivas did occasionally notice, when he emerged after his ablutions, that she seemed put out.

There were restraints that he exercised too. He could not bear the smell of meat being cooked. When she cooked these items, as she did when she could afford to, he had to go out, or retreat into the basement, where the smells did not penetrate, although he took care not to do so ostentatiously. Consequently she did not realize the extent of his aversion to flesh, though she knew he did not eat it.

They were, relatively speaking, prosperous these days, from a pooling of resources. Trading profits, while never dynamic, provided him with enough to live on, while she, not having to stretch a meagre income to cover inflated rents for lodgings, often had a little money left over now. She liked to spend it on food. On fruit, for instance, which she knew Srinivas liked, and which he seldom remembered to buy for himself. On unusual foodstuffs and vegetables that had begun to trickle into the country, eggplant and tender coconut and okra, which she nosed around the markets to find, for the nostalgic pleasure with which he greeted them. On meat sometimes, which she had more or less scrubbed from her previous diet. It was still expensive, the better cuts were out, but now and then she bought a chop, or a little bit of offal, liver perhaps, or kidneys, which she liked with her bacon.

Most days she shopped in the afternoon, returning with her string bag bulging with purchases if it were the end of the week, when she could afford to indulge herself, otherwise shrunk to modest proportions, and the holes of the fabric barely stretched. If he was in (he often was: there was not all that much to keep him in his office) she would call to him and put on a kettle to make them a cup of tea, and range her purchases on the kitchen table for him to see, especially if there was something for him. One day she bought him a pomelo.

'I've bought you a pomelo,' she said, 'and I bought myself some heart. Lamb's heart, it's cheaper than pig's.'

She unwrapped the meat and fruit to show him. The pomelo, pink tinged and tangy. Next to it a dark-red heart.

'It's delicious stuffed,' she told him. 'I wish you would join me, but I know you won't.'

Srinivas was stunned. He could not make it credible. It was not the blood, or the severed vessels, or the juices that oozed: he had got used to it in the war, had taken a course in first aid and even practised it and what burst out of a man was no different to what came from animals. But that this woman should, who was close kindred to him! Careless – or was it oblivious – of the process. The deliberate act, and the blood and mucus pumping out while the animal kicked and twitched and spilled its guts and died and the knives began again, severing and slitting, and greyish-green shit befouled the floor. The trade of killing, the obscene trade, so classified since medieval times, which brought meat to the table. And the business of feeding: people who ate and ate, like this woman stuffing herself with heart, unmindful of mutilation, force feeding, deprivation, the miseries of farm, market, and slaughterhouse; or persuading themselves that animal flesh did not feel, which was the worst horror of all.

Srinivas opened his eyes, which had involuntarily closed. They do not see it, he said to himself, as feverishly forgiving as any missionary; may God forgive them, they do not see it, they do not think about this side of things, otherwise they could not bring themselves to do it.

As she does not, he told himself, because, of course, she is one of them. It saddened him a little to think like this, since they were after all so close, in so many ways; but having given it recognition he would not allow the gap to grow. Live and let live, he said, as indeed Mrs Pickering also often had occasion to say. On this note of mutual forbearance they continued to enhance and advance their living.

9

TOWARDS CHRISTMAS, LAXMAN VISITED HIS FATHER.

He did so to forestall the issuing of invitations or the expectation of them, a stratagem so transparent that Srinivas had little difficulty in penetrating it. As it happened, it was not even necessary, for he accepted facts, these days, more easily than he had ever done, and without that rending and rebellion that had come close to destroying him after his wife's death. What had become difficult was to understand the need for deviousness. Why, wondered Srinivas, did Laxman bother? He felt a little sorry for his son, labouring to make plain facts complicated, and even tried to put him out of his misery by making his own plans crystal clear.

'Christmas is a Christian religious festival,' he said simply. 'I shall not celebrate it. Or expect to celebrate it with others.'

Laxman was vastly relieved. 'Don't know about the – um – religious side,' he mumbled. 'More for the children, really. But with a houseful, you know ... hordes of in-laws. But after Christmas perhaps something ... perhaps we can do something ...' He was getting incoherent, he realized, and he paused. 'I hope you won't be too lonely,' he said, and could have throttled himself for picking the most unfortunate words, in the circumstances, he could have found.

Srinivas, however, did not take advantage. 'Why should one be more lonely at Christmas,' he asked reasonably, 'than at any other time?'

'I only asked,' said Laxman, sweating.

'Besides,' said Srinivas, 'this year there is Mrs Pickering to keep me company.'

It stumped Laxman. He liked to believe he knew all his father's friends and acquaintances, and even imagined he knew the old man inside out. Yet here was some woman being introduced, whose name he had not even heard of before.

'Who is she?' he asked, rather brutally.

'A friend,' replied Srinivas. 'She shares the house with me. Have you not noticed how well kept it is? A pigsty,' he said slyly, 'no more.'

Laxman had indeed missed it, tussling with his other problem. He rose and walked about, taking note of the order and cleanliness and somewhat absently approving it, but far more conscious of strong twinges of dismay. For he had regarded himself the heir: had trodden these boards proprietorially, taking his inheritance for granted, while all the time this dry old stick had nurtured other ideas. Laxman felt aggrieved, and his step was less firm than it had used to be, but as there was nothing he could do, he resolved to be jocular, the way he was with the men at the factory.

'You *are* a dark horse,' he said, leering. 'Now where did you meet her, eh? Come on now, tell all.'

Srinivas remembered that he had never spoken to *his* father in this way, but he accepted that all kinds of speech were used by sons to their fathers in this country and so suppressed his astonishment.

'We met in the street,' he replied truthfully, 'quite accidentally.'

'A pick-up, eh?' said Laxman, and the flint showed, though he stayed jocular.

'If you like,' said Srinivas, 'although the implication is incorrect, since what happened was mutual.'

Then Laxman could not sustain his joviality. He sat glum and sipped coffee and thought about his father and Mrs Pickering, and his thinking was done in sexual terms, with here and there a financial note to add astringency. What was she like, he wondered, this pick-up? Some cheap little tart, he imagined, for he could not imagine any other kind of woman who might find his father attractive; some shrewd whore, he decided, out for what she could get out of the old man. And his father? Laxman stole a look at Srinivas, upon whom the sheen of tranquillity – its first glimmerings – had begun to rest, and drew conclusions that unsettled him. In terms of years, he realized, his father was not old ... middle-aged of course, well into middle age, with the parching and reducing that went with it, the shrivelled-up skin, the pulpy flesh and pouch like a prune; but then women could take anything, cripples, old men, the lot. Laxman shuddered a little and stroked his limbs and dwelt rather lovingly on his own firm swelling body, and sharp jets of acid and alarm shot hot and cold down his spine to think of his father, and the act, and the woman who jeopardized his patrimony, such as it was, since one could not expect very much from a man like Srinivas.

Srinivas was aware. He caught the whiffs of anguish let loose on the atmosphere, and without breaching his own inner peace felt sad for the young man exuding such misery on his hearth. He wished he could help, but the source was obscure, and such was the block between him and his son that he could not ask. He wandered to the window and stood looking out, perhaps for inspiration; and presently saw Mrs Pickering, who was wandering along the street, believing it best not to get in the way of the family reunion, but wanting her tea.

'It's Mrs Pickering,' he said with pleasure, feeling that somehow she would iron things out between his son and himself, she had that kind of power. 'You must meet her. I am sure you will find her a very pleasant person.'

Laxman rose quickly; he did not particularly want to meet the woman, but he was curious to see what she was like.

'Is that her?' he asked, indicating a girl in yellow who was nearing the gate.

Srinivas peered. 'Just behind her,' he said. 'The lady in the brown hat and coat. That's Mrs Pickering.'

Laxman looked, and all his fears melted away. He had imagined a sharp-eyed, sexy tart, and the reality turned out to be this ordinary, middle-aged woman whom no man could possibly want, still less lavish his worldly goods on. No need to lose sleep over her, he decided, and luxuriously allowed himself to collapse into his chair.

But he was wrong, for his father and Mrs Pickering were coming together, gradually, and in the natural manner of these things.

Srinivas would not by himself have made the first move. He had reached that stage in life at which, in accordance with the tenets of the culture in which he had been brought up, one pauses, turning from the restless activity of earlier years to more contemplative attitudes. Srinivas was not averse. He could look back on his childhood, on the turbulent years of his youth in occupied India, and on the period of consolidation here in England as a householder with a wife and children. These were two of the three divisions of life, carefully charted to guide the

young Hindu: and cut off though he was from his roots, its
ethos still held sway. He was therefore ready for the next
stage, the contemplation leading to spiritual discovery,
the sinking of flesh and its attendant preoccupations into
insignificance in preparation for the last adventure. More
ready for it, in the calm that Mrs Pickering's advent had
created, than he would have been in those empty wastes he
had inhabited after Vasantha's death.

But now the calm was invested with a new quality.
Nothing much to speak of, but still. Srinivas was aware of it
when he woke in the morning, and walking home through
the darkening streets in the evening, as they talked quietly or
were together in silence, and when she opened the door to
him, taking his chilled hands into her warm broad ones and
chafing them until the blood began to flow strongly again.
Sometimes he wondered, and scanned her face for clues, but
when she offered the opportunity he did not know how to
take it, or perhaps he was waiting, afraid to risk what was
fragile and subtle between them.

'I asked why you were looking at me like that,' she
repeated, in one of these silences.

He apologized, 'I'm sorry. I'm afraid I didn't realize.'

Then despite herself she was curiously hurt, this woman
with the worn face and colourless eyes. She examined herself
and her body, truthfully, and thought with some bitterness
of the years in which it had been used but never loved, this
body which had thickened and aged and could not, she
accepted, be expected now to please any man. Even so, her
pride was bruised, since she was after all a woman, and she
could not help feeling dispirited.

There were, however, other things, and she busied herself
with these. Christmas was approaching: for the first time in

many years it occurred to her to do something about it, a
thought which shortly crystallized into words.

'They're selling off Christmas trees in the market,' she
said to Srinivas, 'for a few shillings each. I might get one. It
could go in the hall, on the table by the window ... and I'll
get a few things to put on the tree, those gold and silver balls,
they're very pretty, don't you think?'

'What would we want with all that,' he asked, amused by
her eloquence, 'two old fogeys like us?'

She blushed. Self-sufficient through so many seasons,
content to spend Christmas after Christmas alone in bleak
lodgings, yet now some atavistic urge afflicted her.

'I think,' she said, 'it must be the beginning of my second
childhood.'

She bought her tree, and Srinivas, feeling gay, if a trifle
foolish, helped to decorate it with balls and baubles, much
of which he bought himself. They placed it in the window
where passers-by could see, and the neighbours in particular
approved, observing that the occupant of No. 5 had after
all these years become civilized – they baulked at saying
Christian, since there was hardly a pulpit in the land,
these days, which did not thunderously proclaim that the
commercial way in which Christmas was waged had little to
do with Christianity.

Almost one of us, the neighbours said privately, and
stopped Mr Srinivas in the street to tell him how pretty the
tree looked. Next-door-but-one, having the privilege since
they had lived there longest – even before the Srinivases had
bought No. 5 – sent round a scion armed with a concrete
symbol. It was the same youth who had wired their basement,
now a grown man, and he came with a string of fairy lights to

wind round the tree and the old incoherence which he had not outgrown.

'How kind people are,' said Srinivas, moved.

'Yes,' said Mrs Pickering, on an odd note.

Srinivas would not allow himself to be jarred. 'These little things,' he said, 'one is made to feel part of the community.'

'After all these years,' said Mrs Pickering.

'Oh, no,' said Srinivas warmly, 'during the war it was like one big family. It seemed to draw everyone closer. My wife, you know, she did not mix easily, we did not have many friends ... but when we were all sheltering in the basement, the four of us and half the neighbourhood as well, it was quite different. Until then I don't think we really appreciated our neighbours.'

'War is a special case,' she said. 'It has been over a long time.'

'Well, of course,' he said huffily, 'you know your countrymen best.'

'Does one ever?' she asked, and he, who had not known Hindus could murder Muslims but had learned they could, was reduced to unhappy silence. Then Mrs Pickering grew remorseful for having chastened this gentle Indian, and set about trying to cheer him up.

'Just think, it's almost Christmas,' she said, 'which is as good an excuse as anyone can think of to eat, drink, and be merry.'

Srinivas closed his eyes. It was quite the worst thing she could have said. Christmas eating made him think of round-the-clock carnage, and farmyards falling silent, one by one. He concentrated on the bells instead, which were pealing to summon the faithful to attend with some fervour, and rather more confidence than they did at other seasons.

10

MRS PICKERING ENJOYED THE SOMEWHAT PAGAN, slightly peculiar Christmas they mounted between them. So, to his surprise, did Srinivas. Even more surprising, he found himself casting around for other festivals to celebrate. He could not think of any. When his sons had been at school, they had heard of Easter and Michaelmas and Whitsun, but these had been scarcely more than the rumblings of a world with which they had little connection, alien occasions which Vasantha had not admitted to their lives.

The festivals of India? There had been a profusion of these, Srinivas recalled, a richness that rounded out his childhood memories; and Vasantha had brought them with her, complete down to the last detail of correct observance. But it was she who knew about these things, as it had been his mother who remembered to bring out the consecrated vessels and send for the priest, while his father's energies were fully stretched between earning a living and his political duty. Now, searching his mind, Srinivas came upon large areas of uncertainty, not to say blankness. Festival lights had dimmed, and even the seasons in which they had been lit – let alone dates – had receded from memory.

'One does not realize,' he said to Mrs Pickering, 'when one leaves one's country, how much is chopped off and left behind too. The inconsiderables, which one does not even think of at the time, which are in fact important.'

'Small things are important,' she agreed, basking in the sunshine in the garden, in a ramshackle deckchair rescued from a pile stacked and left by previous owners in the basement. 'What, in particular, were you thinking of?'

Srinivas felt a slight prickling of embarrassment. 'I thought we might celebrate', he said a little lamely.

'What?' she asked, assuming he knew.

'That is the point,' he blurted. 'I cannot think of anything. Neither an English occasion, nor an Indian one.'

Mrs Pickering considered, debating whether this deviousness was peculiarly Indian, or merely human; but suddenly, in this pause, she became aware that what he was talking about was loss.

'There can be compensations,' she said, curbing the flip reply that rose to her lips. 'If one is cut off from one's culture there is always the adopted one to draw upon.'

'But you see,' he said, 'we – that is to say, my wife and I – I do not think we did.'

Now, partly through Mrs Pickering, it seemed to him, his mind was opening to the country, which in a way Vasantha had closed off. She – the brisk, weathered Englishwoman – made him see the beauty of a crisp winter morning, where before – infected by Vasantha, shivering in unsuitable clothes – he had been conscious only of a cold that pierced to the marrow; and if he still could not face butchers' shops, he linked these barbaric necessities of a carnivorous people with their great concern for animals – their well-fed, friendly dogs, their plump cats that roosted on walls and windowsills, secure in the expectation of amiability.

During his years with Vasantha – exiles both – he had longed like her for palm trees and oleander, sighed with her for the rivers of their vanished youth, for the ramifications of family they had sustained and been sustained by. Mrs Pickering introduced him to English rivers no whit less enchanting, took him to areas of total peace, added sycamore and even oak to his limited appreciation of rosebay and goldenrod, supplied the underpinning he needed from her own not inconsiderable strength. Obscure longings, nurtured over the years by him and his wife and lingering on, Srinivas now put aside, though gently enough. These had served their turn: had even, perhaps, acted as blocks, preventing an absorption of a country and its people that offered, quietly and without meanness, many compensations.

Warmed by this new understanding, which he sensed had more to do with reality than the effusive feelings generated during the emotional war years, Srinivas beamed upon the neighbours, who returned his smiles but scurried past, embarrassed by too open a show of feeling. This, too, he understood. I am becoming more English than the English, he said, and felt almost as if he could enter their skins. Indeed, his whole awareness seemed to have grown, as if the finest cilia covered all surfaces of mind and skin, ready to pick up messages.

Sometimes, lying in bed at night, listening to the sounds of Mrs Pickering upstairs (it was more an absence of silence really), Srinivas thought of the intangibles by which, little by little, she was rounding out his life, which had become so stiff and barren. At these times he could hardly restrain himself, so great was the rush of feeling for her. But he waited. Waited in the ringing night for hints, knowing it was the best way – if not, for him, the only one. Until one night he heard her come down, and go past his room to the kitchen, and presently knew she was by his door, even if he did not hear. He opened it.

'I've brought you some cocoa,' she said. 'It's so cold, I thought you might like it. But I wasn't sure if you were awake.'

He took the cup from her. He knew – as each knew the other did – it was a cover for nakedness: a provision for thin human hide, offering retreat, if retreat were needed, without undue suffering or loss of face.

'I am awake,' he said, and drew her in.

It took a long time – months were to go by – for them to work out their position in relation to each other, and in relation to the people around them. When they did it was largely without words, in the manner of their generation. Mrs Pickering continued to live in one room on the first floor, and Srinivas spread himself, his books, his boxes, and the cumbrous wooden bed they had shipped out from India in the large ground floor front. The back room they shared.

'I think how we are,' said Mrs Pickering obliquely, 'is the best arrangement. At our time of life. I mean,' she said, 'one gets set in one's ways. Upheavals are for the young.'

Srinivas agreed. They had been derelict, in a way, when they met. They had come together, and in the process had salved and restored each other. But it was a muted process, more an easing of aches than a violent build-up of pleasure, which did not demand the constant stimulus of touch and presence of young love. Even when they lay together it was with a degree of serenity: looking on, as it were, on something which had once been wet and wild, but now was calm.

The neighbours, more cynical, were also more hypocritical about the nature of the relationship. They went along with it by pretending it did not exist, shoring up their sense of propriety by delicate references to Mr Srinivas, the landlord, and Mrs Pickering, his tenant. Youthful goings-on might have made for jealousy and gossip; an elderly pair at it could be ignored, if only to preserve the respectability of the neighbourhood. Also there were the two women, first Mrs Srinivas and now Mrs Pickering, who redeemed their oddities of dress and manner by keeping the house scrupulously clean, as you could tell just by looking at the shine on the doorstep.

'Good thing Mrs Pickering did come along,' said Mrs Glass, doyenne of the neighbourhood, mother of the stammering electrician, who lived at No. 9. 'The house was getting in a state, what I call really filthy, if you know what I mean. You could say it wasn't any business of ours, on the other hand it's not nice, not in a nice residential district like this.'

'Lowers the tone', said Mrs Fletcher of No. 6, who had recently moved into this house.

'Not that I blamed him', said Mrs Glass. 'You can't expect a man, they don't see dirt like women do. Besides he wasn't himself at all, after his wife passed away. The way he went around some of us thought he was afflicted, though I will say I never did.'

'What was she like?' asked Mrs Fletcher curiously, and waited for a description of the strange object.

Mrs Glass considered. 'She was a nice little thing, really,' she said fairly. 'Of course she was Indian. I mean she couldn't help it, could she? But I will say she kept her place spotless. Like one of us, although she wasn't, if you follow what I mean.'

Mrs Fletcher followed these non sequiturs quite easily. Mrs Glass had known she would. As she often said, that was the advantage of living in a good locality: everyone understood, they knew what you meant, you didn't have to spell it out. Mrs Fletcher, full of understanding, nodded and nodded. She thought of the dead Mrs Srinivas, and now and then she blinked, because the vision she had was distinctly fuzzy, she could not even paste a colour on the face.

'Was she black?' she had to ask at last.

'Black? Oh, no,' said Mrs Glass, and paused to get the tint right. 'Sort of café au lait,' she said, proud of her French.

'Pretty?' inquired Mrs Fletcher.

'I daresay she used to be,' said Mrs Glass judicially, 'but towards the end she wasn't. Oriental women don't wear well, do they, that's common knowledge. Towards the end she looked awful.'

'Fat?' hazarded Mrs Fletcher.

'Thin as a lathe,' said Mrs Glass. 'TB, I shouldn't wonder, though they never let on what took her. Mr Glass, when he saw the coffin he said that could be a child they're burying, and he was right, it could have been.'

'Only they wouldn't bury, not being C of E, poor souls,' said Mrs Fletcher.

'Cremated,' said Mrs Glass, 'and I could tell you something funny about that, too.'

'Go on!' said Mrs Fletcher.

'Yes, well, the hearse came,' said Mrs Glass juicily, 'and they carried the coffin out. Mr S. was walking behind, and he says something to the men, of course we couldn't hear what. They carry on and slide the coffin in, then one of them brings out a seat, sort of a hassock it was, and puts that in too, next to the coffin. And – you'll never guess what – Mr S. gets in, into *the hearse,* and sits down on the hassock, and he's holding something in his hands. What's that? I says to

Mr Glass, though I could see it plain as plain, just to check, you understand. What's what? he says, I can't see anything, and of course, his sight not being what it was he can't, but I could see quite plain. It's a tea caddy, I says to him. Just the job for a funeral, he says, and starts slapping his sides. For the ashes, I tell him, and that makes him stop his laughing.' Here Mrs Glass stopped and looked at Mrs Fletcher, to see how she was taking it. Mrs Fletcher felt the look and shifted her eyes, being troubled by certain doubts.

'Are you sure?' she asked, bravely if uncertainly. 'I mean, do you think it would have been big enough?'

'It was a big tea caddy.' Mrs Glass slapped her down. 'What's more, from what our Bert saw, it still has her ashes in it, to this very day.'

'No,' breathed Mrs Fletcher. She could feel her flesh creeping.

'Yes,' said Mrs Glass. 'Our Bert was down in the basement mending the fuse – just before Christmas, it was, he'd just fixed the lights for the tree when it blew – and he saw this box. In fact he didn't see it, being so dark down there and all he tripped over it and it went all over his shoes.'

'What did?' asked Mrs Fletcher.

'The contents,' said Mrs Glass tartly. 'Like sand or ashes, he said it was.' Course he thought nothing of it, just scooped it back and closed the lid and put the box up on a shelf to be out of the way, and told Mr S. what he'd done in case he should go looking for it. And do you know what Mr S. said to him? He said: Oh, yes, that box contains a little Indian soil, that used to *belong to my wife!*'

Mrs Glass was a good raconteur. Mrs Fletcher, earlier doubts stilled, sat on the edge of her chair, thinking about human ash spread over shoes. Now and then she gave a little shudder.

'I suppose,' she said at last, 'it's one of their customs.'

'I daresay it is,' said Mrs Glass tolerantly. 'We can't all be alike, can we? Live and let live, that's what I say.'

Then both ladies sat gazing out of the window draped in nylon in keeping with the times, which went yellow, it is true, but was so much smarter than old-fashioned lace. They felt very close – much closer than they did at other times – just thinking how alike they were, especially when you compared them to other people. People of Many Lands, thought Mrs Glass, as the title of an old school primer swam into view, and felt the same fascinated repulsion she had felt before for the strange customs of different people in distant lands. Though Mr Srinivas, of course, was in England, and almost one of the English, as the English themselves said in their more tolerant moods, bestowing the best accolade they could think of. While Srinivas, more and more now, was inclined to take them at their word.

11

SUMMER CAME AND WENT AND CAME AGAIN, BRINGING with it Abdul the Zanzibari, in a broad-finned automobile imported from Detroit that attracted males in shoals, of all ages from sixty down. Cars were not as thick on the ground as they were soon to be: Abdul was able to park his car where he wanted to, and where he wanted to was right outside No. 5, where it outshone the pre-war Morris parked at No. 9 as well as the baby Austin owned by No. 6 opposite.

Abdul bin Ahmed was, as could be seen and as he had prophesied, doing well. He had moved his trading centre, he informed Srinivas, from Zanzibar to Dar-es-Salaam, whose lively port facilities were more attuned to the growing organization he controlled. Trading stations had been established across the continent, he explained, to supply the commodities it handled. To consolidate these ventures he was in the process of setting up a chain of restaurants in London and other big cities.

'So we approach the ideal,' he told Srinivas. 'We create demand with one hand, we supply it with the other, it is one big smooth operation.'

Srinivas smiled; theirs was an old friendship, he was quite happy to listen. Really, though, he was not vastly interested. He would never be a merchant in the grand manner as his friend was. That needed certain qualities of drive and ruthlessness, which he would have found wearing to cultivate, besides the flair and tenacity which his forebears had passed down to him. Also, overridingly, he did not have the ambition. A woman might have roused it, with her yawning canyons of desire for this and that fostered by the glossy pages of magazines, but neither Vasantha before, nor Mrs Pickering now, belonged to this breed. In a sense both were women of an impregnable integrity, who would have considered it degrading to behave like cup bearers or handmaidens for the furthering of their men's careers, as women of subordinate mentality might imagine it their duty to do. So Srinivas was left in peace to jog along as he wanted, following the modest path he had chosen for himself. Except, of course, when dynamic business in the shape of his son breathed fire down his neck to urge him on, or as now, with Abdul. But Abdul's concern was edged, though Srinivas could not perceive, as yet, in what dark colours.

'Come on, man! Show glad!' cried Abdul, thumping the table.

'I am glad,' said Srinivas, and watched the striking fist, whose ebony uppers showed clefts of cleanest pink, like slashed doublet and hose. 'Truly, truly delighted,' he said earnestly, guiltily aware that his attention had wandered. 'It is good for the country that trade should flourish.'

'Which country?' demanded Abdul.

'Well, England,' admitted Srinivas.

'England! What's the matter with you, man, you can't think about anything else?'

'I suppose I could, but why? This is where I live, in England.'

'It's your country like?'

'It's become.'

'You think so? You think they'll let you?'

'Yes.'

'Then you better stop,' said Abdul, 'because they won't. The British won't allow it. First thing that goes wrong it'll be *their* country, and you go back, nigger, to *yours,* back where you came from.'

'Oh, I don't think so,' said Srinivas.

'Oh, you don't,' said Abdul. 'Well, I see the signs. You been in a pub lately? Know who gets served last, never fail? Why, yours truly. Or coming through Customs – you haven't been abroad lately, man, you just don't know. I don't own restaurants for nothing, I learn. The way they look you up and down and harden up – well, if looks could kill you'd be stone-cold dead and the sheet up over your hairline before you could count to three!'

'The people around here,' said Srinivas, and felt depressed, as violence always depressed him. 'I wouldn't say – '

'*You* wouldn't.' Abdul sneered. '*I* will. I'll tell you what they're saying, right now, this very minute. That black ape, they're saying, meaning me, what's he doing over here in his overheated automobile? Living off our white girls, that's what, stands to reason he must be, else how it happens he can run a motorcar two blocks wide which we can't afford to do?'

'Why do you, if you know they resent it – is it just to annoy?'

'Why?' Abdul's fist was punishing the table. 'Is there no such thing as history? Which tells how, when they were the top dogs, we were the pariah dogs, only it doesn't spell it out specifically? But maybe you think my skin's so thick I never felt what they did to me. Took my land from right under my nose, took my old man first so he wouldn't bleat, took my pride so I never walked with my head up, took my freedom finally. Maybe you even think like they do, that it was all in aid of me – my health, my family, my prosperity. What's come over you, man, that you can't remember, seeing how you went through what I did?'

'What I went through,' said Srinivas painfully, 'is past. The past is over. It is best to forget it.'

'What you're saying,' said Abdul, 'is turn the other cheek. Forgive them, O Lord, as the pastor used to preach, for they know not what they done unto us nor ever will. Well, you carry on. What I carry on *my* back, I carry to my grave. I don't forget so easy.'

Srinivas rose and stood by the window. He did not know what to say to this man, whom the workings of empire had damaged so badly, whose running sores and ulcerated interiors time could not heal. Only, perhaps, people. People like those who lived alongside them in Ashcroft Avenue, who had accepted him and his family in their first floundering days, and come round to help with the weeding and the electricity; who had not known what to say when news came of his son, but had rallied around nevertheless, their faces pale with the strain and misery of fellow feeling, bearing potfuls of tea. People who had borne with him while he stalked among them like a zombie and single-handed created a slum in their very midst. People like Mrs Pickering.

'I know what you're thinking,' said Abdul. 'That I'm bitter. That I should sluice out the bitterness, with some kind of enema like because it's bad for the bloody inside. To me that's fucking saint's talk.'

'The other kind has usually been pretty useless,' said Srinivas.

Now it was Abdul who was stunned. He could not make out this man with the honey-coloured skin, who could go through what he had done and emerge with his faculties intact. However darkly, Abdul understood what these were: the ability to forgive while remembering, a sweetness that consumed the meaner human streaks. Only, how could he? For this same honey skin had been thin, as thin as his own black pelt. He had seen it quiver and flinch as his own had done, and witnessed reactions – in this very house, not all that long ago, before the balm of England had begun to cure old sores – that were intelligible to him, sprung sharp from a common experience. So what had happened in the interim? Abdul pondered, staring at the back of the greying head, which was what Srinivas presented to him, then he got up and joined his friend by the window.

'I've got a suspicion,' he said.

'About me?' asked Srinivas.

'About you,' said Abdul, who was not without some intimations of his own. 'I can see you are content. You've got grace. It makes it difficult for you to see what's not so nice, so you feel safe. Maybe you are, but you need to watch it. Back it with power. The Britons, they respect power, but no money – no power.'

'I don't feel in need of either,' said Srinivas, gently. 'I am not, you see, an ambitious man.'

'Who's talking about ambition?' said Abdul. 'I'm talking about self-preservation. Face it, man, the way you are now, what are you?'

'A nobody, I suppose.'

'Right. You took the words right from my mouth. A nobody. Naked as a born babe. You've got no defences.'

'Against what?'

Against what, he asks, said Abdul to himself. He felt a great sense of helplessness. How could anyone give chapter and verse? There was no way. One went armed in the jungle, that was all. Especially this one, which was yielding up that mixture of bland and terrible as only white men could make it do, wanting only a mouthpiece to set off the mauling.

'I can't tell you exactly,' he said. 'If you can't see, I can't make you. Maybe there's less for you to see, not being black. Seemingly it's the blackness that offends whites more than the rest of the rainbow. All the same, I wouldn't like to go away leaving you as you are.'

'Peaceful?'

'I've got a proposition,' said Abdul patiently. 'It won't mash up your peace. I'm looking for someone who can keep an eye this end, it's what I've come here for. Someone I can trust. Like you, man, I've known you long enough, I know what you can do when you have a mind to it. I'm asking you be my agent. Job with prospects, like they say. Good money, too. Business is booming.'

'What would I want with booming business at my age?'

'Maybe nothing now. But later. When they start talking about how you're clogging up the country you'll want to shut them up. For instance, with how much tax you're paying on the profits. It'll give you a comeback. You need,' said Abdul, and swivelled his eyeballs to show the whites, which as he knew could make his blubbery black face quite fearful, 'to think of these things.'

Srinivas considered, and was moved. A grown man, driven to pulling faces in an endeavour to alert him to danger. Unreal danger, it seemed to him, unreasoned fear of hysteria, of a kind of madness which he could not equate with what he could see and the people he knew. But done for his sake, out of the pure impulses of a curious friendship which had drawn men from two different continents so closely together.

'We think on different lines,' he said, gently.

'Then the answer is no,' said Abdul.

Srinivas came out on the pavement to see him go and there was a heaviness about his heart as he watched him drive away. He knew what it was like to walk burdened with suspicion and fear, had felt the sly corroding hatreds that it bred. If it had been in his power he would have given Abdul the gift he enjoyed – the priceless gift of shedding the past. Sometimes those nightmares of the past caught up with him, in bad moments and in sleep. But Abdul, it seemed, was doomed to them in broad daylight, and for life.

Mrs Glass also watched the departure, peeping over the nylons of No. 9 and relaying to her friend Mrs Fletcher.

'He's going,' she said. 'He's got his flowerpot on.'

'Taking up half the blooming road as if he owned it,' said Mrs Fletcher. 'Do you mean fez?'

'Fezzes look like flowerpots to me. I'm not as ignorant as I look, I hope,' said Mrs Glass. 'What I say is everyone's entitled to use the road and if he was taking up more than his share there's others I could name who do the same.'

'No one's got a monopoly of the highway, that's the law,' said Mrs Fletcher defensively.

'Who's talking about the law?' said Mrs Glass, and twisted the conversation slightly to keep it on the right tack. 'I'm talking about what's going on.'

'What is?'

'Who knows? All I know is what I see with my own two eyes.'

'The place isn't the same.' Mrs Fletcher caught on, at last. 'Full of foreigners, you see all sorts, going around in their big cars. They're the ones with the money these days.'

'Rolling in it,' said Mrs Glass. 'It makes you think.'

'That car!' said Mrs Fletcher.

'These flash darkies,' said Mrs Glass.

'He looked really tough to me, didn't he you?' said Mrs Fletcher. 'I wouldn't like to meet *him* up a dark alley, would you?'

'I would not,' said Mrs Glass, and felt a current pass through her frame which she described to herself as a shudder. 'I would not,' she repeated, to give herself strength.

Mrs Pickering also peeped, from her room on the first floor which overlooked the road. She had retired there because she had deduced from the fez that Abdul was a Muslim, and Muslims, she had been told, did not care for women to be present at business transactions.

In fact, Abdul was quite reconciled to the presence of women, at least in his missions abroad. He had a French wife, a shrewd woman whose business acumen he respected, whom he would have been happy to have by his side at all his complex negotiations. To his regret, however, Odile's availability was not to be commanded. She picked and chose, twisting the lozenge-shape emerald and diamond ring he had given her, while she considered; and often declined England. Abdul had once told Srinivas why: she thought the British were so full of their own virtues that no dialogue with them was possible. Srinivas had not been able to accept this, but because it was Odile, the wife of a friend, he kept quiet. Also, perhaps, because he respected her, the poised, experienced Frenchwoman he had met once, soon after the war when the pair were in London looking around for opportunities.

Going back into the house now, Srinivas wished Odile had been present. The Frenchwoman's composure, he felt, might have gone some way to counteracting Abdul's intensity, the troubled airs he had introduced which, despite himself, continued to saw at the edges of his consciousness. Driven to examination at last, he concluded that his peace was intact, at least its centre: but its shape was subtly distorted, as if he were seeing it reflected in a flawed looking glass. When, presently, Mrs Pickering came down to join him, his heart gave a little jump – elation, or at least relief. She would distract him, he knew, withdraw his mind from incipient lunacy: her stolid figure seemed in itself a bastion of sanity.

'I wish you had come down earlier,' he said. 'Sometimes I find it difficult to cope with Abdul ... he is not an easy man.'

'He seemed upset,' she agreed.

'Was it that evident?'

'Yes. And now he is gone, leaving you upset.'

He had forgotten, he thought, the communication between them. Nothing gave him away, that he knew: he was not a volatile man, and his years in a phlegmatic country, if they had not repressed him, had taught him to enclose his emotions; but he could not control the invisible interplay between them. What, however, were these emotions, whose echoes he could not still, nor prevent her from recording? None, he reassured himself, since his core had not been touched, only some insubstantial outer frills.

'I don't think I am upset,' he said at last. 'It is just that there are things which are best forgotten.'

'Suppressed?'

'Oh, no. Remembered without rancour, would be a better way of putting it.'

'Which your friend is unable to do?'

'He has never really recovered,' said Srinivas, and felt a heaviness, bars of lead riding up inside his chest. 'Some people have not been able to ... it affects everyone, when a country is occupied. Both sides, I mean, overlords as much as inhabitants, it seems to twist them out of shape, out of any recognizable human shape. Sometimes,' he said, and stared at her in what she had come to call that queer fashion of his, 'they do not even recognize themselves. They ask, or at least their compatriots do, how could I do these things? How could such things happen? And nobody knows the answer.'

'In wartime –' she began.

'It spills over into peacetime,' he took her up. 'Some never forget, it discolours everything for them, even their thought. Some are so damaged their vision is affected, they can't see ordinary things as ordinary people would.'

'But many come through,' she said rather than asked, 'end up as ordinary human beings.'

'Oh, yes,' he said passionately. 'Thank God many do.'

'So it depends upon the person.'

'So many things,' he said. 'Upon oneself, and the quality of one's adversary. Upon the experience.'

'Was it bad?'

'For Abdul?' He drew a long breath. He did not want to go into it but there was no alternative, unless he was prepared to jeopardize what had come into being between them. Even to spare her he could not.

'I believe it was,' he said at last. 'His father was sent to prison for subversion. He was an old man, he died there. Abdul was imprisoned too. Not long, a few months. But he took it hard, because it meant he never saw his father again.'

He saw her flinch, but she said, steadily, 'And you? Your experience?'

It moved him. He considered her, and his admiration grew for this plain Englishwoman who insisted, who would not look the other way and pretend it did not happen, but would go on asking these bald questions.

'It was not as bad as Abdul's,' he said, meeting her honestly with as much of his own as he could manage. 'Physically far less, certainly. In other ways –' Suddenly it came alive. What had happened long ago was standing at his elbow. 'One day I will tell you,' he said with difficulty. 'I think you will make the better judge.'

12

THE SPECTRES THAT ABDUL HAD RAISED LAY DOWN again when he had gone. Not quickly: too much life had been breathed into them; but soon enough. When Srinivas looked out of his window his eyes dwelt, if not exactly upon a dreaming countryside, at least upon a macadam landscape of redoubtable calm. With matching people. They helped to lay spectres, the two: the clean solid slabs of pavement, the sturdy houses and brickwork and walls free of scurrility however tempting the cement expanse, and the inhabitants who had created this environment and were, clearly, shaped by it: orderly, level-headed people, who spoke politely and patiently waited their turn to be served in the shops and were good-natured even when grumbling about the shortage of somewhere decent to live, which the papers had begun to be vocal about. Yet a good deal of building was going on, noticeable even in their area. Along the avenue four ageing semis had been pulled down, and in their place stood a terrace of twelve houses, trim and small in the modern manner. At the end, where the corner shop had been, a cluster of maisonettes was rising; and the bomb site where birds and weeds had flourished, on whose rubble Mrs Pickering had sat and wept over a hat long ago one dreadful spring evening, shuddered and rang with the sound of building.

The residents took time off to watch, taking turns at the peepholes the builders had considerately cut in the hoarding, and were occasionally rewarded with a progress report from one of the men knocking off work. All day, all week, bulldozers tore up earth and power drills reverberated. The air, in that dry summer, seemed impregnated with dust, and in nearby houses along Ashcroft Avenue ornaments trembled on mantelpieces, and sometimes the windows rattled.

'It's almost like the war,' said Mrs Glass reminiscently to her husband.

'Bloody sight less dangerous,' said her husband, rustling his paper and putting it up like an occluding shield so that Mrs Glass, foiled, could hardly continue her reminiscences and had to look out to see if she could capture Mrs Fletcher. And was successful quite soon, for Mrs Fletcher, being long married, with a husband who likewise had a habit of lopping off conversations with, in his case, the *Radio Times,* was also out prowling, though carrying a letter for alibi.

'Oo-ooo,' called Mrs Glass, leaning on her gate and waving as Mrs Fletcher went by.

'I must just catch the post,' Mrs Fletcher sang back. 'Be with you in a tick.'

As if the world would stop going round if she didn't, said Mrs Glass acidly, but she waited all the same, being in need of company.

'The van was just drawing up.' Mrs Fletcher returned triumphantly, displaying her conspicuously empty hands.

'Was it important, then?' inquired Mrs Glass.

'Well –' Mrs Fletcher faltered. 'Just a few lines to my son. He's in Australia, you know.'

'So you've told me.'

'Yes. Well, he does worry if he doesn't hear from his mum. He's a good boy, always thinks of us, you know,' said Mrs

Fletcher, suppressing memories of that final row which had flung Fred Fletcher into outer space, or at least to Australia on £10 and an assisted passage.

'You must miss him,' said Mrs Glass.

'Oh, I do!' said Mrs Fletcher.

'It must be difficult, settling so far from your own kith and kin.'

'It can't be easy. Since he went it's given us an insight like, I often feel sorry' – Mrs Fletcher lowered her voice and jerked her thumb at No. 5 – 'for him. Being so far from his folk and all.'

'Yes. Poor man. Though no one asked him, he did come of his own accord.'

'But still.'

'Yes.' Mrs Glass shook her head sadly, and pondered whether to haul Mrs Pickering into it but desisted, because somehow Mrs Pickering had this odd effect on her: you couldn't say how, but she made you step gingerly. A bit superior too: civil, yes, but *un peu* hoity-toity. Instead she said, ditching these staccato thoughts as well as Mrs Pickering, 'It's council flats they're building, up the road.'

'I've heard,' said Mrs Fletcher.

'Rehousing the homeless, or some such scheme,' said Mrs Glass. 'Bert's pal, that's on the council, told him. We'll be getting,' she said gloomily, 'all sorts.'

'All sorts!' cried Mrs Fletcher. 'What do they want to do that for?'

'That's what I said,' said Mrs Glass. 'They'll never be happy here, I said, this is a good residential area, they won't fit it. Especially coming from Jamaica and all, like I've heard. It's not us I'm worried about, mind, I'm looking at it from their point of view. But what's the good of talking?'

'Might as well save your breath,' agreed Mrs Fletcher.

They paused in deference to this sentiment, but as a fresh burst of pneumatic drilling assailed them Mrs Glass had to speak.

'The noise!' she cried. 'You can't hear yourself think!'

'The dust!' Mrs Fletcher grew animated. 'Flies into everything. I've had to take my curtains down *twice* this week. *I* can't get them clean.'

'I can't get them white,' confirmed Mrs Glass. 'The rate they're going there soon won't be a patch of green left anywhere.'

'Green?' echoed Mrs Fletcher, somewhat hazily.

'Everything built over,' Mrs Glass had to elaborate.

'Oh, yes, I see what you mean. Still,' said Mrs Fletcher charitably, 'I suppose people have got to have somewhere to live.'

''Course they have.' Mrs Glass was not to be outdone by her friend, and the rapport between them having worn thin she said she supposed she'd better go now, rather perfunctorily, and did.

The construction site drew Mrs Pickering, as it did many others who lived on the street. Like them she stopped now and again, and stepped up onto the viewing platform as was occasionally possible, or applied an eye to the spyholes, and watched developments.

'Another fortnight and they will be laying the foundations,' she told Srinivas. 'It is to be a block of flats, twelve storeys high, they say. It seems difficult to imagine.'

'It's more difficult to imagine what it used to be like,' said Srinivas, and despite himself a note of regret crept in. For it had been a source of pleasure, that patch of land. Over the years it had seldom failed to delight him, to walk past rows and rows of houses and suddenly to light upon what was virtually a small wilderness, held in check by masonry and assorted rusty ironware that the citizens heaved in, but still exuberant with ferns and vines, buttercup and bindweed, and flowers of a dozen different varieties whose names he never succeeded in learning, and coarse grass in which field mice nested. To see it built over was like seeing a grave filled in: feel the pity of it, experience the same finality.

But he would not say so, as the neighbourhood did, if with some ambivalence of feeling, for although he was so nearly one of them he could not quite command the liberties and licences of the English.

Which they exercised, it seemed, without undue inhibition.

Sometimes he marvelled a little, listening to their indictments of Asia and Africa, watching them wag a stern finger at these dark and delinquent continents while up to their armpits in the same crimes. Crimes against creation, it seemed to him, needing a wholesale scrubout of debauched and rotten conceptions within the brains of human beings, and getting instead societies. Societies for the protection of flora and fauna, to which he occasionally contributed. In a kind of despair. Riveting his gaze on the national show window as the natives did, while behind these narrow enclaves a cruel destruction went on.

Although, not being blind, he could see. He saw whose backs wore the ocelot coats, whose chairs were upholstered in zebra skin, whose presses ate up entire forests, whose money bought the elephant-foot umbrella stands against which store mannequins lolled in West End emporiums.

But he would not comment. His dual affiliation restricted him. It made him aware of incongruity as the islanders were not, and the merging in him of them and us called for an honourable consistency which kept him silent.

There were others who were displaced, besides the birds and bees. Youthful gangs – facsimiles of the four who had turned so terrifyingly into scalp-hunters that haunted day – who had treated the bomb site as clubhouse and trysting place, now had nowhere to go. They had come from the fringes of the neighbourhood, where respectability tapered away into the uncertain realms of prefab and slum, lured by the feeling of space and freedom the site offered them, the absence of authority apart from the flimsy palisade and a passing policeman. Now they mooched about, these incipient men and women with their pinched, rebellious faces, and watched like everyone else what was taking place, a legal conversion of what they had regarded as theirs by a society which they could not bring themselves to acquiesce in, nor summon enough strength to opt out of.

Rootless, sober citizens said.

Sometimes in these lost faces Srinivas saw the faces of his own two sons: Laxman, pleading for total integration, which was both adjunct and essential to his living, which they had not been able to give him; and Seshu, who believed he had murdered to order and gone to his death unshriven, since his parents had no facile absolution to offer. But sometimes it was not this that he saw at all, but images of terror, the faces of the youths who had pursued, grinning, loutish, bent on destruction, fun out of cruelty. Then Srinivas had to take firm hold of himself, and gaze at the masks until they resumed the lineaments of humanity, and make a conscious act of recall which showed what these same youths had turned into, four inoffensive, rather sullen, fairly inconspicuous factory hands; and so reclaim his balance.

The flats were half built – a raw brick tower in a forest of scaffolding with timber-framed holes where the windows would be – when Laxman came to visit. It was actually a business trip, in the course of arranging which he had said to himself it might be as well, while in London, to look the old man up. And see if the woman was still about, what was her name, Mrs Pickering. He had no idea if she would be, since he and his father seldom met, hardly ever corresponded; but in his opinion it was doubtful. Loose liaisons like that (and here he thought of the marriage lines which Pat kept in a mauve scented envelope among her undies in the middle drawer) had a habit of tailing off, even if, perhaps, his father and Mrs Pickering did not quite fit into the lascivious slots of loose living.

So here he was, in his pinstripe grey, and not a hair out of place, and smelling faintly expensive. And here was his father in the same blue suit he remembered, whose pants were shiny about the seat. And Mrs Pickering in her best, a maroon cardigan and a matching skirt in which he, Laxman, had he been a woman, would not have been seen dead. Mrs Pickering, about whom he had been wrong, who was evidently here to stay. Established in the house, presiding over the tea table. Rather bleakly, Laxman acknowledged and admired her staying power, such as he would have applauded the success of any calculated manoeuvre. To judge from her achievement, a woman of unusual gifts, he thought, not entirely unkindly.

Srinivas, uneasy as always in the presence of his son, was embarked upon light conversation.

'Well, how's life?' he asked, quite brightly.

'Fine,' said Laxman. 'How's business?'

'Oh, well. Jogging along, you know,' said Srinivas, and felt steamy under the collar, from the heat coming off the nimbus of failure in which Laxman's probing invariably invested him.

'Jogging along is hardly the answer,' said Laxman, and frowned. 'We find, these days, we have to keep running merely to stay in the same place.'

'It sounds exhausting,' said Mrs Pickering. 'Do you take milk?'

'A drop,' said Laxman. 'Of course, one isn't in business exactly for fun.'

'It does seem a pity,' said Mrs Pickering. 'Egg or tomato?'

Laxman brooded as he ate his sandwich. He had a slight sensation of being outflanked. She's getting at me, he thought, but it was difficult to believe, and he reassured himself it was impossible by studying her exceedingly ordinary face. Soon he even felt a little warmth towards her, for she was undoubtedly responsible for some trace elements of civilization detectable in the place. Commendably kept, for instance. And the tea. Quite a spread, he conceded, running a discerning eye over the scones, the tarts, the well-risen sponge, which Mrs Pickering had spent a good part of the morning baking. It was an even better outcome than he had expected, even if, profiting from bitter experience, he had taken care to warn them well in advance of his coming.

'Splendid tea. Congratulate you,' he said at last, sitting back, speaking in the rather clipped, benign way he used to encourage employees at the factory. 'Must say it does the soul good.'

'I don't think that was the priority I had in mind,' said Mrs Pickering good-humouredly, forbidding her eyes to stray to Laxman's healthy waistline. 'I was more concerned with providing for bodily needs. One grows out of the habit, you know. Two old fogeys like us, we seldom entertain.'

'Then you ought,' said Laxman, describing flourishes for, he said to himself with amazement, this dowdy woman. 'It is a shame to waste your culinary skills.'

Srinivas, listening to them, felt relieved that the day was not going to be as difficult as he had feared. They find each other – he was not sure what; approachable, he settled for in the end: perhaps even congenial, he said to himself. A little warmth crept into him at the thought, relaxing the small muscles in his face which had gone into spasm. All the same he could not find anything to say, so he hovered on the fringes of their conversation, willing to make a contribution should one occur, but not over optimistic that it would, nor dismayed when it did not. Happily they seemed to be getting on tolerably well without him, observing which he allowed his mind to wander equably, immersed in a kind of euphoria.

Torpid, Laxman described it to himself, prickling with annoyance. 'More cake?' he said in a loud voice, and was glad to see he had made his father jump.

'No, thank you,' said Srinivas, and wondered how his son could imagine he would eat the cake, into which half a dozen eggs, those embryonic chickens, had been broken. Mrs Pickering also wondered how Laxman could have forgotten something so basic to his father, but tried to smoothe the spiky edges that the situation had begun to develop.

'You see how little encouragement I get,' she said ruefully. 'You must visit us more often.'

'Yes, and next time bring the children,' said Srinivas, pleased to be able, at last, to contribute to the conversation.

Laxman froze. All but his eyes, which ranged over the room, picking out everything he loathed: the *gulab-jan*, bought by Mrs Pickering from an Indian restaurant at

Srinivas's bidding, swimming messily in a saucer of greasy liquid; his father in a suit such as only Indians wore, too short in the sleeve for their ape-like arms and too wide at the shoulder for their narrow frames; the plain person with whom he had chosen to cohabit, not even troubling to regularize the position. Visit more often – introduce his children to this set-up! –

Never, thought Laxman, who cared passionately for his family, and he twisted his lips to think that anyone, even his father, could be so blind to his own shortcomings.

Then Srinivas saw that it was no use. He had been deluded by a few grains of surface harmony into thinking a closer relationship might be attempted. Not with his son, he accepted that that was impossible; but with his two grandchildren. If I passed them in the street I wouldn't know them, he thought with a pang; but then in an explosion of hard cold light that seemed to fizz out from Laxman he also saw himself as his son did and his son's children would, the children absorbing from the parent as the parent had absorbed from his birthplace: an ill-dressed ancient Indian, deficient in good living and small talk, with whom they would have nothing in common, nor even want to find out if they did.

Mrs Pickering meanwhile persevered. The rifts were almost palpable, but somehow the day had to be held together and she got on with it. It helped that she genuinely liked children – more so, perhaps, from never having had any of her own. It enabled her to put the right questions and evince the proper enthusiasms, and presently Laxman found himself reaching for his wallet to show her the snapshots he carried around in it.

'That's Roy,' he said, subduing the pride he felt in the sturdy children whose faces smiled back at him. 'He's nearly eight. Big for his age, isn't he? And that's the little 'un, taken when she was a year.'

'What lovely children,' said Mrs Pickering warmly, carefully holding the prints by their white margins. 'Roy is very much like you, he looks exactly like you must have done when you were his age. Don't you think so?' she inveigled the shutout Srinivas in.

'Exactly,' said Srinivas, after peering, and dusting off some faded memories.

Laxman frowned. He did not want Roy to look like him. He preferred that the boy should look like his mother, or his maternal grandfather, after whom he was named, since clearly it would be less disadvantageous that way. He had almost come to believe that in fact Roy did.

'Do you think so?' he said, distantly.

'Yes, indeed,' said Mrs Pickering. 'The resemblance is quite marked. Just look at those eyes.'

'A pity,' said Laxman.

'A pity? Why?' asked Mrs Pickering.

It made Laxman feel as if he had entered – at least one-eyed – into a sightless world. They are *both* blind, he said to himself, that's what has brought these two together. Like attracts like.

'Because it's easier to escape attention,' he said with furious patience, 'if one looks much the same as everyone else in the country. It's not a British forte, is it, to welcome foreigners? At least that's the way I see it.'

'Foreigners are foreigners. How can anyone be foreign who is born in this country?' said Mrs Pickering, as if she were propounding a riddle.

'When their skin is a different colour,' said Laxman, as if he were answering it. And he waited, to see what bizarre reaction would be wrung from this odd pair whose responses were so much at variance with his own. Ideally fitted, he could not help concluding, for a kind of world in which they did not live. Nor was he disappointed.

'Ah, well,' said Srinivas tolerantly. 'The British are a reserved people.'

Mrs Pickering's view amazed him still more. 'It would be a dull world,' she said quite straightly, her colourless eyes unwavering, 'very dull indeed, if we all had pale skins and pale eyes.'

'That's all very well, but can't you see, that's just what England doesn't think?' he cried in exasperation.

'Then it's England's loss,' said Mrs Pickering, in her flat, forthright, foolish way that Laxman found so demoralizing. So, like Srinivas a little earlier, he saw it was no use. Nothing to do except pick up the pieces, of his sanity he felt, and depart.

His peace, however, such as it was, was to be shattered at other levels, and with an alarming immediacy.

Borne along in his cab towards the Westbury, where he was staying, he realized their progress was getting slower and slower, until they were barely crawling. He rapped on the sliding panel.

'Can't you get a move on?' he said irritably. 'Take another route or something?'

'Doing my best, guv,' said the cabbie. 'There's jams a mile long in every direction. Demonstrations gwine on, police out and everything.'

Laxman sank back. He knew what it meant. I cannot believe it, he said to himself, as thousands of others were saying, but the crowds, the confusion, the passing banners made him. BOMBING IMMINENT they said, and LAW NOT WAR, and STOP EDEN'S WAR. Laxman groaned. Too late, he thought, too late now to stop anything; and the crowds melted away and in their place he saw the Canal, the narrow blue tongue that split the desert and widened into seas which were the trade highways for his goods.

'Teach them gyppos a lesson,' he heard the taxi driver say with relish. But Laxman could not concern himself with the Egyptians, or British or French for that matter; his concerns were for himself and the family he had founded. Hunched in the dark-glassed gloom of the cab he thought of them, and of the Canal bunged up with stationary ships; and his mind filled with weighty images of crates bearing the Roy-Lax stencilings bumping along on the expensive Cape route. Now and then these images were dislodged, only to be replaced by a scarcely less cheerless one: a picture of his father's house and its unnamed inheritor, a matter he had not been able to broach or settle although it had been a principal item on the agenda that had brought him to London.

13

WITHIN THE WARM, TENDERLY CONSTRUCTED COCOON that life had now come to be, the reverberations of the Suez affair over the strident months of late summer and autumn had reached Srinivas only as attenuated echoes. Until the bombing. Then it hit him.

I cannot believe it, he said as Laxman had done, and images rose in his mind as they had done in Laxman's, but were of a different order. He saw, not figures of expenditure totting up alarmingly at the bottom of ledger columns, but a confused procession in which ships, tanks, rifles, fifes and drums, men in khaki, and the Union Jack all played a prominent part.

Gunboat diplomacy, the Oriental world had called it in the old days, this ominous jingling parade which had been used to intimidate People of Many Lands, who had objected to People of Other Lands ruling them. Called it that again, in his own country, in the upheaval that followed the breaking of promises of self-rule, disinterring that phrase of the nineteenth century in the incensed perception that it also belonged to their own. What did one call it now? Srinivas wondered, and felt a little desolate, a little sick at heart because the name could not but be the same for a pattern which was no different.

Only, this time he was involved. Citizen of a nation which had gone to war without declaring it. A naturalized Briton, who must needs share Britain's guilt. Citizen, beyond any of this, of a country to which he was bound by loyalty, even love, which had reverted to peremptory imperial ways: ways which had shaped his life, been soil and seedbed for his own past anguish.

'One dug a grave and buried it,' he said to Mrs Pickering. 'Thought it was over. But it will not lie.'

'You cannot bury things that have life left in them,' she agreed, not knowing to what he alluded, but grasping the state he was in, whose naked quills rasped her skin, scraped on the living flesh.

'Greed for land, greed for oil,' he said wearily. 'Or maybe just the habit of it. But who would have thought, in this day and age?'

Then she had an inkling.

'Wanting and taking,' she said. 'Is there a closed season for such things? It's always there. Perhaps it appears more barefaced now.'

'Barefaced or below board, the shame is the same.'

'Half the population, according to the polls,' said Mrs Pickering, offering such consolation as she could, 'is against our using force in Egypt.'

'Yes,' said Srinivas, and felt a slight stirring of gratitude for her effort, an ember among the ashes. But it was out before it could warm him, and he felt a numbness riding over his limbs and threatening his faculties. He shivered, and tried to be close to her as they usually were, which would have kept the cold from his spirit; but failed. He tried again, but something had come between them. A wedge that he could not shift, forged by outside events and driven between them, which he could hardly believe could happen.

'What is it?' she asked, feeling the cold as people must who suddenly find themselves standing alone, exposed obelisk on a windswept hill. Doubly vulnerable now, because, like Srinivas, peace had returned only after years of restless, rootless living.

'Nothing,' he said, and his mouth was wrung, purse-strings tight drawn, the contours of an old man.

'I am,' she said, prompted by instinct, which remained sound, 'with that half of the population that is against it.'

'I know,' he said.

But a fundamental knowledge ran more deeply, less audible, more insistent and alienating: for he knew that she came to her conclusion by reason and intellect, whereas his sprang straight from the blood. Blood which came down from generation to generation, holding in solution memories and truths as indestructibly as genes, as demonstrably as slow-worms. Chop it in two, each poor stump staunches the running fluid and after the pain has dulled regenerates, and each new part remembers and performs (heavy with embedded wires and coils), haltingly performs the tricks they have taught the old one.

His blood. Instantly, but through a long conditioning of misery, it aligned him on the side of those attacked, in automatic reaction, spring-loaded by the past, against those nations which had carved up continents, calling the slices their colonies. While she, collating facts and sifting the evidence of a confused situation, came sober and upright and in decent English fashion to her conclusion, which was in essence the same as his own.

Only, they had reached it by different paths: and the difference lay heavy and leaden upon them.

The afternoon wore on. Mrs Pickering brought tea and biscuits; but he could not eat. They listened to the radio, a set well past its prime that belonged to Mrs Pickering. In between the static they heard the announcer's voice giving the casualty figures: two hundred Egyptians killed or injured, a total of five for British and French. In this, despite himself, Srinivas again discerned the old pattern: a ratio of forty to one, forty Oriental lives for each European, the familiar equation with its bitter inflections. Life is cheap in the East. If they didn't die like flies, how could they cope with their excess populations?

Srinivas smothered the echoes, that came up sharp from the past. They did not apply. Whether they did or not, he did not want to hear them, now or ever again. He got up with no object in mind, then produced one.

'It's stuffy in here,' he said. 'I think I'll go out and get some fresh air.'

'It's foggy,' she said.

He had not noticed, but when he went out it swirled about him. He stood for a while to acclimatize, surveying the November gloom through yellowish drifts. A cold-country scene. Trees that dripped, a chill ragged tattoo on the pavement. Ash and elm stripped, branches like blackened brooms rising stiffly out of the murk. A haze about the street lights, which had come on early: each an ellipse of brilliance, shot with streaming particles of mist and light like fireflies. No fireflies in London, though. A pity, said Srinivas, picking his way through the fog. He had not thought about them for years. A recurrent phenomenon of the night scene once and then – in harbour, waiting to sail – seeing them for the last time, starry clusters winging dizzily above the taffrail.

Sailing, and the luminous trails following briefly and being extinguished in the grey vapours of colder seas. Of England, he said to himself: I am in England. Suddenly a gust of unreality swamped him. His head swam. He steadied himself against a lamp post and presently the feeling went, but now there was an overpowering stench. He looked down and saw the dogshit in which he had planted his foot; above, a notice threatened dog owners who allowed their dogs to foul the footpath with a five-pound fine.

Almost retching with disgust, he bent down and unfastened his shoe and holding it by the tongue deposited it in the gutter. Shedding its pair to equalize, he walked on, but now his socks felt clammy and he stopped and pulled them off and left those in the gutter too, a few yards downstream from the shoes.

The pavement was icy under his soles, but walking restored his circulation and he began to like the feel, the grip and slap of toe and heel upon the glistening flags. It was a small thing, but pleasure effervesced and burst like tiny champagne bubbles in his brain. Presently he felt a trifle light-headed. I am disappointed in you, he said explicitly, to the country whose pavements he trod, and he wagged a schoolmasterish finger; I am disappointed and disgusted because you have gone back to your old freebooting ways. Bombing other people's lands. Killing other people. Creating misery. The effervescence on which he rode subsided as suddenly as it had arisen, leaving him sunk even lower than before. His legs however continued to carry him and he allowed them to.

At the corner, turning out of Ashcroft Avenue, he bumped into a small flickering figure in raincoat and hood, and recognized the pale damp face of Mrs Fletcher.

'It's horrible,' he said to her.

'Why, it's you, Mr Srinivas,' she said. 'You gave me quite a start. Yes, it is horrible isn't it? Not fit to be out in.'

'The bombing,' he said.

'I hadn't heard,' she said nervously. He seemed to be accusing her.

'On the news,' he told her. 'They've bombed Egypt.'

'Oh, that,' she said. 'Tell you the truth, I didn't pay much attention.'

'You should have. It is a grave matter.'

She backed a little. There was something stern about him, quite unlike the Mr Srinivas she knew. He looked strange too. No overcoat, in weather you could catch your death of cold in, and everyone else wrapped up to the eyebrows. Her eyes travelled down and she saw his feet. Bare. Like two wet fish on a slab. She wanted to scream, but after all one didn't, not right out in the open street. She stood frozen. He saw her petrified stare.

'Don't worry,' he said. 'I am quite used to bare feet. From my young days, you know.'

It seemed to release her. 'Yes, yes, of course,' she gasped, and dodging around him, scuttled down the avenue.

Srinivas turned and began to walk in the same direction. A fine drizzle was falling, and it seemed to him now the best thing would be to go home. To Mrs Fletcher, however, it seemed as if he were after her. Despite her great fear of looking foolish she broke into a trot, and did not feel safe until she had banged the front door behind her.

Mrs Pickering, who had been on the lookout, let Srinivas in, and she, too, felt better after she had closed and fastened the door. To keep out draughts, and those clammy airs and animosities that nipped her mind, making the eyeballs ache. Or perhaps because it was best for him to be in, a man of his age: a view that gained strength when she saw his feet. Bare, as Mrs Fletcher had seen, with the joints and tarsals whitened and the arches marbled by the cold. Pneumonia, no less, she said to herself, and fetched water, a flannel, warm towels, in an effort to avert it. He watched silently, did what she told him to, immersed his feet in the water and even allowed her to rub them dry.

'Your shoes?' she asked, not too hopefully.

'I threw them away.'

'What for?'

'Dog's muck,' he said briefly.

'Do you remember where?'

'No. I just flung them away.'

'Why? They could have been cleaned.'

'I could not bear to.'

She said nothing. She waited in silence, the water cooling in the basin between them.

'I am used to going without shoes,' he told her.

'I daresay you were,' she said, 'but you have forgotten how to. It was a long time ago.'

'It seems like yesterday,' he said. 'Time has a way of catching up. It has caught up. After all these years it has all come back. I even feel now as I used to feel. Worse,' he said, and peered at her to see if she could understand, 'because now I am on the sinning side, which is more difficult to sustain than being sinned against.'

'What do you feel?' she asked.

'Turmoil,' he said wearily. 'Anger and turmoil, which I believed belonged to the past.'

She sat back, because she too had reached a stage. A time to stop and ask, which each had recognized might come, before the years of silence which had been humane could undergo degenerative changes.

'You keep harping on the past,' she said. 'It crops up time and again, I can always tell when it does because you become a different man. Your past. I know nothing of it, except generally. Generally, it is unpleasant to live in an occupied country, everyone knows that. But what was it like for you? Perhaps it was a bad time to live through, but are you sure? Are you sure it was as bad as you think? It's as well to get it right, because life can go rancid if one is haunted too long.'

Then he saw he would have to go back, dredge up what he believed he had left behind so that they could both see. Only, he had no great heart for it. He did not wish to speak against her people, dissociate though she was from those men, long ago, who had made the decisions; nor to smirch with mean memories the country to which he was in debt, owing it much that he valued.

14

THERE WAS THE HOUSE, THEN, IN WHICH THEY ALL lived. The first *Chandraprasad*, which his grandfather had had built on the salubrious outskirts of the town. He built it there because town was where the schools were, schools which his sons would have to attend, since the men who were masters now looked askance on those traditional ways by which he had acquired his learning. Four pupils to each guru, a rigorous discipline, training that took in aspects of both body and mind and went on regardless of the clock, did not gain their approval. Their seal went elsewhere: to those who sat in classrooms from nine till four, and learned English and read tales retold from Indian history, and passed examinations which entitled them to pieces of parchment and letters after their name like S.S.L.C., Secondary School Leaving Certificate, or even BA.

These men they favoured, which was logical enough, since they had created the system to create such men, who fulfilled a specific purpose: that of stocking the vast army of petty clerks without which no ruling could be done.

In that age of innocence people vied for these favours. In return they were despised, although this stern dawn did not break until some decades later. The old man, the grandfather, needed no favours. He was a Brahmin, a landowner, descendant of a long line of learned men, lord of all he surveyed, a survey which took in some excellent forest land. But somehow a view of the future which remained so steady for him developed a distinct tremor when he thought of his sons. So he sold his village house on the edge of the forest and moved to town with his wife, his two sons, his two daughters, a milch cow and a buffalo, leaving a poor relative encamped in a jungle hut to look after his teak and sandalwood trees in the plantation on the edge of the village.

This same poor relative having, prior to his translation, supervised the construction of the town house, the move was accomplished with minimum inconvenience. Except of course for the old man, who continued to have twinges and hankerings, and longings that settled themselves into aches in his bones, since after all he had been accustomed, until his middle years, to a green and tranquil existence.

These, however, were involuntary feelings. Consciously he had no regrets. His sons, then young teenagers, took to the new living like ducks to water. Naturally bright, their progress at school was studded with prizes of hymn books and Bibles, a success story which they repeated at university. Duly equipped with MAs, the younger son, Srinivas's uncle, became in due course tutor to a deposed maharaja's son; the elder, Srinivas's father, starting as a teacher in the local high school, went on to become a lecturer at the Government College. The old man looked on and was pleased. Sometimes he even felt he had made the right decision.

By this time both sons had married and the children were coming. When the family assembled, now, there were uncles, aunts and cousins, parents and grandparents, Narayan, Narasimhan, Laxman, Nila, Kapila, Chandralekha – the names alone were like a litany and the house, though large, was too small for all of them. When the women grumbled, and sighed for more room, and wondered how better money could be spent than on additional housing, the old man counselled patience. He would not build intemperately, or before the time was ripe.

Srinivas was eight years old when construction began on the extension, which in effect was a whole new house, with interconnecting corridors which delighted the children. Long before, even before they had begun to complain of cramp, the old man had journeyed back to his village to choose the best timber for his house. Each day the two men sallied out: the poor relation from the tent into which he had been cast, the old man from the hut he had commandeered whose thatch was stabler than the flapping canvas. Together they made their survey, selecting and marking the trees to be axed, followed by the woodcutter, an unlettered character who knew the woods as if they were charted plains, and who returned in due course with his team, leading them unerringly to each ringed bark. The felled trees lay, season after season, weathering, for the old man would have no truck with new wood which warped and would not lie true, and could not be planed or dovetailed into structures of pleasure. He, and his family, could wait.

Three bullock carts, finally, each drawn by two bullocks with a relief beast in tow, brought the timber to the town site. The purlin alone – a huge log, with a mighty girth, specially selected – took up the whole of one cart. Rafters and principals came on a second, beams for joists and supports on the last cart – a comparatively light load this, upon which small boys perched. Srinivas watched with envy. He was a small boy too, he would have liked to ride as these children were riding, sons of carpenters and masons whom his grandfather had hired. But he was the owner's son and, besides, he had to go to school.

Even at that early age he knew how important school was. He saw the respect in which his father was held, and at home he often heard the grown-ups speak in commiserating tones, with self-congratulatory nuances, of families whose sons could not get jobs because of a lack of British-type schooling. His sharp ears picked up these undertones, he knew they were doing the right thing, he and his father and uncle who were securing bright futures through education; but sometimes he wondered why those others, who could not get jobs, did not return to the land, earn a living as his grandfather had done, and indeed still did. When he asked, his father looked anxious, and said it would be difficult to explain to a young boy, and his grandfather pursed his lips and eyed him, and then said things were different nowadays; the British were masters, and one had to go along with them and their ways.

Srinivas, at eight, found it difficult to comprehend. How could the British, so alien, so aloof that one was scarcely aware of their existence, impinge upon all these levels of one's living? Besides, there were so few of them. He had seen no more than a handful, driving past in their motorcars, or playing polo in topis (a distant view, this) on the club grounds, and one man with a coarse red leathery face who shouted and cursed at the sepoys he drilled on the maidan. So he wondered, and the reality receded to the grown-up world, not disbelieved but with strictly limited impact.

By fourteen he had a fair inkling. That was the year of the Great War. Britain was fighting Germany, and somehow it seemed as if it were India's war too. At any rate, the factories were turned from assembling tractors and locomotives to producing cannon and roundshot, and taxes went up on everything from salt to cement, and in the towns – even their smallish town – recruiting officers were thick on the ground, spirited men who spoke in ringing tones of the nobility of war, and sent forth their assistants who smothered walls and the trunks of trees and the corrugated iron of men's urinals with stirring posters.

In the classrooms at school there was a good deal of excitement, but not much debate or disagreement; that came later, in college, when they were older. Now they spoke in approving terms of this just war which Britain was waging, for freedom, and against the militaristic Germans, invaders of Belgium, perpetrators, they had heard, of unthinkable atrocities. They even spoke in favour of joining up, not necessarily themselves, of course, they were scholars, and this kind of thing was best left to the martial classes. But they supported the war, and praised the military who supported it, and were proud that their country had contributed over forty crores of rupees towards the war effort in less than a year. Occasionally a voice objected. If the British were so passionate about freeing other peoples, why did they keep such a tight hold on India? But it was a lone, older, cantankerous voice to which, in the full flush of generous and outgoing young adolescence, they did not listen.

At fourteen, besides, there were other things. The house, for instance, which after six years' carping and care was at last completed to the old man's satisfaction. In varying degree they all had some feeling for it, this rambling edifice whose growth they had watched from founding stone up – and further back, some fancifully said, from the seeding of the great teak trees. But in Srinivas, inheriting as his grandfather had done from some remote source, before inflexible patterns had begun to mould natural preferences, the feeling took on acute and tactile overtones of pleasure. If he had not been a Brahmin and a scholar, he would have been a carpenter. As it was, and despite all his handicaps, especially school, he contrived to absorb a good deal about chisels and bevels and gimlets, about notching and cogging and miter joints. More, he even managed to put his skills into practice, so that there were parts in the house to which he could point, if he wished, and claim them as his own handiwork.

When the building was complete he loved every aspect of it, the sturdy, weathered beams whose timbers could be seen supporting the surfaces and ceilings of structure, the heavy resinous doorposts, the polished rosewood swing with a finish like porcelain which they hung from chains in the central room, the timber floor on whose planed surfaces a drawn fingertip would not have coaxed a splinter, the marquetry of light woods and dark, rose and sandal and satin inlays that ornamented doorframes and windowsills.

So there was the house to which Srinivas returned with pleasure after school each evening, passing the barracks on his way, and skirting the maidan, which seemed to have been taken over by the military these days. And there was the child Vasantha, daughter of neighbours, a Brahmin family like theirs except that this branch had gone into law. Lawyers, all of them, father, son, grandfather and nephew, as his brother, father, uncle were teachers and he was planning to be. He could not have said how he knew she was to be his bride, but he did. When he first realized he was not quite eleven; at that age the knowledge lay simply within him. At fourteen it was different. He looked at her with curiosity and speculation, although in the wet, impassioned dreams that were now beginning it was never her narrow, straight body or candid face that engulfed him.

Vasantha also knew. It did not inhibit her. After all, she was only seven. When she wanted something from him, to retrieve a kite from a thorn tree where her inept handling had landed it, or to hold one end of a skipping rope, or even when she was merely bored, she took to calling him husband, a ploy which she discovered yielded satisfactory results for he would do almost anything to make her desist.

'If you don't stop I'll run away to war,' he said to her one day, goaded beyond endurance. 'I'll become a soldier, just see if I don't.'

'How can you?' she said reasonably. 'You have to go to school.'

She had this devastating kind of realism.

'In a year or two, when I finish,' he informed her coldly, 'then I'll go. And when I've gone, what's more, you'll be left without a husband.'

'You can't,' she said.

'Why not?'

She did not answer and he thought triumphantly, even contemptuously, she's not even thinking about it, she's thinking about her kites and dolls, she's only a baby. But the conclusion was too swift.

'You can't,' said this child Vasantha, 'because war means killing people. Killing people is wrong.'

Her view was quite clear, even then. She never changed it. Over the years, unmodified by event or circumstance, it remained an uncompromised statement. Nor could it be otherwise; to her it was an absolute.

Two years later, when he was sixteen, Srinivas sat for his school finals. He passed with distinction in seven subjects, and they gave him a copy of Macaulay's *Lays of Ancient Rome* as his prize.

His father was pleased by the book, with its inscribed flyleaf and morocco binding. In his day, for a similar achievement, they had given him a Bible, an equally baffling choice, which he courteously kept, approving Hindu precepts and principles which he found in the New Testament, though mildly dubious about Genesis. He was even more pleased with his son, who could now go on to college, take a degree, join the higher educational echelons, become a professor or don, begin in earnest that academic career which, more than most others, might preserve him from destructive involvement in national politics.

Destructive it would be, thinking people knew. Britain wanted to keep India; so captive and lucrative a market for her exports was not easy to come by elsewhere. India, however, wanted to be free. The issue would not be decided without a long struggle. What that meant was becoming clear too, spelled out incisively by men preparing for the contest and understandably anxious to avoid that melting away of cohorts which follows the dawn of grim reality. It meant sacrifice, of home and family and career and ambition, and discipline of mind and emotions; it meant cutting free, now and illimitably, of that robust human stanchion, me and mine first. So the father and grandfather and the older members of Srinivas's family devoutly asked to be spared, and clung to the manner of their living which, in these shifting times, had become doubly precious. Involvement, however, already lay waiting, just around the corner, where they could not see what form it would take, only the amorphous shadow.

In college the lone voice had grown louder. Because now they listened, and thought it made sense. Also, as far as Srinivas was concerned, because it belonged to Vasudev, Vasantha's brother, the lawyer's son. Why, it asked, the languid accents of this graceful youth strangely wrapped around sedition, should Britain deny India self-rule? Since it did, why should India cooperate in her own humiliation?

'Yes, why?' they asked each other fiercely.

'Because we are cowardly sheep.'

'Are we? Are we reduced to sheep?' Srinivas wanted to know. But in his house there were no answers. No one dared to give them, because the salary earners depended for a livelihood upon the government, which was British.

Here too, though, questions were forming in the swollen, precarious atmosphere, questions which were about to pitch them out of the walled and pleasant garden they inhabited – were clinging to, if the truth be told, by their fingertips.

15

THE FOLLOWING YEAR, 1917, THE MILITARY BEGAN
to build the road. It was to link the two military cantonments,
one in their town, the other on the coast, and they planned
it like a Roman road running strategically from point to
point to facilitate troop movements.

On the fifty-third mile of its run the road, as envisaged,
would encounter the teakwood plantation belonging to the
Srinivas family, would cut through it for some five miles,
and thereafter resume its unimpeded (save for one or two
negligible hamlets) progress to the coast. Compensation
would be paid.

'Compensation,' the old man said, without vehemence,
with the bleak acceptance of his age, which knew that the
rebellion which was called for was only for the young. 'What
compensation can they give us for purloining what has taken
a hundred years to grow?'

Nevertheless, despite his resignation, he rallied his
energies and travelled down, not so much to witness and
wring hands over what to him was a desecration, but to
hamper it in every way he could. Srinivas marvelled. It was
his vacation, he had accompanied his grandfather with some
hazy notion of supporting him; but the old man, it turned
out, had no need for such underpinning. In thin-soled
sandals, careless of thorns, his snow-white muslin shirt-tails
flying, he strode through the woods, exhorting; and when

he had finished not a single woodsman was to be come by, neither topper nor rigger nor any man who might remotely be called lumberjack, notwithstanding extravagant wage offers dangled enticingly by the harassed civil contractor, so that in the end it had to be left to the military. Then it was over. Skirmishes might be won, but one single old man could not fight a mighty machine with any hope of victory.

The two of them together watched the trees come down. Girths of seventy inches, some of them, more than a century in the making, with heartwood darkened to burgundy and the sapwood bleeding, the sapwood which in the young trees was golden-green and scented, the whole air was scented with their sharp aroma. Then Srinivas understood, standing beside his grandfather among the felled crowns and the crushed white inflorescence, what it was like to be helpless, to be less than master in one's own house, to have not even a voice in the running of one's own country.

'They will tell you with pride,' his grandfather said to him, 'how they have built roads and railways in our country. Well, no doubt they have. The devil must be given his due. But remember too – you must never forget – how it was done, and why.'

This bitter speech was not characteristic of him, and later he amended it. He was, besides, nearing seventy, no age at which to be harbouring malice and high time, furthermore, to be done with worldly affairs and to cultivate those contemplative attitudes and inner harmonies enjoined by the scriptures, for which, indeed, after the buffetings he had endured – town life had taken from him more than he realized – he was ready.

In the Vasantha household no such philosophy prevailed.

'What they have done now,' said Vasudev, blazing, in contrast to the pale suppressed reactions Srinivas was more accustomed to from his family, 'or are about to do – it needs only a rubber stamp and a week or two before the bill becomes law – is to introduce internment without trial.'

Lawyers all, to them it was the final iniquity, a breach of what they had been bred and trained to regard as fundamental, imbibing the creed from the British themselves: the right of any man to remain innocent, and free, until he had been adjudged guilty.

'What will you do?' asked Srinivas. He knew, though. They would do what the nation's leaders asked them to, without hesitation, riding high over obstacles that paralysed other families, such as what to do for a living, which was, after all, not an unimportant consideration.

'What will I do?' Vasudev repeated, and laughed. 'There is only one thing to do, protest. And you?'

'I don't know,' said Srinivas, cagily. But he had a good idea. Soon – ahead of time on the advice of his professor – he would be sitting for his intermediate exam. Then he would take his degree. After that – well, it would depend on what kind of pass he got, but nevertheless a pleasing progression filled his mind, touched here and there with dazzling glints, of MAs and PhDs, and somewhere at the end of this glorious trail perhaps even a vice chancellorship. He hugged these thoughts to himself, more tightly than ambition alone warranted; they warmed him, but somehow there was something not quite right about them, something a little unprincipled to indulge in dreams in these times when appointments were being contemptuously resigned and declined and whole careers wrecked. And so he was wary of what he said.

In Vasantha's household such ambitions as still survived were now renounced. One after another the male members of the family – one a high court judge, another a court pleader, a third a collector and magistrate – sent in letters of resignation. Vasudev, duly keeping his word, organized a protest of fellow students against the hated ordinance, under which, predictably, he was summarily convicted. The women of the family, lacking the opportunity to indulge in such lavish and picturesque action, made their own small contribution. They kindled a bonfire and burned on it every article of what they thought to be British-manufactured that they could find. Silks and cottons, doilies of Brussels lace and crêpe de Chine bought from innocuous Chinese hawkers, were hurled on to the flames as one by one the camphor chests were opened and searched and almirahs ransacked wholesale. It was fun. Afterwards, though, their living somehow seemed less bright. They missed their pretty clothes, the delicate feel of fine cloth against their skins, the radiance thrown off on a woman by brilliant and graceful plumage. Vasantha, in particular, who could not wholly comprehend the reasons for this self-denial, resented the loss. She liked her gay skirts, the play of silk around her ankles, her thin soft blouses, the coin-spotted gauze scarves, meant for her shoulders, which were endlessly useful for playacting and dressing up as princess or royal concubine; and from dislike she moved to a loathing of the lumpish, coarse, off-white homespun they thenceforth wore. But it was a discipline. Singly and collectively they accepted it as they had accepted all the other disciplines and denials, and with accumulating grace. Even Vasantha, who was only a child. She was ten; but already the shadows that were eroding the looks of her elders lay delicate and faint, a forecast of future umber shades, upon her face.

The Srinivas camp watched and admired, if they could not emulate. Smaller sacrifices were within their scope; larger ones, such as they witnessed being made, they deemed to be beyond them. Neither Vasudev, who possibly could not from his prison cell, nor anyone else on his side, ever criticized. The liaison between the two families continued as closely as before, the marriage arranged between a son and a daughter of each reinforcing the link. Vasantha herself hardly ever thought about her marriage. It lay beyond her horizon, like freedom, and returning to old lush ways of living. She played with her celluloid dolls, as her china ones had been smashed, learned to spin, as all patriotic little Indian girls obediently did, visited her brother in prison, escorted by a warder who stilled her fears with sweets he bought expressly for frightened children, and at home continued to torment Srinivas with scandalous cries of husband, banking on her parents' preoccupation to escape unscathed.

Srinivas bore with it, deliberately calling to mind the straits the family were in, and mentally listing the horrible attributes possessed by this child, while daily he grew more conscious of her delicate oval face, the high, vermilion-tinted arches to her feet, from which sometimes he could hardly lift his eyes. His studies were his refuge. He immersed himself in them, shutting himself up in one of the smaller chambers that opened off the central room, though even here sounds penetrated, especially the oosh and swish of the rosewood swing, which was favourite sitting for everyone. Throughout the hot weather he slaved, wet towels wrapped around his brow, sucking the perfumed orange flesh of badami mangoes to sustain him. When he sat for his intermediate examination he was well prepared: even so, the results surprised him. Distinctions in every subject, a first-class pass, first in the whole presidency, his name heading the list of successful candidates.

They gave him a medal for it, which the vice chancellor, a booming man called Drinkwater, presented. He made a little speech first, standing on the dais with his gown thrown back and his thumbs hooked in his waistcoat pockets. He found it, he said, a pleasant task to reward so deserving a young man as Srinivas: a young man whose exemplary conduct, he felt, might with advantage serve as an example to all students – to, he would venture to say, all India's young men – especially those rowdy radicals who roamed the streets to the detriment of their studies, wasting their own and their parents' and the country's time and resources. After this he presented the medal and everyone applauded, the students packed in the hall, porters and peons draped in doorways, the college staff, among whom sat Srinivas's proud father, the assembled parents and friends, among them Vasantha, who had come escorted by her uncle, whose clapping sounded louder than all the rest to Srinivas's burning ears.

But somehow there were uncomfortable flavours, an aftertaste that lingered like a bitterness at the back of the tongue.

Nevertheless they celebrated, Vasantha's clan (or at least its rump, since there had been further brisk removals of freedom-campaigning members) sharing the celebration by invitation. After they had dined, and the leaves on which they had eaten had been gathered up and slung in the buffalo's trough, and the women had begun cracking areca nuts and stemming and veining betel leaves with which to round off the meal, they asked to see his medal. Srinivas brought it out, shyly. It was a beautiful thing, gold, or at least golden, bright and shining in its purple velveteen case. On one side

the words 1ST PRIZE had been engraved. The obverse bore
a portrait of the King Emperor, and an inscription in Latin
ran sonorously around the rim: *Georgivs V Dei Gra: Britt:
Omn: Rex Fid: Def: Ind: Imp.*

'What does it say?' asked Vasantha.

'First prize,' said Srinivas.

'On the other side.'

'George Fifth, King Emperor,' he said, shortly, oddly
reluctant to translate in full but compelled to reveal the
worst, so to speak, the imperial presence which haunted
them all.

'Oh,' she said, and it was all she said but it made him
flinch. He looked at her closely, but her lids were down,
opaque lids which were touched with the tawny hues of the
warm brown eyes they concealed. Concealing eyes, he said
to himself in the heavy silence that invested them, not those
of the transparent child I imagined; and the grains began to
gravitate and mass, single items of evidence coalescing, and
he heard again the sound of her clapping rising thunderously
above the dutiful applause, and knew it had been defiant
and partisan, a stubborn demonstration of fealty in the face
of the tenuous but perceptible feeling in the hall. Then he
put away the medal in its case and snapped it shut and got up
and went out, out of the house into the luminous darkness
of the yard where they tethered the buffalo. A friendly beast
this, with opulent flanks that smelled of butter fat and milk,
a sweet baby smell, and a muzzle as wet and glistening as the
rinsed plantain leaves it had recently eaten, and upon which,
now, he laid an affectionate palm while he sat on a truss of
hay and thought about his bride-to-be. Explored her, and
came with renewed surprise and pleasure upon what he
found, recognizing the subtle change that had not quite

touched the shape of her body, but was already altering the contours of her mind.

'What is the matter with Srinivas?' the family, abruptly deprived of the company of the star of the occasion, asked each other, though perhaps they had more than a glimmering of a notion, but asking all the same to keep the thought from popping out like some bulbous appalling tumour at first incision of the surgeon's knife: the thought that all was not well, that the citadel they had built for themselves could not withstand the creeping malaise that affected the country.

'It is his age,' said Nirmala, Srinivas's mother, soothing, smoothing over with the industry of a master plasterer so that they could be held together, as is the nature of women to do.

That same month the old man, Srinivas's grandfather, died. He did it as he had lived, without fuss, simply lying down to sleep one night on the hard wooden bed he had designed himself and failing to wake up the next morning. Srinivas, who liked to wake first and work in peace before the rest of the household roused, found him with his eyes closed and his jaw fallen, and one arm thrown round the bedpost. It was a favourite position: the old man had liked to feel the carving on the finial, a design of his own which his grandson had executed. The touch of it had helped him to sleep, especially towards the end when sleep did not come easily, and he had turned to it for the last time, in his extremity. The impress was still on his arm: a life-size representation of wheat ears and teak florets which the dying flesh and curdled blood could not efface, though it seemed rather as if death were powerless to erase the indomitable pattern.

Now the new head of the family was Narayan, Srinivas's father, a man no less able than his father before him but with the ground of convictions and certainties cut away earlier from under his feet, leaving him less stable, more tremulous and compromised than the old man had ever had cause to be. He, the grandfather, had always been independent, a man planted firmly on his own two feet. His son was dependent. With the substance of his inherited forest land wasting, crippled by the swathe cut through its vital centre, he was dependent on the government for his living, on the whims of its higher representatives for such grace and favours as accompanied it. Imperceptibly, in small doses, he learned he was inferior. A scholarly man, a senior lecturer at the college, outside the lecture room his company, he found, was seldom positively sought by the British who employed him. No invitation to the principal's home, generously extended to English colleagues, ever came his way, nor in some twenty years' service did he once set foot in an English house. It made him speculate on his deficiencies: on whether his manners were uncouth, or a degree of civilization lacking, or if he simply did not make the grade as a man; and eventually to believe that one if not all must apply. Not, of course, that he craved such intercourse: he had his own circle of friends. But still. The barbed implant might not fester, as it did in less patient men, but it remained a continuing presence.

More painfully, he discovered he was not good enough for the top jobs. As his career progressed, and he saw the higher appointments – headmaster, principal, vice chancellor – going one after another to Englishmen, he gradually came to accept that he lacked the quality of leadership, that these jobs were beyond his capacity. A modest man, he lowered his sights accordingly. It was only when lesser posts – the deputy and assistant headships he aspired to – also passed him by that he began to wonder. It was, however, not a conflagration but a slow ache in his breast, about which he did nothing and did not believe there was anything he could do.

Srinivas, festooned and foundering in question marks like the rest of his generation, found solutions to his father's problems while his own remained intractable. Why could he not do this, why did he not do that? Why, in particular, did he not resign when Platt, who was only a BA, was made deputy principal over his head? Why, having accepted the humiliation, did he continue to dispense courtesy to greasy, usurping Platt, who did not even have the decency to stand down? Above all, why was Vasantha's family not asked to share what they had, their plight being what it was with so many wage earners missing?

This torrid monologue, however, went on silently. Srinivas could not speak to his father in these terms. The respect owed by son to father was instilled into and had become a part of him, he could not jump out of his own framework. At odds with himself he mooned about the place, barking at those who suggested occupations for his energy, and neglecting his studies to think about Vasantha: how much did she miss her relations, was she getting enough to eat? Sometimes he sent her sweets, home-made fancies done up in a newspaper cone, agonized in case she should turn down an offering from a collaborationist house, which in fact it did not occur to her or her family to do.

Could not afford to, perhaps, for their fortunes were sinking. And it was not Srinivas alone, as he thought, who perceived it. His father, too, was agonized, and his agonies were possibly more acute in that he was the head of his clan, the one who made the decisions, the one who dealt with the realities of the situation which included harbouring a family under suspicion and taking on, perhaps for life, the responsibility for supporting it and its subsidiaries. Enough to make anyone shiver, and hesitate – a reaction that roused in Srinivas a disdain, a contempt so incandescent he could hardly contain it, for the moralities of the middle-aged. So what lay between them simmered, consuming the substance of their relationship, and charring the edges of an entire range of family communications until they contracted, mangled antennae that functioned erratically and sometimes not at all.

16

IT WAS 1918. THE WAR HAD ENDED, THE ARMISTICE
had been signed.

Now, they said in India, we shall be free. Britain has
promised, we shall be independent, or at the least we shall
have home rule. It was a simple belief and here and there
simple people celebrated.

In Britain it was different. We must think about it, they
said, and sent simple concepts packing, and put in their
place a complex of abstruse and weighty thought. Reduced,
it meant that for various sound reasons it was not feasible for
India to govern herself.

Not yet.

Not ever?

Well, no; but precipitate progress was not in the best
interests of those concerned.

'What they mean is that they are not ready to let go,' said
Vasudev, and his hands drooped, limp and depressed like his
spirits, which had banked on a swift clean victory and could
scarcely bear to contemplate the vista that stretched, as long
and dreary as everything older men had predicted.

'No matter, the day will come,' his mother comforted,
mechanically, not caring a rap for freedom at this moment
but only for her son, returned pale from his incarceration
but otherwise well. They had treated him well, she felt,
she could not complain, the only legitimate complaint

was over his absence, the months he had been away from her, but even that was dissolved in the happiness of his homecoming. Not only his; one by one the other absentees were returning, having served their term of sentence – which had been half-hearted and mild, the British being nagged by their own consciences – less remission for good conduct.

'It is like the end of a nightmare,' Srinivas overheard his father say. But he was out of touch with events, peering from slits in his academic fortress and seeing little, possibly not wanting to see too much. Blind, Srinivas put it to himself, staring at his father with that glassy, mesmerized look which Narayan dreaded, which made him wonder what he had done wrong now, what manner of reptile he appeared in his son's eyes. Bootlicker, the word came to him. That was the most charitable word in their descriptive lexicon, they applied it to people like him who worked for the British and were polite to them. He sighed, and looked down at his pen-pushing hands, and came close to despising his teacher's patient, prudent mind while Srinivas set his teeth and repeated, speechlessly, blind, blind, blind.

For he felt he, unlike his father, knew what was coming. Not a dawn after nightmare, but another long dark night. Vasudev primed him, Vasudev, whose place was underground, that underground which was the suppressed mouthpiece and keeper of the conscience of the nation, whose friends seemed to be strategically placed and subversively employed in most urban trouble spots.

'They are agitating right across the board,' Vasudev said, with satisfaction but soberly, with a beginning of appreciation for the forces at work, their nature and magnitude with which neither side, as yet, had come fully to terms. 'There have been demonstrations in Delhi and Calcutta ... all over Bengal and the Punjab.'

'What will happen?' asked Srinivas fearfully. His friend's realism, though calm, was much more alarming than flights of fancy, however frenzied.

'Anything, I'm afraid.' It was Vasudev's father who answered, and he used the orotund language of the lawyer he had once been. 'It has always been my submission that when people are activated by overriding emotion their action follows a course foreign to their character.'

Srinivas's father sat quietly listening in a corner – literally, on a battered cane chair put there to be out of the way – while the other three lounged on the broad plank of the rosewood swing; figuratively too, for he knew his opinions did not count and would not be sought, that he was in fact an insignificant man. Sometimes it did occur to him to wonder what all these patriots would do if there were no people like himself, humble providers of rice and roofs-over-one's-head. But it was a thought that came rarely, and after what happened never surfaced again.

What happened happened far away, hundreds of miles away, in Amritsar in the distant Punjab. The facts were fairly straightforward, though terrible; the interpretations varied and the repercussions no one could calculate.

On the 9th of April, two Indian leaders were banished from the Punjab. On the 10th, three Britons were murdered by an Indian mob. On the 11th one General Dyer arrived to take control. On the 12th he issued a proclamation forbidding processions and meetings. On the morning of the 13th he read out his proclamation to the people at certain points in the city, and in the afternoon he ordered his troops to open fire on ten thousand people assembled at a meeting in contravention of his order. The military fired 1,650 rounds and 379 civilians died.

'I did not think they would act so far out of character,' Vasudev's father permitted himself to say. Then he lapsed into bitterness, as people tended to do now, despite some shreds of conviction that still remained that Britain was an honourable adversary. 'Over three hundred lives,' he said. 'A hundred Indians for each Briton. That is their scale, the scale by which they value themselves and against which we are measured. That is what we are up against: not their greed, or their anger, nor land hunger, nor the need to trade, but their arrogance, the mentality that produces such policies and acts.'

Vasudev was more succinct. 'The chips are down,' he said.

From then on, it seemed to Srinivas, the perplexities and indecision which had beset them all suddenly lifted. Each knew what to do, within the structure of his own power whose lines were clear, and did it. It was as if each of them, pieces in a hitherto jumbled-up jigsaw puzzle, saw his slot and dropped into place.

They did it differently. The Vasudevs took their chosen path. They had reached the point where the machinery of this foreign government seemed so odious, so intolerable, that not only could they not take part in it, but somehow they had to stop it working. Somehow, bending their minds and throwing their bodies upon the cogs and wheels to do it, they had to bring the whole obnoxious process to a halt. It led, of course, to prison: but this time for only one of them, the head of the family. Perhaps the problem of jail space was pressing; or perhaps the authorities had become aware of a measure of failure in previous policies.

'This one will fail too,' said Vasudev. 'They take our leaders – they call them ringleaders. But who swallows this double-talk? Not even they, any more. And to whom will they turn when something needs doing?'

'They were not born yesterday,' said his mother. 'They are culling the wage-earning heads. Is that so naive?' And she twisted her hands, yearning to use them in the service of her husband but was deprived, and tried to dwell on the subtleties of the governing race but her mind was preoccupied, jammed full of her deprivation, the sense of loss overflowed at her eyes beyond her control. So she dabbed her splashed cheeks, and the inflamed corners where the tear ducts jerked, furtively, ashamed of her sagging discipline which would not allow her to fulfil her part, while the others pretended not to see and continued their conversation.

Nirmala, Srinivas's mother, listened, but she listened for a break, rather than to what they were saying. She knew what she had to do, and intended to do it, and cast around vainly for ways, not too stark and bald, to introduce what she had in mind, and was haunted, until she hit upon a subject.

'Kunthi,' she said, in a suitable silence, 'has calved.'

It paralysed them. They knew, the event was a week old. How could she connect a buffalo calf to the fundamental matters under discussion? But she did, drawing the strange ends together, as determined in her own way as they were in theirs. 'We have so much milk,' she went on, 'we hardly know what to do with it.'

Vasudev's mother, finally, understood. She was being asked to share, not having a husband to provide. A few strands of pride still held, restraining acceptance, but she was tired. Tired out, she told herself, by the months and years that had gone, and those that stretched with no end in sight, and she began to stroke the flanks of the calf she had been ushered out to see, moved by the small replica, the fuzzy coat a true if soft facsimile of hairy hide, the tiny copy of glossy wet muzzle, the buds of horns like tonsures, minute roundels of dusky suede let into the dove-grey pelt. Gradually it filled her, the sense of something precious, something that could still be found, linked to life and growth and the slow, miraculous processes of continuation, and what was without fell into place, those puny onslaughts of commotion and strife that had worn her down, those rigid structures of pride that had held her upright, in the upright position for crucifixion on an unnecessary cross.

'It would be a relief,' she said simply, 'if you are sure you can manage.'

'Of course, of course,' said Nirmala, with the brusqueness of her embarrassment, and plunged about in the rustling hay as if it needed tossing and arranging, though in fact both calf and dam had been content with the stall as it was and only now raised their heads to complain.

So it was settled, quite quickly, since both families after all came from similar soil and stock, God and spirit were right, food and customs the same, and such differences of thinking and action as still existed were being daily whittled away.

It had come to Srinivas now. As he knew, having seen straws in the wind, and stalks of grass in his mother's hair, and from sundry proddings of his restive spirit: but he waited, not consciously aware of what he waited for, until presently his pride in possession came to balance the revulsion he felt, the same coiled revulsion that was moving all of them. The day it happened he took out his prize, nervously, handling the velvet case as if uncertain of its wounding capacity, or perhaps of his own invulnerability. But when he opened

it and saw the shining medal he felt little: a passing pang
for something that had once been precious, and even that
sprung, it seemed, from another era, in which glittering
trifles on purple beds from imperial patrons had been
important. Gently, though, he snapped the case shut.

'Goodbye, Georgivs V,' he said aloud, not without
affection, and went off to hunt for paper and string, and
to compose a letter at once courteous and candid, which
promised to be difficult to do, to Drinkwater the vice
chancellor.

His father observed these purposeful stridings. In their
present state of amiable congestion, the two families living
together, and people, furniture, and effects crammed in with
abundant goodwill but scant regard for order, it would not
have been easy to overlook such deliberate acts.

'I see,' he said, offering his son the chance to confide, in a
forlorn bid to reinstate himself, he who was the head of the
family but the only one left out in the cold, 'I see you are
busy.'

'I am,' said Srinivas, and his voice was hard, gritted with
the scorn he felt for the gutless man who sat in the chair
without a seat. 'I am returning my gold medal to the vice
chancellor, who can keep it.' Stuff it up his arse, he would
have liked to say, but he could not use such language in front
of his father, which made him angrier still. So he marched
out, not quite shivering the timbers, since he had passed that
stage, but nevertheless closing the door with a decisive click,
to post his protest parcel.

When he got to the post office, however, it was closed. It
was Sunday, he remembered, he ought to have remembered
because if it had not been he would have been in college, not
standing outside this shuttered edifice unable to conclude

an honourable undertaking. It incensed him. What had Sundays to do with Hindus, in a Hindu country? Like everything else, it was, he thought, an arrogant imposition.

Somehow, though, it refused to ring true. Would the British, those indolent religionists, have slapped their sabbath onto a colony for holy reasons? After all they had never shown much zeal for assaulting the Hindu faith. All the way back he worried at it, until at last his recalcitrant mind began to open, to admit that what they had done might have been done for simple considerations, an innocent preoccupation with rest and pleasure unconnected either with arrogance or an exercise in domination.

It was a reluctant admission, subtracting somewhat from the intensity of his revulsion, but he felt better for making it. Truth, and its half-cousin Justice, were acquiring accumulating importance, on a personal no less than on a national level, in exact proportion to the accelerating rate at which both, on both sides, were being eroded.

So it was Monday, 9 a.m. on Monday when the post office opened, before Srinivas could return his medal. By then his father's gesture was two hours old, since at seven o'clock that morning, after bathing and saying his prayers, the older man had laid aside the decreed college uniform of white duck trousers and black alpaca coat, which he had worn since the beginning of his career, and dressed himself in khaddar.

Khaddar shirt, khaddar dhoti, khaddar cap.

He looked, thought Narayan, surveying his reflection in the looking glass, more like a national saboteur than a sober senior lecturer, and he trembled, thinking of what his principal would say, and of the day ahead. The principal, however, had nothing to say. He was a remote man with the ability to spin distances about him, invisible but impassable barriers that kept people at bay, or perhaps their tedious imbroglios.

'I do not propose, Mr Narayan,' he said, his aloof eye scanning the shrinking form of the Indian, 'at this stage to say anything.'

It was Platt who commented, Platt the deputy principal, whose red face was sweaty – as it frequently tended to be – from the atmosphere from which the two of them had just emerged.

'I suppose one has to do these things,' said Platt.

'Yes,' Narayan replied.

'Well, good luck,' said Platt, and nodded, and shunted off nimbly to dodge any thanks, embarrassing confetti with which Narayan might be inspired to pelt him.

Having left home early, Srinivas had not seen his father in his revolutionary regalia. His first glimpse of the strangely clad figure came in the corridors of the college, and his first reaction was querulous. Pipped to the post, he thought with chagrin, and watched the knots of students forming in the compound, adoration rising from them like wisps of burning incense. Then something in him lurched, some great load of badly stowed ballast shifting to correct a list that had hampered him so long; and his own affairs slid into second place. My father, he said to himself, and felt some straightening of kinks that had formed over the years. My father. Who would have thought?

Life was full of delightful surprises.

A week went by. Used to the vagaries of the postal system, Srinivas gave it another. Surely by now someone must have received the medal? he asked himself aggrievedly. But no one said a word. Neither the principal, nor his deputy, nor the vice chancellor, nor any of the professors. As for his fellow students, they went about unconcernedly, oblivious or indifferent to what he had done: no heady incense rose for him, such as they had burned for his father.

Driven, he descended to lowly depths. He asked Ratnam, the exalted peon in charge of the study the vice chancellor used on his occasional visits to the college.

'Parcel,' said Ratnam, well aware of the importance that rubbed off on to him from the top job he had, yet always on the alert to add lustre to it. 'What parcel? How do you expect me to know? Sahib gets a hundred parcels, more than everyone else put together.'

'This shape. This size.'

'Of all shapes and sizes.'

No satisfaction there. None either from Vasudev, to whom he mentioned the matter, as casually as he could and acutely aware of scales, the return of a medal scarcely matching the courting of imprisonment which to Vasudev was every day and standard.

'Well,' said Vasudev, with bald truth, and not unkindly, 'it was no great sacrifice. By the time you sent it back you really didn't want to keep your medal. Besides, do you suppose they'd give you the satisfaction of acknowledging an insult? They're not as feeble as that.'

Srinivas, silenced, accepted this as he had to, truth being an effective damper of such indignation as still struggled to ignite. So there was to be no acknowledgement, no adulation for an act whose value was intrinsic. The deed had been done for its own sake, and the waters had closed over it, and that was that. Life might be full of surprises: it was also, it seemed to him, intent on spelling out its manifold disciplines.

Gradually, from the sheer nuisance of chaotic living, the two families sorted themselves out. Rooms were allocated to congenial spirits to share, to save everyone's sanity, furniture stacked away or rearranged, personal belongings pared to a minimum. The house, which had appeared to sink under goods and chattels, surfaced again: one could see its frames once more, and the spaces it enclosed, and suddenly there was flooring under one's feet, instead of objects to skirt around.

'It is pleasant to have order again,' said Srinivas's mother. 'One has only to look away two minutes – two minutes, no more – for complete disorder to reign.'

'Ah, yes,' said Vasudev's mother, and sighed. 'It is so nice and peaceful here. After our house, you know ... one never knew whom one would find, the place always seemed full of strange, wild-looking young men. They said they were Vasudev's friends, but really you know, I don't believe half of them were. Still, what could one do? In times like these one can hardly refuse anyone shelter.'

'No, indeed,' said Nirmala, hoping she would be spared such decisions, ashamed of herself for such hopes, and knowing all the time that it was creeping up on her: the situation, the dilemma, the same strange young men or, if not, their close kin, whom she found lurking in the labyrinthine corridors of the house and its annex, who straightened up when they saw her and said they were friends of Vasudev or Srinivas. But the problem was not acute, and there was little she could do if it were, so she put it away firmly from her. I will think about it, she said to herself, when I have to, later, and turned to the present, which was not without its own quiet pleasures.

High among these was the presence of Vasantha, whom her son was to marry. A pleasing girl, a pretty girl who would be prettier still if she were not quite so thin, but then who wouldn't be after what she'd been through, poor child. Though child or woman, who could tell? Since it flickered between the two, this shifting light that played upon the open transparencies of childhood, and dissolved and fell upon the cowls and veils of a woman, her wary body, the sudden watchfulness of eyes and lids that dropped over burnt umber depths, and so full circle to the child again, who made straw dollies and sailed them in paper boats, and ate dismaying amounts of butter, sugar, fruit, and curds, and afterwards licked her lips and fingers in simple, total satisfaction.

'You make lovely curds, Auntie.'

'Do I?'

'Yes. Thick and sweet. I wish I could make it like you.'

'It's easy. Anyone can. One spoonful of curd to each pot of milk. Stir it in slowly.'

'Like this?'

'Make sure the milk is just below blood-heat.'

'That's how we did it, Mother and I. But it set sour and watery.'

'Well, I expect you used cow's milk.'

'Is buffalo's better?'

'It's richer.'

'Sweeter?'

'Not really.'

'My mother says you cheat. She says you put sugar in.'

'Does she! Well, I don't. You tell her, not one single grain goes in.'

'Then it must be Kunthi.'

'Quite possibly. She is a superlative buffalo.'

'Or you are a better cook. Are you a better cook than my mother?'

'I don't think so.'

'Are you a better mother?'

'No, of course not! In what way?'

'Would you allow your son to go to prison?'

Such questions, innocent, crafty, leading to this. Suddenly, then, they changed their roles, they were two women confronting each other, and the one who was much the younger was the one with the wider experience. The incongruity spun them round, placing one where the other, by rights, should be. Nirmala the elder asking: 'Would you?' and Vasantha the younger answering: 'It is not a case of allowing or not allowing.'

Now why couldn't I think of that? wondered Nirmala. She felt a little giddy, though not unused to finding herself mounted on this particular carousel since the young, these days, were better equipped than their elders to answer questions that the air seemed to breed. They have more energy, she told herself, shying away from the truth that was striking glancing, uncomfortable blows on her soft-shelled body. More energy, she repeated, and felt herself cornered, more energy ... and, of course, they are not middle-aged cowards like us.

At that moment, however, she felt old rather than middle-aged, and events and people were soon to combine to convert patent cowardice into courage, or at least a passable imitation of it.

17

FACES. FACES THAT WERE SOMETIMES RECOGNIZABLE and sometimes not, features that retained their shape, maxilla and occiput intact but imbued with a quality, a dangerous, friable quality as if collapse were imminent, as if at a tap, no more, on this fragile shell that kept up appearances the bone would cave in, revealing the inner degeneration.

What is the matter with us, asked Narayan, still in the chair that lacked a seat, in his khaddar clothes which after all had turned out to be no more than a gesture of little significance. What is happening, to make us look like a copy of human beings? Like lepers, he said to himself, at the point where flesh becomes sludge, and fled horrified from his own image to his wife, the sanctuary she offered, but gazing upon her pinched features saw that she too was haunted.

Haunted as he was, though differently. For sometimes she saw the face of her son, and the faces of his friends and of strange wild men, but sometimes they dissolved in front of her eyes and re-formed and then she was uneasily aware of unknown identities materializing under familiar features, searched them and came upon flint, seams of iron and quartz that had no place in the make-up of human ore.

'What are you up to?' she asked Srinivas bluntly.

'The question you should ask is what are *they* up to,' he replied.

Which silenced her, since both questions had point. So there was nothing to do but wait and see, like the rest of the country. Both sides, decisively separated into governed and governing, in limbo, waiting it seemed for something to happen.

When it happened it seemed slight: the passing of a vote of support and sympathy, the collection of a purse by fellow countrymen in a far country, both following upon official censure of the man and his act, the general and his order which had cost so many lives. But it aroused an anger that appeared out of proportion, feelings whose intensity surprised even those who imagined they had the measure of their own spirit, its range and stretch and capacity.

'They don't know what they have done,' said Srinivas, who believed the touch paper had been lit, saw large-scale rebellion on the rapidly homing horizon.

'Indeed they don't,' his father agreed, but his horizon tilted differently. 'They do not realize ... they have not thought it through. It is a common human failure.'

'Human failure,' said Vasudev. 'Well. And what was the other, when they shot down unarmed civilians? An excess of military zest? No. It was a massacre, the murder of lesser beings, people of little account in their sight as they now make clear.'

'That act was repudiated and condemned,' said Narayan.

'It is now condoned and endorsed,' said Vasudev, and the question was ripe on his lips, *what is the matter with you that you cannot see things in their true light?,* but he bit it back out of some lingering shreds of respect for this shaky father of his friend under whose roof he sheltered.

'By a few people,' said Narayan.

'By more than you think,' said Vasudev.

'The place is swarming,' said Srinivas.

'With troops,' said Vasudev. 'What for? What do they want to pack the town out with troops for?'

'To preserve law and order,' said Narayan, ashen, assaulted on two flanks, routed and falling back to his dismay on statements he knew to be discredited.

'Some law, some order,' said Vasudev, with the sarcastic inflections habitual to common speech. 'They have the gall, you have to hand it to them.'

'No gall, no empire,' said Srinivas.

'No empire, it is over,' said Vasudev, 'in everything but fact.'

Facts, however, were stubborn. Often they were frightening.

'Is it a fact,' Narayan asked his son, 'that you have been involved in the manufacture of petrol bombs?'

'The police thana is bristling with rifles and ammunition,' said Srinivas. 'You can see the rifle racks if you stand on tiptoe. The window is barred but they have not yet fixed a blind.'

He had learned to avoid straight answers, to stall, to deal in obliquities that contacted reality like a skilful clown, at chosen set points. It was part of a new learning, taken straight from the top, that permeated the country: a whole new acquired repertory of cover words for what, perhaps, was unspeakable.

The only person who could still elicit straight answers from him was Vasantha. Something in her halted the process that hung people up, kept them and their situations helplessly bottled in jelly. One cannot quibble with a child, Srinivas told himself. But it was no child that roused such responses, set fire to a sexuality, already stroked and stimulated by violence, that made him burn and twitch in her presence. Only sometimes her words broke through to him, piercing the quivering sac of his feelings, a cold douche that pulled him up sharply.

'Were you involved?' she asked.

'Yes,' he said, and was aware of Vasudev's disapproval frosting his back, Vasudev whose anxiety was for a whole ring whose safety such disclosures endangered.

'Actually?'

'In a way.'

'Are there two ways? User and producer, soldier and manufacturer?'

Srinivas was silent. He knew he would not raise his hand to kill. That was enough for him, he wished it could be enough for her so that he could come down off his hook, although he knew that it would not be.

'Petrol bombs can kill,' said Vasantha.

'No one was killed,' said Srinivas abruptly.

'Next time they may be,' she said.

'So might we,' said Vasudev. 'So might we.'

Srinivas went away. He had not many retreats left. His studies had gone to pot: he seriously doubted whether he would be able to sit his BA exam at the end of the year. If he looked inward it was upon scenes of awesome turmoil. Those cocoons of spirit from which he might have emerged refreshed were all ravished, shredded and scattered like the nests of experimental mice. He had, once, seen them at it, in a laboratory on a school visit, crazed, mute, vocal cords cut to silence their distracting cries, as he discovered after persistent questioning. They scurried about demented, these small white bruised creatures pumped full of distorting chemicals, tearing their nests to pieces, turning on each other too; their backs bore weals and scratches.

Observe, said the doctor in charge, in immaculate white coat, devil's disguise for the obscene. Observe the alteration in behavioural pattern. Compare it with the control group. And obediently they directed their attention to the control mice, unimpaired velvety females that had constructed small bowers for their young out of balls of surgical cotton wool, and were peaceably cradled in them.

Observe, notice, the interesting changes. That modulated voice, how it conned you! You would never have suspected that what it was talking about was cruelty, methodically practised on a living creature until it lost its instincts, its purpose, its place in creation, and finally its spirit for life. Well, no doubt it was interesting – if you didn't think, never put yourself in those helpless skins, if you rode on surfaces for fear of going under, what you might find there.

But, you see, it won't work, said Srinivas to himself. You must go under. You must look and see. And he stared bleakly at what was surfacing, sleazy mudflats revealed by some receding tide. That is the truth of it, he acknowledged at last; whether one likes it or not, that is the truth.

'It's no good,' he said to Vasudev.

'You mean you aren't up to it.'

'Yes, maybe that's what I do mean,' said Srinivas, and gazed at his hands. User, producer, was there no difference? One felt in one's bones that there was, the feeling was common to millions. Only one's bones lied, as any particle of self or cellular structure could be induced to do.

'I can't go on,' said Srinivas.

'If you can't you can't,' said Vasudev, and turned his back and leaned it against a pillar of the veranda which commanded a view of the distant maidan, dotted at this time – as for much of the time – with tiny strutting khaki-clad figures. 'As you see, it is to be no holds barred,' he said. 'They have called in the military.'

There was an echo to the words which Srinivas placed, and felt his guts lurch. They have called in the military, his grandfather had said, seeing his efforts nullified, and facing defeat, and finally watching his trees come down. The military machine, the mindless destroyer. Destroying efficiently, purposelessly, trees and houses and growing crops, everything whose going could make life wretched, while the real target remained, the spirit that rose like a phoenix, blinking and bemused but alive, again and again from the ashes.

'They don't even fight fair,' Vasudev's ruthless voice went on, remorseless as his sister's. 'Look at them. Gurkhas. Baluchis. They bring in these foreigners to make sure we are cut down without hesitation at their command. The mixture as before, only the general is missing. For how long, though? Yet we have scruples. Some of us,' he qualified, 'are petrified by our scruples.'

Srinivas went away. He fled from Vasudev as he had fled from Vasantha, and from that diminished man his father and the raking questions of his mother. He would have fled from himself too, but he did not know how. More accurately, he was afraid. You could buy Indian hemp in the bazaars but he had seen what it could do. He had seen them high on it, surf-riders in the streets, cushioned off from the harshness of life, blithe and insouciant as he longed to be. But there were others, returned from regions they had themselves opened up, whose minds had gone, stoned to fragments by the experience. He did not want to be like them, ruled by fragments that fought for possession and won at random, submerging them in total impenetrable silence, or abandoning them to howling delirium – to anything, it seemed, from a spectrum devised in hell. His brain was too precious for that: matchless system lodged in the cranium, hoarding somewhere in its twists and convolutions the impress of that elusive entity, his mind, luminous prints to show that something had been there and might be again, close to the mystery of being.

He could not tamper with that. No.

Only, it was a temptation.

Especially now that he was alone, with the unpleasant realization dawning that in the last analysis one would always be alone. All I want is peace, said Srinivas, staring at himself, stranger in the glass; all I want is peace. Is that too much to ask? It seemed so. It seemed so to a good many people, who ingenuously assumed it was a little thing they asked for, whereas in fact in the world they inhabited it happened to be one of the most difficult to come by.

18

THE HOUSE REMAINED. WHEN HE LOOKED AT IT, THE dovetailed structure and interlocked unity, the solid construction which, barring vandals and acts of God, would outlast them all, a vestige of peace returned, like a gift, to Srinivas. Then he, the running man, forgot to run, forgot he was haunted, stood still and allowed it to invade him, feeling somehow as if he had been expanded and refreshed. Like a Japanese paper flower in a glass of water, he described it to himself, able to afford such fancies in these moments when the fretful engine idled, and he closed his eyes the better to feel as he stroked the polished woods, the satin wood sills and smooth teak posts, and slid his foot in widening arcs over the planed timber floor, so glossy, as smooth and glossy as love and labour could make it, until the sensuous sole encountered faults. Flaws, in that prized surface. He opened his eyes.

'Someone has scratched it,' he said in disbelief. 'How careless people are. The floor is all spoiled.'

'A few scratches are nothing. You should see the marks that boots leave,' said Vasudev, roughly.

Srinivas did not understand. There were many things, these days, that Vasudev kept from Srinivas, who no longer belonged. Then he learned. In one night the knowledge came to him, burst in his brain, the full flower of what happened only to other people. Suspected, reported, even believed, but never exploded within the flesh like this. Happening to him now, happening to them. The footsteps that had never stopped at their door, stopping at their door. The dreadful silence as they waited, full of the heavy presence of men gathered outside in the darkness. The peremptory knocking – not knuckles, bone knocking on wood, but something with lead in its composition, clubbing the door.

'Who can it be? At this hour?' His mother whispered, her lips were dry. They looked at each other, frightened. Somewhere close by a dog began to bark and kept on barking, sharply.

'I'd better see.' Narayan rose, head of the family. His face was grey and lumpy, like putty. Srinivas could see his hands trembling as he unfastened the latch and opened the door.

'Who is it?'

'Police.'

Narayan fell back. No one had touched him but he flattened himself, flat against the wall to let them pass. All of them in these moments, were reduced, carved into base attitudes and shrunk into their clothes which no longer fitted but hung loosely on their abject frames, like shrouds. Overpowered by these invaders of their privacy. Eight, perhaps ten of them. It seemed more. They filled the room, towered over the occupants with their presence, the bulk of hobnailed boots, their buckled belts. Overwhelmed, in their uniforms. One forgot there were men under the khaki, as one was meant to do.

One's own countrymen at that, thought Srinivas, unable to raise his lids, his gaze fixed low upon dark-skinned knees. Who would have thought? Somehow it seemed incredible. Less so, though, that the men in charge should be English. Men in command were always English, they had grown to expect that. A pink young man, such as he had often seen playing polo on the maidan, in dusty breeches and shirt that ballooned in the breeze as pony and rider galloped headlong after a ball. But a different being now. Contained within an aura, a glittering envelope of subtle intimidation, and invested in the robes of authority which were coloured khaki. Khaki shorts, khaki bush-jacket, a khaki cap; and in his right hand a cane, a springy malacca which he kept tapping, rap-tap, on the backs and legs of chairs and tables as if they were limbs that would jump to attention.

'Mr Narayan?'

'Yes.'

'You are the head of the house?'

'Yes.'

'We have reason to believe that subversive activities are carried on on the premises.'

'No.'

'No?'

The blond brows rose, only faintly offensive. He had sandy brows, this pink-and-white Englishman, and golden hair, and a milky skin which, clearly, had not long been exposed to the Indian sun. Yet already the climate had worked on him, seeding the blood with imperial implants, potent drugs that bore him to spheres from which he looked down, cold distant eye above the common run: an attitude which annihilated any basis of parity between the two human sides, substituting the split levels of vassal and overlord.

'No?' said the overlord again. 'You are sure?'

'No,' said the vassal, miserably, suddenly and acutely aware of his vulnerable toes and loose white homespun.

Like draperies, thought the Englishman, conscious of the knife edge to his shorts even at this hour of the night, and he slapped at his calves, which were firmed and shaped by the imperial substance of conquerors, or possibly by the puttees wound round them, and surveyed the humans thick upon the scene who seemed to him to resemble nothing quite so much as jellyfish flopped out on a beach.

'There is evidence,' he said.

'It is not possible,' said Narayan.

'That such activities were carried on.'

'Not to my knowledge.'

'You didn't know?'

'No.'

'Or suspect?'

'No. That is to say, I did, of course –'

'You mean yes.'

'I mean that I, that we –'

Narayan faltered, caught in terrible coils. He could feel himself being squeezed, pressed – oppressed – by the weight of this cold white man; he would have given anything to yield, to simply accept guilt and be done. But there was his family, his son especially, before whom he was being exhibited, dangled like an unstrung puppet. So he struggled, desperately, to conduct himself like a man, in front of these eyes that mattered, and to keep himself intact – warring issues that brought out the veins on his forehead, for the truth was that he had known as they had all known, by seepage though not by palpable evidence.

'I didn't know,' he said, and cleared his throat, for his treacherous voice was squeaking. 'I didn't know, but I did suspect. But the climate is such that one suspects everything.'

Smart alec, thought the Englishman, to whom the struggle under that alien skin was not apparent, and he remembered dimly what someone somewhere had once told him, and resolved on no account to tangle in dialectics. Wily Brahmin, he said to himself, won't look you in the eye and say yea or nay, oh, no; and his hands began to itch with a desire to knock down this smallish, brownish man trembling in front of him, though he too held, himself intact, for he could not allow these people to observe him out of control.

'You are harbouring a wanted man,' he said curtly. 'We have orders to apprehend him.'

Then Srinivas was afraid, for his father, for them all, seeing the bunched knuckles, and the raised cane, which in fact ordered the search to begin. He huddled himself in his contracting allotment of space, which was beside the swing, grasping a chain for support and unaware that he was swaying with it until a hand steadied him. He looked down, into the pinched, upturned face, and saw it was Vasantha. She and her mother and his mother and their aunts, all of them sitting on the swing in the centre of the central room, silently witnessing the violation of their home.

Every aspect of it, from top to bottom: its nooks and crannies and hidden places under the floorboards and between the ceiling and rafters where a man might lie, and the cool dark spaces beneath the arches of the connecting corridors and passages where pickle vats stood. They will spare nothing, thought Srinivas, and his head began to split with the sound of trampling feet and splintering wood and he could feel the house shake, the timber frames of its structure shuddering as the trees had shuddered before they toppled, when the axes had touched their pulp. They will tear it apart before they are done, he said, and it was a terrible fear.

But not the most terrible. It had been, but now another took its place, to do with the men themselves, their core and nature, and it was more terrible. Dear God, pleaded Srinivas, or some inner, voiceless part of him that framed meanings void of words. Dear God, he said, and his vision blurred, magnifying his senses, which were saturated with the essence of these men, the hoarse sounds that burst from their throats, from the back of their throats, the deepest part of themselves, and from the odours thrown off by their heated flesh. Dear God, no, he mumbled again, but his nostrils reeked with the smell of what they exuded and his palms grew wet and his groin was slippery in a kind of hideous identification.

He was dizzy now; he felt himself sway and leaned against the wall for support, only it was the swing, its iron links fell ice-cold on his hotness. The shock seemed to clear the dense miasma that had clutched his upper brain, leaving the lower free for excesses. He began to fight it then, the liquefying fear and passion that had worked in him, brought it under control grain by grain.

Control, in fact, incredibly, was passing to them.

The house ceased to rock, or perhaps it only seemed to, from a diminishing of activity. Its nucleus, the feeble group marooned in the centre, had hardened, manufacturing out of spirit and necessity nacreous layers to protect itself. They shimmered, these people, invested in a curious light not unlike the glittering skin that had insulated the Englishman. As he was aware, but he put down these intimations which he mistrusted, ascribing the glare effect to the barbarously naked electric bulbs and the reflective quality of the primitive whitewashed walls.

'Nothing,' he said, and brought his distant gaze to bear. 'We have found nothing so far.'

'There is nothing to find,' Srinivas answered, stabilized by the new inflow of impulses which converged to make him the spokesman.

There was a pause, in which both men grew aware of each other, and of the balance in the fluctuating scene, which had tilted.

'We will take the place apart if we have to,' said the Englishman.

'If you do, you will still find nothing,' repeated Srinivas.

Liar, barefaced insolent liar, thought the Englishman, and he advanced upon the group, quite slowly, though his blood was up, as any decent man's would be.

'Stone by stone,' he said, and panted a little.

Srinivas said nothing. He saw the change in colour, pink gone to splotchy red, and the knife edge crease of the shorts ruined, risen to an apex above the bulging jockstrap. The Englishman also said nothing. He must be slipping, he thought, to be dumbstruck like this. He came closer, swaggering a little to cover his uncertainty. His stick, which had rapped, was also swaggering, uncertain of its function. Suddenly he saw new scope for this exhausted tool in his hand, and bending slightly inserted it under the frill of Vasantha's skirt. What it did to him, this physical act, astonished and alarmed him. He would have withdrawn if he could, but now control had slipped away entirely. The supple cane flicked upward, and the flounces gathered soberly around Vasantha's ankles flew up over her head and left her naked, ready for bed as she had been, of her own though, which was an entirely different kind.

There was a burst of laughter from the men who ringed the room.

The Englishman heard, and burned with shame. Not for what he had done, but because he had lost command of himself and his men had seen it. The house, he felt, was responsible. It had worn him down with its totality of plastic resistance and concealed warrens of retreat and resilience. The house, and these people, and the girl whose skin he despised, though not the secret dark scented flesh he had glimpsed, which had been his undoing. He licked his lips and waited, wondering where there was to go to from here.

Momentarily, only. Split seconds. The time it took for the stunned Srinivas to come to life and throw himself at the Englishman and knock him down, his thin curved murderous fingers itching for the throat, nothing else whatever would do. They fell together.

Hands, a half-dozen pairs, pulled him off and pinioned him. Another half-dozen, brown and white collaborating in this enterprise, helped the Englishman up. The two men stared at each other, in disarray, and breathing fit to burst, and conscious that the distance was closing between them; and suddenly a spark leapt between white man and brown.

I might have killed him, Srinivas thought; I might have killed this man, who is a human being like myself.

Narrow shave, the Englishman said to himself. Fact is, there's a limit to the strains we can load on each other. We both lost control, he thought. We have seen each other naked. He blushed, a vivid scarlet suffusion which made him feel fiery under the collar, and which he could see staining the backs of his hands. He turned his burning face away.

'Let him go,' he said shortly, and began brushing off the dirt and general debris that clung to his clothes, glad to be shaking off the dust of the place.

19

THE MORNING AFTER THEY HAD GONE SRINIVAS started putting the house to rights. He did it himself, staying away from college, whose values became meaningless while this kind of violence went on. The structure, of course, was intact: organized demolition alone would have destroyed the integrity of the building that had gone into it; but the interior, the facades and surfaces, were sadly damaged.

Srinivas restored them, refusing to summon carpenter or mason or plasterer. His skills, acquired as a child of eight and accumulating since then, were sufficient. Methodically, with little emotion, he put back floorboards, righted fallen balusters and railings which had been kicked askew, repaired the chipped panels of the door and filled in and smoothed over cracks and splits in the woodwork. When he came to the floor of the central room and saw what they had done to it he faltered a little, but he carried on. It was only when he had finished, splinters and woodchips cleared away and the floor sanded and sealed and restored almost to its old state, that quite suddenly he began to sob.

Dry husky sobs, on his heels in the middle of the room, that welled up from the deep roots of his being, for what they had the power to do, and he and his people were powerless to prevent: for all that must be relinquished, all the precious frivolities of youth and pursuit of the humanities that must be surrendered to redress the squalid imbalance; and for the dreams he had dreamt, jewelled diadems that had glimmered so brightly over the brows of himself and his bride elect.

It was the last time he wept, during Vasantha's lifetime.

It was also the last time he would allow himself to be bound to, or feel for, possessions: for bits of wood, glass, beads, baubles, metals – even land – all those compositions of matter that would, ironically, outlast the human frame, but in turn be eclipsed by the indestructible spirit that informed it. They might titillate, these lustres, curves and inlays, even soothe and please the surface levels of his mind. They were not again to penetrate beyond.

So he thought, remotely, already receding, like a dying man, from objects that had been of importance at some inscrutable moment of time, and he ran a finger with lingering affection along the grained woods of the window frame whose distorted mosaic he had carefully matched and reassembled – as careful and detached as a robot.

All this time the man who had died lay near, in a camphor-wood chest whose rusty locks had defeated the searchers. They had avenged this rebuff by smashing a number of pickle jars which they pretended, and it might just have been true, were large enough to conceal a doubled-up man. The strong and clinging odour of limes pickling in chillies and brine concealed the odour of his dying, until it became a stench. Even then the locks would not yield. They had not been oiled or used for years, not since Vasudev's family had last opened the chest to empty its contents on to bonfires, and they held on grimly, splitting the nails and staining the hands of those who were trying to force them.

'God only knows,' said an aunt piously, her simple mind not extending to take in more than the corpse of a mouse or a bandicoot, 'how whatever is in there *got* in there.'

That, as it happened, was to remain Vasudev's secret. He had got in, and finally it was the gases manufactured in his body that blew the top out, rather than the ineffectual gashes they were making in it. What they saw horrified them. Being a large family all had witnessed death: but the dead had been washed and cleaned and burned long before putrefaction set in. They had never seen a corpse like this, bloated, with delicate filaments of fungus pushing up from pockets, and emitting a stench that blasted them backwards.

The only grain of comfort they derived – and it was small enough – was that no one of his family saw Vasudev's body. His father was in prison; and his mother sat day and night with her other child, Vasantha, who lay in a hospital bed in a state of shock.

Vasudev took his secrets with him. They did not know if he had been implicated in the explosions that had gutted both military headquarters and the police thana: and if he had been, how deeply. They did not know if he was the wanted man for whom the house had been ransacked, or why or from what he had hidden. In death, as in life, Vasudev revealed nothing, but created an undulating area of uneasiness.

They hesitated even to send for an undertaker.

Srinivas cleaned up, as before. He felt no revulsion at the disgusting state his friend was in. His detachment from accretions of matter, earned during the visitation and its aftermath, prevailed strongly and carried him through. Methodically, without nausea, he disinfected the body and wrapped it in a shroud, trussing it with waxed cord at ankles, knees, waist, and neck. An act which under normal circumstances would have been taken to defile a man of his caste, in these extraordinary times passed without comment. Least of all from Srinivas. His brain, nurtured and tuned to learning, its proper function, was, he suspected, to be deflected to other purposes. What he did with his hands, therefore, concerned him hardly at all.

All of them, not only Vasantha, without knowing it were in a state of shock. Weeks later they realized, when it had lifted, and they looked back in astonishment at what they had done, acts and thoughts against the grain, feats of which they would not have believed themselves capable. As the trauma subsided, feeling flowed in. Rather, they dribbled it in slowly, in case it should rip them apart, picking their way with care and taking stock of themselves to avoid disaster.

'How empty the house seems,' said Nirmala, sadly. She meant the space that would never be filled, since the flux of relations within the house was fully resumed. In fact there were only three absentees, of whom one was part-time: Vasantha's mother. She went daily to the hospital, each time crossing the maidan in a diagonal line, where others kept to the periphery, to disrupt military manoeuvre. They let her pass, somehow afraid of this woman in white with hatred in her glance – even the drill sergeant who, being English, was totally unaware of what the locals thought, or anyhow immune to it. But even he could not altogether escape the distilled hate that emanated from her. So he stood his squad at ease, or even at times dismissed them, rather than tangle with the figure whose presence got him up in gooseflesh, especially along his spine.

At the end of a month Vasantha was discharged from hospital.

She came home paler, thinner, quieter than anyone could remember, but entirely composed. The aunts, who had fluttered anxiously before her arrival, put away the reviving cordials and infusions they had assembled. They saw they were not, after all, to have a swooning girl on their hands. What they did have they did not know, since it lay outside their actual experience, as well as beyond their imaginative grasp. Unnatural, they whispered, watching the clear-eyed, dry-eyed, calm-voiced Vasantha. Father imprisoned, brother gone, the shameful thing that had been done to her ... had she no feeling? It griped them that she should not show any.

Vasantha's mother shut them up. She had seen Vasantha, drymouthed, sleepless, staring up hour after hour at the stark ceiling of the hospital ward. She felt enough had been gone through without the need to mount an appropriate show.

Srinivas backed her, barking at anyone who, however slightly, seemed to him to be harassing Vasantha. It seemed to him, indeed, that she had taken on the quality of some rare and fragile porcelain that would shatter at a touch, though he suspected, too, that at the end of the process she was undergoing she would emerge toughened enough.

But she had grown up. Suddenly, in those frantic moments, nubile and naked before men, her childhood had gone.

It is wrong, said Srinivas, and ached for the loss – to him or to her he was uncertain – of that delicate period of flux between woman and child, deliciously garlanded by each in turn, which had been roughly snatched away. Somewhere, too, grit between the ribs, lay unanswerable questions of what it could do to him, to her, to their lives together: this forced growth that had been completed in the flash of an impulse, and a cane.

Sometimes he dreamed, and awoke sweating in the narrow bed which, because of police visits, could no longer be set up outside on the veranda. It was always the same dream. In it he and Vasantha were lying in their marriage bed, but she was not made of flesh but of some inert wood that he could not bring to life. He could not penetrate her. He was making her cry with his efforts and at the same time she pleaded with him not to give up, to continue until she was made flesh again.

The impressions of night carried over into his waking hours. He felt she was asking for help and at the same time rejecting it. In the precarious atmosphere that prevailed, however, he could not be sure, he could not trust his feelings enough to force the issue. He wanted some sign from her, some encouragement before he could advance, but she gave him none. Where had she gone? he wondered, near to despair: where was that glowing girl who had laughed and teased him, and stretched out her warm hands in crisis to steady him and give him strength? In her place was this encased woman, thirteen years old, who scraped her hair back in a bun, and sat erect holding body and soul intact, and girded her clothes tightly, desperately about her person, and never, not even at night, stripped off her constricting daytime wear to put on the loose flowered skirts under which her body had enjoyed freedom.

Gone, said Srinivas, and fretted himself thin.

Nirmala, feverishly counting her blessings in this era of disaster for the other family, thought her son worried unduly about trifles.

'There is nothing to worry about,' she said. 'The girl is perfectly well, except that she's quieter than she used to be. Is that so surprising? When you're married you'll wonder what you ate your heart out for.'

'Yes, when,' said Srinivas.

Nirmala narrowed her eyes. 'When they say,' she said. 'The family is in mourning. They will fix the day – no doubt after you have passed your exams.'

Srinivas turned away. He knew he would not be taking his exams. Was not capable, did not want to. The very thought turned his stomach, because it was tied up with the whole sick paraphernalia of rule of this powerful, detested government.

20

ABOUT NOW SRINIVAS BEGAN TO FEEL HIS TIME WAS running out. Exactly how, he could not tell. Only, it seemed to him as though things in which he was involved were pushing up, waiting to come to a head. It conferred a certain sharp clarity on people and events. They swam up closer, acquired incised outlines as if cut by a diamond, as if they were to be lifted out and placed, in full dimension and illuminated, in niches along corridors beyond the natural elisions of time.

I feel I am dying, said Srinivas to the shade of the departed Vasudev, who in life, at any rate, would have understood. The prospect of death to him, however, continued to reside in the realms of what happened to other people, and he remained, in fact, in excellent health.

Then, suddenly, it happened: the precipitating event that threw him out, quite unconnected with death, and beginning strangely with fifes and drums.

Fifes and drums, and Indian notes obtruding among the improbable sounds of bagpipes borne on strapping Punjabi shoulders, and those figures in khaki march-marching on the maidan, all through the last scorching weeks of late summer.

'Flaunting their strength,' said Vasantha's mother with contempt. 'Who do they think we are? They frighten no one, whatever they may think.'

'I hope they are not preparing for trouble,' said Nirmala. 'I am sick and tired of trouble.' Sick to death, she wanted to say, only death had stood so brutally by her elbow, nowadays she flinched at the word.

'They are preparing for the Governor's visit,' blurted Narayan, and felt guilty, as though he were privy to moves within the enemy camp.

'Which is a dress rehearsal for the Prince of Wales's visit,' said Srinivas, primed by Vasudev's camp, which was national and respectable, and to which he remained affiliated.

'Princes, Governors.' Nirmala shook her head. 'Something possesses them, to do these extraordinary things.'

'From time to time they have to carry out tests,' said Srinivas, 'to see how popular they are.'

It rocked them. They held their sides, laughing. Nirmala wiped away the tears that rolled down her cheeks. 'One doesn't know whether to laugh or cry,' she said, appropriately.

Afterwards Srinivas said to his father: 'I suppose there will be the usual quota of functions.'

'They are arranging for an address of welcome at the college, yes,' said Narayan.

'Will you attend?'

'I have no option.'

'Then neither have I,' said Srinivas, and was conscious of a sense of involuntary involvement, like a fly observing the tacky trappings of an advancing web.

Narayan was back in the old black alpaca. The message had gone out from the vice chancellor. It was relayed to him by Platt.

'Plain bloody silly,' said Platt. 'Those weeds you wear – what d'you call them – look all right to me. On you, of course. Manners,' he continued surprisingly, 'makyth man, not what bloody rig he chooses to dress up in.'

Narayan regarded the deputy principal with affection. 'I don't mind,' he said.

'It doesn't offend a principle?'

'No. Not noticeably. It's taken a good few knocks already.'

Platt went away looking relieved. Narayan went home and took out the coat and hung it in a draught to get rid of the smell of mothballs. Srinivas saw it hanging there and questioned his father.

'Is that what you will be wearing?' he asked.

'I have no option,' repeated Narayan, and felt a little queasy, perhaps from the combined smell of mould and mothballs. 'Have I?' he asked. His son made no reply.

So here he was, in mortarboard and BA gown, and the black alpaca, which had developed shiny green patches about the seams that glistened when the gown fell open. Sitting on a platform, listening to the drone that was the address of welcome that someone was delivering, among the dignitaries. The Governor, who was the Distinguished Visitor, accompanied by assorted aides, and Drinkwater, the resplendent vice chancellor, and the remote principal whose house he had not once been asked to enter and would not care to now, and the deputy principal Platt, who, being the man he was, could be heard distinctly muttering about Old Panjandrum from the Big City. As he could not, thought Narayan, would not dare even if the word had been familiar because he was not the man Platt was. Not half the man, as his students made clear by their looks as he came in. In his black alpaca. Took his seat in the back row among top people, not because that was what he was, but since he chose to remain of their company.

The company's colour, a Union Jack, was pinned to the curtains behind.

'Clap,' someone said – it was in fact the efficient ADC. Narayan complied. Why not? He was already compromised in so many eyes. That sea of faces. Where was the incense they had burned for him? Snuffed out. His authority sapped, his integrity under suspicion, here as at home. At home his son, not he, was spokesman. Deservedly, the titular head had been ousted.

Without meaning to Narayan sought out his son in the assembly, among the sparsely filled back benches. You must believe me, he said to the filial eye, holding it between the serried heads: whatever you may think there really have been no options open to me. He was trying to work out what the eye replied when he felt a dig in the ribs.

'What the hell's the matter with you?' Someone (probably Platt) hissed at him. Recovering, he saw that everyone was standing. Obediently he stood up too. (What for? Nothing seemed to be happening.) Below the platform, in the right wing of the assembly hall stood the college upright. Poised above the keys, he saw, were the hands of the pianist, waiting. They descended – for the second time if the truth be told – and the preliminary commanding roulade rang out, ready to lead them into the thumping rhythm of the national anthem. Narayan quivered. A hall full of Indians and a handful of Englishmen, and they wanted *their* anthem sung.

It was.

God was duly petitioned to save the king.

The hymn-cum-battle- cry finished. Chairs scraped forward to receive bottoms. Narayan remained standing. There was something he had to do. Leaving his place he advanced to the edge of the platform and opened his mouth to sing. He meant to sing his country's anthem, but realized that unfortunately he did not know it, so he began to sing one of those hymns that ordinary people sang, such as Nirmala hummed as she went about the house.

He listened to his voice as he sang. It was thin, and it quavered. But it captured the attention of the entire hall. Narayan was pleased. He intended them to listen to him and clearly they were listening.

Such was the silence there really wasn't much alternative.

Then the air began to accommodate additions to his tremolo. Incredulity and wonderment went winging through the ether, silent whys and whats before voices could be found.

Unexpected man had created unprecedented situation.

The principal rose to deal with it. Fastidiously he did his job, this remote man, laying a hand on Narayan and hating the human contact. Narayan shook it off. They were all on their feet now. The Governor stepped forward, beating the vice chancellor by a short head. He brought his hand down firmly on Narayan's shoulder to stop him making those distressing sounds, which to him distinctly resembled caterwauling.

When Srinivas saw that hand fall he knew he had something to do.

All of them were doing things they had to do: the peons advancing, the students howling, police converging, and Srinivas vaulting over bench after bench to reach his father. When he did he lifted the restraining wrist and flung it away, making the surprised Governor stagger.

'Your Excellency,' he said, distinctly, 'take your bloody hands off my father.'

Because it seemed to him they had all had enough of these white men's hands that grasped and would not let go –

he, and his father, and Vasantha, and their country, upon all of which that maiming yoke had fallen.

They put Srinivas in the cooler. Narayan, who had begun to babble, was sent to the mental ward of the municipal hospital where Platt came to visit, bearing luscious fruits and cordials which privately he called conscience fodder.

The vice chancellor did not visit. He thought Narayan's conduct infamous, and wondered whether he should sack him. If he were to, however, the students would riot. All things considered he felt that hustling the man off to a lunatics' hospital was the best thing they could have done. It explained his lack of action, and at the same time neatly avoided any loss of face involved in overlooking such lese-majesty. Important, not to lose face, said Drinkwater to himself: it was a most important ingredient in the maintenance of East–West relations.

They let Srinivas out in a week, without preferring charges, at His Excellency's suggestion. He had been made to lose his balance. He did not consider it advisable to parade the loss, or to harp on the insult to the dignity of his high office as some were doing. The Governor was not only a sensible man, he also knew the affair would not end there.

The principal was also a sensible man. He toyed with the thought of expulsion, but discarded it in favour of other disciplinary measures, less likely to invite disorders, which he detested.

Narayan came out of hospital the week after, the first of many sequences of discharge and readmittance. Because he knew this he kept a tight hold on himself so that necessary arrangements could be completed before he was again overcome.

'There is no future left for you here,' he said to his son, without preamble. 'You will be blacklisted in every school and college throughout the country. Government service is out too.'

'I know,' said Srinivas, who had had time to work things out for himself.

'You could still have a career,' said his father, 'elsewhere. They say that England is not a bad place. Platt says in many ways it is better than here. Especially for someone like you.'

For someone like him. A marked man, like a criminal, thought Srinivas with a bitterness that had begun to go stale, but he was more aware of fresh winds blowing, awakening ambitions and bringing opportunities which he believed he had lost forever.

'I'm willing to try,' he said.

'Then the sooner the better.'

'Yes.'

'Don't tell your mother.'

'She has to know, sooner or later.'

'That I – that I suggested it.'

Srinivas knew if he did she would not credit it. No one associated this shrunken man, his father, with the quality of courage, and the habit was so strong they would continue to deny him. Even his last valiant act had been nailed as lunacy, a lunatic folly stemming from what people preferred to call a nervous breakdown.

'I will keep it to myself,' said Srinivas, gently.

For all his determination Narayan would not have been able to cope, but there was Platt. It was Platt who made the arrangements, booked the sea passage, procured the necessary passport and papers, saving Narayan and Srinivas the endless waiting, delays, embroilment with officialdom that as nationals of the country would have been their lot. The wheels were oiled for the Englishman. The immense power concentrated at the peak descended to the last individual of the imperial caste at base.

Both Narayan and Srinivas were glad: they realized they were exhausted men.

Years were to go by, however, before Srinivas felt any gratitude for Platt, the man who had displaced his father.

When they told Nirmala she cried. She cried until she was blind with weeping. She had to wait until the next day, when her eyes were still puffy but functioning, to ask what it was all about and scrutinize them as they replied.

'All my life,' she said, 'we have lived under foreign rule. At least half that time we have opposed it, but we have lived with it. Why has it suddenly become unbearable?'

'Suddenly, there is no suddenly,' said Narayan. 'It has been happening slowly.'

'Under them there is no future for me,' said Srinivas doggedly. He had said the same thing several times already.

'If they are bad to you here, what makes you think they will be good to you there?'

'If they are bad to us here it is because they have bad consciences about us,' said Narayan.

'The same thing may happen there,' said Nirmala. 'Who is to say? Can guarantees be given? If it does happen there will not even be the strength we have had from our family.'

Srinivas grew impatient. He felt he would give way if they argued much longer. 'I must try,' he said brusquely. 'The joint family will no longer do. The plantation has long been cut down. We have clung together and it has served us very well, but it will not serve forever. When I am married and have children I don't want to look over my shoulder to see what is supporting me. I want to support myself, and my wife, and our children.'

Nirmala dried her eyes. She saw terminus had been reached. She began to think of the innumerable things waiting to be done, which stopped her from worrying at the central theme of departure and so falling to pieces.

Srinivas and Vasantha were married in a four-hour ceremony a week before he left.

The marriage was consummated the same night. Because of the state she was in, never having fully shed the sphincter that had closed her off since the night of the assault, he would have preferred to wait, but he could not. When he touched his bride he was so suffused with love for her – for flesh and spirit that were so beautifully conjoined – that he could not hold back. Forgive me, forgive me, some part of his brain cried, but soon he was lost, flooded with sensation which obliterated mind. Through it all she complied. Her body opened for him, accepted his. That was the sum of it. The exultance that he demanded, the heartbeat and tumult, were all absent. It will come, he panted, striving as he had striven in his dreams, sinking himself deep into her flesh until he touched the pulp of her womb. But it did not, then or ever.

In the morning there was blood on the sheets. It seemed like a symbol to him. He showed it to her, full of a tenderness which replaced the night's urgencies.

'Your virginity,' he said gently, 'surrendered to me. Immaculate, unsullied by anyone or anything before.'

She gazed at him, compromised, uncompromising, the look he learned to know very well later, in England.

'That is the physical fact of the matter,' she said.

Thereafter time accelerated, sweeping them along. Days which had dragged began to telescope, nights and dawns following each other with bewildering rapidity – before one even has time to blink, thought Nirmala, assembling furniture and clothing which she imagined Srinivas and Vasantha would need for their lives in England.

Srinivas was to go ahead, to have everything ready for his wife, they pretended. The actual reason was they could not raise her fare as well as Srinivas's passage money and freight charges for the household goods they intended to ship. Vasantha's family was more or less cleaned out. In Srinivas's family Narayan, the principal earner, was on half pay.

'Do I have to take all this stuff?' Srinivas asked cantankerously.

'One day you will be glad of it,' said Nirmala.

She was quite wrong. In the end Srinivas had to pay to have the bulkier items jettisoned, and he only felt glad when he was rid of them.

Soon it was all over: the sorting, the packing, the journey by rail, the convoy in taxis to the dock, the leave-taking, the embarkation. Srinivas stood alone on deck, trying to overlook the misery of the group gathered on the quayside. He smiled at them, he waved, they waved back. His father, his mother, Vasantha his wife, his wife's mother. Under the electric lights they looked quite pale, and he could see tears glistening on his mother's cheeks. Courage, he said, as much to himself as to her, and waved again. He saw her scarf fluttering in reply, but dusk and distance were already cutting

them off, he could not make out her features, the figures on
the quayside were similarly blurred. Soon they were no more
than indistinct dots. Then they were altogether gone. Still he
stood by the taffrail. A galaxy of fireflies were dancing along
with the ship and he watched them. It was a long time before
they gave up and their light trails faded away.

21

'IT WAS A MISTAKE,' SRINIVAS HEARD HIMSELF SAYING, 'if I had thought about it, Mr Platt, if I had considered it *carefully* as I should have done, I would have gone down on my knees to you. Well, perhaps not. It would have embarrassed you, and you would have gone away without hearing me out. Besides, kneeling is not our custom. We prostrate ourselves, you know. We throw ourselves at God's feet.'

'Feet are dreadful,' the woman said.

'The feet are stone,' said Srinivas. 'What else could they be? One cannot expect divinity to be made flesh before one's eyes. Whatever you may believe,' he said accommodatingly, 'I could never believe that.'

'I do not believe,' the woman said.

'Besides, flesh,' said Srinivas, 'would never survive. The devotional needs of mankind, Mr Platt, are too destructive. Even stone does not last, you know. If you look you will see the toes are abridged. In older gods the toenails are eroded up to the quick. All done by touch, just fingertips touching.'

'Horrible,' said the woman, with a clatter.

'Why, it's you, Mrs Fletcher,' said Srinivas. 'You've dropped your handbag. For some peculiar reason I thought you were Mr Platt, but of course he would never carry a handbag. Men don't, generally speaking, do they, Mrs Fletcher?'

'No,' gasped Mrs Fletcher. 'I was just going,' she said, 'Mrs Pickering's here with the doctor.' And fled.

When she was gone Srinivas went back to what was on his mind, but soon the door opened again.

'Nothing but comings and goings,' complained Srinivas to this visitor.

'That going was rather rapid,' said the visitor.

'That was Mrs Fletcher,' said Srinivas. 'She is of a rather nervous disposition, it is difficult to know why. I was talking about Platt – you are not Platt, are you?'

'I am Dr Radcliffe.'

'Yes, well, Platt was a man from my past life. An unusual man for his time, though at the time one didn't recognize it. I ought to have fallen at his feet, you know, touched his toes in gratitude.'

'You're lucky to have any toes left,' said Dr Radcliffe.

'I am no god,' Srinivas smiled faintly. 'Only gods have their toes nibbled away by the devout.'

'No. Being human,' said the doctor, deftly winding bandages, 'you have to be content with frostbite.'

'Kiss of death, touch of life, who knows?' Srinivas smiled cheerfully. 'I am babbling,' he said. His father had been taken away for babbling.

'You have a high temperature and are slightly delirious,' said Dr Radcliffe.' Your wife – '

'My wife? Vasantha? Is she here?' Srinivas was very confused. His father's fate had been written on buff-coloured paper that the telegraph office used. Vasantha's ashes he had himself consigned to the river.

'I am not his legal wife,' said Mrs Pickering.

'Common law spouse,' said Srinivas, giggling.

'My mistake,' said the doctor. 'You are, may I say, in highly capable hands.'

'We are all in God's hands,' said Srinivas, piously.

'Yes, well, I'll look in again tomorrow,' said Dr Radcliffe. How close God lay under some surfaces, he thought with a flicker which could have been envy, though he also felt it was not really very suitable for this climate.

When they were alone Mrs Pickering said: 'You're getting very pious in your illness.'

'In my old age,' said Srinivas.

'No. Old age does not happen in a few weeks.'

'Have I been ill so long?'

'Longer. Over a month.'

'I dreamed about the past,' he said.

'No, no dream,' she said. 'You told me.'

'I wanted you to know.'

'I do, now.'

'Does it make any difference?'

'Why should it?'

'Dearest Vasantha,' he said, and took her hand, and saw that it was different, an old worn white hand, but clung to it. 'I am a little confused,' he said, quite clearly, 'but, you see, you are both people I love, there is apt to be some interchange.'

When he slept Mrs Pickering gently disengaged. After she had finished her household chores, however, she returned, and as gently slipped her hand into his sleeping fist, curling the weak brown fingers over her own.

Some weeks later when Radcliffe called he saw that his patient was on the mend. 'Though convalescence is bound to be a bit protracted,' he said cheerfully, 'which is only to be expected after the bouts you've had.'

'Do you mean bouts of madness?' inquired Srinivas.

'Dear me,' said Dr Radcliffe mildly, 'no. Only double pneumonia and frostbite, in layman's terms. One would have thought that enough to be going on with.'

'I'm glad,' said Srinivas simply, and lay back against the pillows, and slowly, slowly allowed the past to dribble away from between his willing fingers until the fevers and confusions it had brought with it had subsided.

Winter went by. Srinivas's feet were slow to heal, so he spent most of it indoors. To his surprise he found that he missed the cold, that piercing chill that could clean one out like the blade of a filleting knife. The house was indeed cold, but it was a different kind, the black stored cold of still lakes rather than the bite of the open. As soon as he could he squeezed himself into boots, which Mrs Pickering had bought for him, and tottered into the garden. The lesions were still tender, but he could breathe with little more than an occasional twinge, and he managed to hobble about rather better than he expected.

'I ought to have sent for your son,' said Mrs Pickering, easing him into a chair.

'But I'm nowhere near dying,' protested Srinivas.

'At the time when you were. Ought I have done?'

'No, there is nothing left,' said Srinivas. 'Except exasperation.'

'Is that all you feel?'

'I know that's all he feels. I'm not sure what I feel. That I've let him down, perhaps. He would have liked his father to be fashionable and successful, and rich. I'm not cut out that way,' Srinivas smiled faintly, 'even less so now than I was.'

Then Mrs Pickering said an odd thing, smoothing her dress as he remembered Vasantha doing with her sari, and her thighs, his wife's slender thighs, showing up in outline under the silk. Mrs Pickering did not wear silks, only heavy, hairy woollen materials, but she too had blunt and difficult things to say.

'Your son's preoccupations are the people's preoccupations,' she said. 'Affluence is the keynote, the key.'

'To what?' he asked, astonished.

'To being allowed to live in peace,' said Mrs Pickering, with surprising vigour. 'This country has no time for the poor or the old.'

'Do you mean us? Are we poor and old?'

'I mean us,' said Mrs Pickering firmly. 'We may not be poor yet, but we soon shall be. Then even the neighbours won't want to know.'

Srinivas was silent. He had forgotten how long he had been ill. He had not considered how deeply his illness must have eaten into their slender resources. He had lain comfortably in bed, living off Mrs Pickering and the state in a country which reserved its enthusiasm for upright and self-supporting citizens, though it did throw a few grudging crumbs to the rest. He had been culpable.

'I'll start up again,' he promised. 'I'll get the business going again as soon as I can.'

It took, however, longer than he had bargained for. Something – his soused lungs, or perhaps the strain of the past which had welled up so irresistibly – had taken out of him more than could easily be ladled back. Sometimes it was his body, sometimes his mind: they took it in turns to retard his full recovery. On the whole he preferred a physical cause: no one could expect a man to turn out who could hardly get his feet into boots for the swelling. But when his mind lay slack, floated on surfaces of pure sensation like the pads of water lilies so that it was difficult to capture aspects of urgency, then there was nothing visible, nothing he could point to, to explain his inability to get up and go.

'Would you like me to prescribe a tonic?' asked Dr Radcliffe, believing he discerned a familiar request nestling within the distraught recital. He had called of his own volition. The stress of his married life was beginning to tell: it drove him out to his patients more frequently than, at this stage, he cared to acknowledge. His patients, a surprising number he found, were grateful for these visits. They needed him, or the humanity of contact: clung, fastened themselves to his supportive presence with the strength of their inadequacy, or deep deprivation. Some were self-sufficient, sent for him to deal with specific disease and laid their bodies on the slab and sealed themselves away. Others, a good many more than the profession (harping away at being overworked and underpaid) liked to admit, would not send for a doctor if they were at death's door – their relatives eventually did.

This one he did not know. Curious, reflected Dr Radcliffe; one usually got to know a man in the course of a serious illness, it crumbled most defences. This illness, however, had been more compounded than most, part rooted in some acute stress in a past beyond his ambit. So he could not know. He waited to see.

'Would I like a tonic?' repeated Srinivas, after consideration. 'If you mean a spirit base with caramel flavouring, do you really think it would do me any good?'

'Not if you think it merely a spirit base with flavouring and colouring,' Dr Radcliffe smiled, unwillingly. 'However, it is not entirely for nothing that it finds a place in the medical compendium.'

'True,' said Srinivas, and paused. 'I have no objection to an alcoholic base or content, or to tonics,' he offered, out of goodwill to the other.

'I have no objection either to your declining medical advice,' returned Dr Radcliffe.

'If I needed it,' said Srinivas, 'I no longer do ... what I need is magic, some kind of magical elixir ...'

'Time,' said Dr Radcliffe gently. 'Don't rush it. Give it plenty of time, it is a great restorer.'

'Of some things,' said Srinivas.

'Agreed,' said Dr Radcliffe, with a few pricks of anguish whether for himself or his patient he was not quite certain. He held out his hand. 'Good luck, anyway.'

Srinivas took it. It was large and firm, like Platt's, thought Srinivas, only now he came to think of it he never had clasped the hand that Platt had offered him.

It was summer before his body and mind began chiming together.

On a bright sunny morning, full of this new well-being and cheered by the weather, Srinivas went down to open his office. When he saw its state something of his cheer ebbed; he was glad he had taken Dr Radcliffe's advice and allowed plenty of time for his strength to return, for he could see it would be needed. It was not so much the concrete aspects of neglect, which were sensational enough, that daunted. It was the weight of inertia which saddled the place, making him realize the effort that would be needed to get a stagnant trading concern moving again.

Nevertheless, he began. He began with the grimy windows, hoping light would stream in through the cleaned panes to help him. But there was no water; he remembered he had not paid the rates and the Water Board had cut the supply. The tap was dry, its chrome stippled green, but the canister on the windowsill nearby was still half-full of coffee. Reasonably fresh too, he thought, sniffing the contents gingerly, and he thought of his ebullient friend the Zanzibari who had often brewed him a cup, booming about trade and commerce and changing climates while he waited for the water to boil, on the gas ring that was also probably now defunct. He turned the tap to see. No hiss, no gas. No electricity either. Srinivas took out a pad and began to note down what had to be attended to.

It was a long list by the day's end. But the place was clean, files dusted, filing cabinets oiled, spice samples sorted and stored. It was the imponderables that resisted him: what to do, what to do next, the steps to take to set the machinery of trade functioning again. Sitting solitary in the now clean office, Srinivas wished he had kept abreast of market trends, or at least kept up his business contacts. Especially Abdul, he thought, who would have put him in the picture, thrown off plans and enthusiasm which were backed by the cold expertise which had made him a millionaire.

Abdul, however, was abroad, in Africa, selling tourists African-style cuisine which his African friends did not recognize. He read the letter that Srinivas had finally brought himself to write, and thought with some anguish of the opportunities that had been let slip, so many of them, soon after the war, when they were just waiting to be picked up. And now? Abdul sighed; his friend, he felt, cramped his style by his curious attitudes, though possibly he might get by now that he actually wanted to. Throwing an African-type robe over his swimming trunks, Abdul sent for his secretary and began to dictate at length, not grudging the time expended on the lonely Indian for whom he had a deep affection for reasons best known to himself.

Abdul's response put new heart into Srinivas. He began to apply himself to some purpose, calling on old business contacts, paying off as far as he could arrears that had accumulated, taking up letters of introduction that Abdul sent. It was Abdul, too, who put him in touch with the club for Asian businessmen, a bustling place not far from Ashcroft Avenue where he found he could raise a loan without too much difficulty. Abdul provided the collateral. Srinivas would have preferred to avoid this, but he needed the money. He could not build up trading stock without capital, and he had none. To some extent it worried him: old attitudes clung, he felt he did not want to die owing money. It was not, of course, that he was on the verge of death: on the contrary, since recovering from his last illness he had never felt better. Only, he was no longer young but a man nearing sixty, whose tomorrows were even more tenuous than a young man's would have been.

22

TOWARDS THE MIDDLE OF 1965 THEY BEGAN TAKING IN
lodgers.

Neither knew exactly why or when the decision was made.
Possibly cumulative causes were responsible. Prices and costs
were rising, and Mrs Pickering's income, which had once
allowed them to run to small luxuries, now covered only
necessities. The business, though it survived, had never been
dynamic. Now, five years after its resuscitation, its profits
barely kept pace with overheads. Their pooled income, once
liberal, had become little more than adequate. This aspect
they might have coped with but, more importantly, the
house had begun to tax Mrs Pickering.

'It's all these stairs and corridors,' she said to Srinivas.

'We could close off the upper floors,' he suggested.

'They would still have to be cleaned,' she said. 'Anyhow it
seems a shame.'

It seemed sensible to him, but he did not want to argue.

'Shall we advertise?' he asked.

'A card in a shop window,' she said. 'We don't want to be
swamped.'

'Are we likely to be?'

'We shall be, unless we are exorbitant.'

Mrs Pickering smiled and Srinivas grinned back at her.
Excesses, in any field, at their age, verged on the ludicrous.
What they wanted was to get by: Mrs Pickering because she

did not want to be a charge upon the rates, it was her pet nightmare; Srinivas for reasons he could not readily have stated, to do with an even tenor of mind, unassailed by the fractiousness of making ends meet.

Despite the card in a window they were inundated. At one remove as it were, for Mrs Pickering had prudently asked those interested to apply within. This took the edge off the assault, for soon the besieged shopkeeper withdrew the card from the window; but there were those who had already armed themselves with the address and arrived in dispirited shoals at No. 5.

'We could have let the place a dozen times over,' said Mrs Pickering, exhausted, when evening fell. Srinivas was equally dispirited. It had been no easy thing to choose between those who waited, and finally to close the door on the last tired face.

Eventually it was done. After a good deal of upheaval they completed their arrangements, and the lodgers were finally installed. On the first floor, which Vasantha had earmarked for her firstborn son and his family, two rooms overlooking the back garden were let to a young couple. The second floor, which she had intended for the loved Seshu and his line, went to a family of four whose living, so far, had been confined to one room. The umbrella meant to spread over a joint Indian family unfurled to shelter a community of another kind, fulfilling its function in a way unforeseen by its originator.

'It has worked out differently,' said Srinivas. But seeing the strain lifting from faces he could not be sorry at this twist to his life, although sometimes, listening to the unaccustomed sounds that filled the old house, he was seized with a distinct uneasiness about the responsibilities with which he had now saddled himself.

The attic and basement remained. The basement in fact was in no state for occupation, although one day it did acquire an intermittent tenant; an old dirty man whom Srinivas could not quite bring himself to eject. Perhaps he saw in him the man he might have been, but for sundry gifts and graces, not least among them the women who had shaped his life.

After this Srinivas removed himself to the attic, taking with him his books and the old cumbersome wooden bed from India which were all that the increasing simplicities of his life demanded. It afforded him the privacy and the isolation that he needed, which the incursion of lodgers had encroached on, without affecting his relationship with Mrs Pickering, which had always been at two levels, and whose bonds and intimacies went too deep to be easily disrupted.

The neighbourhood looked on, aware of what was happening at No. 5. Privately they commented, some seeing it as a good thing, others deploring all this subletting that turned respectable houses into rabbit warrens. But there were no strident voices. Srinivas was grateful, if not overly so, in the manner of people who after a long buffeting have come to accept that peace is possible. He had no reason to suspect that the era of live and let live was ending: no whisper had reached him. Meanwhile he allowed the peacefulness of living to lap around him, with a mild hope or two and some satisfaction that it would see him out.

23

ALL AROUND THEM, ALL THIS TIME, THINGS WERE changing and continued to change.

As Mrs Glass said, the place wasn't the same. If she hadn't lived right through the changes, she told her friend Mrs Fletcher, she wouldn't have recognized it, she would have walked up the street and right past her house and not known it, the surroundings were that different. But of course she, like the Fletchers, and the Srinivases, and the remaining older residents (of whom there were not many left) had lived through it all. They had lived through demolition, and rebuilding, and road widening, through community planning and trial runs for ring roads. They had seen the elms chopped down along their avenue, and the piles being driven in, and new housing taking the place of the old. They had got used to the traffic, and their truncated front gardens, to the accelerating sounds of the age, and to the sight of perpendicular buildings framed in their front and back windows.

Skyscrapers, Mrs Glass called them.

'Why, you seen those then?' inquired Mrs Fletcher.

'Maybe not in the flesh, but there is such a thing as pictures, isn't there?' said Mrs Glass, glaring.

'No need for acerbity,' said Mrs Fletcher.

'It's acerbity that keeps us friends,' said Mrs Glass. 'Too much sweetness is very apt to get cloying.'

'No danger of that,' said Mrs Fletcher, sniffing.

As there was some ambiguity here Mrs Glass was silent, though resolutions formed to attack on other topics, especially Fred Fletcher, who was now back in England, Australia not having been to his taste.

Skyscraper was Mrs Glass's description. Nobody else called the flats that, since they did not brush the sky, even if they did disrupt the skyline. But they were tall enough: ten, twelve, twenty storeys some of them. Tier upon tier they rose, these concrete quarters for the living, and into them disappeared the exhausted homeless, delirious with the happiness of having a place of their own, though presently they would feel the loneliness of heights, and yearn for gardens and fences to drape their friendliness over, and miss earth levels without quite believing in root causes for their restlessness, and to wonder what it was that ailed them, and to look around for scapegoats.

These were the lucky ones. Those who waited outside, names on lengthening housing lists, looked up with envy, contrasting the comforts of modern living with their own squalid existence, crammed five and six to a room. They would wait their turn, these people. Only a few would attempt to jump the queue which was the yardstick of fair dealing. But their numb misery fermented, waiting for obscene voices to nominate scapegoats on whom they could offload the frustrations of their living.

Over at No. 6 Fred Fletcher was in a state of some frustration. He didn't care who knew it.

'I'm fed up,' he told his mother. 'Fed right up to there,' he said, and drew a finger across his gullet.

Mrs Fletcher bridled. It was her privilege, she considered, to be fed up, lumbered as she was with Fred and six kids, and more being conceived if she was any judge of the noises that came from the back bedroom at night, and the afternoons too, they were that shameless.

'*You're* fed up,' she said, and sniffed. 'You don't want to stay, you don't have to, you know. Nobody's forcing you, neither your dad nor me.'

'Oh, no,' said Fred. 'There's homes waiting I could walk into tomorrow. You would,' he said vindictively, 'cast out your own flesh and blood and it wouldn't worry you nothing, not a damn thing.'

'No cause for swearing,' said Mrs Fletcher. 'I've seen my duty as a Christian and I've done it. Otherwise you wouldn't be here under my roof, Fred Fletcher!'

Fred kept quiet. They had had this argument before. The last time he had shot his mouth and gone to Australia, and it had done him no good whatever. He had not found anywhere decent to live there either, and although he was not what you might call a skilled worker, he had not really expected to work as a road mender, which was the only job they offered him. So he came back, using up the last of his savings and losing his place in the housing queue into the bargain, and went to live with his mother. There was only one thing worse, Fred considered: living with his wife's mother. It did not make him thankful for small mercies. He felt, indeed, that he had been done, though he did not know on whom to pin the blame.

One day he found out, from a mate of his who had had it straight from the mouth of his councillor. The blacks were responsible. They came in hordes, occupied all the houses, filled up the hospital beds and their offspring took all the places in schools. A great light burst upon Fred. Why had he not thought of that? He lumbered out of the pub, in which he had received his moment of illumination, feeling he had been put on his guard against imminent calamity, and determined to be on the lookout. Exactly for what, though, he was not too sure. The blacks, of course: but his mate had also spoken of different habits and alien characteristics, so that he had the confused impression that what he had to look out for was a species of ape with black faces.

As it happened Ashcroft Avenue was rather short on these. Fred had to go farther afield. At the poorer end of the borough he found a man sweeping the street. He was not at all like an ape, but he was coal-black and he had thick lips. Fred felt he would have to do.

'Here, you,' he said to the man. 'You got no right to be in this country. You bugger off, see?'

'I got my right when you lot carved up my country,' said the man, who happened to be a graduate, of London University in fact, doing the best job London could offer him.

'You disputing my word?' asked Fred, and bunched his knuckles.

'Yes,' said the man, and leaned on his broom. His biceps, Fred noted, were huge. His own were not negligible, labouring in Australia had developed them, but they shrank in comparison.

'You watch it,' said Fred, moderately, and stalked off.

His next encounter was more satisfactory. Standing alone at a bus stop he found a thin, elongated coloured youth, whom without preliminary he sent flying into the gutter. Then he turned for home, pleased with the evening's work and prepared to call it a day.

Rounding the corner into Ashcroft Avenue, however, opportunity presented itself again, in the shape of an elderly brown man walking along by himself. His face seemed familiar, but Fred could not place it; possibly it would have made no difference if he had. He planted himself squarely in the other's path.

'You got no right to be living in this country,' he said, and thrust his face close to the brown man's. Beery fumes rose from his nostrils. Srinivas stepped back fastidiously.

'Why not?' he asked.

'You telling me you're English?' asked Fred.

'By adoption,' said Srinivas happily.

Fred, feeling he needed nothing further, lashed out. Srinivas dodged the blow. Fred spun round once, staggered two steps, fell on the pavement and rolled into the gutter. Srinivas ran to help him up. Fred looked up at him from where he lay. It seemed to him a harmless face, but the colour was wrong. He decided he hated that colour, and the man, and the untold evils he and his kind were letting loose in his country, his beloved England which he felt he had never loved so much before, not even when he left its shores for Australia.

'Get stuck, you fucking ape,' he bellowed, and as his rage built up with foul words he channelled it into still more fetid reaches, until a constable arrived, and shared out his disapproval impartially between the two men.

Mrs Fletcher was upset. Her name had been dragged in the mud, no doubt of that. By Fred. Sitting in the gutter, he had been, tight as a tick, shouting and swearing. Filthy language such as Mr Fletcher, if he had been in any state to hear, which he was not, would have been ashamed of his son for using. As Mrs Fletcher was. And a worse feeling for the other thing, to which she could not quite put a name. She sat with her hands motionless, as still as two frightened mice in her lap, while quivers ran through her frame. For Mr Srinivas, and what her son had said to him: to an old man who lived among them, and did them no harm. Unknown to her her lips began moving. They formed words without sound, like tiny balloons in which messages were written. Love thy neighbour, these read, love thy neighbour. When at last she caught their drift Mrs Fletcher agreed. Fred had done wrong. Without cause he had wronged a neighbour. Even if the neighbour was peculiar, which Mr Srinivas was. Kept human ashes in the cellar – which Bert Glass had seen – and something cannibal about his gods (or his people, she wasn't sure which), whose toes were eaten away.

The quivers turned to shudders, threatening Mrs Fletcher's angular form. But she rose. She was a Christian, and would do her Christian duty. She put on her coat and crossed the road and rang the bell of No. 5. Mr Srinivas opened it.

'I have something to say to you,' she said to him straightly, raising her eyelids, which seemed to be weighted, and seeing the old calm face, which eased her. What Srinivas saw was strain, its lines and stresses plain on the harassed, blanched face.

'Won't you come in?' he invited.

Mrs Fletcher shrank. She gazed at his ordinary features, but now she did not see them, because superimposed on them, suddenly, were his two blue feet like fish, which had come slap-slap along the wet pavement after her in the November gloom. But she stood her ground, rooting her legs which wanted to scuttle off sideways around the nearest corner, carrying her to safety.

'It can be said here,' she said, trembling, her limbs like water weeds somehow upholding her. 'It needs to be said, because my son had no call to say what he did. No call at all. You've been a neighbour to us these many years, Mr Srinivas, and you've been a good neighbour, and whatever's been said you've as much right to be here as any of us and there's few as wouldn't be sorry if you were to feel you had to leave because of what our Fred said. And if he hasn't got the decency to apologize,' concluded Mrs Fletcher, her eyes beginning to flash, 'then his mother's got to do it for him.'

Delivered, her tremors eased. It was Srinivas who felt the shafts now, thin lances that cleaved through him, so subtly that the flesh closed over before blood was drawn, leaving no injury, leaving almost no injury, only this that was like the beginning of pain to be lost in unconsciousness as the stunning blow took effect.

Because if he left he had nowhere to go.

Nowhere, he said to himself, and he scanned the pale anxious eyes which were regarding him for reasons that might drive him out, a nowhere man looking for a nowhere city. But the eyes wore a film, a watery film that gave him back his own anxieties, and Mrs Fletcher, who tried, did little better.

'You don't want to pay any attention to Fred,' she said, giving no reasons, only this quavering reassurance. 'He doesn't know what he's talking about. You've got as much right to live here as what he has. More,' she claimed, extravagantly, prepared for any extravagance in order to right a wrong. 'Even if you weren't born in this country, Mr Srinivas, you belong here, and don't let anyone convince you different.'

'I won't,' said Srinivas, and he gazed at her remotely, emptily, until presently her face swam back into focus, a nervous face desperately embarked upon reassuring him.

Do people reassure when there is no danger?

No, said Srinivas, judiciously considering: reassurance is shaped only from the ingredients of existing danger.

'I won't,' he said however, to calm Mrs Fletcher. 'I do belong here now. It was good of you to remind me.'

24

REASONS.

Srinivas sought them, sitting alone in the attic to which he had taken himself away from the red herrings of kindness that Mrs Fletcher scattered across the trail, away from the profound peace that came in Mrs Pickering's company which seduced him from his purpose.

But there were none: no reasons that could be ascertained why Englishmen should want to rid their country of him. None, he said to himself, until something began to stir in him, some knowledge that he could not suppress, which insisted that what he sought did not lie at the end of a rational road. Then he began to grope, to feel his way towards interior realms not to be reached by other routes, where the kernel of the matter resided, and the truth of it could, perhaps, be touched, naked, before it was decked out in improbable garb and sent out to make a respectable, lying entrance.

And he acknowledged, too, that he knew. Somewhere in the coils and folds of his mind had lain subliminal perception, for signs had not been lacking. Only, in the preoccupations of his life – in the savouring of that peace which had been vouchsafed him – and the inward inclinations of his age, he had not permitted them to invade his consciousness.

Pulsing signs, all about him. Erupting like a rash on walls and the backs of buildings, and scrawled tall upon the unwitting blackboards of hoardings so that onlookers could decipher from afar the man-sized messages of hate. BLACKS GO HOME, they said, their fear and hate crystallized into words which opened whole new hells of corresponding fear and desolation in those at whom they were aimed. As now he saw, walking frail through the streets, such was the oppressive presence of rejection. Heard the whispers that he had allowed to brush him by grown into strident voices that preached a new gospel, a gospel he had not heard since those echoes from Germany before the war. He recalled them now, almost phrase by phrase, presenting hate as a permissible emotion for decent German people. Not only permissible but laudable, and more than that, an obligatory emotion, which they summoned up subtly and starkly from a reading of a checklist, or charge sheet, of the differences between men, their customs and observances, their sexual, religious, and pecuniary habits, sparing nothing as they peeped and probed, neither bed nor bathroom nor tabernacle, citing in the end, without shame, the shape and size of their noses, lips, balls, skulls, and the pigment of their skins.

And where was compassion, the tolerance that had touched his life with grace for close on half a century? Gone, he thought, his balance shattered and floundering in the first waves of loss that broke over him. Gone like those direct statements of love and cheerful blasphemy that had once enlivened the scene, which present hatreds had all but swept off the billboards. When he looked from his window now, at the hoardings which enclosed the demolition site, he saw not sad hearts pierced by careless arrows, but the crude drawing of a dangling man.

His sons, in childhood, had drawn just such a man, playing a game called Hangman, which neither he nor his wife had taught them. A game which made them laugh, whose ritual had to be – was – followed punctiliously. Placing the gibbet's upright first, then its supports, next the arm, and the cross member to strengthen it, and finally drawing the shorn figure, round head and stick limbs of the hanged man. No child, though, had scored the graffito that confronted him. It was a grown man who shinned up the ladder that swayed between pavement and hoarding to vent his cave feelings in these cave drawings.

Sometimes Srinivas saw him in the half light of dawn.

At these times, when he had risen to pray, as was his custom, but could not, he saw the grey figure waiting. Saw it emerge from shadows, evading the squad car that cruised through the streets, and rapidly ascending the ladder begin, with the ritual downward charcoal stroke, its baleful indictment.

Of what? Srinivas could not tell. Second only to the emotions of loss that besieged him was the feeling of bewilderment. What wrongs had been done, what crimes committed that called for such punishment? Srinivas searched – himself, others – in that deep manner which was becoming habitual to him, which accepted that seeds of truth were rarely scattered on surfaces for easy picking. But there was nothing. Instead, creeping up on him, truths not to be denied, came strange barbed thoughts. That this bland country owed debts it had not paid, rather than scores which it had to settle. That the past had seen his countrymen sinned against, rather than sinning: crimes that had not been atoned for, nor even acknowledged save by the honourable few.

Where then was his own honour, he asked himself, when he harboured these rancorous thoughts of a country that had taken him in, given him shelter, restored his manhood and his self-respect, and become in the end his own? So he sought to be rid of them but they clung, gummed to him with a strength that defied him. Indestructible, like truth, or matter. Buried, resurrected: the soul may not, but the bones come up. Fit only for burial, he cried, shovelling them back. And he thought of Platt, and the warder who had bought sweets for frightened children visiting their fathers in prison, and the young blushing policeman who had felt compassion for him. But they were not enough. Not really enough. Not enough to lay those other memories, of the forest laid waste, and the young man with his flicking cane and his caste insolence, and the tears that had run down his mother's cheeks when, finally, they knew there was no place left for him in the country of his birth.

I thought it was done with, he said to himself, meaning the stockpiling of rancour, the dreadful meanness of it. Restlessly pacing the room, six steps from the wooden bed to the window with its diamond panes, six steps back. From teakwood base to a view of the dangling man, and back. Curbing these dark emotions, failing. Thinking. Unable to cease, while the grains of peace slid away, that peace he had imagined to be his right by reason of his age and the penultimate stage he had reached in his life. Did one then not have a right to anything? Nothing at all?

He rebelled, and rebellion exacted its own penalty. His body, disciplined to remain in the background, edged forward and made its grievances known. Aches and pains, quiescent or ignored before, began to claim his attention. They settled like sludge in his joints, which seemed to enlarge, and develop club heads, and lose their lubricity. When he moved he creaked.

'I hope you're not sickening for the flu,' said Mrs Pickering. 'There's a lot of it about.'

'I don't think it's that,' said Srinivas, kneading his knuckles, which were painful, and jutted.

'Perhaps it's the atmosphere,' she said.

'What do you mean?'

'It's been so close. Stifling.'

'Yes, perhaps it's that,' he agreed.

Babbling. For what else could this interchange be, between two adults, each meaning one thing, talking about another?

'I'll get out the deckchairs,' she said. 'We'll sit in the garden.'

Was she, after all, talking about what she really meant? Heat, and the humidity? Dealing in the immaterial, this immune islander, unaware of the hostile climate that was wearing him down?

'I'm afraid we can't.' She was back. 'Our visitor's bagged both chairs. He's asleep in one with his feet on the other.'

'Kick him out,' he said, to see. 'He's only an old black man.'

She stood frozen.

'I will, if you're not keen,' he goaded.

She did not move. 'Whatever's come over you?' she asked.

'That's what they want to do, your countrymen,' he told her, and waited for a reply which did not come. Waiting, he considered her, sombrely. Her face was old and wrinkled, and sad. Time accounted for the first, but the sadness was his responsibility. He had put it there, as ruthlessly – no, less mercifully, since precipitately – as time. Man's lashing tongue, rooted in his mouth, as restless as himself, as indiscriminate, as criminal: exquisite organ of sense and delicacy, used for love, for loving, for this. Misused. Suddenly he slumped, rods and stays gone, all the bones that hold a man up.

'Look at it, how it spreads,' he said in despair. 'Even into this house, even to us.'

'To you,' she repudiated.

'And you,' he said, 'are you exempt? Are you immune from the thinking of this country?'

'I feel no different,' she said, so steadfastly that he felt ashamed, 'towards you or anyone else. Nor can I conceive of any circumstances in which I might. I am not the only one either.'

It steadied him. Replenished pools upon which the being depended. A man could crack if they ran dry: feel himself split, and not know the cause. Blunder around searching with throbbing head and bolting heart, what was left of it. Soulless. There was a word for it, only it was not acceptable until its terrifying sense had been expelled. Soul taken from that too. But returning to him: unknown, unknowable, somewhere, invisible, the soft trickle that he could not feel, reconstituting the human being. In his gratitude he stretched out his hands, placed them upon her shoulders, felt the friable bones through the cheap cotton print she wore, knew their frailty gave no clue to the strength upon which he and his burden leaned.

'I'm afraid I lost my balance,' he said. 'Sometimes it's difficult not to be thrown.'

'It's all too easy.'

'Yes.'

'Traps.'

'Yes.'

'That old black man in the basement,' she said, returning them to the point at issue, one of the innumerable aspects of daily living that tended to be overlooked in his present thinking.

'Oh, yes,' he said lamely. Leaving it to her, she would know.

'He's no problem,' she said, 'unless we choose to make him one.'

This, being of sound mind, they declined to do. Tacitly, with an exchange of wry smiles. For there were problems enough, without creating any: little incentive to introduce them here, into this old ugly brick house that somehow transcending its looks was gradually assuming the nobler aspects of a sanctuary.

At home, in Mrs Pickering's company, was one thing.

When he went out it was totally another. Walking through the streets, as he had to, wandering in them as from time to time he felt compelled, a new feeling joined the frailty that could make him cower, walk bent, a man on sufferance apologizing for his presence, like a convict on parole but denied his belligerence.

The new feeling was detachment.

Not that severance from the material which belonged to the domain of the spirit, but a human cut-off engineered from without that made him uneasy, made him peer at the faces going by which had once been familiar but now were remote, belonging to denizens of a world different from his own. Their world. Mrs Pickering's world, which struck most strangely of all. To which she, and they, but not he, belonged. Inhabited an area devoid of meaning for him, but dense with experience for them. It isolated him, cast him in the role of intruder.

Intruder, after ten, twenty, fifty years?

When he went peering among them they confirmed it. Outraged eyeball challenged eyeball, glazing over with rejection. Sometimes he could not take it: he retreated, muttering, relapsed into attitudes he knew to be sterile, from which Mrs Pickering had plucked him. But sometimes, in the very teeth of QUIT and VAMOSE notices, among the ice floes, he saw the colours of humanity, pity and concern in the greens and blues and hazels and greys of island eyes for this stalking stranger that, alternating between hunchback and straight-spine, was himself.

It was different, too, in the club for Asian businessmen to which he went, where he heard them talking, about anything and everything but finally (scratching away at the irresistible sore spot) about the ill will in the country, conjured up and let loose like a respectable spirit in their midst.

'It is not worthy of a Christian nation,' they said, those club members who were Indian Christians, in voices that were less than robust since they knew themselves to be a minority, examples of unseemly conversion in the detested imperial past, though one or two did remember a more honourable ancestry in pre-colonial times.

'It is what one expects of a Christian nation,' said their companions. Without emphasis, since none was needed. Simply stated a fact, the needle of Asian awareness scanning the tape that clattered past, on which were the raised pimples of indictments. Of Pizarro and Salazar, Vorster, and Dyer ... Roll call of history, yet more: a folk memory, insidious stream in the unconscious triggering action for which, later, no reasons would be found. Leave them bewildered, like white-faced loons unable to connect the lifeless bodies scattered around them with any action of their own.

Srinivas listened to them, and he ached. There were strange aches in his limbs, which had not resolved into flu. His mind felt bruised, as if it had been assaulted. Worse, he felt it to be unclean, rank with animosities absorbed from the atmosphere. He wished he could repudiate all they said: in truth he could not. Some things, yes, and he spoke of these in a voice that came thin and strained from his larynx, such was the disbelief against which it was pitted.

They heard him out. They gave the old man the respect due to his age, and in undertones bawled out the fossil's opinions.

'Trouble is, Pop, you've been here too long, you don't know what you're up against,' a young Sikh said, and laid a huge commiserating hand upon his arm.

'Yes, perhaps I have lived too long,' said Srinivas, gently, 'although, on consideration, I would not have thought that a bar to finding out.'

'You should listen, hear what they say,' counselled the Sikh, pitying the mushy sentiment that undoubtedly lay under that thatch of fine white hair.

'I do,' said Srinivas. 'It is unavoidable.'

'The way they say it. Whew!' said the Sikh through bearded lips.

'Every time they start it gets like a furnace for us.'

'Who?' said Srinivas. There had been more than one voice.

In chorus they listed names.

One day he followed their advice and went to find out what they meant.

It was a large hall. He stood at the back because of his vision, which had altered with age. It saw distances, rather than closer ranges. In the distance he could see the speaker, an ordinary man with an ordinary mouth and a tongue in it. Ordinary, all of them, no more than a normal man kept in his head. What was extraordinary was what these organs in unison could do.

Srinivas listened, astounded. It seemed to him like a reading from the Book of Doom that the fearful compile, so haunted was it, so hung with promises of violence and prophecies of calamity to come and exhortations to beware. Now and then, as the words poured out, there was a feeling. It came in waves, and each time more were carried away, you could tell by the way they gave up, surrendered themselves wholly, shrieking, their lungs bursting with fervour. Nor was Srinivas exempt. He began to feel with them. He shook with fear. He felt they were all in deadly peril, all living dangerously, in imminent danger. It affected his feet most strongly. He felt they were scorching, within his shoes his toes curled, he felt like snatching them back from the brink and shouting to his neighbours to do the same, as if like a lot of crass fools they were perched on the crater of a belching volcano. Choking in the fumes, he tore his gaze away, moved it upward from the mouth to the eye, for guidance.

It was cold.

The eye of the sour messiah was cold and hard, like quartz.

For Srinivas the volcano ceased to be. Instantly. The shock seemed to catapult him clear of the atmosphere. As he floated free, attached to some charred scraps of sanity, he spotted, boggling, the identity of the menace. It was people. The peril was people. Not all people, but people like himself, their threatening presence, the presence of their offspring and their offspring's offspring, since their children were only off-sprung, never born decently in bed. Thousands upon thousands of them, threatening millions upon millions of these islanders at every turn of existence, not excluding their very lives.

Srinivas felt it was time to leave the hall. All he wanted to do now was to get out. It was not easy because of the crush. When he tried, using his elbows in his efforts, they looked at him blackly, with menace. 'Please,' he said, 'please excuse me.' At once they made way, battering each other's toes and ribs to save the old man from being pulped. Where had the menace gone that had been written so blackly upon those mobile faces? As he came out Srinivas's head was whirling.

He resolved to ask Fred Fletcher. Fred would know, he had such strong views on the matter he had singled him out and slugged him. He had gone on from there, made strides as it were, he was known as the district's blacks basher, a title which pleased him but was known to distress his mother. Fred, however, proved elusive. He crossed the road when he saw Srinivas coming. Or if he saw the figure of the old man bearing down purposefully upon him he took to sprinting up the road and into the pub that was his home from home. Here, perspiring, he described the dreadful persistence of wogs. Once, cornered by the sudden apparition of Srinivas at the junction between avenue and road, he leapt convulsively on to a passing bus, leaving his mother standing. For all his bulk he was a nimble man. Also, he felt driven.

'You'd think the devil was after you,' said Mrs Fletcher sourly. She had had to cart home a vast laundry bag full of Fred's family's washing as well as her own, which Fred had deposited at her feet before vaulting on to the bus.

'He's a devil. They're all devils,' said Fred simply. Having said it, it became true in his mind.

'What's all this I hear about your Fred?' inquired Mrs Glass.

'What's all what you hear about my Fred?' countered Mrs Fletcher.

'He's going around saying Mr Srinivas has got the mark of the devil on him,' said Mrs Glass with disapproval. 'Hoof, on rump.'

'Never!' Mrs Fletcher exploded. She felt outraged, but she was in a quandary. Fred was her cross, but he was also her son, especially in front of neighbours. 'Fred knows Mr Srinivas better than that,' she temporized. 'It's words being put in his mouth, that's all I can say.'

Safely behind the four (soundproof, she hoped) walls of her house she flew at Fred.

'What've you been saying about that poor old man?'

'What poor old man?'

'You know very well what poor old man.'

'What have I been saying?'

'You know very well what you've been saying.'

Fred wasn't sure. He said a good many things, of which quite a few got blanked out during his pub sessions.

'I'm sure I've said nothing,' he said cautiously.

'You call it nothing, saying an old man's got the devil's hoof baked on his bum,' cried his mother.

'I never.'

'You did!'

'Did I say that?'

'You know very well –'

'All right, all *right*,' cried Fred. Must've been properly sozzled, he said to himself, to come out with a thing like that. Like something weird out of the Bible, which no one, except possibly this dotty person his mother, could believe in. He, Fred, certainly had no time for theological devils. He meant the real ones, the human ones that drove a man to Australia, and generally made life hell.

What, exactly, though, had he said? He worried at it, gloomily, fearful for his reputation as a proper bloke and wondering if they called him a nut case behind his back, and soon, tracing the source of his ills, grew even more vilely disposed towards his tormentor, Mr Srinivas, and through him towards all his ilk.

25

AT NIGHT MRS FLETCHER PRAYED.

She knelt on the faded Brussels carpet of her living room, since the bedroom was engaged, and offered up prayers for her husband, who was stricken and for her son, that he might be granted Christian love and understanding. These were constants in her prayers, included after she had recited the Lord's Prayer two or three times, to make up for the gaps where her mind had wandered. They had been so for several months. Constant theme, principal burden, of her supplication, the two had been. But latterly she noticed other, insidious, prayers appearing, like side dishes at the main offering: entreaties for her husband to be taken, pleas for her son to leave her. In the beginning she had resisted. Of late she admitted them. 'In case worse should befall, O Lord,' she had taken to adding, addressing herself directly to all-knowing God, who would understand what she meant.

'In case, O Lord,' she finished, raising her voice a little to make herself clear. Then she rose, dusting the detritus of cotton carpet off her knees which formed as fast as she swept it up, and unclasped her hands and smoothed her hair – as if her husband would notice, but it was too late now to break the habit – before going into the bedroom where he lay.

Like a cabbage, she said to herself, as she frequently did. 'Nothing but a vegetable,' she had overheard them say in the hospital, and that was what swam at once into her mind.

A large white bad-smelling cabbage, speechless, helpless, waterlogged, that she felt – insisted – was her duty to bring home to tend. Did so, too. Washed and fed and put clothes on the subhuman thing, and even looked into its eyes. Not for long though, for she saw not the hoped-for glints from these windows of the soul, but a jellied reflection of the soused brain. It put her off after they told her: off brains, that is; she had liked calf's brains, done with a parsley sauce, a nutritious dish she had enjoyed preparing and eating. It did not put her off her husband, nor her duty to him.

Only, lately, she found herself failing: her strength not what it was, to carry on. The prayer came in her weakness. It moved her lips before she could stop them. At first she suspected the devil: then it came to her the devil could not operate coupled to the Lord's name on her lips. Now she did not try to stop them. Now that she did not she thought the eyes looked different. Grateful, as if their owner knew what she was up to, asking for them to be finally extinguished. So she beseeched with renewed confidence, ending on a note of anguished humility. 'Yet not my will, O Lord, but thine, be done.'

That night she could feel it was close. So she kept vigil, sitting up straight on the slatted chair beside the bed on which he slept. By dawn it was over. She listened to the sounds of his dying, and when all was silent again she got up and bent over the body. The eyes were open: dying must have awakened him. Carefully she drew down the lids. Then she did not know what else to do. So many deaths, so many in her family had passed away, but they passed away in hospital where green screens were drawn behind which nurses did the necessary. Nurses. Mrs Pickering, she remembered, had once been a nurse. Presently, at a slightly more decent hour,

Mrs Fletcher put on her hat and coat and went down to call her neighbour.

Mrs Pickering had given up praying soon after her first marriage. Her prayer at that time had reduced to one theme: one long impassioned importuning of God to release her, by death, by anything, from her marriage. When she realized that this was no longer prayer, and could not be deemed to be so by any conceivable God, she ceased to pray. Later, when she was free, and empty, the years having washed away her substance, she attempted to fill the void by prayer but found she had lost the habit.

On this night it revived. Or perhaps it was the urgency of need, which opened like lacunae and rapidly latticed her being.

'O Lord,' she began, and could not continue. Because what needed to be vouchsafed was so diffuse, so vast, to do with rethinking by whole races and each individual within it, with sin by omission or commission, undisguised by semantics, by those strange somersaults and acrobatics of muscular apologists. 'O Lord,' she began again (anything, anything to start the flow): and what came was a child's prayer: 'Now I lay me down to sleep, I pray the Lord my soul to keep.' She recited it to the end. Nothing more came, so she sat with her face in her hands, listening to the house. There was always something to listen to. The shuffling and snuffling of people in sleep. The faint groaning of wood – stairs, doors, floorboards – easing up on the stresses and strains of the day, contracting not in concert but fitfully as the coldness of night seeped through. Sometimes she heard the snores of the basement man who, when drunk, could be heard all the way up to the rafters; sometimes, from the attic, the soft footfalls of Srinivas.

Srinivas, pacing. Shoes removed, his feet set on this painful pilgrimage. For what, she asked herself, what purpose was served, what manner of mind could sentence a man to this? She mused over it, huddling herself in a blanket, but came no nearer to understanding. Nut case. The word burst in front of her suddenly. It was a word that she frequently heard used, though not by people of her generation. It described exactly, mentally, physically, the nature of the man who would so condemn a fellow human being, a man whose kernel, were one to come upon it, would be similarly enclosed, in the hard shell case of a nut. She settled down then, touched by an impulse of pity for an unhappy breed of men, her anger ebbing.

Overhead the pacing went on. Ball and heel, up and down. Softly, so as not to wake the sleeping house. But it was growing louder. So loud that it woke her up. She listened. The footsteps had ceased. Someone, she realized, was knocking: a timid knocker, to judge from the indiscriminate flurry of muffled knocks. Mrs Pickering went down to see, still swaddled in the blanket in which she had fallen asleep. Mrs Fletcher, in coat and hat, in the grey dawn, met her surprised gaze. The two women, each suffering the symptoms of interrupted slumber, each wondering at the other's odd attire at this hour, were locked in silence for some moments. Mrs Fletcher broke free first.

'It's Mr Fletcher,' she said. 'He's been taken.'

'Taken ill?'

'He's passed away,' said Mrs Fletcher, depressed. 'I was hoping you could come. To help like. Being a Sunday, you know, the undertakers ... I don't know if they ...' Her hands were describing feeble arabesques.

Mrs Pickering nodded. 'I'll be around in a few minutes,' she said, briefly, since despite the blanket it was cold standing on the doorstep.

Mrs Fletcher watched while Mrs Pickering worked. She would have helped if she had known how, but she did not; a dead man was very different from a sick, live one. She felt she would have been grateful too, if she had not felt so numb. Gradually, though, curiosity nudged away the numbness. She watched, with interest, Mr Fletcher's face emerging from under razor and flannel: clean, chalk-white, shaven. She had almost forgotten what he looked like. During his illness he had forbidden her to touch his face, threshing and struggling if she approached with a sponge. Before that there had been those years of hiding behind magazines and newspapers. Now he was revealed. Familiar body, forgotten face. Plugs of cotton wool in all the holes, as if Mrs Pickering expected him to ooze.

'Do they leak?' she had to ask.

'In case,' said Mrs Pickering, and bound the big toes together, making a neat figure-of-eight with household twine. Like some ritual, it seemed to Mrs Fletcher, watching her neighbour's weaving fingers. 'He's Baptist,' she said at last, dubiously.

'Makes no difference to the corpse,' said Mrs Pickering. 'It stops the legs rolling about,' she added, seeing Mrs Fletcher's consternation.

Mrs Fletcher was vastly relieved. Mrs Pickering was, true, one of them, but on the other hand she did live with Mr Srinivas, an Indian, some kind of pagan, though he was a good man, but his religion, all those gods ... you couldn't be too careful. So Mrs Fletcher made her nervous bows and scrapes towards and away from understanding, while Mrs Pickering contemplated the correctly laid out body of Mr Fletcher and wondered about people. People who lived and died, witnessing neither birth nor death but running wildly for cover as if its processes might contaminate their hygienic envelopes of existence. But caught in the end, each one, in total loneliness, while the fainting relatives bolted. Mrs Pickering could almost have smiled, but Mrs Fletcher's solemn eye was upon her and she lost the inclination.

Srinivas was also in the habit of praying, but it had long ceased to be either verbal or formalized and was simply a communion. Not always, sometimes. Sometimes it was greater. When, sometimes, rarely, his mind was cleansed and concentrated suddenly he would be pervaded, his mouth filled with the name of God, his eyes, his soul, his entire being merged into the dazzling light which bathed the whole of creation. Minutes, seconds, he could never tell: its reality he never doubted. When it faded, traces lingered; while they did, for hours or days, moments of ineffable peace could still be touched, the precious shimmering residue.

Mostly it was not so. Mostly it was less, intense human petition graced by a brief benediction. Gradually, then, flesh would fall away, to be replaced by spirit: fragment of spirit granted awareness of a vast and radiant entity of which it was part, seeking union but unable to enter, but refreshed by awareness, the fragile encounter.

When there was neither, the spirit howled.

Of late there had been nothing: the name of God no more than an ordinary wafer in his mouth. He knew well enough why. Because he sought personal favours, contrary to the meaning of prayer, contrary to the tenets of his religion. His longing for peace, the craving for rest, insinuated themselves into his wordless communings until these ceased. Were blocked, since being so contaminated they could not be deemed to be communion with any conceivable deity.

Tonight was the same. He could not sleep. Restlessness, the curse of the age, stood him up, made him pace. Up and down the attic, caged man, padding softly. But now and then the floor creaked, increasingly loud as the night deepened. Darkness reached its peak, and passed. There were other sounds now, of sleep grown shallower, and the first stir of birds still in sleep. Presently there was another, the slight swish of tyres on tarmac. He went to the window. In the darkness a darker density revealed the shape of an encumbered man.

Moving like an automaton – for he could think of no valid reason for his actions at all – Srinivas put on his slippers and went down the stairs and into the street, using his latchkey to let himself out.

A fine dew was falling, the pavements glistened. Something else glimmered too, from low on the ground, shining lines that radiated from a hub. He peered again, and picked out the outline of a bicycle propped against the curb. Its spokes attracted whatever meagre light there was and shone. Curious, he thought, how there was always light, even in pitch darkness, when one was out in the open: as if day absorbed a sheen which it slowly released during darkness. There was a source here, though, which he singled out: the dim glow of a low-wattage bulb burning behind the drawn curtains of No. 6. Mrs Fletcher, of course: she went in for miserly lighting, the house flickered uncertainly through the worst glooms of winter. Mr Fletcher must be worse for a light to be on, he thought, and recalled the knocking he had half heard and dismissed. Then there was a creaking of the ladder and everything else passed from his mind.

The ladder creaked each time a foot was placed on one of its rungs. Seventeen ascensions to reach that point on the hoarding where the downward stroke began. He stood rooted, and listened to the squealing chalk. So loud in the quiet dawn. Shrill, like cord being sawn. The spinal cord, as the pithing rod passed. How many strokes, though, to cut down a man? Gibbet, rope, noose. Slogans, speeches, accusations. The one, he thought, was as deadly as the other, only its authors did not, could not, acknowledge it. For how could they, these sour crusaders who needs must demonstrate the righteousness of their cause or suffer defections in their following ... so they called them warnings instead, issued with the welfare of the black minority in mind. Ah, words! How they could twist! Lies falling like autumn leaves from the mouths of gentlemen and judges, as the common man knew, as he, Srinivas, knew from listening through two wars and the battle for independence. Steeped in it as he was why, now, he asked himself, should his stomach crawl?

Let it pass, let it pass. Srinivas was suddenly weary, standing alone in the shadow of his house in the empty dawn. The encounter he had subconsciously sought, the confrontation with the virulent cartoonist, this he no longer wanted. Nothing would be achieved. What could each say, that would make sense to the other: the one explain his hatred, the other his bewilderment confronted by it? No. They would merely be faces with round Os for mouths that spouted endlessly, chattering at each other in different codes.

Weary. He had slept, Srinivas remembered, hardly at all – finding himself swaying on his feet reminded him. Yet somehow he had to see it out, be witness to this childish, vengeful mimicry of an execution. Soon done: fewer strokes were needed than he had imagined. The last stick limb, the starfish hand, were drawn. The chalk lines gleamed white on the grimy hoarding, as stark as the deed, as the emotion that dictated it. Briskly, some appetite appeased, the executioner descended, looked around furtively, shouldered his ladder, mounted his bicycle, and pedalled away quickly. An ordinary man, save for his message, hatred for blacks. A minority man. Or perhaps the majority of ordinary men, white men, carried the same curdled message in their hearts? Srinivas pondered, grown cold in a cold country, nothing to warm him in these debilitating moments of pre-dawn, no one beside him on the stony pavement who might, perhaps, seeing the chill gathering in bluish penumbra about his flesh, have chivvied him in, or taken his hands and chafed them, as Mrs Pickering would have done.

No one like that at all.

But as, at last, he turned to go, the two men pounced. They were big men, or perhaps they expected resistance, for under their weighty palms Srinivas was borne down almost to the ground, then bounced up, ridiculously, as they released their pressure. Totally surprised, he gazed at them blankly, noting irrelevant details like the straps of their helmets which bit into their chins, the excellent quality of the blue-uniformed sleeves that rasped his face.

When they had bobbed up, the two policemen and he, they had to wait, to recover their breath. Then the younger of the two, who was a constable, tapped him on the arm.

'Will you step this way with me, please, sir,' he said correctly.

'What for?' asked Srinivas.

The sergeant, middle-aged, leathery-faced, looked around. There were no witnesses. 'You're under arrest, sir. Start walking.'

'What for? Where to?'

'Wouldn't you like to know?'

'I have a right to know.'

'What would you like to know?'

'Where you're taking me.'

'To the station,' said the constable.

'On a picnic,' said the sergeant. 'We're going on a picnic, us and you.' When they were like this it would be bloody. Srinivas's nerves jumped. In the pointless, primitive way of nerves they connected what was happening to ancient, fifty-year-old scenes. Interrogations and beatings. One scene in particular, out of a series, of four men and a boy who would not answer questions. The four men in khaki with him, who were being matey. They joked with the boy. They joked among themselves as they beat him up, when he could no longer respond. When they were boisterously funny the beating was the worst. Cowering in adjoining cells they discovered this. Later experience confirmed the discovery, which they observed and filed away as an inexplicable fact. Because they were young, all of them under twenty, and innocent for their age, as the present violence-nurtured generation could never be, they did not know that brutality and laughter needed to keep close company, to preserve the sanity of the perpetrators.

Deliberately, Srinivas killed the memory. What relevance did it have to the present? That was India, an occupied country, a half-century ago, at a time of inflamed emotions. This was England, where such things did not happen. Because he felt tolerably robust about this Srinivas challenged the policemen.

'I've done absolutely nothing,' he said, 'I can assure you –'

'We saw, with our own eyes.'

'What could you see? I've been standing here –'

'We saw. With our own eyes. Didn't we, constable?'

'Yes, sergeant.'

In spite of himself Srinivas's heart began thumping: the spirit no help, worn out, poor bird, by this cynical assault.

'You're making it all up,' he said.

'Making it up?' The hand on his arm tightened, jerked him around and brought his eyes on a line with the sergeant's accusing finger, which pointed to the dangling man. 'See that? That's incitement to violence. Couldn't believe it was you, if we hadn't been watching. Could we, constable?'

'No, sergeant.'

'It's ridiculous,' cried Srinivas. 'No one will believe you. It says "Hang the blacks." How could I ever say that? Only a white man would.'

'Cunning bastard.' The sergeant eyed him, and his face was bland.

Srinivas began to freeze. They were twisting it, and they knew what they were doing, and they knew he knew they knew. His blood, which had been hot and angry, slowly ran cold. In this icy climate what he had clothed, out of a diminishing stock of remembered decencies, stepped out naked with clear, sharp outlines. What was happening was England. England, he said to himself, incredulous, but accepting. As it was now. Swept by a blight, the dreadful stains everywhere. You could see the blotches of corruption, eating into all that had once made it great, a greatness composed of tolerance and implicit freedoms which had simply been, a part of being – a part of *his* being which had been woven into consciousness and living without need for overt manifestos, and now was departing.

Leaving another climate, in which defences were advisable for survival.

'You're unlucky,' Srinivas said gently, and pointed in turn at the window behind which Mrs Fletcher's light burned, even more dimly now because of the half-drawn blind. 'You're unlucky, because there are two women there, two Englishwomen, who have been up all night with a dying man and have witnessed all that has happened, and who will be prepared to testify for me.'

The sergeant swivelled sharply, towards the window, then back to Srinivas, looked him straight in the eye and outstared him. 'I'm sorry, sir,' he said, 'I'm afraid we've made a mistake.'

Totally unruffled, he restored his helmet to its correct angle and prepared to move off. The younger man, however, shuffled his feet, and turned bright pink, recalling to Srinivas's mind another policeman, a fair young constable who had rebuked him for polluting the Thames, and turned this fiery colour when he saw it was a bereaved man he was unwittingly harassing. But he had blushed from innocence, not guilt.

Long ago, when people still felt shame, before the material here and there had begun to go shoddy.

When the two men had gone Srinivas remained where he was for quite some time. Standing on the pavement, his back against railings, as sitting on the pavement and lying down on it were also current cults, perhaps for not dissimilar reasons. The few passers-by, in big-city custom, paid him little attention. Presently the sun rose, quite bright for London at this time of year. In the strongish beams Srinivas studied the backs of his hands. They were stained, or at least outlines were visible, like watermarks.

Why had he lied about them to himself all these days?

As he had lied to the policemen, as they had lied about him, lying meshed thickly into living, a part of the quota of daily cunning accepted, like calories, as a requirement for day-to-day existence. Common man adapting to climate, no better now than gentlemen and judges.

Srinivas looked down again at his hands, the blotchy beginnings of disease, the penny-sized areas of decreased feeling, and felt unclean as if somehow they reflected the meannesses of the situation, which possibly they did. Then he thrust them out of sight, his old, cold hands deep into his pockets, and went into the house and up the stairs with as little touching of its timbers as could be managed, and sat alone in his room with a view of the dangling man for company, to compose himself for the forthcoming visit to Dr Radcliffe.

26

MR FLETCHER WAS BURIED, WRAPPED IN A SHROUD, encased in a coffin, embedded in the earth.

His widow went to his funeral riding in a shiny black Bentley. In another rode Mrs Pickering, with Srinivas beside her, wearing gloves on his hands. For Mrs Fletcher had insisted.

'After all you did,' she said, her pale eyes flickering, looking anywhere but at the woman she addressed, while invisible words scrambled around saying: after what *Fred* has done, so hectically that it brought the blood to her cheeks.

'I did very little,' said Mrs Pickering, with truth, but unable to deny the gesture, whatever it was, that this wan, courageous woman was making.

'I am a sick man,' said Srinivas, also with truth, though the full extent of it he could not reveal.

'A short service, it will not take long,' said Mrs Fletcher, limp but stubborn, and lied on an inspired note. 'Mr Fletcher would have wished it.'

Mr Fletcher's wishes, of course, had not been ascertainable for some considerable time and now never would be, but Fred Fletcher made his own view plain.

'If that bloody wog goes anywhere near my father's grave there'll be trouble,' he declared, banging the table and breaching the reverent membrane that hung, as frail as a caul at imminent birth, in this hushed house of the dead.

Mrs Fletcher did not deign to reply. She gazed at the drawn blinds and her lips tightened, but she suffered in silence. After the funeral, she promised herself, and made nebulous, daring resolutions that rocked her even as she sat.

Srinivas also postponed. He set up the interment in front of him like a deadline, before which there were certain things to do, and after which there would be certain actions to take. For the three-day respite thus gained he made up a meticulous timetable, plotting each hour and filling it so that it could lead to the next, and the next, and so reach, without undue severity, redemption date of the bond he had sealed with himself.

The third day went by. The date was advanced to the fourth and the fifth, then indefinitely. Keyed up to deeds, his hours carefully charted, Srinivas felt there was nothing with which to continue. He grew hollow, from want of substance with which to mould existence, while the inner surfaces of his body and mind were stretched and glazed with the tension of the situation, and what had been respite took on the aspects of nightmare.

Meanwhile Mr Fletcher also waited, all stiff and unknowing, on a trestle table rigged up in the crowded funeral parlour. They had embalmed him once, just enough to render him innocuous yet presentable; now they carried him to inner rooms and gutted him thoroughly, in the interests of hygiene in general and their own health in particular.

'Can't be too careful,' said the funeral director to his assistants, 'in this business. See what's happening?' He twitched at the sheet and uncovered Mr Fletcher's hapless middle, around which a furry girdle was sprouting. 'That's putrefaction. Damn and blast their bloody guts.' He meant the gravediggers, whose strike had brought the corpse to this plight, though the newer of his assistants, concluding falsely, thought the wording unseemly, but soon had his faith revived by his director's manner on the telephone.

'Oh, no, madam,' he was saying, as he had already said to several distracted bereaved, in tones which blended concern nicely with reassurance, in a voice pitched – but not so low as to render him incomprehensible – at that reverent level proper to this transit camp of the departed. 'Oh, no, there is no difficulty, our premises are more than adequate, and if I may say so, madam, you would find everything most tastefully arranged ... that is, if you would care to visit?'

Most would not, he knew; they ran from death, but dead bodies really had them bolting down the aisles. He banked on it, though for safety's sake he did set aside one smallish room, in which three coffined corpses were on show, capable of rapid substitution and disposed like wares in a Bond Street window, which effectively demolished any suspicion of congested counters within. Nicely done, he thought to himself; very nicely done indeed. Not for nothing were his premises crowded.

So Mrs Fletcher composed herself to wait, with a certain bleak cheer that, unlike some, she had at least got her husband as far as the undertaker's.

In the fifteen days before the gravediggers took up their spades again Srinivas's resolve wore thin. He did not know. He imagined it to be as sturdy as when he had conceived it. He drew gloves over his disfigured hands, and sat beside Mrs Pickering in the third black Bentley, the first two being full of Fletcher family. Discreetly, shapes behind curtains, the neighbours watched. Odd, was the consensus of opinion.

Not even her own family, Mrs Glass said darkly, let alone kith and kin; Mrs Fletcher could only be assumed to be not quite all there. This verdict her son thoroughly endorsed, adding several refinements of his own as he climbed, glowering, but impotent in the face of his mother's indomitable resolve, not to mention her possession of the roof over his head, into the car after his mother.

Srinivas was not aware. He sat remotely, and watched the familiar streets go by, and absently raised and smoothed the nap of the armrest which was suede, once some animal's hide, now dove-grey and lush under the yellow gloved tips of his fingers. The blinds at the window were drawn. He could not remember a car having blinds except –. Except in India, he thought; long ago, in his youth, he had seen motorcars with flowered curtains fluttering at the windows, in which Muslim ladies rode, ladies in purdah who were as total a mystery to him as those English memsahibs who festooned themselves in mosquito netting: throat, face, topi, all bundled into one large steamy globe. Yes, India. A far country, thought Srinivas, gently, to which he would not return. Gently, too, he felt the bottle in his pocket, filled with the white powder of tablets he had bought, and crushed, and carefully funnelled in. But he had no feeling about it: the bottle, the tablets, were only agents, he could not transfer to them the weight of his resolve.

No feeling then, nor even at the graveside, or for Mrs Fletcher, who he knew had been relieved of a burden. Others, though, were moved by him, Fletcher mourners who had not been infected by Fred's phobias felt sorry for the thin old man in his striking gloves and faded coat who looked, they said to each other in suitably subdued tones, so sad, worn out by the death of a neighbour and friend.

The looks, however, were false; the wear was not due to Mr Fletcher, whom Srinivas had scarcely known and would not miss, but was caused by the strain of unscheduled waiting. The long wait for a stranger's funeral, which had pared away not only his visible flesh but also the bones of his resolution, leaving a kind of wickerwork which his blindness imagined intact.

After the funeral, he had said to himself. It was after the funeral now. Up in the attic Srinivas waited for Mrs Pickering to return; she had gone to Mrs Fletcher's to partake of something – baked meats, he thought she had said, but could not be sure. He had been invited too, but had declined. Between the uncertainty of what baked meats were (he had his suspicions) and the certainty of Fred's animus, even the need to be close to Mrs Pickering ceased to be overriding. So, alone, he waited, and pale yellow sunshine flooded in and bred light on the polished surfaces on which it fell, of which there were not many, only the posts of the bed that were shiny from hands, the many hands that had touched and rested upon and wrestled with and finally lifted and shouldered the awkward structure across two continents, and the exposed oak beams of the sloping ceiling which had acquired the glossy patina of age. Eschewing passion (kindled, once, by the sleek dovetails of a structure he and his grandfather had raised, and deliberately killed after its desecration) yet both, house and bed, were dear to him. As such he had bequeathed them: the one to Mrs Pickering, by whom he knew it would continue to be cherished, the bed to his son Laxman, though here he entered an area of doubt.

Laxman. Srinivas shook his head, not over the shortcomings of his son, which it never occurred to him to include in any reckoning, but about the gulf that had opened. Inch by inch, territory had yielded: as years went by yard after yard with increasing speed were gobbled up, until the chasm appeared. Canyons, up whose rocky sides neither could clamber. Created by mighty forces, one would have thought, would one not? Questioning himself, Srinivas smiled faintly. Trivia was what these forces were composed of. Made up of manners, accents, the food one ate, the clothes upon one's back (for not all Laxman's invisible strictures had gone unremarked), the pathetic grains piling up to become a force. What granules, then, had gone into the shaping of his momentous resolution? Srinivas smiled, genuinely, faintly, once again, as he gave himself the answer. The colour of his skin, which had begotten the dangling man; and the configurations upon it which marked him out as diseased. These grains, so mighty, grew pathetic even as he named them.

So deep was his reverie that Srinivas did not hear Mrs Pickering come in, nor her footsteps upon the stairs, nor see her figure framed in the open doorway. She had to speak to rouse him.

'Oh, there you are,' she said, in some kind of relief.

'Yes.' His mouth was suddenly, terrifyingly dry, faced by the practicalities of the situation. Philosophy had vanished.

'I was worried.'

'Why?'

'You looked so strange.'

'No.'

Condemned to monosyllables, it seemed to him, when what he needed were strings on which to thread the meaning of his act. Because, somehow, one could not bring it out baldly. For one's own preservation it had to emerge comely, as Dr Radcliffe had done it, the announcement illuminated

like the miniature of an old manuscript, even if comely was
the last thing, in honesty, one could say about death.

'Perhaps I did,' he managed.

'Did what?'

'Look a little strange.'

'Yes. Funerals are apt to induce these feelings.'

At last he saw a way. 'It was my funeral,' he said, 'induced
them. I have decided to end my life.'

She studied him. Alarm, which had made her catch her
breath, was already almost under control.

'What for?' she asked, and removed her hand from her
breast, which had ceased to heave.

'It is time,' he replied.

'Who is to say?' she said. 'It is not for us.'

Her calm, the decency of her manner, leavened the horror
of the situation. As suddenly as he had been terrorized,
serenity returned to Srinivas. As, like a blessing, it had done
in the surgery, dispossessing the doctor, composing his
patient.

'It is time,' he said simply, 'when one is made to feel
unwanted, and liable, as a leper, to be ostracized further,
perhaps beyond the limit one can reasonably expect of
oneself.'

He rose, and drew her to the window, from where they
could view the dangling man – his outlines at any rate, since
council workmen had been sent to wipe the slate clean as
they were sent almost daily, an ineffectual routine reflected
in a certain perfunctoriness of performance.

'You see,' he said.

'A few barren men,' she replied, and stood thickly,
rebutting all that they represented, squalid policies to which
the decent and incorruptible qualities of her constitution

could clearly never be party. 'Is one to become a leper to oblige them?'

Then he did not know, became unsure as to whether it had been imagined to oblige; wavered and stared at his hands, which wore yellow gloves. Lemon-yellow. The shop had sold them, from old stock it had no ready sale for nowadays, and he had not objected. Though, as he now saw, they glared a bit: were, perhaps, too vivid for their purpose. As she, too, saw: had seen riding in the Bentley – indeed, had been unable to avoid – and had wondered, ascribing the donning of such gloves to some quirk, or a mistaken notion of appropriate apparel.

'To oblige, no,' he stammered. 'But, you see, it has happened.' And became calm, understanding that what was masked was real, whatever the chemistry of the change.

Under the gloves was disease. He took them off and showed her.

'The hospital has confirmed,' he said, 'Dr Radcliffe's suspicions, as well as my own knowledge which, I am ashamed to say, I have been fighting for some time.'

She remained standing. Lashed, it is true, by the same gales that had howled about his head, atavistic urges and old refrains that put bell and clapper on a man and sent him wandering. But standing. Her manner obdurate though wisps were flying, wild grey strands of hair escaped from coils and pins and pitching around in a frenzy. She tucked them back.

'It is curable,' she said.

'At my age?' he reminded. 'Are the means endurable, even if the end were not in some doubt?'

'Then what will you do?'

'I have told you.'

'That is the last,' she said flatly, 'of many solutions.' And she sat down to consider, the strength of her resolution forming like armour, some iron cladding of spiritual manufacture that would manifest to uphold her, right or wrong. Then he knew, in the middle of his own maelstrom understood better than he had ever done before why they made such good settlers: clung, where lesser mortals would have scuttled, and chipped and hammered away until whole landscapes altered, and original inhabitants turned into displaced persons.

'It is,' he ventured nevertheless, 'the only solution for me.' Wavering still, and conscious of draughts, and of holes enlarging in his decision, but aware all the while of a welding of their views.

'No,' she said again. 'That is not the solution.'

'What is?'

'Treatment,' she said, and would not meet his eyes. 'It is the only way.'

'I have already rejected it,' he said, with a bitterness born of disenchantment, having relied upon her strength but now, it seemed, to be driven back upon himself. As she had been. As all are in the end. A lesson which he at his age should have learned, only, Srinivas confessed to himself, there are these threadbare patches, these liquefying weaknesses of the soul.

'I have thought about it,' he amended, 'but being old, it is not easy, since there are not many years left, and one would not wish to eke them out in prophylactic isolation.'

'Ah, no,' she said, rejecting, rejecting with all her might, which though formidable might yet prove powerless. 'No. They would not condemn you to that.'

'Their concern would be for the community, as it is right it should be,' he said, gently, because she was upset, being unused to defeats of this nature, or subjugation, as he had been. 'It would not be fair to override their interests for the sake of one individual.'

'The community,' she said – fought on, and would continue to fight, he saw, long after he had given up, 'need not be affected. You could be isolated here as well as in wards and cells, which are enough to drive anyone, as you have been driven. I would care for you, I am trained. There could be no objection, and the community will not be at risk.'

'They will think they are.'

'The doctors can correct their beliefs.'

'Nevertheless. They will believe what they want to believe, and there will be trouble.'

'In which case nothing need be revealed,' said Mrs Pickering, 'there is no onus on anyone to bring a hornets' nest about their ears.'

'But the others,' he cried in despair, 'they will be endangered. Or think they are. The house is full.'

Of encumbrances. As it should not have been, as his instincts had known, but he had overborne them. Barnacles, which one supposed salved the hulk, but in fact anchored the man whose destiny was to rise free.

'There are the tenants,' he said again, bleakly.

'They will have to be given notice,' said Mrs Pickering briskly.

'What can one tell them? They will want to know why.'

'Nothing,' she rejoined, 'as nothing can be told. We are not compelled to give reasons.' She mused for a while. 'I foresee little difficulty,' she said, 'as all the lodgings are furnished.'

27

BECAUSE SHE WAS CAPABLE, HE LEFT IT TO HER.

As he was not. Incapable of cruelty, and shrinking from it, so that others must come. Walled in the attic he saw the dual turrets of their nationality rising: she who could harden at will, and inflict suffering in the name of need with little interior damage; and he, whose whole ethos being set against violence must allow others to do what was needed, or be destroyed by inner convulsions.

Getting that woman, the tenants muttered, as they met on landings, or passed him on the stairs, as perforce they had to in the course of living. Getting her to do his dirty work.

It is not like that, he answered, begged them silently for understanding. It is one's teaching, which does not breed toughness: the lacerations would go so deep as to rip one apart.

But they tossed their heads and went by. They knew what Indians were like. Sly. Wolves in sheep's clothing, no less. Look at him then, a prime example. Going around looking as if someone had kicked him in the teeth while he was busy kicking them out. And days went by, and their homelessness looming ate up charity.

'Driving about in Bentleys,' said Mrs Glass, summing up the foaming resentments. Also, because it rankled. Being left behind terylene curtains, while *he* was rated among the mourners.

'Why, has he got a car, then?' asked obtuse Mr Glass. He knew of whom she was thinking, possibly even better than she did, by certain strains that entered her voice, but he could not track all the twists of his wife's conversation.

'Has he –!' said Mrs Glass. She felt severely tried, but she rallied. 'No, of course he hasn't. Though he could have had, with all the rents he's been collecting all these years. Sitting pretty, he's been.'

'Then why's he giving them notice?'

'Who knows?' said Mrs Glass, and attacked vigorously on another front. 'It's a scandal, no less. Throwing them out like that. After all these years. It shouldn't be allowed.'

'An Englishman's home is his castle,' declared Mr Glass, somewhat mystifyingly.

'If he was English it would be,' said Mrs Glass, 'but he isn't, is he?'

Mr Glass felt there was some fault here, something that was not quite right about these statements, but as he could not immediately put his finger on it he remained silent, enabling his wife to resume.

'It's these people,' Mrs Glass said, and her lips kept turning inward – she had to stop now and then to blow them out again because she was not hard, no, she could not allow her mouth to give a false impression. 'These immigrants. They keep coming here, who asked them? One day they're poor, living off of the rates, the next they could buy us all up.'

'What should they do then?' inquired Mr Glass. Bent, she could see, on being tedious.

'Live ordinary,' his wife answered, after thinking. 'There is such a thing as a middle course, isn't there? No call to go flaunting themselves in Bentleys.'

'Who is?' asked Mr Glass.

So that they were back where they were.

Over at No. 6 it would not be, Mrs Glass felt in her bones, very much better. For Mrs Fletcher could not be trusted these days. Not since her son Fred. It had upset her judgement, that had, Mrs Glass considered: made her speak up for these people more often than was proper. So you couldn't be certain with her, which made one uncomfortable. No way of knowing, said Mrs Glass, aloud, and surprisingly, which way that cat will jump. But it would be exciting to find out. Better than nothing. Infinitely better than Mr Glass. A gleam entered Mrs Glass's eye, which was usually rather dull. She got up and put on her coat, which had a matching hat, driving hatpins into the velvet and through her somewhat sparse hair to stabilize it on her head. Then with a glance of hatred at the newspaper which shielded Mr Glass she left for No. 6.

Mrs Fletcher presided over the premises. She had done so in fact for quite some time, but with Mr Fletcher's going it was, as it were, official. She sat alone in her parlour, which she had not quite trained herself to call the lounge, and daily filled out, cheeks and calves, and the hidden areas around scapula and clavicle, all those hollows and depressions scooped out of her by her husband's long, speechless illness. She was not aware. She believed what the neighbours said to her. You look worn out, they told her, which was the correct thing to say, you couldn't after all tell a widow she looked well, it wouldn't be proper. But they saw the bloom and fill, and in a secret, obscure way, disapproved.

Not, of course, that much could happen. It was too late. Mrs Fletcher was not young. But the sag and droop were gone, and the bones jutted more softly, so that sometimes she stroked the base of her throat for the pleasure, and her forearms, throwing back her sleeves as she had ceased to do in her husband's presence, before he was stricken, for fear of inflaming him. The kind of inflammation that had bred Fred. She would not have wanted another like him. Sometimes her mind could leap over her son, describing a somewhat dizzy arc to alight on his children, whom she loved. Mostly, however, he stuck, a central and insurmountable factor of living, as her husband had been. But whereas Mr Fletcher had lain like a log, Fred loomed. She was ashamed of him.

Ashamed of her only son was what it amounted to. Nowadays she admitted it to herself, openly, and not only in the secret recesses of her being. Ashamed, ashamed of Fred, who bashed human beings, the refrain rang in her head. Often she wished he would go away: simply cease to be, like going back to Australia, for instance. Sometimes she even succeeded in imagining this state of bliss. The tranquility, the absence of stresses that were bending her mind, so that it could recover its correct tension, like her spine, whose ligaments had been stretched and wrenched with all that stooping and turning of the waterlogged body, which of late had resumed its natural pattern and no longer ached.

Ah, the relief of that, dear God, murmured Mrs Fletcher, and placed a hand on the small of her back. Her head began to nod, and she allowed it, sitting upright in her chair. These days she could, there was nothing to prevent her, no body to sponge, and turn over, regularly, on the hour. Mrs Fletcher dozed. The sunlight filtered through the curtains and fell on her warmly, and she dreamt of her grandchildren who were warm and sweet in her arms, only Fred forbade it, she felt he did it out of spite, or perhaps in case their grandmother infected them. But when he wasn't there she could entice them, she kept a jar of bull's-eyes on the mantelpiece, and rattled the sweets to make them come. She could hear them now, clicking against each other like pebbles. But she was shaking too hard, at this rate the pinstripe satiny surfaces would all be pitted. She stopped, and woke. It was only, after all, someone knocking.

Mrs Glass had knocked in a subdued way on the widow's door. Then more loudly. Deaf as an adder, or else they're rowing, she said to herself. By this time she was hammering quite strongly, the lion's head knocker going like a flail, so that she did not hear Mrs Fletcher at the door and all but fell in when it opened.

'I wondered if you'd heard,' she said lamely.

'Half the neighbourhood, I should say,' opined Mrs Fletcher. 'Come in.'

'Yes, well, I will.' Mrs Glass recovered her balance. 'Thank you. If you're sure I'm not intruding.'

'Quite sure. I was just thinking of making myself a cup of tea. Will you join me?'

'Just what I could do with,' said Mrs Glass, and meant it, perceiving in Mrs Fletcher's restored form more opposition than she had expected for certain assaults she intended to make. And would, moreover: she had not come this far only to turn tail. Mrs Glass bristled at the thought, and braced herself.

'Have you heard?' she asked in good time, when second cups of tea were steaming on the table.

'I have heard rumours,' said Mrs Fletcher, and stifled the name of Fred. 'I have not been out much myself.'

'They're true,' breathed Mrs Glass. 'They're being turned out, all of them. Been given notice to quit, no less.'

'Is that a fact?' said Mrs Fletcher, cool, but breathless.

'It is,' said Mrs Glass, and waited.

Mrs Fletcher said nothing. She studied the backs of her hands, as if, thought Mrs Glass, she had nothing to answer for. All that sticking up she had done, when it was best these people should be kept in their place. As she had tried to tell her, but some people cannot be told.

'Two families made homeless,' she said, and bobbed her head, up and down, up and down, to ram it in. 'For no good reason. None, that is, that has been given.'

'Given or not there must be,' said Mrs Fletcher, thinly, but managing.

'Who knows?' said Mrs Glass, and eyed her pious friend. 'All I can say is it's not Christian. But then he isn't, is he?'

'He is a good man,' said Mrs Fletcher.

'Funny way for a good man to behave,' said Mrs Glass.

'I expect he's got good reasons,' said Mrs Fletcher, her reedy voice picking up as it went along, 'what you and I know nothing about.'

'Maybe,' said Mrs Glass, and glittered formidably, above the fragile teacup and saucer she held balanced in her hands, 'but is it a decent one, or is it a case of getting them out so's to sell at a fat profit? Because that's what's going on, you know, up and down the country. Exploiting us, that's what they're doing.'

'Mr Srinivas isn't,' said Mrs Fletcher. Explicitly. And gripped the edges of her chair for strength, but moved her thighs until they concealed the whitened knuckles, so that Mrs Glass should not see.

Mrs Glass did not. She felt only the power which seemed to have welled into her friend's unlikely body, which sixth sense had warned her about when she came in. She preferred to put it differently. Pig-headed, she said to herself, and finished her tepid tea, and went away.

Mrs Fletcher saw her out, quite sweetly. She pulled her chair up and sat by the window and, at intervals, saw her friend's form zigzagging down the road as she went into this house and came out of that, the green feather on her hat nodding and dipping. Spreading tattle, said Mrs Fletcher, and decided to act as champion for Mr Srinivas, her neighbour, for whom she had no great love, other than what was enjoined, but there were certain things one did, whatever. Contemplating, her nerves began to twitch, as they did when Fred bawled, but she put up her hands to the base of her throat, which had been filled, and at length subdued the corybantic pulse.

Mrs Glass had no great hate either, for that matter. She did, she felt, what she had to, bearing in mind the issued warnings of leaders of opinions and moulders of men. Watch out, they said, for bloodshed, so Mrs Glass went out and about to make sure.

So the two ladies were pushed, one to champion, one to condemn, when what was wanted was something of a different order, to do with certain recognitions of human need and nature which at one time had been known in Ashcroft Avenue as live and let live. Days, and graces, which had gone or were passing, as everyone on all sides absolutely agreed.

Because his mother made his life such hell Fred often went to his home from home, which was the local.

He would have liked to live there, but as the licensing laws did not permit he did the next best thing. He planted himself on the threshold at opening time, and the landlord threw him out when it was time to pull down the shutters. It suited Fred. Not so much the exits, which he seldom remembered, but his entrances, which were vivid, and sweetness itself in his mind. He swelled when he entered. Airs and essences that a man needed, emptied from him by spiteful jabs from mother and wife, seeped back and rounded him out in the beery, breezy atmosphere. A man among men, he put it to himself, though what he felt more like was a king entering his kingdom.

Sometimes there were contenders. These were usually working men, who looked askance at the lounging Fred and asked him at what he laboured. But sometimes, happily, he could introduce subjects on which he was the undisputed expert. The blacks, for instance. Or persecution. Not of himself: that had begun to pall on his listeners, besides which there were some – he could hardly believe it – prepared to side with that bitch of a mother of his, and even put up with her philosophies. Fred ruminated, one thick wet lip thrust over the other, both elbows on the stained oak table, while he tried to gauge the temper of the evening. Because he had to get it right. Even one degree off, Fred knew, and he was liable to find himself strung up instead of the correct party. That was no fun, and fun was what one needed, what indeed one came here for, since his home and the country were no longer fit for Britons like himself. Fred peered through the soupy, homely atmosphere for signs of infiltration. No, no darkies, nor barrack room lawyers to steal his thunder. Only, he saw, his cronies, some natural, some made, contented faces bent over pints of beer he had ordered, it being his round, and he having been lucky with the horses. He plunged.

'You heard what that flipping spade's done,' he demanded, 'to that little old lady that's been living in his house?'

The landlord was behind the bar, polishing glasses. He leaned over the counter and said, crudely, 'What's he gone and done then: screwed her or something?' And laughed uproariously, just thinking of that old pair at it was enough to kill anyone.

Fred frowned. He liked laughter – he thought of himself as a robust, laughing man – but not when he had other things on his mind, or when it was aimed against him, as from certain ringing tones he suspected it might be.

'He's slinging her out,' he said, when everyone had subsided, and gone back to swilling his beer. 'Putting her out on the street. After all these years, and she not a day under seventy.'

Faces rose like moons over the rims of pint pots. Of Mike and Harry and Joe and Bill, and all of them were appalled, as Fred was pleased to see.

'Told her to go,' he capitalized. 'It's his house, see?'

They saw. It was inhuman. Only a monster could.

'Next thing,' said Fred, 'he'll be packing them in. His own kind, twenty to a room. They don't mind, like we would. You wait.'

'There should be a law,' said Joe, gloomily.

'Poor old soul,' said Harry.

'Who?' said the landlord, squeaking his cloth over the glasses.

'Number 5,' said Fred, not allowing names to pass, or sully, his lips, 'has chucked the old woman out.'

'No,' said the landlord, and hung the cloth over his shoulder.

'What?' said Fred, checked in full flight, and annoyed.

'Not her,' said the landlord. 'You must have it wrong. It's the tenants he wants out. *She's* been there since I can remember and that's going back some. He wouldn't do that to her.'

'Her as well,' Fred insisted. He felt a little dubious, but he wasn't going to be put off. Not when he had just got going on this important topic, which was what you could expect of the blacks if you let them. No. 5 for example. Ill-treating his tenants, and especially a helpless old woman. That, Fred felt in his very bones, really drove the thing home: he wasn't going to water it down for the sake of detail, or for any interfering sons of bitches. 'Her as well,' he repeated firmly. 'I heard it direct.'

'Bleeding shame,' said Joe.

'Wouldn't do that to a dog,' said Harry.

'Old lady, did you say?' asked Bill, and pictured a crabapple face, which for no reason at all reminded him of his grandma, whose face had resembled rather some whitish moon vegetable, whom they had put in an old people's home, so that he would have preferred to drop this line but it was too late. The others had fastened their teeth in it and were dragging.

'Not a day under seventy,' said Joe. 'Didn't you hear what Fred said?'

Fred blossomed. They had listened to him, they paid him attention. All his cells, muffled by presences – his house-owning mother, and his carp of a wife – threw off their cowls and rioted joyously. Fred rose up with them. He felt impassioned, and thumped the table until the beer ran.

'An old woman,' he cried. 'Could be your mother or mine. What harm has she done him? But she's out. Just like that. Not so much,' he said bitterly, 'as a roof over her head, which none of you here knows what it's like.'

As he did, from that time in the antipodes, and since then from fanciful descriptions his wife gave him after one of his quarrels with his mother, when they were all under threat of just this fate.

'An old woman,' Fred underlined, 'out on the pavement.'

'Like one of them slums in Calcutta,' said Harry, 'which they showed on telly. It was disgusting.'

'There's homes,' said the landlord, from the fringes of the conversation.

'No', said Mike violently, and his neck slowly thickened. 'No homes.'

'I'm not talking about Calcutta,' said the landlord.

'Who cares about fucking Calcutta?' said Fred, and grew frenzied. 'I'm talking about London. What goes on in it. It's disgusting. The way we're being pushed around. Whose country is it?'

'Up the Union Jack,' jeered the landlord, and flapped his teacloth in Fred's indignant face, though he could see which way the current was flowing. A pity, he thought, that bonehead, and came as near to loathing Fred as a man of his nature could, not only for the present but for the past which was full of incident, scuffles and breakages and the humping of stertorous bodies for which he would not be paid a brass farthing. But he saw the run of it, and ceased his flapping, and turned his back like a diplomat and began stacking away his glasses, keeping one fervent eye on the clock.

While the currents swirled, muddy, and rancorous, and full of disenchantment, with undercurrents whose pull those who were paddling did not judge, this being unfeasible from present stances, or predilections.

'It is a crime,' said Joe, dabbling a toe.

'Should be stopped,' said Bill. 'It's up to us, really.'

'Country's going to the dogs, like Calcutta,' said Harry. 'Then where'll we be?' he asked reasonably.

'Bloody swine,' said Mike violently, coming up suddenly out of his silence. 'Deport the whole bloody lot.'

Fred masterminded, and got to thinking, and thought of the leaders whose aims he was spreading, and that perhaps he, Fred, had missed his vocation, seeing the kind of support he could drum up in four hours flat. A good evening's work, he felt, and a satisfaction of some substance accompanied him on his way back to his paltry quarters and his wife. For now it was not only people like himself, and what this implied he knew from revelations during intermittent bouts of honesty, whose following he secretly scorned: it involved also solid, worthy citizens like Joe and Harry. Fred began to glow. He felt upright in this new company he kept, and his hands were like toast in his pockets as he weaved his way home. People shifted to give him room and Fred accepted, urbanely, his thickset figure moving within the rings of avoidance it created like a fitful, ill-coordinated ghost.

28

DAYS WERE SHORTENING.

His own, or the season's, Srinivas was not quite convinced, but developed a porous quality which allowed the absorption of both messages. His mind, free as he was not, drifted like a sponge: it picked up what they were saying, these people among whom his lot had been cast, even when he could not hear them, and it told him when the globe of sun hung directly over the battered gables of his house even when he could not see it. Though, of course, he did see auburn flares in the sky, and hear the occasional expletive flung up at him, and no doubt these were pointers.

Time is running out, said Srinivas, testing for sound, and it seemed to him that here and there along the line it did ring true. My days, he went on to experiment; my days under these rafters, my days beneath these skies; but now the sounds were clanging and jangling and he could not tell. So he rested, and folded his hands, which were encased in gloves of a sepia hue that matched his unalloyed skin, to please Mrs Pickering, whom the flagrant yellow had finally offended, and watched the speckled black creatures that had colonized a corner of his windowpane, clustering against the wood frame like a moulding of minute ornamental grapes.

Of the genus *coccinella,* his son Laxman had informed him. He must have been about eight or nine then, and already his eyes were slanted, looking askance at his two parents who belonged to a despised subcontinent. When he was ten Srinivas put him right about the sub, which Laxman had imagined meant below in degree. It made little difference. The boy preferred to believe the version of his English contemporaries.

Seshu, who was different, even at five, unlike his brother knew a whole host of English poems and songs which neither of his parents had taught him.

Ladybird, ladybird, fly away home
Your house is on fire, your children alone

he crooned to the little beetle, bearing it in delicately on its boat of leaf, and transporting his father, who still ached now and then, to his own boyhood in that same forsaken subcontinent. There were beetles there too, of course, universal like sparrows, or cats; but they were richer, brilliantly lacquered, and gilded, and chromed, whereas their cousins chose garnet, redeemed only by a few bright spots.

But charming. He must remember, Srinivas noted, to tell Mrs Pickering not to clean the window. She liked to do it for him, more perhaps than was necessary, to keep his view clear, though this was already extended beyond the simple frame and transparent glass and the thick ranks of aerials marshalled against the sky. Nevertheless he was grateful, for at certain times the rays of the sun came clear through the shining pane to fall orange and oblique on his flesh, and at others, if he stood upon a chair and squinted down before the light failed, he had an unimpeded view of people going about their business. How they went at it, these pale, determined people! Driven by cold, and whatever consumed them, whipped along the streets by sudden squalls and what burst in their brains. Did they stop to ask where? If so – if at all – it was done not in full view but privately, within four walls, between the twin turrets of their temples and in the roundhouse of skulls. From which they emerged to push on, their eyes swimming in the wind. And their breath coalesced. Ran to thought and unvoiced word. Hung in the air like icicles.

Something was building.

Slowly.

It had not reached him yet but it would. As Srinivas was aware, up in his eyrie. Meanwhile, as he must – as one must, as all do – he slept and he woke, and he ate the food that Mrs Pickering set before him between heated dishes, and the polar cold came in in bluish drifts and would have settled except that now and again he was moved to dispel them. Then he would rise, and run his tongue over his blistered lips, and chafe his wrists, and so coax in a little warmth to enable him to continue.

'It's this bally fire,' said Mrs Pickering, accusing the gas jets, which in fact functioned efficiently. 'I've always said there's nothing like an open fire.'

Which was true.

The truth also was that she was aware, more directly than he. For her nodding acquaintance with Mrs Fletcher had ripened. You could not, after all, lay out a body between you, with the hapless limbs flopping and gaping, without the ice cracking. Or so Mrs Fletcher felt, laboriously constructing a rickety structure to bridge the two houses and ascending it gingerly to beckon and welcome Mrs Pickering.

On this troubled day there was a welcome, but somewhat clouded over and hidden by the invitation she felt obliged to issue.

'Since you will soon be homeless,' she said dismally, offering her roof, which was already stretched and not, after all, made of elastic. But offering all the same, and chastening those infra voices within her that were raising healthy objections.

'What do you mean?' asked Mrs Pickering.

'When your notice expires,' said Mrs Fletcher. 'It is not easy to find a place. I would not like you to think you have nowhere to go.'

'What notice?' asked Mrs Pickering. Sharp as anything.

'To quit,' quavered Mrs Fletcher. Perhaps she had got it wrong, she thought, as she often did.

'You must be out of your mind,' said Mrs Pickering crisply. Her hair was flying. Wiry strands leapt, out of control, from the teeth of her tortoiseshell combs. If Mrs Fletcher had not been made to feel so stupid she would have been quite afraid.

'It's Fred,' she mumbled, 'what he's been saying. I should have known better, but you don't, do you? When it's your son. I mean if you can't trust your own flesh and blood. But I wouldn't let *her* blame Mr Srinivas,' she said, picking out what was solid, and even seemed to shine a little beneath the grime, from the morass in which she was floundering. 'I told her he must have good reasons, being a good man, for whatever he's doing. Though what these are,' she gasped, being on the verge of infringement, 'one simply has no notion.'

'None,' said Mrs Pickering. She seemed to be glittering, even worse than Mrs Glass, thought Mrs Fletcher, who was fast becoming an expert in these matters. She shrank back from those spiky, dangerous sparks that appeared to be emanating, which would burn holes in her skin if they fell, she knew.

'Fred is no good,' she confessed.

'What has he been saying?'

'That you are to be thrown out,' said Mrs Fletcher, and snivelled a little, at least in part for her friend.

'It is a lie,' said Mrs Pickering composedly. 'If you can,' she said to the collapsed woman, 'out of charity it ought to be nailed for what it is.'

Mrs Fletcher agreed. Only, she lacked the power, but resolved to trust to prayer to make good the deficiency.

'The lie is spreading,' Mrs Pickering told Srinivas.

'Which one?' he asked. One way or another there had been quite a few.

'That I'm to be thrown on the mercy of the parish.'

'To the wolves, that implies,' he said, and laughed, but the joke miscarried, took on disagreeable life in the room as he spoke. For both, in varying extent, had heard some prowling, though Mrs Pickering would continue to discount her sentience until forced.

'It ought to be nailed,' she said, 'for the lie that it is.'

'What does it matter?' he said. 'If one does not stick, they will find another.'

For ingenuity grew rife, before a lynching, it being vital to crush the rearing conscience with a weight of rhyme and reason.

'Nevertheless it ought to be,' she repeated stubbornly.

Srinivas agreed; only, like Mrs Fletcher, he suspected that they might not possess the necessary power. Possibly Mrs Pickering felt so too, although he detected no sign, only some tattered signals of strength in the cast of her chin, which jutted, and a certain squaring of the load-bearing shoulders.

'It would not be easy,' he dared to suggest.

'There should be a law, to help,' she rejoined.

Then he perceived that she too was running: running to law, as Mrs Fletcher did to prayer, from a feared or acknowledged inadequacy.

Running man, it seemed, had acquired a running mate.

It dislocated him. He put out a hand, since he could not speak, for his mouth was wracked by pity, the slack lips baulked at every attempt; and presently felt it taken. So they remained, while amber light filled the room, and it seemed to him that they flowed together as young people do, in a commingling and creation of strengths of which neither, singly, was capable. For now other currents were being generated, strange ones that passed from her clasp and galvanized even his gloveful of bones. Then he grew bold, and felt that whatever was building could be dismantled, and looking for confirmation found it in certain laminations of her eyes, which were bluish, and tempered with the qualities which were needed to carry one on. Life is still sweet, he said, to himself, to her, and his mind stretched itself and stepping delicately, tender gazelle, went forward into the spring and he thought it would be pleasing, after all, to see the ladybirds clustered on his windowpane spreading their wings and testing for flight, and flying away to safety.

29

MRS PICKERING HELD HER NAILING CEREMONY, WHICH took the form of a meeting with the tenants, and achieved nothing.

They listened to her politely – the ingredients for uproar were missing from that austere room – though they felt she had a nerve, considering. For it was they who were being thrown out, not she: they who were the losers in this terrible fight for a dwelling place. What did they care if stories were going around about the old woman being thrown out too? They had not said it, it was not up to them to correct what others said. Their concern was for themselves. What about us, what about *me,* the lonely faces asked, each walled up in its own suffering. Surveying that rebellious, anguished sea, Mrs Pickering began to doubt her action, and even herself, until a young woman rose, and said, bluntly, above the noisy gurgling of the baby in her arms, as blunt as the instrument with which ideals must be clobbered, 'I have to look after me and mine. If I didn't, they'd go to the wall. So I do, and I don't care what happens to the others. I wish I could, but I can't. Do you understand?'

'I do,' said Mrs Pickering, who turning the matter over, did indeed perceive that it was the mood of the country, in which all of them were implicated, she no less than the others.

'If one could only reach the people and tell them the truth,' she said, nevertheless, to Srinivas, 'it would make all the difference.'

'People believe what they want to,' he replied.

'If there were some method of broadcasting,' she said.

But the only broadcasts were about bloodbaths.

Which did not help.

Mrs Pickering, undaunted, joined forces with Mrs Fletcher, whose efforts though earnest tended to be spasmodic, and the stalwart landlord at the local, and those few who were prepared to stand up and be counted. But their voices came thinly, and were hardly to be heard against the chorus that swelled from the community, led by the furious top notes of Fred.

'Bloody bastard,' he said, in his best English, of Srinivas, and sometimes, when Mrs Pickering was nowhere within range, for he was quite afraid of certain incendiary qualities to the woman, he liked to add, because of the gratifying effects it produced, 'Poor Mrs Pickering. Fancy doing that to a homeless little old lady like her!'

'That young couple too, got a baby and all,' said Joe.

'Yes,' said Fred.

'And the family with the four kids,' said Harry.

'Yes,' said Fred.

'Not forgetting the feller in the basement,' said the landlord.

'Yes, poor sod,' said Fred again, and only remembered afterwards that the feller was black, and felt aggrievedly that he had been trapped into ignoble sentiments.

But nowadays, as he could afford to, he quickly forgot such aggravations. For he was riding high, the breath of success sweet in his nostrils. The currents that bore him aloft, their nature and composition, remained obscure; once or twice he did wonder, but the process so jarred him that he eschewed the exercise as unfit for plain, forthright men like himself. The plain man was pleased with what was plain: the drop in the number of his detractors. They had dwindled, Fred noted, or had fallen silent, while his company multiplied. Stretched out as luxuriously as could be managed on the lumpy mattress for which his mother expected him to be grateful, he felt with some justification that his working days were over. No longer did he have to tout around for good men to fight the good fight: they offered themselves, body and brawn, to him. People who had once shunned him stopped to listen when he spoke, or even came expressly for that purpose. For Fred, once reviled, had become respectable. He had acquired a status within the community which it had hitherto denied him. Fred breathed deeply, and pressed on with his company.

The company was motley. As Mrs Pickering observed in the course of her tireless peregrinations up and down the district, conducting her lonely campaign. In its shuffling ranks she saw, with the eye of her experience, and some intuitions not to be distrusted, the lineaments of the deprived, the disaffected, the hopeless, the haters, the ambitious, of exploiters and the exploited, cruel scorings upon faces which, later, would rise like welts upon the skin and call for whipping boys and reparations.

Some came from the high-rise flats, whose foundation stones she had watched being lowered from the jibs of towering cranes, seeking an outlet for the unnameable maladies that afflicted them; some from the tenement blocks on the fringes of the district where boundaries met, and boroughs were as skilled as single citizens in shifting the burden of civic responsibility. Some came sober, their faces and overcoats buttoned up so that you would not have known, until they revealed their hands, which held those lethal black balls which, when the time came, they would cast. Until such time they stood, half furtive, half bold, shoulder to shoulder with those who came done up in leather, brittle and crackling with hatred.

Sometimes she was afraid of those glistening skins, as people can be of buckles or belts, or boots, or black shirts, or silver knobs upon malacca canes, symbols from which auras arise long after time has quenched their power. So she shivered now and then, but sometimes, too, she was wrung by the anger and the hunger on those faces, which could, she suspected, as easily swing towards compassion, be lit by fires more generous than those which now consumed them.

Then, weakened, she would sit down on a bench to recoup her energies and to reflect, spreading a newspaper if one were handy, or wiping away the rime and frost that beaded the slats. At these times, if she were left long enough, she could pretend, return to the leafy avenue that Ashcroft Avenue had indeed once been, and believe all was as before. Often, however, a passing policeman, nervous for no reason except, perhaps, through absorption of the atmosphere, would ask her to move on. Once, outraged, she attempted a challenge, in terms which Fred had frequent and touching recourse to in conducting his vendetta.

'Why should I? It's a free country,' she said.

'Being a focus of trouble, so to speak, madam,' the officer replied.

Mrs Pickering felt dazed. A curious state of unreality enveloped her, akin to what Srinivas had been swamped by at his confrontation, as if the world was bent, so that those who walked straight were led to wonder if it was not they, after all, who walked crooked.

She, the focus of trouble.

What, then, were these others, summoned and fomented by Fred, who gathered in muttering groups and exchanged views about the colour of oppression? She rose, however, and moved on, from some failure of that incandescence that fuelled her energies, or perhaps from a respect for the blue uniform which remained a beacon, even if its elements glowed less brightly, and now and then gave off questionable whiffs.

So the edifice, which in overflowing moments they had imagined might be dismantled, grew. As it grew it consumed, whittling away at the solid structure of the old house which had weathered two wars and supported five generations but now began to assume the properties of a shell. Its form endured, and even provided some scraps of cover, but the substance grew tenuous, and textures that had once been thick and meshed developed fretted qualities whose openwork a finger, one felt, could poke through.

'The place needs attention,' said Mrs Pickering, rubbing a toe over the creamy bubbles of rot that lined the wainscot.

'Yes,' agreed Srinivas.

He could not, however, put his mind to it. His mind was on other things; it considered illusions, of men and the castles they built, himself in particular, and the houses on two continents in which he had lodged, which each when the time was ripe had repudiated the contracts of security to which it had not in the first place been signatory. Yet one persisted. How one persisted! He sighed, and looked about him at the attic, which had once presented aspects of solidity. Its walls were fragile now, reduced by the general paring away that was taking place. Was it really here, he asked himself, that he had sought and found refuge? He pondered, and was lost in wonder that these rafters and laths, which were so patently made of paper, could ever have seemed to promise him more than the flimsiest physical shelter.

'I will get an estimate,' Mrs Pickering proposed. For she could see she would get no help from this dreamy man, who like the rest of his people gave up the ghost when there were practical things crying out to be done. She went at them herself, taking down lino that curled up at the corners, and stopping up cracks that appeared in the framework of, these days, the much-slammed doors. Soon, however, a modicum of shame disrupted the complacent vigour of her labours: not because of her strictures upon an old sick man, but that she should join those spiteful endeavours that sought to slap down a general pattern of shortcomings on races or nations. So she subdued her efforts, banging and hammering less to show him and more to achieve her purpose, the spirit of her indomitable person reluctantly bowing to acknowledgements that a proper humility must be born again and again out of repeated submissions and humiliations.

30

AS THE SEASON ADVANCED SRINIVAS BEGAN COUNTING the days, towards release or dissolution he was not quite sure, but allowed the flavours of what was to come to wash over him. Sometimes, to his surprise, they were extraordinarily tender, tinged with rosy delicate hues, redolent of roses, as if the wafery walls to which his world had shrunk had developed subtle, petalled linings. These he placed, accurately enough, if wistfully, as the combined product of a sedulous mind and the substances circulating in his blood. Sometimes, however, they were sharp, like singed flesh, or the cyanide odour of bitter almonds. The source of these flavours he could not define, having temporarily lost the faculty, or perhaps unable to believe the monstrous nature of the emanations that rasped against his membranes, though occasionally it did occur to him to consider if, indeed, it was intended for him to enter the reeking cubicles of self-destruction.

'It will be easier when it is over,' said Mrs Pickering, breathless from climbing the stairs, of which nowadays there were altogether too many, although in her time, which had not been all that long ago, she had taken them in her stride. 'It's the waiting that gets on one's nerves,' she said, avoiding his eye, which might disclose other causes and consequences.

'Yes,' said Srinivas, and stroked his arms which were peppered, full of the needles that pumped mercury into his system. Or so Dr Radcliffe had told him, in those simple terms which he had learned from his patient were best, preferable in his interest, if not in one's own, to retreats behind comfortable shrubberies, glossy evergreens of superiority and dog Latin. Mercury. Quicksilver in the blood which, Srinivas assured himself, made him sluggish: heavy eyes, heavy lids that would not lift to confront Mrs Pickering.

Sometimes the two of them were full of avoidances.

'It doesn't help, being cooped up,' suggested Mrs Pickering.

'Are there alternatives?' he wanted to know, for snow was falling, handfuls of flakes flung thickly against the windowpane; and saw from the set of her shoulders that she considered there might well be.

'Not in *this* weather,' she said, furiously. 'But it doesn't *always* snow, does it? We do have good days?'

Shouting, although that great white whale of cold which pressed down and muffled made it unnecessary.

To oblige her, but dubiously, Srinivas began, when the weather was less foul, to go out again. Over and above, that is, his regular visits to clinic and hospital, which he had thought sufficient, but which she dismissed.

'Like going to a factory farm,' she said, sweeping these drawn-out and denigratory processes into appropriate bins. 'Where they put one's soul into deep-freeze,' she amplified, out of a vocabulary and territory which had been extended and were not strictly her own. For from cohabiting certain qualities had rubbed off onto her, she was unafraid of thoughts, and their expression, like soul and spirit, from which Christians like the Glasses, for instance, sped like rockets.

So Srinivas ventured out again. Not by day, for fear of contaminating his peers, which he did not wish to do, but at daybreak when their claims on the city, prior to the daily renewal, were only tenuously staked, or at night when the streets were empty, a macadam landscape strangely interloping under the violet, snowbound dome of sky.

He seldom went far, for fear. He kept close to that shell, his house, into which he could bolt, he assumed, and vague images did spring to his mind, less of an ascending drawbridge that would protect him from the natives than that of some opaque, impregnated sheet hung from the sky that would spare them a sight of his ravaging presence.

'You are becoming altogether too sensitive,' said Dr Radcliffe reprovingly. He decided to blame it on race. 'Over-sensitive, like the rest of your people,' he said.

'Does that surprise you?' asked Srinivas, composed like an emaciated Buddha in the doctor's study. 'One's responses are influenced by one's fellow men. To some extent. It is shameful, but not, would you not agree, altogether avoidable?' and he made a basket of his fingers, which were naked in front of the doctor, who was disciplined not to mind, and also unavoidably unpleasing.

Dr Radcliffe, being honest, did not argue. His own responses, he suspected, were forged by those of his wife. Into impermeable obstinacies that insisted on bringing this patient home, or at least to that part of it – his study, which he also used as his surgery – to which she would not lay claim, even if the rest of the house stood in her name. For Marjorie objected to the old man's presence – diseased, she suspected, or anyhow unsavoury, not knowing but imagining the worst, and her skin creeping, or as close to this phenomenon as she could manage, skin and the silvery hairs upon it undulating, like a crawling caterpillar.

She disinfected the hall with a spray after he had gone. However late it was, and it usually was late at night.

'You can't tell with these people,' she said. 'They don't look too clean to me.'

'If you can't tell,' said her husband, 'why do you?' Fire on ice. Or something equally uncalled for, thought Marjorie, and would not stoop to reply.

To Srinivas it seemed warmth, charged particles that streamed from the man and lit fires here and there, where they were needed, within the chilled lacunae of his bones.

'Do you think,' he said, from the depths of the armchair into which he had been urged, whose coarse slub closed round and consoled his angular form, 'that it was intended we should meet?'

'No,' said Dr Radcliffe bluffly, from an opposition that sprang instantly armed against any such notion. And grew still, reflecting. Planes of his mind opening and revolving, a shimmering mobile. For it seemed as if there might be some glimmering of a plan, from the way in which each met a need in the other, muting the despairing wolf that howled in each breast.

'Would you deny me?' asked Srinivas, an utterance that seemed to form and rise, encouraged, from the glow in the room.

'No,' said Dr Radcliffe straightly, not bothering with pretences as to what was meant.

By sequestering himself in his room, and seeking and keeping to selected places, and living within the robust circle of Mrs

Pickering's presence, Srinivas sought to spare his hide. Or so, in those derisive moods which from time to time afflicted him, he liked to put it to himself. But the wily picadors stalked him, discovered his habits and vulnerable spots, and came within.

One morning, at daybreak, when Srinivas returned from his walk there was filth on the doorstep.

He felt ill. He leaned against the railing, and nausea came at him in waves. When it had ebbed – quite soon, quelled by the overpowering need for action – he went in, collected a pail, newspapers, rags, a bottle of disinfectant, and letting himself out as quietly as possible, stripped off his gloves and cleared the mess. Then he washed and scrubbed himself, restored bottle and pail to their place in the cleaning cupboard, and went up to the attic.

Sitting on his bed, he began to tremble, more forcibly now from a lifting of restraints he had imposed, without which he could not have functioned. And yet, he said, it is nothing, and splayed his hands wide in witness. A Brahmin's hands, which in their time had not baulked, which had washed and laid out a decomposed corpse and thought nothing of it. Were they now, at the behest of other men, to be considered defiled, returning to terms he had long repudiated?

But still.

Excrement.

It is nothing, he repeated to himself, shivering from weakness, his hands hanging. Nothing, he repeated, and beads of sweat forced themselves up from the pores of his skin and hung there, shamefully, bright globules that the white icy atmosphere could not absorb.

Mrs Pickering noticed the ghost of a smell, which lingered in greenish wraiths around the portals despite all the weather could do. It did not really register until the second or third time, and then she saw someone had been at the bottle.

'What have you been doing?' she asked him, her nostrils pungent with pine essence, with which he had been liberal that morning.

'A little cleaning,' he answered. 'The doorstep was dirty.'

She did not probe, having reasons. Fears, as great as his own, of discovery, which from mutual nakedness might involve both in ruinous disintegration. As a woman may withstand rape, but not before the eyes of her children.

For, from avoidances, they had moved on to hiding things from each other.

Twice a day, at breakfast time which was a movable feast, and again at two in the afternoon, Mrs Pickering intercepted the post. At these times she could invariably be seen hovering near the front door, in the checked apron she had purposely bought, with the big patch pockets into which she could whisk, an instant after they had landed on the doormat, or as quickly thereafter as her creaking framework would allow, missives their fellow citizens were sending. Some for Srinivas, some for her: the favours evenly given, and nearly all obscene, with an obscenity not to be gauged from the neat English writing. The neater the writing, she learned, the worse the contents: the more innocent the envelope, the more vicious the enclosure, outdoing those that were more explicit and came black-edged, like mourning cards. Learning, learning: the span of life too short, she felt, to take in all. Continuing, nevertheless. Coming upon depths, in herself, and in others, depths, cavities, capacities, realizing that the whole spectrum was open but saying, each time, bewildered, who would have thought? While conceptions dissolved in the chemicals of blood speeches, took on gross forms, and were admitted as decencies in the marketplace.

Ah, yes, the days of the Roman carnival were not over. Whatever one might think. Mrs Pickering often thought, her pockets bulging with letters which later, watching her opportunity, she would put on the boiler.

'The postman often comes, these days,' observed Srinivas.

'Yes,' said Mrs Pickering.

And pine essence rose, hung like a green curtain between them, accusing.

Sometimes, it seemed, nothing could quite purge the stench.

'Shit on the doorstep,' Fred told the company.

'Who said?' asked the landlord, looking around the public house, and wishing he could choose his company.

'I'm telling you,' said Fred. He wished he could liquidate this geezer, whose voice buzzed about him like a wasp. He turned his back on the bar.

'They'd do anything,' he said, continuing the lesson in enlightenment. 'That's these black buggers in an eggshell.'

'Nutshell,' said Joe, scratching his head, from which flaky scurf drifted down and floated like rafts in puddles of slopped beer.

'Nutshell, then,' said Fred. 'They'd do anything, they would.'

The landlord came around. 'He's got no reason to,' he said, to Fred's face, which was ruddy with ripe emotions.

'Stop at nothing,' said Fred, facing him, as he had to.

'Fouling his own house, don't be so stupid, you must be barmy,' said the landlord.

'To get the tenants out,' said Fred, doggedly, but beginning to perspire.

'They're going anyway.'

'To speed them up.'

'No need to. Only a few weeks to go.'

'Who cares blasted why,' cried Fred, tried beyond endurance. 'I seen what I seen. Shit on the bloody doorstep, and it's him what's responsible.'

'Dirty sewer,' said Joe the spotless.

'Immigrants,' said Mike. 'Filthy mob, bringing their filthy habits with them.'

'Ought to learn them a lesson or two,' said Joe, 'hygiene and that.'

'Ought to be kicked out,' said Fred. 'Who invited them here?'

'You be careful what you're saying,' said the landlord, congested about the face from some convictions of equity which, he felt, this clown was assaulting. 'Just you watch it, or they'll have you for incitement to violence and not before time.'

'What, me, for speaking my mind, in my own country?' cried Fred, striking his chest as if bronze notes might ring forth from these breastplates in defence of free speech, if not the homeland itself.

'Yes, you,' said the landlord, a lip bulged with loathing. Fred felt damped, but he cast around and came up triumphant.

'That would be discrimination,' he said, and swaggered a little from uncertainty. 'Yes, that's what it would be. Discrimination against the whites, which is an offence in the eyes of the law.'

For, from assiduous study of trendsetters in these matters, Fred was becoming fluent in certain arts, notably that of the involution of the meanings of words and phrases.

One day it was not dirt laid against his door but a small grey mouse.

As if I were guilty of murder and this my punishment, said Srinivas, for it pierced him, and he picked up the tiny creature which lay stiff and quiet on a quilt of snow, having been done to death. Placed on his hand it covered the palm, the gloved palm from which a feeble warmth exuded, which one would not have guessed from the chill it enclosed, but ice crystals that pointed the fur were melting, there were droplets in the cupped leather. We shall both be sodden, you and I, he said in the hush of snow, to the silenced creature, quite forgetting that skin and pelt whether alive or dead are impervious. Proofed against water, dust, dirt and grime, the entire detritus of existence from which, allowed to preen, which is its power by right, it will emerge shining. Until split from within by gases, or the acids of thought, or the massed unconscious, or broken, crushed as this one had been.

There was blood where heel had ground into skull, a rusty arc of half-moon, incomplete for lack of space on the grey nap. He felt it, gently, with a finger: those indents upon the bone, or was it upon himself, a man, all men. A shallow depression in the cranium. Concealing it with his hand, as some deeds must be for self-preservation, he began to sway. Standing on the doorstep, in the snow, face gone to bone and his hands aping some makeshift casket, Srinivas rocked, and was seen by a passing neighbour whose memory stretched, reminding her of the long-gone Indian woman who had also teetered, mauve tints under her skin, clutching an unopened letter, in full view of the world. But she did not feel inclined now, as she had then. One of them, got no right to be here, got no backbone either, from the look of things, she said to herself and went by, aiming her contempt at a point between his shoulder blades as she passed, to avoid the two pairs of eyes meeting.

Srinivas felt the glancing blow, a stroke upon the sensitive tympan he carried within him, which the times had brought into being. He heard footsteps crunching away through the slush which sun had created out of snow on the pavement. Soon there were others, more and more of them, reminding him of where he stood. Fumbling for his key, made awkward by the glove and numbed fingers, he let himself in and went up to the attic.

It was morning, full blown by now, an hour at which he did not allow himself out. The sun, watery but revealing, was high on the horizon. Too late for disposal, he excused himself, looking down at his burden, the minute corpse that continued to weigh him down. Then the sun, the sin of being abroad under it, no longer seemed to matter, and picking up a box of matches from the mantelpiece he went down the stairs.

At the last bend in the flight he encountered the blunt young woman with the baby. She would have bumped past him, having angled her basket of shopping for that purpose, but she saw the dangling tail and stopped.

'What have you got there?' she asked, sharp with suspicion, having heard the rumours that were circulating.

'A dead mouse,' he told her.

'What are you going to do with it?' she cried. Backing, and squeaking, this sensible woman with her basket, as if he might pop it down the front of her blouse.

'I shall burn it,' he answered her, gently. 'It seems the best thing to do.'

'Why not chuck it in the dustbin?' Like decent ordinary people would.

'It would smell.'

'Yes,' she said. 'Of course. How stupid of me.' Flustered but mollified, and making amends, flattening herself against the wall to give him unimpeded passage, and holding the basket she had intended to jab his ribs with safely over his head.

So he passed, stooping, under the creaking wickerwork, and along the corridor into the garden, at the far end of which the incinerator stood. It seemed very large and uncaring, by comparison: blackened and empty, its two-inch grid coated with ash and ice, its open maw waiting.

He felt it would not do.

Nearby was flat ground. He fetched a shovel and cleared a circle. The snow, turned by the shovelling metal, revealed yellowish tones, an underbelly stained by hues that seeped up from the earth. The ground was black and hard, and entirely suitable. On this, carefully, he prepared a bed – a bier, a pyre – of crumpled paper and criss-cross twigs built up to receive and embower, and consume, the body.

Windows along the avenue overlooking back gardens began to be occupied. Faces appeared squarely at panes, wondering what he was up to. They stared at the fire he had kindled, which was small, and rather dull, a damp affair of smoke and smouldering twigs rather than a hearty blaze, and said it was a fire hazard, which was the best indictment, under the circumstances. Until Mrs Glass hit upon something.

'Some kind of rite, like,' she said.

'Don't be so bloody daft,' said her husband.

'He put a toad on it. Or something similar. I saw him. Explain *that* away,' said Mrs Glass. Her spectacles were glinting.

Her husband hunched his shoulders, and himself into them. He had a way, as if he could bear no more, which Mrs Glass found insufferable. She continued to suffer, however, rather than cut short her viewing, although in fact Srinivas had almost finished, except for sprinkling the ashes, and then he was done.

That evening when Mrs Pickering brought up his supper Srinivas told her.

'Yes,' she said, absently, removing the covers and eyeing the risotto, whose texture was soggy instead of grainy, due, she felt, to the butter congealing on the journey up three flights.

'It was dead,' he said.

'Yes,' she said again. Those stairs. Took it out of one. She would be glad, she knew, when it was over, an end to all this carting and climbing and they could settle down as people of their age were meant to, the two of them established on the one level. That, she thought with a glimmer of a smile, would make a refreshing change, and she eased herself into a chair, so taken up with this delirious future that she quite forgot her knees, which creaked.

But he whisked it away from her.

'It was killed,' he said. 'It had been killed and left. I am of course, in a way, responsible for its death.' Owlish, she thought, his eyes enlarged and luminous in his head, and solemn.

'Well,' she said, shortly, from being severed, 'it was only a mouse.'

'Yes,' he said, stiffly. Sitting stiffly beside this stranger, who could think this, her horizons being bounded, the boundaries those of a narrow white ethos which, unable to assimilate the totality of creation, or perhaps finding it inexpedient, introduced puerility in its own image. In the shape of grids which it laid upon natural patterns. Yes, he said to himself, a grid. Straight lines which divided, severe compartments designed for infant comprehension, attaining a sterile lucidity that eliminated confusions in the mind. So then there were areas for compassion, and for indifference, of conservation, and expendability, of animals to cherish and experimental animals, and (extending the same line, after all, an imaginary line drawn straight through the cerebrum) white men and other men, the degree of concern for each being regulated by the grid.

Committing blasphemy first, the first crime, by claiming men to be made in the image of God, to whom were all actions, and acting accordingly, to justify all.

And the loss, he thought, it involved: so great, so terrible. Shall I, he asked himself, tell her? That a mouse has entitlements no less than a man? He abandoned the idea. Mrs Pickering would not run barefoot down corridors, she was not built for that. It would come out in other ways: in those freezing crystals about the eyes, and an untouchability, all ball and spikes like a threatened hedgehog, which he felt he could not endure. Not now, at this moment in time, which was fraught for him.

'Wanton killing,' he said nevertheless, to get it straight, as some things must be got.

'Pretend,' she said. 'Just pretend it was in someone's larder and killing it was a necessary job.' For she was tired out. A mouse, she felt, when there were other matters. Really, some people, the way they tore themselves to pieces over nothing. And she began to clatter, dumping dishes and glasses on the tray, and the plate with the risotto which, she noted, had been only partially eaten, the remains not only wearing a glaze by now but buttressing the sides of the pottery. She would have to soak it, she saw, and the sooner the better.

But he could not let go. The burning thing was fused to his flesh, like napalm.

'I cannot,' he said, tripping over words which can both indicate the way and block it. 'I will not put my name ... I will not be cause for even one more to be laid at my door.'

She ceased to clatter. His distress stood out, a human monument on the plains of another's bafflement, which she could not ignore.

'What can one do?' she said gently. 'There is a limit.' Setting limits, which went against her nature, to ease him out of a situation, though she quaked from a fear, a superstitious dread that in the mysterious way of such processes she might be shredding her own strength.

But he, by now, was beyond her pull. He was being pushed, or led, or perhaps even struggling forward of his own volition, towards a confrontation. When he reached it he was alone, as he had surmised he might be, and from some vast distance wished it could have been otherwise, from the undoubted comfort to be drawn from her presence, but the vital nature of the engagement overpowered such considerations.

It's his decision, Mrs Pickering said to herself. I cannot stop him, even if I knew what he intended, which I don't. She waited, teasing the soft fringe of the napkin on the tray until she saw it was all in strands, its silky cohesion undone, and blaming him, became fretful, and was finally driven to ask.

'What is it?' she said.

'Deception,' he answered, showing his hands. 'Suppressing the truth was where it began. It must be revealed, which is quite simply done.'

'No,' she said, and began to be afraid. 'No. It won't help. There is, after all, only a little while to go. What can happen in that time,' she said bitterly, 'that has not happened already?'

'A lot,' he said, 'more than I can allow. More than I can bear.'

'It won't stop people,' she said, and drooped, her shoulders dragging her down as if weights hung from her hands.

'I must try,' he answered, and was gentle in his turn. 'I have, you see, no choice.'

She did not see. What she saw was reefs, manufactured oyster beds over which, for unfathomable reasons, people hauled their protesting bodies. But at least she knew, she told herself, as she watched him stripping off his gloves. She knew, and extracted one or two drops of cheer from the fact, to what unnecessary act of folly he was committed, and could at least prepare to parry the blows that must fall in consequence.

31

THE WOMAN WHO SQUEAKED AND BACKED WAS
stricken. Motionless, speechless. Turned into a pillar of salt,
she felt: a salt madonna, clutching a salt infant in one hand
and hanging on to the oak newel-post with the other.

'There is no cause for alarm,' said Srinivas kindly. 'I can
assure you, I have been assured, it is by no means an instantly
communicable disease.'

'Yes,' she said. He, after all, had rehearsed his speech
while she, except for this sole syllable, had lost both words
and will.

'That is the reason, and no other,' he went on. 'It is right
you should know, and wrong that I should have concealed it.
Whatever else has been said, that is the truth, to which you
were entitled from the beginning. Only,' he said, and began
to jangle, the supple lines on which he had strung his phrases
tangled and jerking. 'Only, you see, it is not so easy, not an
easy thing at all, one's human quality, being what it is, does
not allow ...'

'No,' she said. She could not take her eyes from his hands.
Her eyelids were hoods which, he saw, were determined
never to lift for him, resentful hoods over blanched cheeks
which, he knew, could come alive, be flushed and full with
the delight of living, in the right company. What she saw
was the monstrous intrusion from a far country into a
wholesome climate: something hideous and medieval that

she had not known existed and did not want to know about, except insofar as it had rooted itself in front of her and could not be avoided. So they stood, desperately, a despair of dissimilar origins binding them, until she found release.

'What did you want to come here for?' she asked him bluntly. Bluntness was her weapon, as me and mine were her strength.

Then she was running from him, she could not run fast enough in her mules, her heels were clacking upon the stairs, at each rise there was a flash of bare pink fleeing instep.

A door banged.

Srinivas followed in her wake, through air which was turbulent, filled with the debris of panic, which pulverizes, and floating filaments of mock marabou wrenched from the hem of the desperate gown.

Turbulence. It could, he had heard, shake an aircraft to pieces: thousands of pounds of sumptuous jet cracked from nose to fin, the spinning cones and the mighty chambers of thrust and lift torn out bodily and hurtling through silver cloud. The frail human craft continued, however, to ascend: somewhat buffeted, but holding together, no visible rifts or burst seams in the superstructure, so that Srinivas was moved to a new respect for the hardy components that went into the human frame.

Or it could not have survived, he reflected, those accretions of the years: millions for the race, and the decades settling like silt ever more heavily on pairs of individual shoulders. It would long since have perished, or snuffed itself out, unable to contemplate the magnitude of living, as he himself had considered doing. Yet here, too, were subtleties: the sly advancement of reasons against – weighty reasons of total irrelevance – while the vital invisible game went on, which was to do with clinging, with working out one's destiny, impenetrable and impossible unless life were to continue to spin itself out.

So Srinivas continued to ascend. He went up the stairs that taxed Mrs Pickering, and round landings; and up the last flight, which was narrow and steep, the bare timber plainly demarcating, and coming to his quarters, took up residence again in the bleached white cell of his isolation. Here, through the walls that had been thinned, but still as if from distances, the sounds of the house floated up. Ordinary sounds of waking and washing, running water, creaking springs, a gurgling cistern, the sizzle of food in frypans, giving way to sounds which were infused with urgency, banged doors, shrill notes in voices, and footsteps as frantic as they could be on the cord in the corridors. He listened to them as they came to him, remotely, not quite detached, but with free connections that allowed him to drift further and further away.

I am a stranger, he said.

I have been transformed into a stranger, said the unwanted man, and examined a pair of hands whose stigmata would be the excuse.

For what, at the end of these assimilating years, can the terminal product be said to be? Srinivas asked himself, and rose from the bed of teak to view from his window the human congress that denied him. An alien, he replied, speaking for them, in the voice that – if somehow, suddenly, he were to be catapulted among them now – they would use. An alien, whose manners, accents, voice, syntax, bones, build, way of life – all of him – shrieked *alien!*

Returning to his bed, he began to drift again, disoriented, such is the power of suggestion, and feeling the tug of another country, which the years had rendered tenuous, to which he was nevertheless being slowly ferried.

India, he said. It could almost have been its balmy air that coaxed up his jugged flesh.

Something, anyhow, got him up. He rose, and bending double, hauled out from under the bed the tin trunk in which things were packed, useless things which even the dustmen would not take, sealed jars of coconut oil with which his Indian wife had kept her body supple and moist, sandals little more than a sole and a thong, the patent pumps which had been imagined the correct equipment for London pavements. From this dented but indestructible box, which smelled of metal and ancient vegetable fat that greased its hinges, after some groping he extracted the thin white mull dhoti with the quarter-inch gold border which his mother had slipped in. Intending him to wear it, though he had never worn such clothes. Could not, under the circumstances, in those Indian days, with the debris of colliding forces showering down on them.

Trousers were more practical. Even in the most ardent houses.

Later, London forbade.

There is a time and a place for everything, said Srinivas, surveying the snowbound scene below him. Quite deftly, considering, he tied the dhoti about him and arranged its fluffy white folds.

In the middle of her chores Mrs Pickering became aware of certain quirks in the natural silence of the attic which called for her attention. Postponing the rice pudding she had planned, she brewed a pot of tea instead and took it up, to see what he was up to.

'I thought you might like a cup,' she said, softening towards the blameless man with the jutting bones who stood by the door.

Then she saw his regalia. Looped about him waist to ankle. Like some kind of sheikh, she said to herself, while somewhere, remotely, she marvelled at the instinct which divining so accurately had sent her up, though she herself would never have dreamed.

'You're dressed up, I see,' she said. It lamed her, in fact, to see those baffling clouds of unsuitable muslin.

He took the tray from her shaken hands. 'These are the clothes I would wear, were I in India,' he told her soberly.

'But you're not. You're in England,' said Mrs Pickering. She had a way of standing which eroded, made one question conduct of whose propriety one had previously been entirely convinced. But he, too, stood his ground, which from tireless communing and journeying had been tamped down and rendered substantial.

'The people will not allow it,' he said. 'It was my mistake to imagine. They will not, except physically, which is indisputable, have me enter. I am to be driven outside, which is the way they want it. An outsider in England. In actual fact I am, of course, an Indian.'

'No need to parade it,' said Mrs Pickering. 'Is this the best time to choose? Why do you?' she asked – had to ask, although her bones were beginning to ache with inklings.

'I cannot pretend,' said Srinivas. 'Why should I? My wife,' he said to the anguished Englishwoman, 'never did.' Had gone about, in fact, uncompromised to the day of her death in nine yards of sari and sandals irredeemably Indian in style and cut.

Mrs Pickering, having little further to offer (except agreement, which she withheld for fear of egging him on to further excesses), sat down beside Srinivas, while between them the tea cooled in the cosy brown pot which was, after all, a symbol of hospitality. And Mrs Pickering felt a yearning, which began in her arms and spread to and filled her whole being, to be hospitable, to pile all the hospitality she could find, all that had been grudged and doled out and denied, onto those denuded shoulders beside her.

As she could not, she got up, time and tide being what they are, she said to herself, and went down the stairs to get on with the rice pudding.

The simmering vanilla pod climbing up invisible trellises was scenting corridors and halls when she remembered a message and returned to the attic to deliver it.

'News of your health is spreading like wildfire,' she said, stony about the mouth from his rejection of her advice.

'I have noticed some comings and goings,' he admitted.

'There was bound to be, I warned you,' she could not resist reminding him.

'You know your countrymen best,' he said. 'Do I smell rice pudding for lunch?'

But she was not to be fobbed off.

'I hope at least,' she said, in tones that expected nothing, not even such minimal prudence, 'you will not think of going out, at least for the time being.'

Being committed he kept silent.

'You won't, will you?' Silence was, evidently, for cowards.

'I'm afraid I have to.'

'Not in those clothes.'

'Yes.'

'It's asking for trouble.'

'I have a date,' he began, theatrically, but her presence discouraged drama. 'I have promised to see Dr Radcliffe,' he ended on a falling note.

'It can wait,' said Mrs Pickering.

'No,' he said, 'I must,' and she saw that his knuckles were whitened and jutting, bulwarks of his will which she would not thwart.

'Well, if you must, you must,' she said, and dusted off her skirt on which fluff from the ancient trunk had settled, and went off to take such action as she could – which, she said to herself, heaven knows is precious little.

Over at No. 6 Fred Fletcher gauged that his time was coming.

Pod's about to burst, he said to himself, though the picture that formed was rather of buckshot flying, spinning pellets sprayed from the exploding capsule to pepper the flesh. Fred enjoyed shooting, though not the lead on which, once, biting into pigeon pie he had broken a tooth. He enjoyed dreaming too: not the night variety, which he could not control, but daydreams, which could be made to fit. In these dreams, which came to him quite easily – he had only to lie back comfortably, and allow his eyes to glaze over – he was always the top man. The Governor. Governor General. His Excellency the Viceroy. In cockaded hat, erect on a dais, one arm, over which gold braid fell in thick loops, raised stiffly in white, acknowledging the homage of dark millions.

Fred felt he could do it. Born to command was the luminous phrase that lit up his mind. Why, even here, in England, which was mostly white – as one had to concede, whatever predictions one threatened one's public with – did not the inhabitants of Ashcroft Avenue, not to mention the side alleys, rise up as one man to follow him? What, then, could he not rise to if the millions were black!

Cocooned, and slightly jumbled up in this glistening trance – the lumpy bed transformed, the moony mother who interfered and forbade disposed of – Fred became convinced. He could see himself. He could hear. Boss, baas, bwana, sahib. Fred allowed some top names that he knew to slide over his tongue. They tasted ambrosial. He closed his eyes, and went higher, if shakily. Your Honour. Your Excellency. In dazzling duck, with a retinue.

'Fre-ed!'

Frederick pulled the pillow over his ears and continued, though in a lower key.

People said these days were over. Fred did not believe. He had seen pictures. Of the Jubilee in Delhi, which Mrs Glass had hung in the lounge, in which you could see the Native Princes bowing and walking backwards out of the White Presence. Mr Glass had hooted loud and violently when he had pointed out this detail, and Fred had told him off. It was not amusing. It was how things ought to be. How they were in countries he respected. South Africa, for instance. Or take Australia. On second thoughts he did not think he would, the Aussies being such an irreverent lot, cracking their sides when he was at his most serious. But deep down they knew what was what, Fred felt. Kept the black fellers in their place, for one thing. Only a handful left now, which only a few fools could pretend wasn't a good thing.

The blacks. Jumped-up jerks who didn't know their place. Getting above themselves, they were, like that bastard at No. 5 his mother was soft about, who thought he could shove people around. Well, he'd have to be taught different.

A lesson, to warn him and his kind.

Lessons were what he and his friends were preparing. Were ready with. Ready to hit back – against what he did not define, but his arms would lash out he knew, the biceps were bulging. His face, under the pillow, began to feel bloated. He could hardly breathe for thinking, thick congested thoughts that were seizing him up.

'Fred!'

Fred removed the pillow. 'Yes, what,' he said, grudgingly, in the way he and his wife communicated with each other. But for once she was different, made live by news, she could hardly wait to tell what she'd just heard, the words flew out like flustered starlings.

Fred listened, which was also rare. Perhaps he could not speak for feeling. He felt for his wife, and his children, and his kith and kin whose health, life and living were in jeopardy. His heart enlarged and took in more, the whole of civilization, the whole of Western civilization, which in his judgement – such as it was, and he would not claim infallibility for it – which in his judgement No. 5 was imperilling. Fred's head throbbed. He began to feel very hot and dry. His lips were like crackling.

His wife, who knew the look, vanished.

Fred did not notice. He was all coiled up inside. It made him lunge, rather than rise, from his bed. There were mighty creaks from the springs, and Fred's boots thudded on the floorboards like falling boulders.

It alerted Mrs Fletcher. She had, in fact, anticipated these sounds, and prepared for them by stationing herself near the door with her shawl drawn right up to her chin, which tended to quiver.

'Give way,' said Fred, addressing his mother as if she were a road sign – some ruddy obstruction, anyhow, in the path of his intentions.

'Where're you going?' inquired Mrs Fletcher.

'My business,' said Fred.

'You touch a hair of that old man's head, Fred Fletcher, I'll tan your hide for you,' said Mrs Fletcher, quaking.

Fred did not answer. He was in no mood. The messianic mantle had descended upon him, it made him untouchable. He shoved his mother aside and lurched out.

So the two men, who had little in common, and were not on speaking terms, at least as far as Fred was concerned, were borne towards each other, in roles each had drawn, perhaps, when lots were being cast.

Fred fairly bounded along. His footsteps rang with the sense of mission. His heels struck sparks from the frozen pavement. Those who were about shrank a little, and thought of America where, as they had seen on telly, violent things happened. They had to remind themselves they were in Britain before elements of composure returned, and even so unpleasant intimations continued to harass the fringes of their minds.

Srinivas floated, or so at times it seemed to him, and certainly to those who saw the thin figure wafting along the wintry streets in a diaphanous cloud of muslin. The cloud gave off whiffs, of coconut oil and sandalwood paste, causing nostrils to wrinkle, and conducting the owners to places vaguely east of Suez which they would visit with pleasure, or distaste, according to preference and a dash of conditioning. The smell transported Srinivas too. It could not bear him away wholly – its influence was waning, or perhaps the atmosphere on which it fell was sharper – but it took a part of him, which touched down now and then, a toe trailed fleetingly over tropical soil. The substantial part that remained trod (soberly shod – for the sandals had disintegrated), trod, in conventional shoes, light and firm along London's pavements, through a landscape that was frozen.

Everything was frozen, in tints of ash and absinthe. Cindery walls, and damp that crept up greenish above the snow humped sallow against air bricks, and trees which had ceased to drip and become encrusted, with boughs that frost had split down to their waxy inner wands, and brittle bark.

A scene which showing no slit or sign could quench your belief, thought Srinivas, in blue, or the tenacity of green, or sun, or a season to come which would be crammed with bounty, fresh and cordial air in which leaves rustled, and purest unfurling greens.

If, indeed, there was to be such a season for him, thought Srinivas, who wished to believe, as he slipped and slithered to his destination through sullen, ice-bound vistas. Too sullen it seemed to him, and iced up as far as the eye could see, ice in the gutters, and cladding the railings and wastepipes of houses, and bearding the undergrowth which gave off smells, the oppressive smell of decomposing leaves and something hidden and rotting. The odour was everywhere. It hung in the motionless atmosphere but percolated, all but defeating those Eastern whiffs which the folds of mull, clammy by now and accepting unsuitability, were still discharging.

For Srinivas was still airborne, intermittently, at least in his mind, although he was distinctly hobbled about the ankles by his dhoti, which clapped about wetly and made him mince.

Fred, in duck, met Srinivas, mincing. They might have passed, such was their preoccupation, but for the mull, which was whitish in the gloom, and definitely out of place.

'You,' said Fred, to make sure.

'Yes,' said Srinivas, returned to earth like Fred.

'Black bastard,' said Fred.

'No,' said Srinivas, out of a passing care for accuracy, though such matters were of no consequence.

Then Fred was signalling, in case this withered basket wanted to make an issue of it, great muscular waves to summon engulfing seas, in response to which the greyness yielded the shapes of Mike and Joe and Harry, and to sustain them others, vigilantes rustled up for the occasion and faceless in the murk.

'I've been looking for you,' said Fred, thickly.

'I know,' said Srinivas, mystified by the paraphernalia of rejection with which Fred was cluttered, but preparing to affirm.

32

IN HIS STUDY WHICH DOUBLED AS A SURGERY AND WAS
also, perhaps, his refuge from the well-appointed house, Dr
Radcliffe awaited the arrival of the thin old man who, from
years of somewhat spiky education in these matters provided
by the country, could be trusted to arrive on time.

His patient.

Or was he? Dr Radcliffe wondered. So thoroughly now
had their roles become jumbled that it was difficult to tell
who, of the two, was afflicted. Only, it was clear, the presence
of each was sought by the other, and welcomed.

Welcome, he thought. Then he tried not to think of it
because of what was going on, but the air would not allow it:
the air which came in reconditioned from the filtering plant
and could be seen to be blameless.

Nothing, declared Dr Radcliffe.

Something, he admitted. Because after all he had instincts,
his calling had developed them, otherwise how could he
sense the obstruction when nothing but indigestion and an
innocent abdomen lay palpitating under his hand?

Hell, said Dr Radcliffe, and reached for the bottle
of Haig which he knew would ameliorate nothing. Put
it down and instead opened the publication which had
come that morning, and could have been absorbed but for
correspondence that caught his eye. It was solicitous. He
read on. It concerned itself with the welfare of the sick, who

might fall into foreign hands. On their behalf it inquired into the qualifications of those who tended them, their medical skills, their command of English. It hazarded – for facts were facts, and must be faced – that these might not, perhaps, come quite up to standard, the standards of Britain which the world envied.

Dr Radcliffe returned the journal to its rack. He felt a queasiness in the pit of his stomach, which from its pitch he judged arose from a complex of sources. Srinivas, who was late. The atmosphere, which was not conducive. Hell, said Dr Radcliffe again, forcefully, and composed himself to wait but what hung suspended would not let him. Soon he rose, and parting the curtains peered. There was little to be seen except chilled streets, and murk. Little, or nothing; but he could deny the thing no longer.

Marjorie, in her new turquoise wool which went well, she was thinking, with the gold-flock drawing room wallpaper, heard the study door go and went to confront her husband in the hall, or perhaps to cut off his escape.

'Must you go?' A hand at her throat, which was swanlike but badly strung, to emphasize some importance. 'The Maitlands will be here any minute.'

'I'm afraid I must.'

'A patient, I suppose.'

'Yes.'

She hated him. She hated his patients who got in the way of vital social engagements, though she suspected he used them. Excuses, excuses! her entire being cried.

'I suppose some wretched woman's chosen to have her baby.'

'Yes.' As always he took the easiest way out – whatever she suggested, to save going into things.

'Or is it that hideous old man you've taken a shine to?'

For she could be coarse when they were alone, or when she felt the prick of the goad he used, she felt, on her defenceless flesh.

'It could be,' he said. Looming – his stature seemed to have increased, or she had shrunk, and no wonder, looked down on like that – and planted on the rug on the parquet of the hall, one ankle deep in wool pile. 'It could be. I only hope it is.'

'Well, if it is don't bring him here,' she cried, distracted – the Maitlands due any minute, herself tied to this lunatic, that disgusting old tramp, her trials all but overcame her. 'Don't bring him here, because I'm sick of him, do you hear. Sick!'

This time he did not answer. She heard the door click, and the modulated whine of the car's engine, and somewhere in the distance the wail of police sirens, then the Maitlands' Merc whooshed softly around the gravelled drive and remoulding her face she resumed her life.

The officious police panda, lights flashing and sirens screaming, overtook and passed the cruising Rover, but it was the dipped beam of the Rover's headlights which picked out the lamp post to which the man had been bound.

Securely tied, as Dr Radcliffe could see, though reddish mists were swirling in front of his eyes, with electric flex that wound around from ankle to neck. Trussed up, this man, like a fowl, except for his head, which had been on a level with the litter bin clamped to the post but lolled forward now on its elongated stalk of neck, and dripped. Thick black pear-shaped drops that oozed rather than fell, and falling congealed in brittle tongues on the frozen flagstones.

So much Dr Radcliffe saw as his metal box carried him on – before the brakes could grip and bring the car to a halt. Then he was out, the screech of his own tyres still shearing through his head, running, his feet slithering on the pavement which was patchy with ice and strewn with grimy, bedraggled feathers.

Feathers, and that black, thick liquid. The reeking stuff was on his hands, ruining his cuffs and nails, tacky between his fingers and the blades of the surgical scissors with which he was hacking – for want of anything better, frantic for time – at the electric flex.

'Can you see all right, sir?' The panda, coming round, had caught up and disgorged its men.

'Yes, thank you, officer.'

Constable Kent held his torch steady, but his face was blanched. He was glad he was not alone. Eye on the job, he still kept himself aware of his mates, two fanning out to search, the third in the car bringing it up so its headlights could be trained. What a job! The officer was steamed up under his cap. Not in all his three years with the force. A good thing that trembly old woman had come to them. Mrs Fletcher, that was her name. He, Bob Kent, had taken her for a bit of a crackpot, but the sergeant, no flies on him. Of course they'd all been expecting trouble, those speeches did send the fur flying. But this, in this day and age! Who would have thought, even if funny things were going on.

'If you could steady his head,' said Dr Radcliffe.

The constable put down the torch. He felt a little queasy, but it was his duty. He put his hands on the sticky mess. When he felt the skull, though, he forgot about the mess. It was like a baby's, so helpless, and rolling on its neck.

Constable Kent felt his hands becoming gentle, alongside the efficiency which his training gave them.

'I hope we're in time, sir,' he said cautiously.

'I hope so, yes.'

Never let on, medicos. Still, it must be difficult to tell under all that. Vile stuff, tar. And feathers all clotted up in it, he could hardly believe in this many feathers.

Mrs Glass, ringside of the smallish crowd – twenty or thirty, she reckoned, you couldn't expect a full turnout this weather – was also riveted by the feathers.

'Like as if a chicken's been killed and plucked,' she said to the person next her shoulder.

'Yes,' said the person.

'In full view. It's disgusting,' said Mrs Glass.

'Yes,' agreed the person.

'Prefer them oven-ready, myself,' said Mrs Glass to this approving stranger. 'Never could stand the sight.'

Of blood, she meant, but she would not say the word. Nor sight of feathers, which came off clean in the scalding vats where they soused the half-dead – though half-alive – birds. Nor nothing like that. 'Just couldn't,' she said.

'Nor me neither,' said the stranger, feeling sicker than ever and wanting to move, but wedged.

They had all become a little wedged, what with wanting to see, and the coppers wanting them to move on, and shuffling along a bit to keep them happy and then edging back. Move along indeed, when they had fetched out special, on a night it wasn't fit for a dog to be out in.

The coppers thought so too. They stamped their feet and turned up the collars of their greatcoats and felt for the man roped to the lamp post who was dressed, for Christ's sake, in cheesecloth.

Quite a few coppers, Mrs Fletcher noted. She stood by the police car, shivering, until one of the constables fetched a blanket from the waiting ambulance and draped it over her shoulders. Then she shivered even more. For the thing had grown, she saw, looking about her at that valley of pallid faces, and gone out of her control.

Wedged like everyone else, but more uncomfortably – he was, in fact, crouched centrally under a berberis bush – Fred experienced similar emotions.

The thing had got out of control, he felt.

They had not had time to make a proper job of it. That Rover swooping down unexpected like it had had shaken them rigid. Then the cops. He hated cops. And that mob out there. He hated them worse. You couldn't shift an inch but one of them was sure to notice and bawl. But he had to, soon, or bust, because of the spines all over the blooming bush. Just his luck, he couldn't help thinking, to pick that one. Though come to think of it he hadn't had much choice.

Now and then Fred shifted, cautiously, but however cautious the bucket clanked. Lumbered with it, he was. He had nicked it off a builder's yard as being just what was wanted, after that plastic pail of his mother's had fallen apart, sizzling and curled up like a rasher in a frypan. Odd he hadn't reckoned on that happening, considering what he knew about pitch, which you couldn't tell him nothing about. Boiling tar, thought Fred, which bubbled as you spread it. On those Sydney roads he had done. On the nobs of those that had it coming to them – . Fred stopped. That last clank had been very loud, from his having slipped off. Fred crouched lower, close to the soggy ground, chin on the brim of the bucket. He wished he had ditched it, as well as some other things, but there hadn't been time. Bucket, shovel, uncoiling flex and flame gun – he could feel them, every one, eating into his flesh.

At length, as nothing happened, Fred lifted up his head again and peered through the berberis at the crowd. It had grown. Talk about overpopulation, thought Fred morosely. He looked around, as far as his barbed crown would let him, to see what he could see, and spotted Mrs Glass, whose spectacles were flashing, and Mr Glass, whom he didn't care for, and his nibs the landlord from the local and – . Fred took another squint. Yes, it was her all right, his mother, he couldn't mistake her moo-cow dial. Bitch, thought Fred, but he shrank a little, the way she'd been of late you couldn't help the shudders.

But he'd learn her too, one day.

If not sooner.

Fred's face twitched at a memory. The pail, for which he could just hear her hollering. And the quilt he had slit. That patchwork thing she drooled over, which he had dragged into the yard and cut up. How the feathers had tumbled out of the silk! Plump as a stuffed goose one minute, next minute flat as a pancake with the flaps hanging open. The memory warmed him for a little, but soon the cold crept back, his toes were numb and the handle of the shovel was wicked in his ribs and Fred had only one wish, that they would all hurry up and clear off and leave him free to get out of this freezing hellhole.

It preoccupied Dr Radcliffe too. The weather was the enemy, in a patient this old, rather than the spectacular mess. He worked as swiftly as he could, but he was hampered. Hands like ice blocks, and that infernal tar over everything, and yard after yard of clammy linen. One of my pottier patients, thought Dr Radcliffe grimly, but knowledge of the man refused to reinforce the opinion.

Nearly through, though, thank heaven.

'Have you got him?' asked Dr Radcliffe.

'Yes, sir,' confirmed Constable Kent, winding his arms around even more tightly. He had grown quite reckless, and did not even think now about what the tar was doing to his uniform.

Some warmth, human perhaps, as well as from blue serge, was trickling through to Srinivas. It revived him. Where am I? he thought of asking, but, really, he knew: the area between his house and the doctor's was familiar stamping ground. He could tell without even raising his head, which he could not do anyhow, because someone was holding it firmly. Within that clamp he could still feel it weighty, like a football. And gummed up, a gum which smelled heavily of resins. All over his hair. Now why – ?

In a rush, it returned to him. Fred Fletcher, who had found him, having been out looking. That bit was clear, and being frogmarched along the road, and footsteps at his heels, more than he thought possible, a determined posse out to show him how unwelcome he was. He knew, he remembered wanting to tell them, but a blur intervened, followed by a sharp image of Fred ladling out dollops, and the stuff thick as a batter for drop scones refusing to come off the shovel, and Fred ranting at it, or himself, it was difficult to know. Then the snowstorm, bird feathers fluttering, falling, succumbing to the viscous fluid, lying clotted in it. Srinivas shivered.

'Are you all right?'

'Yes,' said Srinivas. 'I'm all right.'

'Is he all right, sir?'

'Suffering from exposure, I have little doubt,' said Dr Radcliffe, censoriously. 'The sooner we get him to –' Hospital, he had been about to say, but what he knew made him pause. Hospitals would not want to know. This unusual patient of his, with his unusual lesions, would be sent merrily on the admission round.

'– to my surgery,' he finished. 'It's nearer.'

The Maitlands had departed.

What else could you expect, ask people over for drinks and have them hang around indefinitely until the host thought fit to return?

Marjorie smoothed her dress, and waited. When she heard the car she held herself in, even more than she was already doing, because she did not want to burst into tears, which she was fully justified in doing, until she had said what she had to say to him.

When she heard the front door open she rose. Her heart was knocking. All this emotion was bad for her, she felt – she was of an age for coronaries – but nevertheless she slipped her feet into the court shoes she had slipped off to ease the bunion on her big toe, and went into the hall to intercept her husband. But she was brought up short. She even screamed a little, without realizing, a bleak yelp which touched a chord of sympathy in Constable Kent.

'Sorry to barge in, madam,' he said, comfortingly, 'at this time of night. There's been a spot of bother, but I'm happy to say it's not too serious.'

'Oh, good,' said Marjorie. She brought it out, though her jaws were locked. She could not, she told herself, take it in. It was too much. That diseased old man whom she had forbidden, swaying between her husband and a policeman. Covered in oil like a seabird washed up on a polluted beach, and reeking. In her hall, on the parquet, next to the rug.

From the corner of her eye she could see blackish stains sprouting in between the curly pile, and spreading.

Marjorie said nothing. She could not. Not in front of the policeman. Later she would, she knew, and so for that matter did Dr Radcliffe.

33

THE ENTIRE PARISH, IT SEEMED, WAS WORN OUT.

It was as if each of them had been sucked up in some great vortex of emotion, whirled around, and flung down to lie floundering and gasping, the breath knocked clean out of their lungs.

Even those who were not directly involved were seized up and spun dry. Like the landlord of the local, who knocked back glass after glass, dispiritedly, unhopeful of remedying the dehydration from which he diagnosed himself to be suffering. Like Mr Glass, who felt worn out simply listening to his wife, who was still wrapped up in feathers.

'Like some kind of rite,' she began to tell him.

'Oh, belt up!' fell from Mr Glass's weary lips.

Even Laxman, who lived peacefully and at a safe distance from his father, or so he had dared to think, was not spared.

'I feel exhausted,' he said, indicating the sober paragraph in the sober paper to which he subscribed. 'Thoroughly exhausted. There just seems to be no end to the old man's peccadilloes.'

'What a terrible thing to happen to him,' said Pat, unable to repress a shudder down her spine which she knew – her husband often told her – was soft.

'Yes. I suppose,' said Laxman, glumly, 'I shall have to go down and sort things out. As if there isn't enough to do here. It's enough to tire a saint.'

Being human he did, indeed, feel quite prostrated. Pat saw the medlar tints accentuating around her husband's gills and sought to placate him.

'Shall I pack your case?' she asked in a wifely way, living out the auxiliary role for which, she often thought, women were best fitted.

'No,' he said, and became cantankerous. 'I can't go just like that, you know. I've a hundred things to see to here. The old man really can't expect me to be at his beck and call.'

'No, of course not, dear,' said his wife. 'Why not,' she suggested helpfully, 'ask him to stay with us?'

'Ask him to –! Well, I suppose I shall have to,' said Laxman on a ruined note, and made up his mind to do so in a way that would preclude the invitation being accepted.

Abdul the Zanzibari, cushioned by numerous aides and the comforts his wealth brought him, seldom felt the wear and tear of ordinary daily living. Yet, oddly, his sentiments when he heard the news (not from the papers, which he seldom read, his reading level being what it was – what the exigencies of a revolutionary situation had made it – but directly from a visiting member of the Asian club) closely echoed what a good many people in Ashcroft Avenue were saying.

'It wears you out,' he said, 'completely, man, completely. To think of what one could have done! ... but he did not want it.' And he gazed at his wife, the beautiful Odile, who in his eyes graced and outshone even this opulent Parisian apartment, and waited for her to inspire him as he could trust this rare woman to do.

'It is, of course, your Indian friend?' said Odile, and plumped up a bolster to support a back whose bones were not as spry as they had been, whatever her husband might think.

'It is,' said Abdul, and thought of his friend, to whom this thing had been done. Once, in his salad days, he would have felt humiliated. Now the day for such feeble emotion was over, it was time for anger. He could feel it kindling in its familiar pit, burning up from embers which had never been extinguished.

'Well, go, *chéri*,' said Odile, and put her arms around the burning man, whose bitter chocolate flesh she had known and adored for over a quarter of a century. 'Go to him. The way you feel, it is necessary that you should stand together.'

I'm sick and tired of Fred, thought Mrs Fletcher.

It was a mutual feeling, of long standing, but now it had begun to flare, fiery streamers that reached out from a central ball of fire and excoriated them.

'It was you, all right,' said Mrs Fletcher.

'It wasn't,' said Fred doggedly. 'It must've been the tenants. The way he's treated them they had every right. It's more than flesh and blood can stand, what he done.'

'What you did, you mean,' said his mother.

'I did nothing,' said Fred. 'You ask the police. Go on, ask them,' he dared her, boldly, for they had hauled him off to the station and grilled him and he had come out of it alive, which meant they had nothing they could pin down on him.

'I'll ask Mr Srinivas,' said Mrs Fletcher.

'The police already have,' said smug Fred.

'When he's fit,' said Mrs Fletcher significantly, 'I'll ask him then.'

'You do that,' said Fred.

It was the best he could manage, all crisped up as his mother had made him feel.

The next day was worse.

His mother found the pail which had let him down behind the potting shed where he'd hurled it, not expecting her to go down there in the winter, which she never did.

She brought it in to show him, holding the tarry plastic between tongs as if it were contaminated. Her face was working.

'Now deny it, if you can, Fred Fletcher,' she said.

Her voice was awful.

It took it out of Fred to compose an answer.

'How do I know how it got there?' he said sullenly. 'It's been planted more than likely ... someone with a grudge. I've got my enemies, for Christ's sake, haven't I?'

'Christ sees,' said Mrs Fletcher. 'Nothing is hidden from Him. Nor from me, Fred Fletcher.'

She spoke with such intensity that he felt as if, indeed, the solid bone of his skull had clarified, gone transparent like bacon fat under a grill so that she really could peer inside him.

'It wasn't me,' he mumbled, making for the door, but she was there before him, blocking his escape.

'You smell of it,' she said. 'The smell of tar is on you, and the blood of the Lamb. You'll never wash it clean. Born and brought up in a Christian household, Fred Fletcher, you have supped with the devil, you have brought shame on this house.'

'I've done nothing I'm ashamed of,' cried Fred.

'Tar and feathers,' continued Mrs Fletcher, 'like the primitives do. Heathen practices, such as savages carry on, not having seen the light.'

Fred could endure no more. His brainwave, a primitive deed? It really jolted him. Thrusting his mother aside, he burst out of the room and made for his own, where he flung himself down on the bed. Heathen practices. Such as natives went in for. He only hoped those who had aided him would not know. Not only Mike and Joe, but those respectable people he had been courting, whose company he found rejuvenating. Fred pulled the pillow over his face and lay there, quivering.

34

SRINIVAS'S STAR, UNLIKE FRED'S, SHONE FOR HIM.

Somehow, he escaped pneumonia.

Somehow, under the blood and tar, there was no serious injury.

'You're a fortunate man,' said Dr Radcliffe. 'More fortunate than you realize,' he felt bound to add, for what he had seen had frightened him. The work of a mob, he felt, defining mob as many: many hands involved in a crude and repulsive act of violence. Against an old man, he said to himself incredulously, to prove what? Achieve what end? Dr Radcliffe shook his head, which had remained stuffy since the occurrence. It is difficult to know what it is all about, he said to himself: no, really I don't. But something, a suspicion, or it could have been knowledge itself, kept crashing around like a wasp imprisoned inside his skull, round and round the contracting rim of revelation.

Mrs Pickering agreed with the doctor. Undoing bandages, she saw that the gash on the temple left by Fred's shovel was healing cleanly.

'You're lucky,' she said. 'It could easily have gone septic,' she added, severely, for she too had been badly frightened.

'Perhaps tar is some kind of disinfectant,' he suggested.

'Yes. Perhaps that was in Fred's mind when he chose it,' said Mrs Pickering.

Srinivas made no answer. Fred's name had not passed his lips; he felt he could not allow it. He said instead: 'Mrs Fletcher would like us to go round one evening.'

'What for?' Mrs Pickering was quite surprised.

'For tea, I daresay,' said Srinivas, and fished out the scribbled note. 'When I am better, she says. I am better.'

Now it was Mrs Pickering who was silent, a silence that dragged, heavy as a trawl along the seabed of emotion.

'You go,' she said at last. 'I cannot face him.'

Because she knew, as most people knew, each of them contributing elements of pity, shame, fear and dislike of involvement to erect a citadel of silence.

It blocked the police. They could not institute proceedings, they said, for lack of evidence.

It soothed Fred. He dwelt, if not comfortably, tolerably within its somewhat tarnished walls. Memories of unfinished business, the berberis bush, being lumped with natives, these dreadful memories he buried as quickly as he could. Being rid of them allowed him to look back on his exploit with unsullied enthusiasm. Sometimes he glowed, his linings swelled agreeably, from thinking of that, and from thinking of his cleverness in covering up his tracks so that no one had been able to pin anything on him.

Sometimes other reflections modified the radiance, suggesting (actually the police told him) his immunity was due less to his own skill than to people keeping their mouths shut. Ah, but why do they, Fred learned to counter cunningly, conducting the dialogue with dignity within his own cranium: why do they! And images of his kith and kin rallying around him rose in his mind, warming images in which he wrapped himself and soon restored the radiance.

Until he walked straight into the trap his mother had set for him.

Trapped, he said to himself, outraged, jammed in the tiny hall between her and his enemy.

That leper from No. 5 and his bitch of a mother, who had plotted, the pair of them, lain in wait for him knowing the time of his comings and goings. Fred was speechless.

Mrs Fletcher, however, had no difficulty. Iron filings, it appeared, had entered her system, were holding her upright, stiffening the vulnerable chin, at least until she could finish what was begun, whatever might come after.

'Mr Srinivas,' she said – even her voice had run to iron. 'Now that my son is here I would like you to tell me, in front of him, if he was involved in what was done to you.'

Srinivas could not answer. Not at once. He was transfixed, he could feel the cord rising, spiralling up from his ankles towards his throat. I am choking, he wanted to say, but he could not raise his head which was lined and coated with lead. If he did, his neck, he knew, would snap, like a pumpkin stalk whose fibres had been blanched and stretched to their limits by the swollen fruit. So he let his head loll to and fro in the surging mists until, suddenly, the lids of his eyes which had been loaded with darkness grew lighter, grew rosy-red one would have said from the contrast, under the beam of headlamps, and a strength not his own took the weight of his skull. Then Srinivas lifted his head and looked at Fred, whose eyes were glittering and watery, and watching him.

'Was it Fred?'

Mrs Fletcher had not finished and would not finish, it was clear, until she had been answered, because it had become necessary to her – essential for continuance – to prevail. So she stood, firmly, in the small unheated room which had begun to reek like a cell, and would continue to stand, as both men could see, until worn down, though whether they or she was open to conjecture.

'I'm saying nothing. Come hell or high water I shall not budge one inch,' vowed Fred, and he dug his toes in – so far as he could, into the unaccommodating lino – such was the power of his oath, or fear of succumbing to the devilish pressure his mother was applying.

Srinivas's strength was nurtured by memories.

Memories of this timid woman faltering on his doorstep, chilled by half-truths and the simple lore of Anglo-Saxon peasants and rendered too fearful to come in, but brought to the threshold and held there by the essential nature of her message. Trembling, poor thing, an ageing fawn, without benefit of youth but touched by the same dazzling brush of fervour and pugnacity, and standing and delivering. Somehow. Affirming in quaking accents conclusions, scraped painfully out of experience and the overlaid core of her breed, which were to do with the intrinsic quality of human beings.

'You are my neighbour,' Mrs Fletcher had said.

As she would go on saying, as she was saying now, a straight statement which had taken on the aspects of an address of welcome, or it could even have been the format of a reborn world.

'We have been neighbours a good many years,' said Mrs Fletcher. 'You must tell me if it was my son.'

Then Srinivas was able to answer, if he could not quite steel himself to meet her gaze.

'It was not your son,' he said.

The two men remained – locked, it seemed, in this strange conspiracy. Vitreous eyes, upon whose convex sludge the arteries had started to rupture and run, looked into brownish orbs that bore corneal rings, the milk-blue nebulae of age. Both pairs questing. Then Fred began to writhe from what he saw, an internal lashing and twisting that could find no outlet, so much so that Srinivas, to whom the workings of hatred had been made plain, could endure no more.

No more, he said to himself: I can endure no more. I am quite worn out. So he withdrew himself, and rested.

35

THE TWO MOTORCARS WHICH CAME EVERY DAY AND parked nose to tail outside No. 5 provided something of a relief to the hard-pressed residents of Ashcroft Avenue, whom the ructions of the week had exhausted.

They could talk about it, they imagined, safely, without fear of blundering into shrouded places, those oppressive zones of taboo which the situation had bred in each of them. Or without danger of treading on corns, which seemed to have proliferated, for no doubt about it a good many toes were tender.

'Wonder what's up,' said Mrs Glass, mildly, and sighed for what had been taken out of her – the stuffing, Mr Glass had suggested, but she did not care for that, it made her feel hollow, like a drawn fowl. Partly it might be that, she allowed, but partly she sighed for someone like Mrs Fletcher, with whom she could exchange news and views, in ways congenial to both.

But Mrs Fletcher, though available, was changed.

She, who could once have been trusted to take every hint, missing no spoor but following Mrs Glass unerringly into the most congested hinterland of her thought, now baulked. Would stop at the merest pebble, which anyone else would have stepped over, build it up into a mountain, and stand in front of it, arguing. Or become wilfully blind. Pretend not to see what was staring her in the face. Sometimes, though, one had to consider whether she really didn't see, for no doubt about it, her friend, never the brightest, had distinctly got a bit dimmer.

Still the old days had been good. A good old gossip, nothing like it for getting rid of the cobwebs. She had her husband, of course, but it wasn't the same. For instance –

Mrs Glass's form, drooping nostalgically one side of the curtains, stiffened. Someone was emerging from No. 5. A very black black man, whose face she could not remember, since they all looked alike to her, but she did remember the flowerpot hat, years ago though it was. Which Mrs Fletcher had informed her – as if she didn't know – was a fez. Mrs Glass bristled at the memory, but then she softened, the ruffled quills lay smooth again, thinking of the agreeable chat that had followed, and of the many more they could still have if only Mrs Fletcher ... and here, indeed, Mrs Glass could almost hear the conversation in which she, for example, might say, 'Look at that Rolls' – at least she thought it was a Rolls – and wonder who it belonged to, and Mrs Fletcher, latching on, would say, 'Look at the owner, one might have guessed, the likes of *us* couldn't afford a posh car like that!' And then they would wonder what the country was coming to, and treating themselves a little allow the shivers to run up and down their spines, exchanging on how blacks would soon be taking over the country.

But those days, which had been cosy, or perhaps even innocent, though of course there was nothing to feel guilty about now, were over.

Other times other pleasures, sighed Mrs Glass, too dispirited even for French. She would have sunk into a reverie but for the week's events, which kept poking in, and none too scrupulously. All in the past, she told herself, and kept pushing them back to where they belonged, but nevertheless they went on buzzing in her eardrums as if they were by no means over and done with.

My head's all stuffed up, felt Mrs Glass.

No peace, she moaned, standing lonely by the window, cotton wool in the limbs if one could but see, until she spied another visitor going up the Fletcher steps, and then her limpness left her.

It was the fourth visitor, unless she had missed one, which she didn't think likely.

Something's up, said Mrs Glass again, more forcefully this time. Her spectacles began to glint, and she became very shrewd.

'It's a gathering of the clans,' she told her husband.

'For crying out loud!' exploded that exasperated man.

'They're reckoning up,' persisted Mrs Glass. 'Each side's counting its supporters, that's what's up.'

Then Mr Glass, for once, had to concede she might have something there. No peace, he grumped to himself, and retreated behind his paper to savour whatever remained.

The visitors were Mike and Henry and various other friends of Fred's, whom he had not been able to contact, having twisted an ankle on the slippery lino of that hellhole, otherwise the hall, from which he'd been trying to bolt. They came one at a time, as instructed by Fred, for fear of Mrs Fletcher, and commiserated with him. Sometimes they commiserated about themselves, and about others too, notably No. 5's tenants, whose time was nearly up. And Fred listened – the topic absorbed him – and thought he perceived signs, and now and then even attempted – somewhat clumsily, for he had to feel his way – to shape out of what was still inchoate the form and contours of reprisal.

Mike had been and gone.

Now it was Joe.

Young Joe stood outside, where his father had told him to stay. He stood in the gutter, at a point equidistant between the two cars, and rotated slowly, trying to decide which of them he would buy, if he had the money.

Abdul, his tarbush at a jaunty angle, its black tassel swinging, saw the boy sandwiched and frowned.

'You there,' he called. 'You want to be killed, carry on right where you are.'

'I'll carry on where I please,' young Joe shouted back, in a routine way, without taking offence. He often hung around cars, and people often bawled him out for it. 'Is that your car, mister?' he asked, emerging from between the bumpers.

'Certainly is,' said Abdul, recognizing a kindred spirit. 'You like it?'

'Not half,' said Joe, and his face shone. 'I never seen a Lincoln before.'

'Lincoln Continental,' said Abdul briefly, and opened a creamy door. 'Come for a spin?'

'You must be joking,' said Joe, miserably. 'My dad would tan me.'

'Man's right,' said Abdul. 'It's dangerous, taking rides with strangers.'

'I've been with strangers,' said Joe. 'It's you.'

'I'm infected, like?' said Abdul.

'You're black,' said Joe. 'My dad says black men are animals.'

'You don't want to libel beasts,' said Abdul. 'You tell your dad whiteys are devil's spawn,' and he cuffed Joe's ear for him, but in a way that showed that he, too, meant no offence.

When the Lincoln had driven away young Joe turned to the car that remained. It deserved his full attention, he considered, being what it was – a Jensen Interceptor, no less – which he'd only ever seen in an old copy of *The Autocar* before. He walked around it two or three times, admiring its points, then he tried the door, just to see, but it was locked. When he took his hand away he saw the chrome trim was flawed. It quite upset young Joe. He glared at his offending fingers, then retreating the whole bunch so that there was an overhang of sleeve he began polishing the chrome with his coat cuff.

'What are you doing?'

Young Joe didn't even jump, he was too absorbed.

'Some birk's left his fingerprints all over the trim,' he threw over his shoulder. 'I'm getting it off.'

Laxman sized up the boy; he was good at such things. Besides, he quite liked children.

'I see you recognize quality when you see it,' he observed.

'I know about cars,' said Joe. 'You don't often see a Jensen,' he offered, 'around here.'

'D'you like it?'

'It's a beauty!'

'Hop in and have a look around,' said Laxman, opening the door on a fine scent of leather.

Joe slid in. He couldn't help himself. They spent an absorbing ten minutes going over the dashboard together. Whenever he remembered about his father, which was not often, Joe ducked his head.

'My dad would slay me,' he confided, 'if he could see me.'

'You're not doing anything criminal, are you?' said Laxman.

'I dunno,' said Joe. 'It's me dad.'

'What about your dad?'

'He'd blow his top,' explained Joe, 'if he saw me with a black man. He hates blacks. Especially if they're rich. It makes him hopping mad. He says it isn't right, them coming here and doing us out.'

'Oh,' said Laxman, and breathed heavily. 'Why aren't you at school?' he demanded forbiddingly.

'School's closed. Heating's off,' said Joe.

'Why?'

'Tanker drivers' strike. When I grow up,' said Joe, cautiously, prepared for changes in this mercurial stranger, 'I'm going to be a tanker driver.'

Laxman didn't hear. He was in his car, revving up with as much noise as could be induced from the high-precision engine. Above the purr his thoughts, tuned to a different pitch, seemed to roar in his ears. Me and mine, the family unit: over the years these were concepts he practised, to which he had given his considered blessing. People like us: that too, surely, could be endorsed. Laxman tried it out. *People like us expect certain standards. People like them don't expect and couldn't support our standard of living.* He found it unexceptionable.

But Them and Us?

As he drove he glanced now and then at the hands on the wheel, his hands, not even brown but the finest, palest Brahmin, or elephant, ivory.

But regarded, apparently, as black. Black Them, doing White Us.

If Joe had been available he would have felt the flat of Laxman's hand, which itched. Though of course he was only a child. Children had a knack, however. They said out loud, while their elders whispered.

Whispers, shouts, sayings, combining. Into Them and Us. He, as English as English could be, converted into Them by criminal illiterates.

Nonsense, said Laxman, quite robustly, looking about him at the congested if elegant appurtenances and accoutrements of Bond Street through which they, he and his Jensen, were spasmodically proceeding. If he were to step down among them this instant he would, he knew, be accepted. His voice, syllables, accent, syntax, the clothes he wore, his manners, his style – all would proclaim him to be the same. If not superior. Distinctly so, if one considered his intellect, as opposed to that clumsy colander the father of the child who had crossed him undoubtedly carried around in lieu of a brainbox.

But somehow as he drove an uneasy feeling rode along with him, as if he were being propelled towards some camp, or ghetto, which the country was assiduously being urged to construct, and into which he would be thrust, whether or not he belonged.

When he got back to his hotel (for no longer could he, any more than Abdul, suffer Srinivas's tea-and-bun hospitality) Laxman went straight up to his suite and kicking off his shoes, which deserved better treatment, lay on the bed with his eyes closed and his body flaccid.

He felt used up. As used up in a matter of days as any of the residents of the Avenue who had lived with it, and could at least show some cause for the deep trauma which paralysed and crippled them.

But what had he to do with it? A man like himself, a pillar of the community, employer of thousands, a magistrate and member of the Hospital Management Committee, and as all these integral to the nation? It made him rebel. Made him want to retch, this indiscriminate humping and clumping that lined him up beside people like his father, this ludicrous tentacle which, thrown up from the unspeakable doings of an odious neighbourhood, was threatening to hook around him and drag him down. Into what, he was not sure. But something, which instinct roughed out as mire. Laxman heaved, and the admirable bed, which might have been created for trauma and tantrum, took its beating with an uncrushable silky aplomb and rippled voluptuously back into shape.

The muffled thumps his fist was making returned Laxman to himself. His distracted soul, which had been hovering, suspended above his unhappy body, twanged thankfully back into place. He opened his eyes and looked at the ceiling, which was white and immaculate, and untenanted. Then he rose, bewildered and, he felt, ruined by all this, and rang for service which being smooth and efficient and of his world assumed in his mind the rounded nature of a lifebelt.

Lying back in his bath, his head reposing on the plump foam rest, with the jade globes melting between his toes and at his elbow the tall tumbler whose amber tints tangled entrancingly with the lapping greenish water, Laxman slowly felt himself coming to rights.

He belonged.

Whatever anyone might say or think or do he knew he belonged, and where he belonged. To the country in which he was born and lived and laboured, not in some reservation rustled up within it. Whatever fathers of sons or sons of bitches might think, suitable inmate for a ghetto he was not, and did not intend to be. Emerging cleansed from the water, in a rosy glow, in a cloud of essence, under the flesh which hung flabby despite roughing up by loofah and towel, Laxman's bones were determined.

What he had was his, not to be eroded, or lawfully robbed, or relinquished in a despairing submission to such process. If it came to a fight, fight he would. As he had in the years of establishing himself. As, foreseeing he might have to again, all but unknown to himself he had assembled, as shrewd and meticulous as his great-grandfather who had planned and planted and supplemented the forests upon which the family fortunes had rested, cogent dialogue as his instrument.

Powerful instrument, with which to flay those who would harry him into the role of refugee, pile his belongings onto a cart, and bid him join the departing caravanserai.

Oh no, said Laxman.

Not on your nelly, he said, as coarse and pugnacious as he knew very well how to be.

It was all the more taxing, therefore, to be confronted the next day by his father. In a dhoti. With a bandage swathed about his head. Hopeless material, Laxman considered, from which to mould any kind of defence. Dough, when steel was needed. He walked about censoriously, renewing acquaintance with the hideous roly-poly bolsters with inward shudders, his footsteps, which should have been crisp, falling dully upon the wooden floorboards whose underside was undoubtedly soggy with fungus.

'I cannot for the life of me see,' he harped, 'why you should have aroused quite so much ill-feeling.'

'It rose,' said Srinivas simply.

'Yes, but I still don't see why,' persisted Laxman. 'Unless you went out of your way. No sane person would do that. Why did you?'

'Did I?' Srinivas wondered. The precise need to relive the whole exhausting process eluded him. 'Yes, perhaps I did,' he said. Then some insuppressible instinct – it could have been a desire for justice – overcame his reluctance.

'It was, to some extent, fomented,' he said. 'Besides, of course, eviction is bound to cause ill-feeling. Understandably. It is not easy to be homeless.'

'One is driven to wonder,' said Laxman, 'all the same, why you insist on turning them out. After all these years. Choosing, if I may say so, the most unfortunate moment.'

'Because I have no choice,' said Srinivas, and seeing there could be no more holding back brought it out baldly. 'I have contracted leprosy,' he said, and apologetically extended the evidence.

Laxman reeled. The papers had not reported it, no one had told him. He was gasping. His flesh had become jittery. A joke in bad taste, he tried to convince himself, while the sepia gloves he had striven to overlook drove home the message.

A grubby pair, soiled and concealing, which Srinivas had resumed wearing to spare others.

I might have guessed, thought Laxman furiously. He had in fact suspected, from hearing the rumours, but had resisted, refusing to countenance that even his father could be capable. But clearly was. Capable of indiscretions of a mind-bending order.

His father. Laxman's thoughts grew shrill, considering the man.

Coming to a country, he said to himself, doing his best to offend it. Sticking out like a sore thumb, instead of decently integrating. In those clothes. Flaunting a common-law spouse and a bevy of impossible friends. Without even the money that might earn his transgressions forgiveness. Crowning it all by contracting, of all things, this medieval disease. The only thing in its favour, it struck him, was that it let him out of issuing invitations, tepid though he had intended them to be.

'I – must think about it,' said Laxman, thickly.

'I have been – deeply touched,' said Srinivas, with difficulty, because it was no easier speaking to his son now than ever it had been, 'that you should have come down to see me through my troubles.'

'Do you think I had much option?' cried Laxman. His eyes were starting out of his head, confronted with innocence of quite this enormity. 'The papers have already got on to the fact that I am your son!'

Your son, your son, the wafers of the old house trembled and whispered, and Srinivas shivered with them, and bled, and the white drops fell within him where they could not be seen, for the fissure that gaped between him and his flesh, though it could also have been between himself and the country which had, until not so long ago, been loved as his own.

'Coming to this country,' said the woman who had set out to support her daughter through the ordeal of eviction, 'acting as if you owned it, oppressing *us*.'

'If we do, we have learned from our masters, madam,' said Laxman, selecting from his armoury.

'Go back where you belong,' said the woman.

'I belong right here,' said Laxman.

'That's the gratitude we get,' said her husband, shifting ground, 'after all we've done for them. Given away millions in aid, we have.'

'Loans,' corrected Laxman, 'totalling one quarter of one per cent of the gross national product. Lent at rates of which a back-street moneylender would be ashamed. It is, in any case,' he said coarsely, 'less than a hundredth of what has been lifted or looted.'

'The war,' said the man, who was livid. 'Gave our lives for you.'

'Over two million of our men,' said Laxman, 'took part in the war. Fighting for Britain, which was threatened. As I did.' Here Laxman grew very frosty indeed, and looked his adversary up and down. 'So did my brother,' he said. 'He was killed, driving an ambulance, when he was twenty-one.'

There was a silence, for the dead perhaps. Then the husband rallied, in fact he became so furious he ground his teeth.

'You're going to cause an explosion,' he said thickly, 'you and your sort.'

'You mean you are,' said Laxman. 'You'll be blown up with it, what's more, you and your sort.'

He regretted having to say it, for it went against the grain, which was English, but altogether glad that he had answers, and defences, and even attacks, which prudence had accumulated in the wary subconscious over the shabby years. As one has to, said Laxman to himself, when the options are closing. Fight, or go under. There were certain satisfactions, too, in the consciousness of a job worth doing being done well. Doing one's homework always pays off, noted Laxman, not by any means for the first time, as he climbed into his limousine whose hide upholstery made slight crooning noises against his thighs, adding little finishing touches to his contentment.

36

IT WAS FRED, NOW, WHO PROMENADED.

As best he could with his flaming ankle, which was puffy under the bandages, and sent piercing twinges shooting through his calf and all the way up to his armpit. Driven, it seemed, from his home, or by his own devils, and walking them out of his system. Limping. Up and down the streets, which were muddied and damp in this bleary season, and along the pavement, which had been spattered, and scrubbed, and returned to its normal umber but for some lightish patches in the stone. Past the lamp post which might have yielded a solution, and the gabled house which could have been haunted, such was the shadow it cast on his spirits.

He crossed the street when he came to it to escape the spell, but sometimes, late evening, when the sun was low, the lengthening shadow would get him, reach out stealthily from across the road and plop down purple and bruised on his frightened flesh. Assuming shapes, of a toad, it seemed to the cringing man, or the tracery of scars of inflicted wounds, or the sly configurations of insidious disease.

He has made me into a leper, said Fred. Dried out, and shaking. Licking his lips which had thinned for want of goodfellowship, and striving to visualize the healed pink firm flesh beneath the concealing swathes while under his agonized scrutiny it turned, was turning, was in fact whitish and curdled, and pitted like corpse flesh when fingertips pressed.

Never, cried Fred. Running, or wishing to, but hobbled, and stumbling, and hating. Hate. The reality of it, by comparison. For now he saw with a bulging clarity that heretofore he had only been playing at it. Playing at hate, this raw thing that had burst from its glistening caul and was running furiously at his side. Banging at his ribs from time to time, and monstrously grown since birth. Fred was not afraid to look; if anything he laboured to keep up with this thing streaming its bloody membranes that galloped at his flanks, and the wind went whistling through his teeth.

People who saw him coming in the gloom gave the plunging figure a wide berth. He crashed into those who were less nimble, or underestimated the purpose of peg-leg, or simply did not see him in the darkness. These, caught unprepared, he sent spinning.

'Why the hell don't you look where you're going?'

The hurt voices trailed after him. Fred did not really care. He bought himself a torch with a powerful beam but it was not for them, it was to get him over the stretch of benighted pavement. When he reached the invisible boundary he would stop, and press the button and slide it along the silvery runner until it held, and shine the torch, its full concentrated exterminating beam, at the eye that watched from the attic.

But the panes, which were a smudgy black from not having been cleaned, smouldered back at him, while continuing to spy. Or so Fred was convinced, as he limped, and lurched, the dazzling if impotent exorciser in his hands executing erratic patterns that seriously alarmed the residents.

Sometimes, in the throes of this most fraught enterprise, the ankle would give way. Then Fred would sit on the curb, and curse, and nurse the twisted bone, and tuck in the straggling flaps, and split the night with his cries of never. Never, never, his soul cried, and the word seemed to fork in his mouth so that it tumbled out differently, sometimes as *You will never make me a leper*, and sometimes as *I will never let you forget you are a leper*. Until his wife arrived, before the police could, shamefully pushing a wheelbarrow under cover of darkness in which to cart away this hamstrung father of her children to decent concealment under the despised roof.

Mornings it was easier.

Never, said Fred, more soberly, and clearly, and bolder, flanked by Mike and Bill and Joe, and braver from certain further pronouncements by the leader.

Oh no, he said, in the piccolo tones his brass could assume, rippling the muscles of his chest which the string vest obligingly revealed. Oh no, you don't outwit *me*. *You* are the leper.

For as days went by there were chinks to be seen, which night cloaked, holes in the decent chain mail of citizens where light, of the manufactured kind at which he was specialist, could be levered in. Multiplying signs, in this breaking season, as tar faded from flagstones, or was swallowed up by the willing quicksands of memory, and the beach lay quivering and clean, and ripe for messages. Sometimes Fred was so exhilarated he leaped like a plump salmon right off the mattress, long before midday, sending the iron bedstead squeaking on its castors to the corner of the treacherous lino floor.

'How's it going, Joe?'

Dipping a toe to feel the temperature, before plunging.

'Not too bad, mate.'

'The tenants?'

'They're mad. Got every right to be.'

Because, somehow, righteousness had to be present, or dragged in, however suspect and slimy the ropes.

'The neighbours,' said Fred. 'What d'you think?'

'It's like this,' said Mike. 'The way I see it, you have to keep at them.'

'It's not fair,' Fred tried out. 'Coming here, spreading foul diseases, keeping mum about it till he was found out. Mothers and children involved.'

'That's right,' confirmed Mike. 'And the removal vans fixed up and all.'

'The removal vans,' repeated Fred. 'Ah, yes, those. That day'll be the day,' he said, in a hushed way, as if light, which he had been wooing and coaxing, had at last begun to pour in.

He could hardly wait to be out and about his business.

'All this roaming and roving,' his wife complained. 'Where's it all going to lead to?'

'Just you wait and see, sweetheart,' said Fred, rippling, and resplendent, and glittering, and throwing off dangerous sparks from the cone of hatred rotating, now, at quite a respectable speed within the abrogated human casing.

And the days went by.

37

'THAT PRIMITIVE IS BANGING HIS TRIBAL DRUM,' SAID shrewd Laxman.

'I can hear the beat of the tomtom,' he said amazingly, and sat prim and disapproving, in his pointed shoes, and his Savile Row suit, and the hat from Lock's which he kept twirling for want of somewhere suitable to set it down in this dowdy house of his father's.

'Is best, man, when the tribes has to be summoned,' said Abdul, showing his teeth, which were white and chiselled, and he too twirled, the silk tassel went round and round with the tarbush in front of Laxman's repelled, if fascinated eyes.

'Do you think so?' he inquired, in his best English manner.

'You don't?' asked Abdul, aghast.

'All this shouting and swaggering,' said Laxman. 'Hardly a day goes by without some sort of rumpus. It's so *emotional*,' he complained. 'It simply isn't civilized.'

'You think,' said Abdul, who expected little from the father, but had hoped for better from the son, basing such faith, or hope, on the evidence of the Jensen. 'You think,' he repeated earnestly, tapping the dove-grey hand-pressed crease, 'it is a civilized war they are waging? Getting the bully boys out when the pigment shows?'

'No,' said Laxman, going abruptly from best English to basic yeoman, while retreating a knee.

Abdul melted. The two tough faces, shrewd, limousine-owning, made-in-Britain Oriental faces were coming together, and mingling, and acknowledging, and generating the energies of a common purpose.

Mrs Pickering coming in and seeing them like that was, in a remote way, comforted, because there are after all, she had discovered, limits to self-sufficiency, and justice, and even to what one can do.

She had brought tea, on a tray, in a dress which did nothing for her, though indeed as both men became aware little needed doing, such was the linchpin that upheld and sustained the composed figure. Like steel, of a quality yet to be invented, thought Abdul, while Laxman, entangled though he was in fastidious perception of externals, of clothes and hair and the profusion of grave-marks poured on the ageing skin, was also embarked upon revisions and acknowledgements of a kind he had submitted to once already.

Such revisions as Mrs Pickering had to make – and there were some, she admitted – she carried out without undue convulsion. Strength, she knew, was desirable, even essential, and certain transparencies in Laxman had early on made plain to her that he possessed the requisite strains. It was the father, however – the thick impregnable indestructible core of him which was sometimes felt, and sometimes revealed – it was this that dominated, not the son.

'Dr Radcliffe will be down in a minute,' said Mrs Pickering.

'It may take a while,' she admitted, as the wrinkled skin formed on the fourth cup, for she had seen the doctor, and the two of them up in the attic, and their attitudes had not encouraged any belief in time being a factor in their deliberations.

Dr Radcliffe had in fact completely forgotten.

He sat with his housebound patient, in a somewhat moribund chair, advising him, it would appear, though it could also have been the other way round from the dizzy if subtle rapidity with which from time to time they switched places.

'Fresh air,' said Dr Radcliffe. 'You ought to open the window a little. It's a bit stuffy up here, don't you find?'

'It's a little too cold,' said Srinivas, 'don't you think? For the ladybirds.'

'Ah, yes, the ladybirds,' said the doctor. What extraordinary, he thought, if perfectly legitimate problems, beset ordinary human beings! His fingers, without his authority, ran up the shape of a prayerful steeple. 'Of the genus *coccinella*,' he found himself saying.

'So my son told me,' said Srinivas.

'Really?' said Dr Radcliffe. The elegant, prosperous son. One might have guessed, he thought.

'My younger son,' said Srinivas gently, 'whom you never met, preferred to call them ladybirds. Like my first wife,' he was moved to continue, for no apparent reason. 'She, too, was before your time. A difficult woman, in many ways. Obdurate, some thought. Or perhaps steadfast, I have never been able to decide. What I am is in part, of course, due to her influence.'

'As one is,' agreed Dr Radcliffe.

'As she, in part, was moulded by circumstance.'

'We are all, to an extent, creatures of circumstance,' said Dr Radcliffe.

'You would have found her,' said Srinivas, smiling, 'even more difficult, if possible, than I am.'

'I do not find you difficult,' said Dr Radcliffe, and grew a little breathless. 'You do not present any difficulties,' he said, and juggled deftly, 'except in certain contexts.'

'Can one be taken out of context?'

The doctor juggled again, or wriggled, he might have been wearing a hair shirt from the movements he made. Then he forced himself to be still, seeing there was nothing for it but to plunge.

'My wife,' he blurted.

'Whom I have met,' said Srinivas.

Whatever flowed could have been healing or shattering, if only the distinction had been clear. Unable to distinguish, Dr Radcliffe ran blindly, he ducked down the first alley that offered escape.

'As your medical adviser,' he began, and this normally fertile alley that had stretched in front of his mind shrivelled instantly to nothing.

He stopped. Important people had medical advisers. People like this one queued in gale-swept corridors like sheep at a dip, and waited for the deity to appear.

'As your medical adviser,' he resumed with humility, and was swept over the weir which had loomed too late, 'I would advise you to go away until it is over.'

'Where?' said Srinivas.

So that they were stuck, the two of them in this bog, afraid to move for fear of sinking without trace, until somewhere in the tacky mess a ferment began, which both perceived, a stirring of latent misery to do with promises which had been sought, and given, in a haven of rough slub and euphoric

light, but had not at any time, within their context, been
really capable of redemption.

The doctor burst out first.

'If I could,' he said, and handfuls were clinging, the mud
he flung at himself. 'The house is big enough, certainly ...
but, you see, I am not free, any more than anyone is free.'

'I had no right to ask,' said Srinivas.

'Every right,' said Dr Radcliffe, and examined his hands,
those culpable things, into which men flung themselves.

'I have to deny you,' he said at last. 'I am denied myself.
I do not know why,' he continued fretfully, 'or what it is all
about.'

But he did know, quite precisely, beyond belief though
it was. It was to do with preservation. With preservation,
or conservation, or hoarding, of curly pile carpets, and
landscapes, and Rovers, and milky privileges, and wealth,
and even health, but, above all – the essential salt – those
intoxicating powers of derision which allowed one man to
look down, from a height, at another.

Selfishness, or you could call it a corruption of the soul,
pronounced Dr Radcliffe. He was something of a purist in
these matters, and in many ways a masochist as well.

38

SO IT WAS TO BE, THOUGHT SRINIVAS, WITH A SOFT free-fall of affection, his sole and final abode as, perhaps, he had always suspected it might be.

The solid edifice of Indian woods with whose planing and polishing he had once had a hand, the smart, curt hospice of Laxman and Pat, the desolate coops of quarantine, the rough slub harbour hung with the oranges and golds of evening light, each in turn had come forward like dancers, and smiled or grimaced, and invited and withdrawn, leaving the gaunt old house in possession.

Srinivas had no objection. The two of them, it and he, waxed and waned if not together, at least in some kind of communion. Both were very frail now, leaning, and insubstantial, but clearly girders and bones would continue to support each other as long as need be. Even if neither fortress nor refuge was to be coaxed out of them, as had been made clear.

'You will outlast me,' he took to saying, slapping a sturdy beam. Or sometimes he wagged a finger and said with conviction: 'I will outlive you.'

Either way was acceptable, considering. For, after all, a great deal had gone on under these rafters: the knowledge of peace, what it was like, and war to provide a leavening, and sorrow which in a curious way pointed up the happiness, and loving and being loved – not once but twice – which by any reckoning was more than most men dared aspire to. So he counted his blessings, and stopped up his nostrils insofar as he could when the stench of the ghetto rose too sharply, and dwelt on the webs of gentleness that still prevailed in the land, could still be found, obstinately clinging, their delicate fabric belying their strength and resisting all efforts of Fred and his henchmen to foul them.

Only, there were times.

Sometimes, when Fred shone his torch, the virulent beam would infiltrate, penetrate the glass and bear down on the tight, white eyelids of his sleep until he woke. Then he would lie still in the discordantly illuminated room, while the light wobbled and scanned and finally raced over the ceiling and abruptly plunged into darkness. Once, though, when he woke, or seemed to, his limbs would not allow him to lie. They sweated, and twitched, and drew him up out of his bed and took him to the window through which the beam played. But when he looked out it was gone. Instead he saw a billboard, similar to the one which had displayed the dangling man, save that this one was washed white, a coagulated white like dead eyelids on which marsh lights were dancing, a greenish fire which flickered and flared and began, as he watched, to emblazon a pattern of destruction.

Burning, make ready for burning, the green fire read, or spelled out, as it fizzed along the billboard. On reaching the edge the fireball paused, but was pushed, or fell, and went careening over the precipice in a final explosion of sparks.

When uncovering his eyes he looked again the street was ordinary. Empty, and dark from a withdrawal of the baleful light, but furnished as usual with bollards, and lamp standards, and illuminated road signs, and a crossing beacon winking in the distance, all those reassuring objects placed upon the earth which conceal, and even quell, its molten core.

Srinivas returned to his bed. He lay down, and pulled up the covers, and closed his eyes, and by these simple acts sought to reduce the strange terrors of the night, and presently succeeded, presently stilled his silly imperfect stampeding heart.

But the green flares continued to drift, swaying and grazing against his eyeballs.

'You were restless last night,' said Mrs Pickering.

Morning demolished visions; he refused to believe.

'It was a dream,' he told her. 'A frightening one.'

Mrs Pickering's arms, exposed to the elbow for efficiency, were plumping up pillows and straightening covers which had become unusually rucked up that night.

'It is curious,' she said, 'how what hangs in the air, over a quite incredible radius, can shape into dreams and nightmares.'

'You too?' he had to ask, for he could not believe, from her sturdy arms, and the way she thwacked the bedclothes.

'Oh, yes,' she said. 'Sometimes I am quite frightened by my bad dreams.'

If he could have offered her then the whole, unsullied, crystalline world in its pristine freshness he would have. Being powerless he said, gently, 'There is no concrete evidence, is there, of any danger?'

'No,' she said. 'There is nothing concrete. But real danger is never born of anything concrete. There are only words in the beginning.'

It brought them together. Oak and teak mingled, were sustaining each other, arms twined in a dazzling effusion of love and strength even if the one pair was somewhat thin, and both were indubitably old. And Srinivas knew, in the glow their throats and breasts had kindled, that what they had could not have been, not by one half, but for what they had gone and were going and would go through together.

The following day words spewed out.

A speech.

An explosion.

Lethal dust from the deliberate detonation, sly little ugly globules, hung suspended in the atmosphere.

'I hope,' Mrs Pickering said, looking up from the brass she had taken to polishing to stem, or at any rate deflect attention from, the creeping decrepitude of the old house, 'I hope you will not go out looking for trouble.'

'Oh, no,' said Srinivas, 'why should I? It will come to me.'

'Or for your own good reasons,' she said. 'Promise you won't, until it is over.'

'Will it ever be?' he wondered.

'Oh, yes,' she said in her confident way. 'A few more days and the tenants will have gone. We shall soon be over the hump.'

He, however, could not wait, because he was not too sure. Besides, if the truth be told, he could not resist the lure of the lovely, soft-budded season that was upon them. If he had to lay down his life, he felt extravagantly, he would, just to walk freely once more.

So he did. He walked fearless, and also slightly drunk, in the limpid airs of early light, noting the unfolding signs, lines of deepening green which traced the openings of buds, and downy growths, and curly vines, and the flow of colour – a wholesale conversion to colour – which, extinguishing greys and duns, had begun to flush the opaque closures of petals and pour into, and fill, the clefts and cups of early blossom.

Sometimes he could not bear it. He would tremble, and retreat, such was the tenderness, or perhaps it was the contrast. Then he would resurrect other vistas, of heady oleander, and flame flowers that lit whole avenues of trees in summer, and they would come, obedient if wavery from distance and time, but unable to take their place. For Ashcroft Avenue, which disowned him, or at any rate would have preferred to divest itself rather than suffer all these convulsions so bad for the constitution, in fact, as it happened, was the owner.

Those who saw the lonely figure were moved, they could not have said why, but dubbed the feeling irrational. After all, they consoled themselves, the laws of our land are the best in the world, our standards are the highest of anywhere on earth. Best, highest, rang in their ears and refurbished tarnished consciences.

And, as they said, you cannot co-opt human nature.

Not this side of democracy: or short of Belsen. Either way, you cannot.

Some were downright offended. They hurried by, with their coat collars up, and would have spat to rid themselves except that by-laws made it an offence to spit in the streets.

'I hear sly-boots is up and about,' said Fred to Mike and Joe and Bill.

'What you worried about?' demanded Mike. 'We're seeing him off, aren't we?'

'We had rats once,' contributed spotless Joe. 'We had to smoke them out. Once you get rats on the premises,' he said, 'you gotta smoke them out.'

'Only solution,' said Bill, though his mind shivered behind the curtain of what this solution might be.

'Come the day he'll get his,' said Mike, cutting short because of its crudity.

So in common with a good many residents they began counting the days to comeuppance.

39

THE DAY BEFORE, FRED FLETCHER WENT OUT TO GET himself a coat.

He felt the occasion warranted it, but there was the question of money. He could depend on Mike and Joe for a good many things, but not money. He was forced to approach his mother.

'Yes,' said Mrs Fletcher, 'we are all a bit short, one way and another.'

She was worn right out, really quite bent. What death, release from that stranded grey whale, her husband, had put back was taken away with interest by the constant presence of what she privately and silently called that gorilla, her son.

A beast, with no hope of salvation, with a brood – lovely bouncy babies, actually, with a beauty of great innocence and mystery sprung from this apish hulk – that tied her hands. Mrs Fletcher, who had once looked up for guidance, and even deliverance, nowadays pitched her aim much lower and simply prayed, each morning and night, for endurance.

'It's essential,' Fred said, to that dry biscuit, his mother.

'What for?' she asked.

'My business,' flashed Fred, not thinking.

'Your business is evil,' said his mother, and turned her grey face to the wall.

But you can't keep a good man down, thought Fred, riding on the top deck of the red omnibus, his pockets bulging –

full, anyway – with money taken from the housekeeping, from the purse kept hidden, but not beyond the scope of Fred to ferret out.

At the Circus he got off the bus and made his way along Glasshouse Street and Beak Street, both of which were familiar to him, to Carnaby Street, where, someone had happened to mention, a coat such as bewitched his mind's eye might be procured. But as he hobbled along, peering and coveting, it became clear to Fred that Carnaby Street didn't want to know, or at least had little to offer in exchange for a week's housekeeping. Nothing, at any rate, that was not firmly behind plate glass. Nothing for honest citizens like himself, though plenty, apparently, for the foreigners who jammed the place, shiny parcels under their arms. Fred's temper began to rise. He stood like a stump, as awkwardly as he could, obstructing the narrow pavement until a shove from a couple of hefty sailors sent him flying. Once set moving, however, he kept going.

He kept going, his mind full of foreigners, until he was lost in the depths of Soho. And there, on a barrow, in an open-air market, so casually flung he instantly knew it came within the housekeeping, was what he had dreamed of. Scarlet, and gold, with loops, and lanyards, and braid, and a broad white buckskin crossbolt.

It could have been the regimentals of a trooper, touched up by a fanciful theatrical costumer.

Or the livery of some faithful, obsolete retainer.

Or it could well have been the vestments laid, somewhere, sometime, on proud vice-regal shoulders, or so Fred, who had seen pictures and saw visions, became convinced.

It was a bursting, riproaring representative of the Queen that rode home on the bus. But purposeful, and determined, and dedicated solely and totally to the welfare of his people.

That night Fred went out with his torch and a bundle.

When he reached No. 5 he went down the stairs to the basement. Ice had broken, black water flowed between. He walked carefully, shining his torch and crunching. Afraid, but forsworn, and upheld by his oath.

In the basement all was ready, slipped in earlier by faithful lieutenants. Fred shone his torch approvingly. The watery beam bobbed over the uneven floor, pausing to consecrate where it fell on the simple array of essentials for the job. Laid out like instruments, these innocent objects of release, and waiting for the act to commence that would resolve the problem.

At one stroke of his hand. The encompassing power, the enormity of it, resting like a world in his palm. Whole worlds, contained within shells or skulls, in his custody. His. Fred swelled; he could feel the size of it, in his pants, and against the turtleneck of his sweater. He could hardly wait, he felt, the moment of release, or redemption, but the day was not yet. The day of the monkey, said Fred, soft and bellicose and baring his teeth. He stood like a thick wet pillar in the darkness.

A sudden sharp snort as of a heavy sleeper disturbed him. At first he thought it was himself, but when he held his breath the throaty grunting went on, if on a descending scale. Paralysed though he was Fred was nevertheless moving. Advancing, he convinced himself, although in fact a retreating foot had reached the stairs before he remembered about the black man, the feller in the basement on whom, unknowing, he had lavished his sympathy. Recovering, though his heart still thumped, Fred began in reality to move towards the sound. Cursing, and feeling around with his foot for the torch, which in the shock he had dropped.

Twice he fell over; once neatly, landing on a pile of wood shavings; once brought hard up against a boiler, with its plumbing attached in twisted leaden coils, abandoned in the middle of the room. Flailing to save himself, his hand fell on the torch, which he clutched, and the two of them went down together. It's an ill wind, thought Fred, picking himself up from the floor on which black water had dripped, and not quite evaporated. He was damp, but the torch, which still worked, restored him. He shone it on the corner from which grunts, staccato but rich, were still rising. It lit up, as he had surmised, the slumbering features of a black man.

Soundly asleep, this coal-black creature – darkness itself, it seemed to his onlooker – and occupying a deckchair which Fred, having seen, instantly craved. From craving to appropriation was a matter of simple progression. Gripping an edge of the tattered canvas, Fred flicked, a firm upward flick of both wrists which tipped the black man on to the floor. The expelled object, done up in rags to resemble a bolster, fell without a sound, and still without uttering – its snores swallowed up in this nightmarish onslaught – began to roll towards the wall. Fred kicked the insensible thing a couple of times to encourage it along, using his torch to aim square at the ribs, then with a sigh of achievement he sank into the requisitioned deckchair. The canvas smelled a bit: cat, and rotting fibres, and what Fred immediately isolated as black man, which mingled with certain sour exudings of his own; but he was not deterred.

'Stinking sod,' he grumbled, and quivered a nostril in token disgust before settling to his vigil in the vacant, warmish hammock.

Towards morning Fred got up and began to be busy. There were a great many things to do, the thought of which brought an absorbed, devotional look to features which the cold had somewhat crimped.

The fire, for instance. Long before it was scheduled to consume, its reflections lit his cheeks, sent glowing runners to relieve the thick pallor of his flesh, warmed his hands which were numb but engaged in building. It could have been a purposeful pyramid that those tingling tips evoked: a mausoleum, custom-built for bones, or a sputtering volcanic cone which, if it buried its base, was specific about its slopes, which crackled, deep in woodchips and cindery shavings.

Fred intoned as he worked: a low sound between psalm and dirge, slashed here and there with distinct notes of incantation. Now and then he broke off, to give a subdued yelp, or suck a finger, for the wood was alive with splinters. Evil, insidious needles that could not pierce the skin but got under his nails, so that he had to stop, tear himself away from the loved edifice to crouch by the grating, under the grey filtering light, and extract the malevolent sliver.

All the time the black man watched.

Like a turnip, thought Fred, who did not mind, no more and no less than one would have minded the scrutiny of a row of cabbages, or any object of wood or stone. Except that this one had pretensions, rudimentary human skills that could be put to use.

'Here, you,' said Fred, and lumbered over. 'I gotta thorn, see. In my flesh. You remove. Savvy?' He was good at languages, especially pidgin.

The black man seemed not to understand. He rolled up his eyes to show the whites, in a way that Fred found disgusting. There was a distinct smell of meths.

'Bloody soak,' Fred muttered. He nudged the hulk with a toe.

'You do what sahib says, understand?' he said. 'Or else.'

This time the black obeyed. His hands, for a drunk, were reasonably steady; his skill, if rudimentary, sufficient.

Relieved of the splinter, Fred mellowed. There were also his thoughts, bumbling around agreeably in his mind as he put the finishing touches. Sprinkling his edifice from the seized green-glass bottle, since Mick and Joe had neglected to provide. Dribbling the volatile liquid finically, like holy water, for only dregs remained, and the precious droplets falling like rain on the wood curls, which drank them up and sent up aromas: odours, vile on the black's breath, transformed and rising sharp and tangy like essences. Fred could not have enough. He took his fill, expanding his chest, and shaking the bottle to extract last drops, while the black watched.

All the time the black man watched.

Presently Fred was done. Or almost. The reflections were dancing on his skin now, a greenish opalescence struck from sage glass and pale light, as he put down the bottle and knelt to open his bundle. Trembling, his hands and hams unsteady as he drew it out and held it up, the scarlet thing in all its glory. There it hung, from the twin masts of his arms, its stiff red folds casting a light such as the cavernous room had never seen in all its years as a cellar.

The effulgence reactivated Fred, petrified in the figurehead and timbers of some ship. He could hardly wait. His fingers flew, buttoning and unbuttoning. In no time at all the coat was on his back, arms into sleeves, braid hung in heavy trusses of jet and gold, the buckskin belt sloped smartly across both shoulders and crossed whitely over back and breast. For Fred had blancoed the straps. He had also polished the brass. Buckle and buttons winked from throat to crotch, and were answered in scarlet, coruscating and determined not to be outdone.

But the two together were lost, could not hold a candle to the splendour that invested Fred. It lit him up, from within and without. The scarlet runners were confirmed, but absorbed and overrun by the glow that had begun to spread, crimson and gold like a sunset across the entire surface of his skin. He shone, Fred felt: was born to lead, he knew with utter conviction. So he would. He would lead his countrymen in the fight to overthrow the evil, hidden forces that were threatening them in their homeland.

It was a flushed, dedicated figure – somewhat dusty about the knees, and with certain signs of an addled egg beginning to manifest, but nevertheless imposing – that rose stiffly in the greyish gloom and advanced towards the kindling.

The black man continued to watch, soundless, motionless. He could have been some object carved from wood or stone.

40

AT PAVEMENT LEVEL FORCES WERE MUSTERING, IN THE perfectly permissible shapes of men and women.

They drifted up – nothing hysterical about the English – they came in twos and threes to declare themselves, and to take up positions against what was being done to ordinary people like themselves, they said, ordinary decent people; and they sighed. The air was full of sighs on this sad occasion.

Shawls were much in evidence. Also a handcart or two, to trundle away pitiful possessions, it might have been inferred, but for the solid figures of rag-and-bone men that were to be seen leaning against the shafts, patiently waiting for pickings. There could be no denying, however, the presence of refugees. They loitered, pale and somewhat shadowy and not without undergoing certain subtle alterations, irresistibly in the minds and hearts of the onlookers. And were brought out and unveiled presently, in their new garb of pitiful English who were being harried, turned out of their houses and thrown on to streets.

By foreigners, people said to each other. By means too foul, others added, to tell about, although it was made clear smears had appeared on tenants' doors. Of human excreta, no less. Varied by leprous exudings deliberately spread on banisters.

'Bloody Jew,' one of them (new to the district, a phoenix from a livid era) burst out, but was quickly squashed as a racist. Since no one wanted those ovens to be lit again, besides which it would introduce some undesirable blurring of roles, between oppressor and oppressed, between patriot and racist, which they were not and would never countenance being. No; what they wanted was a little weeding out, and a little elementary justice, in the pursuit of which they were gathered here together.

Poor things, they said accordingly, concentrating on the victims, and they waited with bursting hearts for the persecuted to appear whom they would usher away, it was implied, under compassionate canopies to welcoming hearths and homes, if only such had been available.

And ladies in single occupancy of roomy houses kept quiet, except for sighs.

It was to be an occasion, it seemed, for sighing.

The police were unconvinced. They were grown men, who could crack the code hidden in speeches. They nursed their suspicions, and held themselves alert within the neutral walls of the station, which after all was within a stone's throw. Because, all said and done, what could you do, apart from dispatching a couple of squad cars to keep watch from the sidelines as had already been done, since you can't change human nature?

Constable Kent felt differently. He had held a painted skull in his arms, thin as an eggshell it had been, as easily crushed, and once you have done that, his instincts told him, it is bound to make a difference. He thought he would go down and see for himself.

'With my blessing. You'll need it,' said his sergeant. 'You must be daft,' he added, frank but mild.

Daft or no, Constable Kent had to do as he felt. He put on his helmet, making sure the strap was well up his chin in

case of bricks, and sauntered off to Ashcroft Avenue to see
what he could see.

Strolling, if deliberate, from his three solid years in the
force, his long legs taking even strides – never do to show
what you felt – P.C. Kent was carried easily along the avenue.
When at a point opposite No. 5 he stuck. He could go no
further. For absolutely no reason whatever, unless it was that
his boots had melted and been poured into the pavement.
Stood cemented, his heart thundering, listening to his
whimpering body and exposed to a strange sense of being
unprotected in the presence of evil, the kind of situation
in which, he had observed, Catholics will pause and cross
themselves.

As he would not, not being a bloody Papist. But petrified
all the same, a blooming blue pillar.

He could have been surveying the scene, it relieved him
to think. Which was only normally nasty, no more than he
had been led to expect.

Why, then, this extraordinary fear which had leapt up,
sprung straight from outworn, medieval notions of evil, and
nailed him to the pavement?

Stuff and nonsense, said the perspiring constable, and
brought the whole stolid weight of his training to pick up
his boots and set them moving in the right direction.

The right direction for him was of course towards the
crowd, which he observed approvingly was well behaved,
and of moderate proportions. Decent local people, he
convinced himself, pacing the fringes with measured tread, a
lost capacity now blessedly restored to him. Decent-looking
men, and respectable women who had covered themselves
against the weather, or to ward off the unpleasantness
inherent in current proceedings. Because no doubt about

it, eviction was a miserable business, although what was happening was by no means that. People would persist though; he could hear them. A few wild ones, the usual bully boys, these days you got to expect them, thought Constable Kent, cool under his helmet. He began to hum, under his breath, as he paced. A policeman's lot, he hummed – from Gilbert and Sullivan, he believed – is not a happy one, bong-bong-bong.

But after a little – quite soon actually – he stopped. His heart was not in it. Or possibly it was because of the stench. Something rank, his instincts, rather than his nose, informed him. He examined these elusive creatures suspiciously, to sec if they were running away with him, or what. But no, there was no denying. So the constable began to poke and pry more closely, and saw faces that he knew, blanched in the cold March light, and a good many that he didn't, or couldn't recognize under the dark flow of emotion, and looked for – and failed to see – the provoking forms of Fred, who had gone underground, and Srinivas, who was aloft.

And was lulled.

'I hope,' said Mrs Pickering to Srinivas, 'you will stay put.' And she drew out a little wobbly teapoy and carefully balanced on it the cup of coffee she had brought him, since life must go on, at all cost, as it has a way of doing.

Srinivas looked out of the murky window at the numbers milling below.

'I intend to,' he said.

For a while they were quiet, sipping coffee, and nourishing the flow between them which, when they were together like this, never failed to join them. Then he said, speaking out of that core which she could have worshipped, but more often resisted – which both resisted from time to time, from certain inhibitions, certain injunctions against what in the English climate could have appeared theatrical: 'It exists of course ... if it did not we would not experience these warnings to be on guard, as we do.'

'Oh, yes,' she agreed at once in her blunt way, 'evil exists, all right.'

'But it burns itself out, eventually.'

'Oh, yes,' she agreed again. 'But I don't think the ashes that were left in Germany gave comfort to anybody, do you?'

Soon she rose, made restless by ashes and incinerators.

'I think I'll go and take a look,' she said.

'Look,' he began, covetous for the flowering light that would fade with her going, and rapped himself sharply. 'Look after yourself,' he finished, releasing them both for normal, ordinary activities.

What these were, in the extraordinary situation ballooning up about them, thought Mrs Pickering as she descended, could be anybody's guess. She put on a sensible wrap, because robust as she was it was a raw morning, and went out into the arena to see.

For, clearly, pavements, like people, were more than they appeared to be, whatever their surface guise. This grey stretch, for example, laid placidly along frontages and forecourts of houses, had been transformed into a theatre, the ringing flagstones might have been boards under actors' feet, on which players were acting out their parts. The woman, for instance, who had come to support her daughter, was playing the part of Mother – suffering, enduring, universal Mother figure she might have been, a madonna of the ages.

'You gotta look after your own, haven't you? Your own flesh and blood?' she was saying. Throwing a shawl, or some equivalent melancholy garment, to embrace the shoulders of her child, and her child's child – all three of them – who were in any case very well swaddled.

'That's right,' the assembly, in its role of chorus, replied.

'Things have come to a pretty pass,' said the madonna, 'when you gotta make room for strangers. Eh, love?' Chucking the bambino, her grandchild, under the chin.

'That's right,' chanted the chorus.

The daughter, however, was dubious; she was, in truth, having some difficulty with her role, which refused to be reconciled to what she knew.

'I will say he always treated us fair,' she managed, this sturdy young woman who had squeaked, and run, and been reassured, and was beginning to feel ashamed. 'Always,' she gasped, to subdue the qualms that were threatening her.

But the crowd only put it down to her decency. They were a decent people. They listened to the mother, who had not finished, not by a long chalk, she intended to have her say.

When Mrs Pickering, who had been cleaving her way through dense and determined citizens, reached her side. So full of contempt she appeared to be spitting. Like a cobra, thought the woman, though she hadn't ever seen one. Venomous. It only had to touch your skin and you were done for.

'Haven't you done enough damage?' Mrs Pickering asked.

It was so frightening the madonna fell back into the arms of the multitude, but those arms shoved her back again, she was standing upright on her own two feet.

'It's not what we *done,* it's what we have to *suffer,*' she was given courage to say, and even managed to bristle a bit before dismantling the woolly tent that had covered three generations and departing.

But the girl with the baby remained, next to the old woman. She was struggling to speak, her mouth was opening and shaping above the tender downy fontanelles of her infant. No sound, however, came, or if it did was lost at the insistence of the crowd, which didn't want to know. So she shut up, closed her mouth and lowered her eyelids which were waxy, and fringed, the lashes rested like curved fans on the dead cheeks.

Mrs Pickering was staring; she could not look enough, it seemed, at those concealing eyelids of candlewax white. It was at this point, she was to realize later, that her terror began. Suddenly, as she looked at lids which were falling like shutters, it began to jet and spurt, setting as it fell into ice, ice sprays around her heart, and freezing splinters in her blood, and coating the sockets into which the heads of bones must fit, which blundered around instead, slipping and slithering.

But she was running. Somehow.

Whimpering, she realized, and stopped that. Ripping the sensible wrap, she realized, but careless, and the cold coming through the rents which she did not feel, because now she was burning as she ran – raced – towards her object.

Ignited, it seemed to the unhappy crowd, scorched at one end while squeezed at the other by the equally determined passage of a similar, if lesser, object.

For Mrs Fletcher was so feeble, and bent, and bloodless – her face was quite yellow – and bowed from whatever burden she was carrying, it was a wonder she could walk, let alone whizz along as she was doing. Looks, however, can deceive, as those who felt her elbows readily conceded, for she was in fact thrusting quite strongly towards Mrs Pickering.

The two women, whose quality was such that it silenced the assembly, met in the centre of the arena in which sweated odours of fear and cruelty – a distinct reek of circus – had begun to be evident. And Mrs Pickering was cruel, twisted into and contaminated by the prevailing climate.

'Where is your godless son?' she demanded. Accusing, attacking the woman who had given birth in innocence, and laying at her door ills for which in all conscience – or any shred of it – she could not be responsible.

'I don't know,' said Mrs Fletcher. Something was trickling out of her – molten sawdust shovelled into the quaking case to propel it this far – in the presence of the stronger woman. She was, she recognized, about to collapse, but would pass on the torch before she did.

'I've been looking and looking,' she gasped. 'I know he's up to no good but I don't know where to find him.'

And toppled, allowing those who clustered to spring into action, calling for water and space, and some even wondering if they dared practise their first aid upon the fainted woman.

41

IT WAS ABOUT NOW THAT FRED, DRAWING ON THE white gloves he had pinched overnight from his wife, struck the first match.

It went out.

At his fourth attempt (cursing each failure, and the glory of scarlet threatened by smuts, as he anxiously noted) the flame held steady long enough to light the damp balls of crumpled newspaper studding the base of the pyramid, which began to burn.

Rather feebly, though.

Whereas Fred had envisaged flames.

In his mind's eye bonfires were blazing, great warning beacons lit at the summits of hills, answered in kind from mountain to mountain, a ring of fire, protecting the beloved coast, which did not square with the wretched heap of kindling flickering weakly in the mouldy basement.

Fred walked about, swearing, and smarting (there was smoke in plenty, if little flame) and poking the pyre with a wooden paling torn from his mother's rotting fence. Now and then his efforts, or oaths, were answered: a tongue would uncurl, and leap, and give Fred a golden foretaste as it flared up the sides, only to falter as it reached the soggy remnants of fence generously piled on top.

He could trust his mother, Fred felt; trust her to thwart him at every step. In his rage he began to tear away the remaining palings, leaving himself with a truncated cone from which wisps of smoke were rising. You couldn't have smoked out a mouse, unless it was by the smell. That stench. Fred glanced suspiciously at the black man, crouched in a corner with his back against the wall. But no; it was stronger, closer. It was himself, he realized: the rubber of his sandshoes and his wife's household gloves were heating, softening, exuding pungent odours prior to dissolution; the soles, indeed, were smouldering at the edges.

I give up, said Fred.

Only, a Briton doesn't know when he's beaten.

Luckily, there was water: blackish drips collected in dips in the uneven floor. Fred squelched about in his quenched shoes, rebuilding with his bare hands. More urgently now, because time was pressing. Because any minute some bastard would notice and bawl. Especially once the crowd had dispersed and there was nothing to occupy attention. Though Mike and Joe – he could rely on them – would keep it milling around for some time yet, giving him the chance to get clear. One wasn't prepared, after all, to roast for a cause. Or be caught for it. He'd be for the high jump then, all right, juries being what they were, especially obstinate British juries, whom you couldn't convince about anything once their eyes started popping over corpses. So emotional, they wouldn't see what was best for the nation.

Fred wasn't emotional, but his breath came in gusts as he built his mausoleum, this monument to himself that no one would see. Under his blackened hands the truncated cone grew swiftly. He packed it well this time, with abundant garnishings of newspaper, and the firewood Joe had laid in, and whatever fuel he could find. Roving in the semi-gloom, held up now and then by his tangling accoutrements, he came across a whole box of candles, and a pile of disintegrating deckchairs stacked against the wall which he heaved on to his pyramid. Underneath was treasure, in the shape of a second bottle, green, and full, and evidently belonging to the black, who started a low bleating, as of deprived lambs, as he saw it lifted. Fred hardly heard. He was absorbed, remote, taken up in the business of what could be last acts or rites; and besides there were the glottal sounds the liquid made, jerking out of the broken-necked bottle on to the canvas and timber frames which formed the peak of the pyramid.

At last Fred's work was well and truly done. The trail of screws and spills of paper leading to the mountain lighted at first match. It began to wriggle, a golden worm, along the clammy floor. Fred stepped back to view. He could not linger, but must. Just for a little, to warm himself by golden light.

When the fiery worm had begun to rear, and the air was fluttering with the soft grey moths of destruction risen in its wake, Fred turned to go.

It was his firm intention.

Something, however, prevented him. It held him firmly, and as he turned its grip tightened around his torso. Fred swore. He was not frightened yet, but not calm either, as he twisted about in the thickening atmosphere to free his crossbelt from the pernicious plumbing of the disused boiler. If he could see, he knew, it would be simple; but his eyes had begun to stream, the drops landed wet and black on his scarlet, he could have wept for the state it was in but for his own, which was worse. When in the very middle of distress – cuffing at smoke, and wrestling with coils behind his back – he saw his saviour.

Still in his corner, a figure of wood and ash, the black man sat.

'Hey, you, sambo,' called Fred. (Not too loud: subconscious vestiges of disapproving British juries restrained him.) 'I'm stuck. Give us a hand.'

The figure had not stirred. It was alive, though. Breathing.

'Hurry up, mate,' cried Fred anxiously. Watching the worm, which had grown, and was loping along at a rate. 'Haven't got all day, you know.'

The figure continued to sit.

'For God's sake,' cried Fred. He had to tear the words out of his gullet. 'You wouldn't let a human being roast and not lift a finger, would you?'

No answer.

'Would you?' Screaming.

The black man rose. His round black eyes were swimming, filled with tears right up to the inflamed rims. This image carved out of ebony could, it seemed, feel. It could walk too. It was walking. Softly, rising and falling on the cushioned balls of his feet, the black man vanished.

Fred was left.

Wrestling within his golden temple, with the gold lights dancing on him, while the coils tightened. Those loops and trusses of braid and buckskin, binding him to the writhing iron pipework. In this terrible conspiracy. If he could shed, Fred felt, wrenching at the cross-straps with scorched fingers, sinking his teeth in blanco, biting on buttons. But buckskin is, after all, hide: it would not give, it allied itself to buckles, and straps, and epaulettes, and held him firmly.

Half-blind, now he could not hear. But he could feel the screams going up the furred chimney of his throat, calling on God and man. Out of the choking labyrinth of his lungs they rocketed, exploding on air jampackcd with its own sounds, of rushing draughts, and the raving insanity of fire, and of snail shells splitting on the brazier of blazing palings. And crammed, it seemed to Fred: stuffed full of shapes that fluttered and flapped, trapped in the darkening vault, above the pyramid of fire.

Like bats out of hell, thought Fred, and kept watch on the charred scraps of paper through crafty, smoke-filled eyes.

42

UNTIL THE TIMBERS BEGAN TO GROAN SRINIVAS HAD no inkling.

He stood by the window, whose diamond pane cut him off from the incisive sharpness of opinion, but was not persuaded because, after all, it had never been words alone but touch and tone and the spirit in which they were kept in solution which conveyed human impulses. Persuasion, moreover, is for the young, who are tender, and bruise easily, he told himself, and need to protect themselves.

Though armourplate might have been what the occasion demanded.

Against the blurred invective that rose, and now and then pierced the old man, who had persuaded himself he was as tough as old boots, as he stood framed by the window, watching them swarming below, the hive which had been stirred to anger by the firebrand of words, and waited for what was thrusting to come to a head. As it would, he recognized, with or without his presence, or participation, because once the seed has been planted the crust of earth must bulge, and break, and everyone take the consequences.

Or so he consoled himself, by what was in some ways a quite frightful thought, as he lay down on the old teak bed which had begun, he noticed, to creak, for all that its wood was so well weathered. Like himself, he thought, inspecting the clothed skeleton: that blunt blunderbuss, his hand, whose power was nearly spent, and a chestful of sluggish ribs, and legs which were almost past it, though the worn pistons would continue to chug along, obeying his will which was adamantine.

Soon, however, he wearied: could not really be concerned with these, which were of no consequence, but came out in a sudden sweat for what was. Cold drops forcing up in that moment of doubt, lying chill in the pits and hollows of his frame, chill ponds in which a mind could drown, until, fighting off the advancing tentacles he began to examine himself, closely, minutely, a formidable inward dredging that left him exhausted, but calm, convinced that within the barrel of bones the man himself remained intact.

Srinivas slept.

The splitting of timber woke him. A snapping of twigs it might have been, he woke without violence. Lay, languid, on teak, while smoke came up in little tendrils through the floorboards, drifted, and draped the bed legs, and coalesced to form a floating mattress. If he were to step down it would swirl up above his ankles, he thought, and was reminded of sunny childhood days, in a boat, on a lake, on which mists had risen and scudded, suddenly, almost between dipped oars so that the blade that went in clear came up dripping and smoking.

Smoke. All hopes, and expectations, and even spectres of dread, condensed into these fleecy scrolls which were already changing their nature. It might have been difficult to believe, otherwise. But the white was tinctured with yellow, and the tender drifts were swollen, and were charging heavy and sullen against the joists of the supporting structure which were not yet ready to yield.

You could almost hear the pounding.

Muffled sounds, somewhere on the outer reaches of his mind, which had prudently unhinged itself, Srinivas was relieved to find, and was hovering, aloof from the distress inherent in the situation, somewhere near the beleaguered ceiling. So he allowed his carcass to rest, watching the clouds mass, and lying on the smoky pallet, until recalled by primary duties, notably to the living. Unable to deny them he rose, reluctantly abandoning the cradle which could have lulled him, and groped his way, somewhat groggily, to the door.

Here he stopped: was brought up short by panels opening in the wood – or possibly in the chambers of his mind, it did occur to him – to reveal a triptych of faces: Vasantha's, which kept watch, and Mrs Pickering's, whose wrung features beseeched him, and Seshu's, whose lips were forming words. Of the three only Seshu spoke. Srinivas heard him quite distinctly.

'The ladybirds,' he said.

'I had forgotten, in all this confusion,' admitted Srinivas.

'I will be with you in a moment,' he said to Mrs Pickering, and made his way back to the window.

Outside, snowflakes were falling: quirky March weather. Too cold, he thought, peering through wreaths of smoke; but the architraves felt hot under his hand, and in the upper moulding the little beetles were clustering closer. There was nothing for it then but to shatter a diamond pane; which he did, with the legs of the wobbly teapoy which were nowhere as feeble as had been imagined.

He could not actually see them go, of course, there was too much in the way: but as each pair of wings opened for flight he had the distinct impression that the wet premature cuticles were drying out, were hard and enamelled as if fired in a kiln. He very much hoped so: he had become fond of his little colony.

When the ladybirds had flown – at least the window frames were empty – he had to see to himself, who was also a living thing. With his remaining strength he began to feel his way out of the attic whose fabric was now quite frail, you could tell from the tapping and moaning of its timbers, the solid oak become as frivolous and light as balsa, preparatory to bursting into flame.

It was going to be a race, Srinivas could see.

When the Jensen drove up, joining the Rover and the Lincoln and the three removal vans with tailboards down and household effects piled right up to the top, Constable Kent began to feel that Ashcroft Avenue was fast approaching Piccadilly Circus for congestion.

Laxman thought so too, as he nosed his way along, looking for parking. Too many car-owning people, he considered, in fact altogether too many people for so meagre an occasion.

Gathered for no good reason, he felt.

Idlers, he attempted by denigration to scale the feeling down, but it would persist, the shaven flesh of the nape of his neck was cringing, as if from draughts. Rubbish, said Laxman, irritably, and parked badly – too near the corner, and a rear wheel riding the curb – which further increased his annoyance. He ought, he felt, to have stayed put, and allowed the old man – misguided architect of his own misfortune – to get on with it. Instead here he was, in a dreary suburb, among a smelly crowd, making his way towards the group of three men who would be in a position to tell him, he hoped, what the old man was up to.

The group consisted of Abdul, whose Lincoln had beaten the Jensen to the last decent parking by a short head; and Dr Radcliffe and Constable Kent, who were special friends by reason of their recent, close collaboration.

The three, one could see, were concerned, but putting a face on it, or, possibly, reluctant to drag in what was nebulous and might be entirely imaginary, since they were after all grown men.

Laxman wholly approved. He hated anything running amok, but looking at the three solid forms it was plain there was no danger of that. The doctor certainly would not; doctors were worse than traders when it came to money, but they were trained not to panic, and they kept their voices low. The policeman was large, and young, but could be relied on, Laxman felt. In Plymouth he relied absolutely on the force, contributing handsomely, and ungrudgingly, to the Policemen's Widows' and Orphans' Fund. Abdul, true, was less admirable (that fez!) but possessing a Lincoln undoubtedly vouched for a basic soundness. Laxman actually felt sunny, his bluish nape had stopped crawling about his collar, as he nodded to the three.

'And how is your patient?' he inquired, affably.

Dr Radcliffe turned. The prosperous son, he saw, and could have groaned but for other matters that were bludgeoning him.

'I wish I knew,' he said simply, and his heart quailed because the knowledge could have been come by so easily, so peacefully, merely by sanctioning the shelter a fellow creature had come to him for, and been refused. Instead here he was, implicated in profane proceedings, observer at a carnival at which he had connived, which was about to begin. For Dr Radcliffe had no illusions.

'I called to see,' he said in exculpation (only there was none: nothing, now, to be had so cheaply). 'I have been a little anxious ... I'll go up,' he said, 'when the dust's settled a bit.'

'I hope,' said Laxman, whose cheer had unaccountably begun to ebb, 'there won't be any fireworks.'

Somehow, though there was nothing whatever to suggest it, it was as if their minds were bent on flames, reflecting a glimmer that lay beyond the horizon of admitted senses.

The policeman, made uneasy, cleared his throat. 'We're keeping an eye,' he announced, and his eyes roamed, looking anywhere except at the reflecting surfaces that were giving off these shattering emissions. 'Though we're not,' he said, 'expecting any trouble.'

'No trouble?' said Abdul, and his nostrils, which were thick, and squat, and ugly in the sight of some, but sensitive beyond anything such blindness could conceive from the ceaseless abrading that went on, began to twitch and flare as if assaulted by the odour of bad eggs being broken into a cracked and dingy basin. 'No trouble, when the bully boys are out?'

'No, sir, no trouble,' said the sweating constable. 'Nothing serious like. Nothing we can't handle.'

After which there was nothing to do but wait, and hope for a miracle that might retrieve the situation, whose criminal nature each had secretly conceded even if not all were ready to call it a hopeless case.

So they disposed themselves gingerly, four very different vigilantes, strung together on this fleshy tape slashed with curious spiritual insertions, and grew, and gradually dominated the scene, the four ordinary beings shuffled into the coils of colossi, perhaps by the grace and fervour of their intentions, or possibly because the landscape was so mean.

Laxman spotted the sensuous tendril of smoke sprouting lazily from the grating. Pretty, and innocent, a flaxen curl above the pavement which he watched between the movements of restless limbs, while what was feared crept closer, advanced on subtle pads until, suddenly, the two were clapping together, fear and reality locking into one in hideous, deafening copulation.

Then Laxman knew. At once, and as perhaps he had known all along, from a dreadful identification. Knew what was up, what had been allowed in behind deliberate backs and veiled eyes, for you cannot, Laxman acknowledged, arrange a picnic, let alone a liquidation, without active and passive participation. So he began to push through the crowd, thrusting savagely against flabby bodies and cowering minds, made savage by recognition of those minds whose configurations were his own, formed in the same schools, and from the same soil, water, air, and atmosphere, and with similar concentrations and precipitations. Minds that wished to eliminate, or be rid, or repatriate, while closing off from the actual horrors of the solution.

Which are not for the squeamish.

Laxman could have despised them, were it not that he was the same.

Or almost the same except for the dusky skin – bequeathed him by the old and culpable man who was even now paying the price for it jammed up in the attic – over which, even in these distraught moments, Laxman could have wept.

But he carried on, as others would, and some were already attempting, since no amount of marshalling or regimentation of blood, or emotion, or upbringing, or brainwashing, can wholly douse, in everyone, or for all time, the primal leap of human fellow feeling: flesh feeling for flesh.

For Srinivas had been seen, through the diamond pane, in distress it was surmised (quite rightly, for he was preoccupied, at that point, with the fate of the little colony), and smoke had begun to belch.

When Laxman began to plough his way through the crowd, the first impulse of Dr Radcliffe and Constable Kent was to follow him. Both, however, were trained to put first things first. The constable raced the squad car, to summon the fire brigade, and reinforcements, recognizing the limits of even his huge, if dedicated, frame. While Dr Radcliffe, with the spear twisting in his side, and the white drops crying to be staunched, was turned away from the attic to minister to the moaning, flaccid, collapsed body of Mrs Fletcher which a frightened posse had brought to his attention. So Laxman, like his father, was alone when he reached the portals.

Although, of course, a fair number of citizens were there to urge him on, themselves holding back when they saw how it was, a state of affairs for which firemen are best fitted.

Laxman went on alone, doing what he had to do, exhilarated in a sober kind of way by the severe freedom of choice which had narrowed down to this one austere path, whereas normally he would have been saddled, slung about with the pros and cons of every question, without which he would not have dreamed of taking a step. Now he kicked in a window, and climbed through to the hall.

At this point several things were happening. The fire in the basement, which had been nibbling and darting, and emitting more smoke than flame, reached the pulp of the pyramid which was soaking in methylated spirits, and erupted with a roar that swamped the uttermost cries of Fred. In the attic Srinivas, an intermittent wraith draped in billows of smoke, was shattering the windowpane which curved out – part still trapped in its lattice of lead – and fell at the feet of the crowd in a shower of diamonds. And Abdul, who was old, and wizened, and could neither run nor climb, but was resourceful from long training, had peremptorily requisitioned the ladder of a watching window cleaner, up whose rungs the imposing figure of Constable Kent was wobbling in ascent.

Laxman knew little of this. He was part way up the stairs, and the whoosh of the fire blew him up the remainder of the flight. At the landing he paused, afraid of the terrible sounds that were issuing, whose demonic notes seemed to him to be rising from pits, and could have unstrung a less impermeable man. Laxman, however, had developed a hide to cover the deficiencies of his inheritance; besides which there was no retreat, for by now the staircase base, and the slender rods of banisters, and the newel-post to which the young mother had clung, and the handrail which had been said to be smeared, all were aflame in what could have been a final purification by fire. So he turned his face resolutely and went on, until he reached the door of the attic, which was jammed.

But weakened: the panels in the wood cracked, by heat, or the efforts of the man who lay crumpled inside, and affording easy entry. It was exits, though, that preoccupied Laxman as he burst in, and braced himself to pick up his burden, and nearly hit the ceiling when he did, the body was so light.

By now the paint was beginning to bubble.

Fanned by great gusts of wind and flame Constable Kent hung on to his post. He had climbed to the second floor, which was as far as the ladder would reach, and smashed in a window, and would have clambered in but that he caught sight of Laxman, who seemed to have come to a standstill, being in fact at the end of his resources.

Laxman could not possibly have heard the glass break, but he saw the figure clamped to the perilous ladder through holes that had begun to gape in the fiery structure, and knew at last which way to turn.

'He's as light as a feather,' he said thickly, and passed on his burden to the constable who, as it happened, already knew.

When the three were safely down the firemen began playing their hoses on the burning building, and would in time get the fire under control, though those most concerned were scarcely aware, being preoccupied by the old man who lay, for all his lightness, as he would continue to lie, like a stone in the pits of stomachs.

The stomachs would heave, later, when they brought out the body of Fred, which was soaked, and charred, and snarled up and altogether unsightly.

But Srinivas was untouched, which somewhat spared the onlookers. Even his fine white thatch was barely singed, although metallic tints did show where it caught the glitter of fire, as his head lolled against the burly shoulder of the policeman.

The rasp of the cloth was familiar, thought Srinivas, as the feel of it penetrated the fibreglass in which each of his senses seemed to be wrapped, and he coasted along through the memories that were crowding him until at last he came to the one he was seeking.

'Constable Kent,' he said, quite clearly, as he felt himself put down.

'Yes, sir,' said the constable, and dragged a ruined sleeve across his eyes, which smarted, leaving a cleanish furrow upon his grimy, decent face. And stood back, having laid the old man on the coarse grey blanket on the stretcher that waited, to make room for Mrs Pickering.

She knelt beside him, in silence, in the quiet cameo that had been carved in the very glare of the flames, with her hands over his, and the almond light filtering through the flying strands of her hair formed a silvery aureole in which they were joined, until she tucked them back.

When the time was up. As perhaps at the moment only she, and the doctor, and of course Srinivas, knew.

Constable Kent did not want to believe.

'Not a mark on him ... I thought, I hoped ...' he floundered in his misery.

'Shock,' said Dr Radcliffe, briefly, and rose, dusting off his knees, but the granules of disgust accumulating, he saw no reason to spare anyone, least of all himself. 'He is dead,' he said ruthlessly, 'and we have all had a hand in it.'

Mrs Glass thought it unseemly of him, not to say a downright lie, but circumstances restrained her. She had levered herself to the forefront of observers, and now came forward in the role of comforter.

'Weep, dear,' she said to Mrs Pickering, and would have embraced her but for the searing light that seemed to flow from the older woman. 'It will make you feel better.'

'You can believe that, if you like,' said Mrs Pickering.

'Don't take it too hard,' said Mrs Glass, nervously.

Is that possible? wondered Mrs Pickering, whose mind was crammed with images, of the fallen weak and helpless, and of their sons, and sons' sons, who would not be content as Srinivas had been but could be trusted to raise Cain – if Cain had not in fact already been raised.

'You mustn't blame yourself,' said Mrs Glass, sweating.

'Blame myself,' said Mrs Pickering. 'Why should I? I cared for him.'

And, indeed, that seemed to her to be the core of it.

ABOUT SMALL ✖ AXES

Founded in 2010 HopeRoad's mission has been to promote new literary voices from Africa, Asia and the Caribbean.

The name comes from a road in Jamaica where Bob Marley lived and which is now home to the Bob Marley Museum at 56 Hope Road.

In exploring themes of identity, cultural stereotyping and disability we bring neglected voices from the margins to the centre of the page in a range of books for adults and young adults.

Hard fought changes in attitudes are currently been reversed. We feel the need to launch a new imprint, Small Axes: inspired by the Bob Marley song, Small Axe: a well sharp axe ready to cut the big tree down. The imprint will mix post-colonial classics that helped to shape cultural shifts at the time of their first publication with titles by contemporary authors that continue in the tradition of rebellion and contesting the canon.

We hope that these books not only give pleasure, joy and entertainment, but that they also help to open minds and attitudes to diversity. We are pleased to be publishing in a period of cultural flux when more and more voices from outside the mainstream are being heard.

If you would like to support our work, please stay in touch online and via social media, details below.

Rosemarie Hudson, *Publisher and Founder of HopeRoad*
Pete Ayrton, *Editor Small Axes*

hoperoadpublishing.com | 🐦 📘 📷 @hoperoadpublish

Other HopeRoad Titles
You Might Enjoy

TERRORISM EXPLAINED TO OUR KIDS
Tahar Ben Jelloun
Translated by Aneesa Abbas Higgins

'Morocco's greatest living author' Guardian

COMING NOVEMBER 2019

Terrorism Explained to Our Kids is Tahar Ben Jelloun's impassioned, succinct explanation of the seductions and dangers of terrorism in the modern world. Exploring all forms of terrorism in both a historical and contemporary context, the book addresses complex and pressing questions in an everyday, accessible language. Because Ben Jelloun understands that terrorist acts come from the perpetrators' deep sense of inadequacy, his arguments are all the more powerful. He places a high value on the importance of secular values, with which he believes Islam is compatible. This is a powerful, timely plea for tolerance and understanding.

TAHAR BEN JELLOUN is an award-winning and internationally bestselling Moroccan novelist, essayist, critic, and poet. Two previous books in the series explained Racism and Islam to a younger readership.

978-1-9164671-1-8 | £8.99

INDIAN MAGIC
Balraj Khanna

'The young Mehra's story reminds one
of *Tom Jones* and *Lucky Jim*. Brilliant!'
REGINAL MASSEY

When Ravi Kumar Mehra MA steps off the train at Victoria
station, London, in the autumn of 1962, he is fully equipped
with the all-important work permit and five pounds in his
pocket. A brave new life lies ahead! He's 23, educated, good-
looking - a real Star of India. What can possibly stand in
his way? Disillusion soon sets in, for the Mother Country
turns out to be a hostile place in which non-whites are not
welcome. But the kindness of strangers helps Ravi to walk
tall - and after six days of sleeping rough, his luck changes, for
the Indian Magic curry house is recruiting for a dishwasher.

When Ravi falls in love, life takes a more dangerous turn,
for the girl in question is an English Rose, and her father is
unhinged. Anything could happen.

Balraj Khanna was born in the Punjab, India, and arrived in
London in the Swinging Sixties to study English. One of the
most admired painters of his time, his novels include *Nation
of Fools*, which was judged at the time as 'one of the 200 best
novels in English since 1950', *Sweet Chillies* and *The Mists of
Simla*. Balraj lives in London, UK.

ISBN: 978-1-908446-28-2 | £8.99

THE CONCUBINE
& THE SLAVE-CATCHER
Qaisra Shahraz

'A delightful collection provoking laughter and
melancholia' Mei Fong, author, *One Child*

Ten powerful stories are set on several continents and at different
periods in history. A well-meaning Abolitionist learns the sordid
and violent truth about slavery from her African servants in
Boston USA. The sundering of India and Pakistan in the 1947
Partition is revealed when a Muslim boy is adopted by a Hindu
family during the chaos of mass migration. A young university
student finds her engagement broken off because her fiancé's
family disapproves of her Western attire. The horrors of the
Holocaust are writ large in one pregnant woman's experiences.
With each unique story, Qaisra Shahraz captures and enriches us
with her wisdom and storytelling magic

QAISRA SHAHRAZ is a British-Pakistani award-winning novelist
and scriptwriter. Among her many accolades are the prestigious
National Diversity Lifetime Achiever Award for Services to Literature, Education, Gender and Interfaith Activism; she is rec-
ognised as one of 100 most influential Pakistani women in the
'Pakistan Power 100 List'. Other books by her include *The Holy
Woman*, *Typhoon*, *Revolt* and the short story *A Pair of Jeans*.

ISBN: 978-1-908446-61-9 | £9.99

DESI GIRLS
Edited by Divya Mathur

This collection of short stories focuses on the theme of Indian women living abroad and how each one copes with the customs and expectations in their adopted countries. The eternal dilemma is: whether to cling to their Indian culture, discard it completely, or learn how to adjust and compromise. It's a challenge! These very different tales of courtship, marriage and betrayal, of losing and re-forming one's identity while trying to live up to Indian ideals of behaviour in an alien environment, contain all the vibrancy of India herself.

Divya Mathur is a multi-award-winning author who works for interfaith and intercultural understanding. She is the Founding President of Vatayan: Poetry on the South Bank, a charity which encourages poets worldwide. Divya lives in London, UK.

ISBN: 978-1-908446-44-2 | £8.99